ALMOST NEVER APART

Adrianna Schwab

contents

1. Chapter 1 — 1

2. Chapter 2 — 9

3. Chapter 3 — 18

4. Chapter 4 — 28

5. Chapter 5 — 38

6. Chapter 6 — 49

7. Chapter 7 — 58

8. Chapter 8 — 66

9. Chapter 9 — 77

10. Chapter 10 — 86

11. Chapter 11 — 96

12. Chapter 12 — 106

13. Chapter 13 — 117

14. Chapter 14 — 127

15. Chapter 15 — 136

16. Chapter 16 — 145

17. Chapter 17   155

18. Chapter 18   166

19. Chapter 19   177

20. Chapter 20   186

21. Chapter 21   197

22. Chapter 22   206

23. Chapter 23   217

24. Chapter 24   227

25. Chapter 25   238

26. Chapter 26   248

27. Chapter 27   257

28. Chapter 28   266

29. Chapter 29   276

30. Chapter 30   287

31. Chapter 31   296

32. Chapter 32   304

33. Chapter 33   315

34. Chapter 34   323

35. Chapter 35   333

36. Chapter 36   342

37. Chapter 37   349

38. Chapter 38   359

39. Epilogue   369

CHAPTER 1

Despite my desperate attempts to avoid it, it turns out becoming an adult is inevitable.

A gap year wasn't my idea, it was Aiden's. Obviously. I had no idea what to study at uni, so I thought giving myself a year to figure that out would be enough. Besides, I could've hardly turned down my best friend of fifteen years when he asked me to accompany him on the biggest adventure ever, right?

Turns out I still have no idea what to study, but the decision hasn't waited for me, so I've settled on English. It's the kind of degree a lot of people settle on, I think.

There was no decision to be made by Aiden. He'd wanted to study Psychology from day one, and he'd deferred his offer from Cardiff Uni to take the gap year. He had it all mapped out. I, on the other hand, manically applied to wherever would take me while struggling for Wi-Fi in our crappy, overpriced New Zealand hostel.

I never actually thought I'd get into UCL, even with some help on the inside.

I'd happily repeat mine and Aiden's year touring the Southern Hemisphere forever, but I also feel like I've aged about ten years over the course of one. In trying to avoid adulthood, we somehow fell headfirst into it because it turns out living and working halfway across the world on a low budget demands a lot of responsibility.

Uni will be a walk in the park, right?

Mum dropped me off at my accommodation half an hour ago, and I've spent every minute since staring at my unpacked bags. I figure I'll get around to them eventually.

Each student assigned to our flat found one another online through some meet and greet Facebook group UCL set up, so I know nobody else is moving in for another few days. It was totally intentional; I want a few days alone to get my shit together.

Besides, it's not like I don't know anyone in London.

I'm still staring at the piles of unpacked items when my phone starts turning warm in my pocket. It's all in my head—my phone's not overheating—but my fingers are twitching as I try to resist temptation.

I don't want things to be weird—I don't want to make things weird, and sending a text within moments of me arriving in London feels weird. Instead, I continue ignoring the mountain of stuff I need to organise, and head outside to explore the streets of Central London.

I end up in a cafe, and in true English student style, it's one attached to a cosy bookshop. I've got a bunch of uni registration tasks to get through, so with nothing but a hot chocolate and a croissant to keep me company, I find a small table in the corner of the bright cafe.

It turns out I may be worse at being a mature, independent student than I thought. No matter how many times I click the connect button on my laptop screen, the WiFi is non-existent.

'You've got to accept the terms and conditions,' a voice suddenly pipes up, and I turn from my screen to meet the eyes of the blue-haired girl sitting at the table beside me. 'They've royally fucked up by making the text and checkbox one shade lighter than the background.'

She smiles as she leans over, then hovers her index finger over a space on my screen. I squint, and—Oh, shit, yeah. It's right there. A grey checkbox with some text beside it. I click on the checkbox, and a green tick appears.

'Huh, yeah, that's a fuck up on their part,' I mutter. 'Thanks.'

'I'm guessing you're a first year, right? Either that, or you're the first student to ever go a whole year without visiting Dolly's cafe.'

I laugh an awkward, slightly embarrassed, laugh. 'Not a record holder, just clueless. And new.'

'Well, hey, I'm Margot,' she says as a warm smile bursts onto her freckled face.

'Mia,' I reply with a grin that matches hers.

'Margot and Mia. Cute. You've moved in kind of early for a first year, right?'

I shrug. 'Wanted to steal the best cupboard and fridge spaces, y'know?'

Ugh, that was painfully unfunny. Great start.

Margot laughs, likely out of pity. 'Good call! Has no one else moved in yet?'

'Nope, just me,' I reply, and her face softens with a semi-sad look, her brown eyes wide.

'Got any plans for this evening?' she continues, and I shake my head. 'Correct answer! Housewarming party at my place. Only caveat is you'll have to deal with us second years, although one of my housemates is Welsh, so you should feel semi at home.'

I stammer. I was not expecting a house party invite this fast, or well, at all. Aiden's the one who aces making new friends, not me.

'That's really sweet of you, thanks,' I reply, then laugh. 'Is the accent that obvious?'

The girl smiles, then lifts her hand in a so-so motion. 'Kinda.'

It takes me a whole ten seconds after leaving my flat that night to regret agreeing to attend Margot's party. I'd assumed she was just being nice when she invited me because who the hell wants some snotty fresher at their house party, right? Margot does, apparently.

We'd exchanged numbers at Dolly's, and my phone vibrated with a text from her an hour before the party started. It was sort of a blessing, really; prior to receiving the message, I'd been torturing myself with whether I should give in to temptation and send the message I'd been thinking about sending since I set foot in London.

Before I know it, I'm standing on a street corner in Clapham while staring wide-eyed at a London townhouse. Dressing for a house party is always a nightmare, so I've played it safe with a semi-casual dress, but I suddenly feel like I'm drowning in the oversized, faux leather jacket I've paired with it.

I shut my eyes, then sigh.

'It's a party, Mia. Just a party,' I mumble as I open my eyes. 'You've been to plenty of parties in the past.'

Some more eventful than others.

Before the thought can snowball, and before I can chicken out, I take a sharp breath and step towards the short staircase leading to the house.

If I'd had an ounce of sense, I'd have messaged Margot to pre-empt my arrival. The front door is opened by a total stranger who doesn't question who I am. He just opens the door, blinks a few times, then walks away. Largely out of awkwardness, instead of turning on my heel and saving myself from any embarrassment, I step inside.

I always find it easiest to judge a party by its music, and to my relief, it's an indie artists nobody's heard of, not a dubstep that makes your ears bleed kind of soiree. I'm not sure my anxiety could've coped with the latter.

I spend the next ten minutes silently weaving through groups of people who, unlike me, know what the fuck they're doing here. It's a sizeable uni house, one that triggers memories of a different uni party I attended a few years back when I was too young to be at one. Although, it was my older sister, Livvy, who ended up passed out on a bedroom floor before it hit eleven o'clock, so maybe age has nothing to do with it.

I give in a few minutes later to text Margot a hey, I'm here! message, only to delete the exclamation mark moments before sending because it feels a bit much. I regret that about two seconds later.

The ground floor is open-plan, and I don't spend too long searching upstairs because the second floor contains nothing but bedrooms and a couple of bathrooms, so it feels intrusive to linger. From what I can tell, the third floor is an attic bedroom, and I figure I best not risk breaking into a stranger's personal space.

Despite my attempts, there's no sign of Margot, and so I end up sitting alone in a bathroom within fifteen minutes of entering the house.

'Great start, Mia,' I mumble to myself as I sit on the closed toilet seat, and I lean my head back against the white wall. 'Well, this has been fun.'

I haven't used the toilet, but I flush it anyway before standing to wash my hands. Again, for the sake of performance.

As I emerge into a crowded second-floor hallway, the only decor being a stolen traffic cone and some empty bottles of alcohol, I take a sharp breath. I need to make my exit look casual, stealthy, and not at all like a friendless loser disappearing into the night.

Why did I even kid myself into thinking this was a good idea? I'm way out of my depth here. I'm clenching my jaw as I toddle down a flight of stairs, and although I know not a single soul has their eyes on me, it feels like I'm the star attraction at a zoo. I know zero people at this party, and hell, I don't even know the person who invited me. I'm pretty sure Margot invited me out of sympathy as it is, which is plain embarrass—

'If you're looking for the bathroom, then I'm sorry to say you're rather lost.'

The world crashes to an abrupt stop.

The music halts, the laughter ceases, the party and the people around me no longer exist as time freezes, and I'm dreaming—No, screw that, I'm hallucinating.

It's him. Six foot-something, bright green eyes, messy, dark blonde hair. Preston. Standing right there at the bottom of the staircase.

This must be some kind of fever dream.

'What the fuck? I can't—How are you... Where—What the fuck?'

'A hello would suffice.'

'Fuck off.'

'Or generally anything without fuck in it. Was your language always this abysmal?'

He's sucking in his cheeks, making his sharp cheekbones pop, and the way his lips are tightly pressed together is enough to tell me he's trying really hard not to laugh.

I don't even think, I just crash down the remaining steps, fling my arms out, and propel forward as if I'm falling. Preston's response to my embrace is to freeze as suddenly as the world around us did moments ago. I forgot he's not exactly the hugging type.

I briefly consider releasing him, but it's been a whole year. Screw that.

'No, seriously, what the hell?' I question as I finally pull away.

'You're the one in my house,' he reasons.

'Wait, you live with Margot?'

Shit. Margot's Welsh housemate. It's literally Preston.

'Yeah, we met in a Quantitative Research Methods lecture last year. Dreadfully boring.' He pauses. 'Quantitative Research Methods, not Margot.'

I'm still convinced I'm hallucinating.

'When did you arrive in London?' Preston continues. 'You should've called, or sent—'

'Damn, Mia, I'm impressed,' a high-pitched voice interrupts Preston, and I tear my eyes from him to see Margot in the kitchen doorway. 'You sniffed out the other Welsh person within a few minutes.'

I arrived twenty minutes ago, but I figure correcting her would be socially questionable.

'It's—We know each other already,' I explain, poorly. 'From home, I mean. It's...'

It's complicated.

'It's crazy. Small world, right?' I conclude.

Margot's grin broadens, and she's practically gleaming. Her eyebrows raise as she glances at Preston, who's silently leaning against the staircase, before turning her attention back to me.

'You've known him a while, then? We definitely need to catch up on that later. The guy's an enigma.'

I couldn't stop the laugh that bursts from my mouth if I tried. I turn my head back to him, and his lips twitch. He's so obviously trying not to smirk.

'You? An enigma? How out of character.'

'Has Euphemia told you that she's a comedienne?' he bites back.

Margot's brow furrows, and I swear I can see her brain's working out in real-time.

'Is that what Mia's short for? I've never heard that before.' Her face softens. 'It's pretty.'

I hear Preston clear his throat behind me, and I swear to God, if he so much as thinks about—

'It sounds rather like an STD, don't you think?'

CHAPTER 2

'I bet your room's the attic one.'

I don't know why the hell that's the first thing I say to him when we step into the house's small back garden, but it is.

Preston responds with a tiny smile that gives nothing away. 'I'm dying to know the implication behind that statement.'

We're standing in the corner closest to the patio doors, and I'm looking—no, staring—at his side profile as he gazes towards the back of the small garden. It's near-empty outside, bar a few groups of people and some lone smokers. I briefly anticipate Preston joining them, but he's not smoked for well over two years.

'Not so clever now, eh?' I goad.

His nothing smile reappears, but he still doesn't look at me.

'Am I right? About your bedroom?'

'Yes.'

Ha. I knew it. I don't know what it means or why I want to feign the idea that it means anything in the first place, but I play along with the charade.

'Can't believe you bloody pulled the STD gag with Margot. It took you literal seconds. That has to be a record.'

Finally, Preston cranes his neck to look down at me. The nothing smile is replaced by the lopsided smirk I've not seen for a year. A fucking year.

He shrugs. 'You should surely expect no less from the occupant of an attic bedroom.'

Damn it. He's playing me at my own game. I'm about to scoff a response, but as my eyes meet his, I lose myself, let alone my train of thought. The night's shadows are failing to diminish the curiosity in his bright eyes, and his hair is messier than I remember it, his posture straighter, or maybe he just fills out his clothes better now.

I break my trance with a, 'I'm convinced I'm hallucinating.'

'Perhaps you are.'

'Not helping,' I grumble with an eye roll, then turn away from him with crossed arms. 'You're less lanky than you used to be.'

'Was I ever lanky?'

'No. You're just less lanky now.'

'In the kindest way possible, Euphemia, what the fuck are you talking about?'

At that, we both start laughing. Whatever game we'd been playing melts away, as if we've communicated some kind of telepathic truce, and God, I want to hug him again.

We talk. I'd say how long for, but I don't keep track. None of what we say is new information. While I've not seen Preston for a year, I've spoken to him every day. In hostels with shit signal, hotels Aiden and I definitely couldn't afford, via letters when there were no other means of communication, through brief text messages hastily typed at the back of night buses, from the comfort of Mum's living room before and after my trip to the Southern Hemisphere, and the depths of my bedroom at Dad's place in an attempt to zone out his drunken ramblings from the floor below.

Even when we couldn't communicate in a traditional sense, there was always something. A bullet point jotted into a journal so I'd not forget to mention it later, a scribbled note on my hand referencing something he'd find funny or interesting, a half-asleep, typo-filled sentence in my phone's notes app because I knew I'd otherwise forget what to say when I got the chance. We never stopped talking, really.

It's not until a new voice steals my attention that I remember where I am.

'How are you guys not freezing?'

I heave my eyes from Preston to glance towards the patio doors, and Margot's standing there with raised eyebrows. Preston and I sat onto the ground shortly after we started talking, so I imagine we look like naughty kids as we gaze up at her.

'Is it cold?' Preston answers on our behalf.

'It's practically arctic. That's the thing with these summer nights, right? Sun all day, and then no clouds for warmth when it pisses off.'

Margot's not wrong. As I emerge back to reality, I'm rapidly realising that the hairs on my arms are pointed upright and that my teeth are chattering.

'Besides, the night's practically ended and I've still not stolen Mia away so that she can spill your deepest, darkest secrets.'

Preston responds with silence and a faint smirk, but his focus doesn't shift from Margot, and I figure she's accustomed to this kind of response from him because she doesn't bat an eyelid.

At least, that's what I think his response is until I sense his chest rise to my left.

'You make it sound like I killed a man.'

I'm so thrown by the comment that I barely register Margot reaching her hand towards me, nor do I process myself taking it and letting her pull me up. She says something—to me or to Preston, I'm not sure—and then we're inside, but I don't remember stepping over the threshold into the house.

'Most people have left, so the good news is that there's heaps of drink leftover.' She looks at me over her shoulder as she guides us into the kitchen area, a wicked grin on her face.

'It's—Sorry, what time is it?'

'Uh, like, two.'

I freeze, my eyes widening so much that I'm stunned my skull doesn't have to expand to make space for them. Thankfully, my abrupt pause isn't too weird because we've reached Margot's destination of a kitchen counter.

She laughs as she starts inspecting abandoned liquor bottles. 'You guys were out there a while.'

'I thought an hour, maybe. Not three.' I shake my head. 'Shitting hell.'

'You like white?' Margot chirps.

She presents an unopened bottle of sauvignon blanc, and I nod, partly out of politeness and partly because my taste buds are still at the alcohol is alcohol stage of my life. She keeps talking as she grabs some plastic wine glasses from the back of a cupboard near the floor, then jumps back up.

'I did consider interrupting earlier in case, well, y'know...'

She halts her wine pouring to turn back to me and gesture into the air, but I'm drawing a blank.

'I figured you guys might've been a thing in the past, that catching up was a bit of an out of politeness scenario—trust me, been there, done that.' She made a faux spewing motion. 'I bumped into my ex in freshers' week during first year, and it was the worst experience of my life, so didn't want to leave you swimming with no lifeboat out there.'

My eyes widen again, and shit, I need to stop doing that. 'Oh, no–God, no, never–No.'

Margot's plump lips part to flash a set of white teeth. 'I won't tell him you were physically repulsed by the thought, don't worry.'

I resist the urge to palm my own face, and instead, say, 'not in that way. It'd just be weird because we're such close friends. Thanks, by the way, for checking because the hypothetical scenario of bumping into an ex at a party full of strangers makes me want to slowly peel my skin off.'

Shit, Mia. Not a normal thing to say.

Margot, seemingly unfazed by my questionable analogy, hands me a glass of wine. 'I have to admit, what I misjudged as disgust did throw me because he's really fucking attractive.'

'Oh! Is–Are you guys...?'

I take a sip of wine to avoid her eyes, and my heart's suddenly beating out of control because I'm not sure if I'm asking out of politeness or awkwardness. Preston would've told me if he was seeing someone, wouldn't he?

'My boyfriend also lives here, so that'd be awkward,' is Margot's response as she laughs. 'No, I honestly thought Preston was asexual for the first six months I knew him, but I think he's just selective.'

God, two-years-ago-Mia would've found that comment fucking hilarious. Present-day Mia, however, finds it painfully intriguing.

'Joe—my boyfriend—is convinced he's in MI6 or something, and I think he's only sixty percent kidding when he says it. Preston's just... difficult to figure out. I mean, he's not exactly a talker, right? Not in a shy way, least I don't think so.'

She pauses, I think for me to confirm her statement, but I take too long to realise this and so she continues.

'Anyway, yeah, he...' Margot purses her lips as if trying to feel for the right word, 'He never demands attention, but it always somehow falls on him. On the rare occasion he does speak, it's like not a single word is filler, as if he's thought about every syllable. Sorry, it's—Am I talking shit? Does that make sense?'

Nothing's ever made more sense.

'He draws you in just by the way he exists.'

Margot clicks her fingers, then points in my direction. 'Exactly! Wait, shit, I need to write that down. Joe will fucking love that.'

A smile breaks onto my face as Margot props her wine glass onto the counter, then hastily types into her phone. As if perfectly choreographed, the brief silence is interrupted by a tall, chestnut-haired guy appearing by Margot's side, who I quickly discover to be Joe.

We chat until my wine glass is empty, at which point I announce to Margot and Joe that I'm going to head home. It's pretty late, I'm shattered, and I've got loads of unpacking to do tomorrow considering I ditched doing any today. They offer to walk with me, but I assure them there's no need.

I find Preston before I've even started looking for him. He's sitting at the bottom of the staircase near the house's front door, a hardback in his hands and a pair of glasses perched on his nose. How anyone is getting up and down the stairs with him there is beyond me, as is how he can possibly concentrate on what he's reading with the music blasting around the house.

'You know you don't have to push the I'm not like other girls vibe this hard, right?' I comment with raised eyebrows. 'On that note, please don't tell me you're still stealing strangers' glasses.'

'You're colder than I remember,' he observes into his open pages, then lifts his green eyes to look up at me with a grin. 'And I'll have you know my eyesight has become considerably more dreadful since college, so no theft necessary.'

'That's something, at least,' I reply. 'Anyway, yeah, I'm heading home. I'm exhausted, plus I think I'm still reeling from you appearing from nowhere with zero warning.'

'I have a tendency to do that,' he murmurs as he closes his book, then jumps to his feet. 'I'll take you home.'

I stammer. 'Oh, no, it's–that's fine. I live super close; literally a ten minute walk, which is insane because you live here. Ten minutes away. As in, how weird is it that I coincidentally picked student accommodation so close to your house without knowing your address beforehand?'

Jesus Christ, Mia, at least try to sound like you've got more than two brain cells.

Preston doesn't bother humouring me with a response beyond another smile I can't read. He hands me my jacket from the coat rack beside the front door, and it's not until we're walking along the pavement outside that I realise I've got zero idea how he knew it was mine.

I'm convinced he'll disappear—potentially forever—if I don't, so I invite Preston into my flat. I make a deflated ta-da! hand gesture as we enter into the communal kitchen-living room, regretting it within half a second.

'Students are gross, so I figure you should appreciate it while it's clean.'

Preston's inspecting the kitchen area when he murmurs, 'I don't want there to be any obligation on your part to associate with me.'

I freeze, and try my best to not explicitly show how thrown I am by his comment. Not that it matters; he's seemingly transfixed by the electric hob.

I stammer. 'You don't actually think that, right?'

Finally, he turns to me, his eyes wide as if the possibility of me willingly being in his company is some alien concept.

'I literally sought out Wi-Fi in the middle of a Cambodian jungle a few months back to send you a picture of Aiden in speedos. Does that seriously scream obligated to you?'

His wide-eyed expression drops, and his lips quiver into a small smile. Despite the shift, he still only looks semi-convinced.

'You don't have to is what I'm saying.'

'I want to.'

I hadn't noticed, but we've both stepped forward. If I lifted my arm, I could probably touch him.

'If you want a fresh start,' he elaborates. 'I won't be offended.'

'I could hit you sometimes.' I roll my eyes in the most in-your-face way possible to get my message across. 'Honestly.'

'Nothing good ever comes of violence.'

I narrow my eyes as I close the gap between us, then lift my chin to glare at him.

'Is that a quote, or just you talking shit?'

Preston holds my challenging gaze, and the silence can't last more than a few seconds, but it feels like hours.

Eventually, he smirks, then says, 'Martin Luther King.'

For the second time that night, I force Preston into a hug with no warning. He clearly hates this one as much as the last, possibly more so, but as with that one, I couldn't care less.

Within minutes of him leaving, I'm burying myself underneath the thick duvet of my new bed. I ordered him to text me when he arrived home, partly due to safety concerns and partly due to me still being convinced he's a hallucination, and he's right on cue. Exactly ten minutes after he left, he sends me a message.

Home

I reply with, Don't strain yourself

Ha

You never shut up, do you?

And you never confirmed whether anyone's ever told you your name sounds like an STD

'Asshole,' I mutter under my breath.

I'm in the middle of replying when my phone vibrates with another message, this time from Margot.

Hey gal, you get home all okay? Loads of fucking weirdos in London. P.S. Can't believe you left me hanging on revealing Preston's secrets

I gaze at my phone screen, the amusement from reading the first half of the message quickly obliterated by the second half.

She's kidding; I know her comments about Preston's secrets are entirely related to the fact the guy's one giant, walking riddle, but still, my pulse quickens. I couldn't untangle his response to her when she found us outside if I tried. Why the hell would he make a comment about killing a man when, albeit accidentally, he has?

CHAPTER 3

I t takes Aiden a total of five days to visit me in London, and I'm confident only fifty percent of it is an excuse to see Preston. Sucks for him because Preston is visiting his mum and brother in Cardiff this weekend, as he does most weekends.

I remind Aiden that I've told him this several times, but he categorically denies any knowledge of it as he lugs an offensively large suitcase through Paddington station. Anyone would guess he was staying for a month, not two nights.

'What was the reunion like?' he asks as we bundle into some bus seats. 'Hot, passionate, and sweaty, I assume. Please don't feel like you've got to spare any details for my sake.'

Despite travelling on a Central London bus crammed full of strangers, Aiden doesn't feel it necessary to lower his voice.

'Speak up, yeah?' I reply dryly. 'I don't think the old lady on the top deck quite heard you.'

'Holy mackerel, the man's wasted on you, Mia, honestly,' he whines. 'I totally get that you're an interim thing while he figures out his deep-rooted feelings for me—'

'—I'm not listening—'

'—but you could at least try to play along.'

By the time we arrive at our stop, everyone on the bus knows about Aiden's sandwich preferences in questionable detail, that the guy he hooked up with last night has six moles formed into a perfect circle on his right arse cheek, and that I'm a virgin. So that's nice.

As Aiden makes himself at home in my empty flat, I toy with prodding his brain about the events at Margot's party. More specifically, what to make of Preston's I killed a man statement. I settle on keeping the conundrum to myself, mainly because Aiden's in the process of trying to pile as many sofa cushions atop each other as possible.

'So this Margot girl lives with Preston? Are we meeting her at their place, then going to the bar? Have you seen his room? What's it like?'

I assume Aiden's questions are directed at me, but he's talking into the pillow tower.

'Y'know, Aiden, I think you're somehow more obsessed with Preston now than when you were sixteen.'

He finally turns his attention away from his pillow tower and flashes me a big, white smile. He juts his arms out with jazz hands, only for the pillows to crash from the sofa and onto the floor.

'Shit,' he mutters, then scratches his shaved head as he stares at his mess. 'I'll fix that.'

As he starts throwing the blue pillows back into place on the sofa, I answer his initial questions.

'Margot lives with Preston, we're meeting her at the bar, and no, I've not seen his room.'

'Weird. Would've thought you'd have used his room for your reunion se—'

'Piss off.'

Aiden starts giggling, and I warn him that if he makes one more Preston-related crude joke, he'll be sleeping in a tube station tonight.

I spend too long getting ready. It's my first night out in London, and while Margot assured me that it's a fairly casual few drinks at a bar vibe, if anything, that makes it worse. How does someone dress for a fairly casual few drinks at a bar? It's neither here nor there, so I settle on a little black dress.

'You look hot,' Aiden assures me as we're leaving my flat.

'You always say that,' I point out.

'It's always true.'

'Shut up,' I reply, which is our version of thanks.

'You don't think this is a bit much?' he asks as he slows his pace, then waves his hand over his electric blue shirt.

'Um, absolutely not. Are you kidding? It looks so good,' I assure him. 'If you don't get hit on by some super hot guy tonight, I'll eat my own fist.'

'Shut up.'

See.

The bar we're headed to is in Soho, which from what I can tell, is where most Central London bars are located. At least, the ones that are worth going to. The streets become increasingly crowded as we approach our final destination, and I'm digging my nails into Aiden's arm as if my life depends on it. We shove ourselves through groups of people high on life, and I imagine various substances, and I clench my jaw as I force down the nauseous sensation in my stomach. As someone who hates crowds, London may not have been my most sensible choice of uni location.

I can finally breathe again once we reach the bar.

'Have you spoken with your dad much since moving here?' Aiden asks after a bouncer requests our IDs.

'Nope,' I reply without a second of thought on the matter.

'He still stalks my social media,' Aiden continues. 'The guy must think I'm a clairvoyant or something, that he can speak to you through me.'

I laugh—or at least, I try to laugh. I think I laugh, anyway. I contemplate opening the father-shaped can of worms, but figure now may not be the best time to analyse why I've ignored every single message and call Dad's made since I moved here.

As we step into the building, I'm relieved to discover there's far more breathing room here than there was in the streets outside. The venue is decorated in a roaring twenties style with gold on its walls and a long mahogany bar, and there's a band playing jazz music in one of its far corners. The round tables dotted around the room are full for the most part, and I scan them for Margot's recognisable blue hair.

Only, Margot's not the first friendly face I spot. I'm too busy questioning if I'm hallucinating for the second time this week to say a word to Aiden as Preston's eyes meet mine from across the room, not that it matters. Aiden's spotted him.

No word of a lie, he sprints. We're talking full-blown, no hesitation, giving it his all running. Preston somehow manages to stand up before Aiden reaches him and his all-encompassing hug, which I've got no doubt he hates. By the time I reach them, Aiden's speaking at a hundred miles an hour about God knows what with Preston.

'Sorry,' I apologise. 'I promise I didn't intentionally spring Aiden on you with zero warning.'

'I told him Aiden was coming, don't worry!' Margot pipes up from a chair to my left as Joe laughs from the seat beside hers. 'Hell, the knowledge motivated him to attend two social occasions in one week—a miracle!'

Preston's response is an obscene hand gesture flashed towards Margot without his eyes so much as twitching to glance in her direction. It's quite impressive, actually.

Aiden finds Margot's comment even funnier than I do, so while he's distracted with her, I turn back to Preston.

'I thought you were visiting home this weekend?' I say over the music.

'I am,' he confirms. 'Leaving tomorrow morning.'

'Oh, it's—I—Sorry, I assumed you'd leave today.'

'It's okay,' he replies, his voice low and deep—deeper than I remember. 'I didn't specify.'

I hadn't even thought to mention our plans this evening to Preston, nor let him know that Aiden was visiting for the weekend. In hindsight, I'm not sure why. Before bumping into each other earlier in the week, we spoke every day, but our communication has been sporadic since. It's as if seeing him filled a space that had been left vacant for so long that it was all too much all at once, as if I'm still trying to manage the excess.

'So you're a hermit now, are you?' I say teasingly.

The concept of Preston missing a social event feels alien. Hell, a few years ago, it wasn't a social event unless he was there—only, no. That's not right.

It wasn't a social event unless Zack was there.

I still do that, sometimes; get elements of the fictional, and all-around dreadful, alter-ego Preston created tangled with the real version of him.

'I always have been,' Preston says in response to my goading. 'You must be confusing me with someone else.'

He can still read my mind, then.

His green eyes are searching mine, but I'm not sure what for, and it's not until Aiden calls us over to sit at the table that we break the spell.

It's evenings like these I'm grateful for Aiden because at no point does he stop for air. It gives me plenty of time to settle into the rhythm of the situation without any pressure to contribute much.

The majority of the talking happens between him, Margot, and Joe. Mine and Preston's conversation is, for the most part, silent glances at each other as we sip at our drinks, or smirks exchanged over something ridiculous Aiden says. I asked Aiden not to talk about Preston's past on the walk from the tube station because it occurred to me that I've got no idea how much Margot, Joe, or anyone in London for that matter, knows about him. Based on Margot's comments, I'd hazard a guess of it being fuck all.

'I had some concerns that he might've become more reserved with age,' Preston comments as we're standing at the bar together to place our last orders. He gestures his head in Aiden's direction. 'I'm relieved those concerns were unfounded.'

'He'll be on his death bed and still endlessly talking shit,' I reply, a little less eloquently.

Preston's eyes remain on the wall of liquor bottles behind the bar, but I spot a small smile crack onto his lips via his side profile, which I'm trying not to stare at. It's as if a year of not seeing him in person has triggered an urge to imprint his features to memory.

'You're allowed to laugh at my jokes, you know,' I say, forcing my eyes away from his face. 'I promise everyone will still think you're cool and mysterious.'

'The risk is far too great,' he replies, and curse him for not rising to it.

Preston stands upright as he catches the eye of one of the barmaids, and she's opposite us within seconds. I awkwardly stand to the side while Preston places our drink orders. She flirts a little. He acts oblivious.

The barmaid turns to prepare our drinks, and as she does, I'm about to pass comment on his feigned ignorance. Only, Preston opens his mouth before I do.

'You look nice,' he murmurs, but still doesn't look at me.

My head tells me to thank him, but my mouth must not get the memo because I instead say, 'I think you're supposed to say that at the start of an evening.' Thankfully, I catch myself and add, 'but thank you.'

'What's past is prologue.'

'Right.'

'Shakespeare, if you were wondering.'

'Of course it is.'

This time, he gives in and laughs. It's light and lasts seconds, but I'll take it. Finally, he turns his head to look at me, and maybe it's the unprompted compliment he just gave me, but I have the sudden urge to check a mirror.

Margot and I are the first to finish our drinks, so while the guys tackle theirs, I follow her to the smoking area. She offers me one, but I decline, then spend too long deliberating whether I should explain I joined her outside purely for some fresh air to say it aloud.

'With respect to Joe, I think I'm in love with Aiden,' she says as she exhales a puff of smoke.

'Same, don't worry,' I reassure her. 'Sucks we're not his type.'

We both laugh, and I hope she misses the blatant relief in mine. As someone who's notoriously bad at making friends, I was convinced I'd spend my university years alone. It's early days—Margot may realise the extent of how big of a loser I am and drop me—but I have faith.

She juts her cigarette towards me. 'You've got good taste in friends. Extremely varied taste, but good.'

'I don't know what you're talking about.' I shrug. 'Aiden and Preston are practically twins.'

We're laughing again, and Margot sits down onto the wooden bench below us.

'It's nice, actually, knowing he had you last year,' she says as a gush of smoke bursts from her lips, and my gormless expression must communicate I've got no idea what the hell she's talking about. 'With Preston, I mean. I'd only known him a few months so wasn't like I knew what normal was for him, but it gets pretty obvious when a person literally drops off the face of the planet for, like, two weeks, right?'

I'm frozen on the spot, my mind whirling at a hundred miles an hour. What's she talking about?

'When was—When did you start noticing him acting weird?'

'Late November, I think. I've got zero idea what his deal was—and not asking you to spill, obviously—but he didn't show up to any lectures or respond to messages. My friend who lived in the same uni accommodation said he basically locked himself in his room the whole time.'

I'm desperately hoping my expression is hiding the dread filling my body. I couldn't spill a thing to Margot if I wanted to. I know nothing. I try scraping together my memories from last November when I was travelling around Indonesia, but nothing jumps out at me. He seemed fine.

Only, I know he wasn't fine because when Preston isn't fine, he disappears.

My eyes don't leave Preston when we return inside. I'm trying to read him, but as always, I'm coming up short. Every expression is perfectly measured, every gesture nonchalant, every comment calm and collected.

As we're all leaving the bar together ten minutes later, I take an opportunity to, in short, ask him what the fuck?

'Why didn't you tell me things got bad last year?' I try as we trudge a few steps behind Margot, Joe, and Aiden. 'Margot told me about November.'

I barely catch it because the look disappears within moments, but an uneasiness flashes through Preston's green eyes.

'November,' he murmurs, but doesn't take the word anywhere.

'Preston?' I try again, this time forcing his gaze to meet mine.

He holds it long enough to say, 'November was fine. An adjustment period.'

'You're not making sense again.'

He releases a light laugh, which disperses the heaviness in the air, albeit only a little.

'Uni was still new and things had changed significantly in a short space of time. It won't happen again,' he reassures me, but I struggle to take his word for it.

I understand where he's coming from because over the course of six months, he left the young offender's institute, moved in with his mum and brother, then moved to London and started uni. Adjusting to the chaos won't have been easy, and I wasn't naive to that reality at the time—it was why I got into the habit of speaking with him every day while Aiden and I were travelling. He always assured me he was fine.

'Does...' I begin, then clear my throat. 'What does Margot know? About your life before London.'

'Nothing significant,' he answers in a heartbeat.

He doesn't have to elaborate for me to understand what he means, and he's ultimately confirming what I'd already guessed.

She doesn't know a thing. About his family, about his attempt on his own life, or about him taking someone else's.

'Does anyone?' I try.

I don't have to elaborate, either. He understands my question.

'No.'

There are a million things I want to say to him, but not now. I glance at Margot, Joe, and Aiden strolling ahead as they laugh into the sky. Not here.

'You should've told me about November,' I say instead. 'You promised you'd tell me if things got bad again.'

There's a pause, and I'm worried he plans to make the silence permanent. My eyes are on Aiden's back as he bounces ahead when I hear Preston take a breath beside me.

'Sorry.'

'Just... Just tell me next time, okay?' I reply as I stop, then turn to face him.

He mirrors my action. 'I'm a little offended by how overtly confident you are that there'll be a next time.'

There will be a next time, I think, I know you, and there will be a next time, but I don't say it.

Instead, I scoff, then declare, 'you no longer have the excuse of me being half the world away, so don't even try to play it down, yeah?'

CHAPTER 4

UCL's induction week passes like a storm. I'm jumping from building to building and darting between introductory lectures, all the while barely having time to come up for air. I can't complain; I've brought this all on myself. The threat of FOMO is so strong that I wound up attending basically everything the uni could throw at me, messy nights out included, and it's not until the Friday that the storm becomes weatherable.

The only thing I have to worry about today is the societies fair, although it'll be a miracle if I sign up for anything. While the concept of missing out shakes me to my core, I also have an insatiable desire for as much alone time as possible. I'm a notoriously conflicting person, in case it wasn't obvious.

I've attended most of the induction week's events and parties with my flatmates, who've now all moved into our shared flat. Thankfully, everyone seems sane, and the biggest qualm I have so far is with one of the guys who I'm convinced is a figment of my imagination because I've only ever seen him once. He must have a private kitchen in his room or something–I've got zero clue how the man eats, otherwise.

I'm taking a break from my flatmates for today and attending the fair with Preston. There are stalls upon stalls being haunted by enthusiastic society reps wearing fluorescent purple t-shirts across campus, and within ten minutes of exploring them, I realise he loves this shit. We've passed fifteen society stalls so far, and I swear Preston's signed up for over half of them.

'So, tell me,' I begin as we stop beside the agricultural society's stall. 'How do you plan on being in a million places at once every week?'

'I'm not going to attend any of these,' he replies as if my suggestion was absurd.

While I stammer, confused, he scribbles his name and email, then drops the pen onto the agricultural society's table with a wink in the direction of some poor guy who gazes back like a rabbit caught in headlights. I figure he's not used to someone signing up in such a blasé fashion, nor is he used to someone so effortlessly charming doing so. It is the agricultural society, after all.

'Not knowing when the dawn will come, I open every door,' Preston utters as we begin walking again. 'Emily Dickinson.'

I blink. Sort of like a brain-dead goldfish.

'I'm signing up to receive their monthly newsletters. If something piques my interest, I can dig deeper.'

'So what you're saying is that you're chronically indecisive?'

'Don't forget insecure,' he chimes in.

I fail to hide a smile, so resort to looking at the floor. 'You've gotten funnier over the past year or so. Well done.'

'Thank you. The prolonged distance from you has had its perks.'

'Actually, I take that back; you're a cun–'

'Hello!'

I jump at the sound of a chirpy voice, and I'm stunned into a halt by a smiling blonde woman, who holds out her hand. I hesitantly shake it, and I'm suddenly horrified that I may have gotten myself caught up in something when I realise she's wearing a purple t-shirt.

'Dana,' she says as she releases my hand, her smile unwavering.

I'm not sure what else to do, so I reply with, 'Mia,' in a way that sounds more like a question than an introduction.

Her attention shifts to my right where Preston has stopped beside me, and it's at this point my bewilderment dampens. Dana's hazel eyes brighten, and a light laugh escapes her pink lips. She without a doubt knows him.

'Is giving a first year a societies fair tour your excuse for not volunteering as a rep?'

Her eyebrows are raised as she speaks, and I'm either reading too deeply into this exchange, or she's flirting. I resist all temptation to glance at Preston to gauge his reaction. Instead, I focus on the stall a few feet ahead of us, and its banner reads Typewriter Magazine.

'No, I just didn't want to,' Preston replies, which makes Dana laugh, and I'm not sure she realises he's being dead serious.

His green eyes meet hers, and while casual, it's a look filled with enough warmth to give the impression that he's hanging onto every word of the conversation. In response to Dana's laugh, he flashes a tiny smile, then runs his hand through his light, wavy hair in a way that's inexplicably mesmerising.

Dana turns to me, which in hindsight, is a welcomed distraction. 'Do you want to join?'

I stammer. 'Oh, I'm—It's—Sure, yeah!'

I neglect to tell her I have no idea what Typewriter Magazine is, and instead, smile politely as she hands me a pen. I can sense

Preston holding in a laugh as I sign my name and contact details, and it's not until we're out of earshot that he gives in to it.

'Shut up,' I grumble. 'She was way too perky to say no to.'

'It's a current events and creative writing magazine, by the way. Opinion pieces, essays, short stories, and poetry submissions primarily,' he explains, his voice low and smooth. 'I'm its editor. Something to pass the time.'

'Something to pass the time screams editorial passion,' I comment with an eye roll. 'At least you actually show up for this one, I guess, not just get off on their newsletters. Also, is it really that obvious that I'm a first year?'

He laughs, which makes the corners of his eyes crease. 'Your permanently wide-eyed expression exudes curiosity, albeit with a hint of fear.' He pauses. 'No one beyond me has yet realised that's just your face.'

'I definitely take my you've gotten funnier comment back.'

Despite my argument, I have to look at the floor again to hide a smile. We pass another few society stalls, the majority of which Preston signs himself up for, and I quickly learn that the only reason he doesn't sign up for the astronomy society is because he's already a regular attendee.

'I still don't understand why you went for economics instead of a degree in physics, or some variation of it. You love that shit.'

'Study something I love?' he queries, eyes wide, and I nod. 'What a bizarre suggestion.'

He frowns, clearly thrown by the idea. It amazes me that I'm still surprised when he says something that makes no sense.

'Y'know, I'm convinced I'm still the only person you expose...' I vaguely gesture towards him. 'This to.'

'You're quite the detective.'

His tone is measured, his placid expression unwavering, but he's without a doubt goading me.

'Piss off,' I snap, but the nudge I give him barely makes him flinch.

Once we're finished at the fair, we return to Preston's house. It's entirely my doing—I was badgering him about seeing his infamous attic bedroom until he agreed to give me a tour.

'You didn't even have to tie my hands together this time,' he murmurs as he unlocks his front door.

'Or smack you across the head with a lamp.'

'A lot less fun all around, really.'

We're both snickering as we step into the house, and if anyone were to have caught the last ten seconds of our conversation, they'd think we'd lost our minds. I'd not blame them, either. Maybe the reason Preston is so secretive about his past is because nobody would believe him in the first place.

His room is everything I expect, but it still draws my breath. There's not an inch of wall in sight because if they're not covered in posters, they're decorated with photos, and if they're not decorated with photos, they're hidden behind piles of books. He has a worn, wooden bookshelf beside the doorway, but for the most part, his literature is stacked in piles that don't appear to have any sense of order. Although they're not set alight given it's the middle of the day, there are at least ten—maybe fifteen—candles dotted around, and I'm suddenly dying for it to be dark so that I can witness the room illuminated.

The air smells of autumn, of spice and wood, and there's a large window letting afternoon sunlight into the cosy space, while a desk and chair occupy a corner on the opposite side of the room. Given it's an attic, it's more spacious than other student rooms I've seen over the past few weeks. At the back of it is a mattress—no bedframe, which I barely bat an eyelid at—and piled atop it are bunched up sheets, the bed's pillows discarded messily across them.

I don't think I've ever seen anything more him.

Instead of attempting to vocalise my awe, I tease him with a, 'you could've at least made your bed,' as I wander into the room.

His footsteps follow me as he says, 'much like unpacking, a made bed is too final.'

I roll my eyes, not that he catches it because I've got my back to him and he's busy fiddling with a stereo near the doorway. Before long, an unrecognisable Welsh indie song—one of Gwilym's, I think—has interrupted the silence. . I scan his walls and notice that there are some drawings among the posters and photos, ones I assume are Matty, his little brother's, creations. Either that, or Preston needs to brush up on his art skills. The photos are mainly those of Matty and Anwen, his mum, but some feature friends—some of him with Margot and other uni friends, some of him with friends back in Wales. Some of him and me.

I double take at the sight of myself, and it's odd—I wasn't that much younger, nor do I really look much different now. My dark hair's a little shorter and I've figured out how to style its kinks and waves, but I've got the same blue eyes, fair skin, freckled nose and cheeks. Despite this, it takes me a moment to recognise myself in Preston's photos. Our before feels like a lifetime ago.

'Dana seemed very fond of you,' I comment, somewhat absent-mindedly as I spot a photo where she features alongside a bunch of unfamiliar faces.

'Dana's fond of everyone,' he responds from behind.

'I'm so not buying your oblivious act,' I say, then turn to face him.

Preston has his back to me as he throws his navy jacket over a coat hook on his bedroom door, but I stay firm. As he moves towards me, I hold his gaze until he gives me his full attention.

'I don't get it,' I continue. 'Margot said she thought you were asexual for, like, half a year, and you've not even semi-flirted back with anyone who's tried it—and I've seen multiple people try it.'

His response is silence, his gaze unwavering. Our roles have somehow flipped, and it's now Preston holding my eyes hostage. If it was anyone but him, the quietness between us would be awkward.

'I'm not the kind of person who has girlfriends, Mia.'

'It doesn't have to be, y'know, a relationship,' I say with air quotes. 'Not that I'm encouraging any playboy Zack-like behaviour because fuck that, but you know what I mean.'

'Do you trust me?' is his reply.

I blink, then narrow my eyes. 'Yes.'

'Then trust me.'

I wait a moment for something—anything—but he doesn't reward me with further explanation. I bite my tongue because I don't want to push and his romantic relationships, or lack thereof, aren't really my business.

'Maybe you're onto something,' I muse. 'I had a date with a guy I met during a fresher's event last night, and I'll never get those two hours back. You have a lot to answer for on behalf of your kind.'

'Sincerest apologies. I take it the London dating scene isn't matching expectation?'

'Totally hopeless. Might need you and Aiden to do that desperate, creepy thing guys do where they pay a sex worker to take their mate's virginity.'

'I don't have the financial means to afford that,' he says, deadpan. 'Sorry.'

I turn back around to hide my laughter and move towards his desk, which is the most organised part of the room. There are a couple of Matty's drawings piled neatly on the wooden desk's right-hand side, and as I shuffle through them, I notice that some are short stories.

I smile to myself, then turn back to Preston, who's now leaning back against the large window, his hands in his loose trouser pockets.

'He sends me these too sometimes.'

I gesture some of the papers towards him, and he responds with a smile—one of his rare sincere ones.

'There I was thinking I was special.'

I laugh as I turn back around, then return the papers to Preston's desk. There are various medication packets stacked at the back of it and I recognise one as an antidepressent, but the others have unfamiliar names. I'm about to shift my attention to an astrophysics textbook when I'm distracted by something beside Matty's drawings and stories.

'You've got an unopened letter here,' I murmur as I lift the envelope to my face and inspect it for clues.

'I know.'

I turn on my heel, then wave the letter in the air, but his back is to me as he cracks open the window at the other end of the room. The air that bursts through it is cool, the breeze a refreshing relief.

'The address is handwritten, so it won't be junk or anything,' I offer.

'I know.'

He still doesn't turn to face me, and he's shutting down—I know his vagueness is a sign of him shutting down, and the breeze from the opened window can't compete with the heat racing through my blood as I feel the worry creeping in. The Gwilym song that was playing has switched to a slower one, as if the speaker can sense the shift in atmosphere.

'What is it?' I try. 'Why are—Do you know who it's from?'

Finally, he turns to me, and as he does, the tension in my bones eases. His lips twitch upwards, but they never break into anything beyond a slight smirk.

'Please, Euphemia, do resist convincing yourself that I'm about to throw myself out of a window every time I say something remotely ambiguous.'

'Haha,' I mock, then cross my arms, the letter still in hand. 'You're an extremely easy person to worry about.'

'Diolch.'

'Croeso.'

His smirk grows. 'Look at you, practising your Welsh.'

'Everyone knows croeso,' I point out. 'Not that you're welcome is even the right response to your thank you.' I huff. 'You're not welcome, you're infuriating.'

'And your name sounds like an STD, but let's not get bogged down in the details.'

As always, I figure it's best to ignore him.

'Seriously, who's this from?' I wave the envelope again.

'How do you propose I'd know that if I've not opened it?' he counteracts.

'Because you'd have to be ridiculously unhinged to resist open-ing a handwritten letter from a stranger,' I argue. 'Granted, you're ridiculously unhinged, but I don't think even you could resist opening this thing.'

He slowly tilts his head, and the weight of his gaze forces me to hold my breath without realising I've done it until my head feels light.

Finally, he releases me with a, 'touché, Euphemia.'

'You're being such an ass with this,' I groan with enough drama to win myself an Oscar. 'You're not having some secret love affair with a Norwegian woman or something, are you? I'd recommend video calls given we're, y'know, not living in the Stone Age and every–'

'It's from my dad.'

I stammer. His dad. His dad? I rack my brain for any reference he's made to his father in the past, but come up short. I've never asked, either. With everything else that has always been going on with him, I didn't want to pile on any more shit, especially anything dad-related given the situation with Matty's father. It's never felt like the right time to ask him about his own dad, but a sense of dread is rapidly overtaking me as I realise that's awful, isn't it? To have never asked him about his father, after everything.

In my bewilderment, Preston's turned his back to me again, this time to peer out of the window, or to at least look like that's what he's doing.

'I don't–What?' I stare at the white envelope in my hand, and it's heavy–it suddenly weighs a tonne. I flick my eyes back up to Preston, who's still staring out of the window. 'When did you receive it?'

'Last year,' he utters, and his shoulders raise with a slow inhale. 'November.'

CHAPTER 5

Typewriter Magazine's weekly meetings occur at six o'clock every Thursday evening. I discover this at approximately five forty-five on the day of the first meeting, courtesy of Preston, who reminds me I signed up for it in the first place. He insists there's no pressure for me to actually join the magazine, but the way he laughs at me over the phone convinces me to attend the meeting as a big fuck you for laughing.

I'm already on campus after my final lecture of the day, so meet up with him minutes after our phone call. I follow him like a lost puppy to find the seminar room the society has captured as their meeting space for this academic year, all the while insisting I have nothing valuable to contribute to the magazine.

Preston's response of, 'me neither and I'm its editor,' is oddly reassuring.

We're the first to arrive, so we grab one of the room's larger tables near the whiteboard. The silence feels loud as he retrieves his laptop from his backpack, and I'm chewing my lip as I watch him log into it.

I've not brought up the letter from his dad situation since I found it in his bedroom, and I'm toying with whether now is a good time to do so when the room's door swishes open. Two girls I don't recognise wander in, and as they introduce themselves to me, I realise I've missed my chance.

The room fills up quickly, and it's Dana who officially kicks the meeting off. I watch and listen so intently that I forget to blink several times, but I'm confused by the end of it. It's obvious why Preston's the magazine's editor; he already had a detailed plan for the year's first issue that everyone ate up, had suggestions for who should do what within that plan, and had the perfect answer to every question thrown at him. Only, as conversation became casual and everyone started chatting about their summers, current events, plans for the weekend—anything that wasn't magazine-related—he shut off.

He pulled a bloody book from his bag, popped his glasses on, then started reading in silence. I don't think he uttered a single word. Once everyone has left, I'm watching him with narrowed eyes as he packs his things away.

'Is there some rule about the editor being neutral?' I ask.

'About what?' he questions, then turns to me as he throws his bag over one shoulder.

I wave my hand in the air. 'The world? It's like you hit your off button once the magazine shit was done.'

He doesn't respond, at least not beyond a short, airy laugh. With little warning, he turns and moves towards the door, and I have to scramble to grab my bag and follow after him.

'No rule,' he says once I've caught up with him. 'I prefer not to engage.'

'What?' I ask, but get no response as we leave the university building.

As we're walking through the streets of Bloomsbury, dodging students and tourists while we make our way towards Goodge Street station, I try again.

'Why?'

'Be less curious about people and more curious about ideas,' he replies, and frankly, I could hit him. 'Marie Curie.'

'You literally ask me if anyone's ever told me my name sounds like an STD every time I see you,' I argue. 'Seems very people curious to me.'

'I've not done that today,' he hits back. 'Although jokes aside, has anyone ever passed comment on it?'

'Shut up!' I half-groan, half-yell, which earns me some concerned glances from the people passing us on the street.

Meanwhile, Preston is giggling like a schoolgirl, and if it wasn't so nice to see him so relaxed, I'd likely shout again. I'm beginning to wonder if it's not just his history he's hiding from everyone in London, but himself. It would hardly be the first time.

The weekend following my first Typewriter Magazine meeting, Aiden visits London a second time, despite it not even being a month since uni started. The fact his visit coincides with one of the rare weekends Preston isn't visiting home screams intentional. He insists he had no idea, and I insist on teasing him about it throughout the entire journey to my flat.

'I owe you a visit to Cardiff,' I say as he dumps his suitcase into my bedroom.

He scoffs. 'Fuck that, we spent the first eighteen yours of our lives there.'

'I should also visit my parents, even just to check that my dad's, y'know, alive.'

Aiden's brown eyes soften as he sits on my bed. 'Have you still not spoken to him since you moved here?'

I shake my head, which prompts Aiden to open his mouth again, but I'd rather pluck my fingers from my hands one by one than go there, so interrupt before he can say a thing.

'We nominate one movie each for tonight, by the way, so choose wisely.'

'Holy mackerel, no pressure then,' he grumbles, and I laugh as I dive towards him, knocking him over until we're lying in an awkward, tangled embrace on my bed.

We're having a sleepover at Margot and Preston's tonight, and the plan is to spend it binging movies and not actually sleeping a wink. In short, every tween girl's dream experience. It was my suggestion, one I regretted moments after blurting the words to Margot because God, who suggests that? Only, I'd never seen someone respond so enthusiastically to anything in my life. At least, not until I told Aiden we'd be doing it when he visited.

We walk to Margot and Preston's house in our pyjamas with no shame whatsoever, although our sleep attire is semi-hidden by the uni hoodies we've thrown over our torsos. When we arrive, Preston opens the door with a poorly hidden snicker.

'At least we're dressed for the occasion,' Aiden huffs, then nods towards Preston's jeans and t-shirt.

'I sleep without a shirt on,' Preston rebukes, and he's walked right into a trap he should've spotted from a mile away.

'That is not the strong argument you think it is,' Aiden scoffs.

Preston rolls his eyes as he gestures for us to enter his house, but Aiden's response is to jump—literally leap into the air—and hope to God that Preston will instinctively catch him.

He does.

Aiden wraps his legs around Preston's waist, who then carries him into the living room without hesitation, despite Aiden being at least two inches taller than him. He even spends the short walk asking me how I'm getting along with the proofreading task he assigned me for Typewriter Magazine. Once Preston returns him to the floor, Aiden begins arguing his case for why Shrek 2 should be tonight's opening film, and it takes everyone about ten seconds to be convinced.

The living room isn't a huge space, but it's big enough for Margot to have assembled a duvet and pillow mountain between the long sofa at the back of the room and the TV at the front of it. It reminds me of the one we created during a movie night at Robbie Morrissey's house a few years back, when Zack was out in full force and their friendship—if that's even what you can call it—was hanging by a thread. It's not me who draws any parallels aloud, though.

'Like old times!' Aiden, who's sprawled across Margot's creation, beams up at Preston and me.

'Don't tell me you've already broken your overnight-no-sleep-movie experience virginity,' Margot says from the foot of the makeshift bed as she slaps her hand over her heart.

'Sorry!' Aiden calls over to her.

I'm laughing as I glance at Preston, who's sitting on one of the black sofa's arms, and our eyes briefly meet before he looks away.

'I don't remember,' he says quietly, then stands before disappearing out of the room.

I dart my eyes to Aiden, who I plead caught that, but he's busy wrapping himself in one of the big, white duvets like a giant burrito.

On the bright side, this movie night runs far more smoothly than the one Aiden referenced. Zack makes no appearance, at no point does anyone smash a full bottle of alcohol on the kitchen floor, nor does someone disappear for an hour to return drunk out of their mind as they're spiralling, so by all accounts, it's a win.

Although, after Aiden's comment and Preston's reaction to it, I'm finding it difficult to concentrate on any movies. It doesn't help that I'm bunched up against Preston because I'm at the far end of the makeshift bed, and the alternative is being bunched up against the hard edge of a cupboard.

'Sorry,' I whisper to him after one especially sharp, accidental elbow nudge.

'We can swap if you're uncomfortable,' he murmurs, and my stomach flips at the sound of his voice so close to my ear.

'It's—No, it's fine!' I reply with too much enthusiasm.

He can see right through my feigned positivity because he starts chuckling, and given the movie we're currently watching is a psychological thriller, it's not at the TV. He wordlessly takes my hand underneath our shared duvet to lift my arm, then rests it on his side, and when he releases me, my fingers are brushing his thigh as if anything firmer might start a fire.

'I'm not infectious,' he whispers, and I relax my hand, my fingers settling on the rough denim of his jeans.

I'm relieved beyond words that it's dark enough for him to not catch my blush. It's not a big deal. It's so obviously not a big deal, but with the intensity of his reaction to Aiden's reminiscent comment lingering in the air, my mind is racing at a pace I can't keep up with. We return to silence, neither one of us uttering a word as Margot, Aiden, and Joe argue over how they think the film will end. When it's our turn to predict, I don't dare glance at Preston as I give my answer, or take my eyes off Aiden on his other side when Preston shares his thoughts. I just keep my hand motionless on his thigh, not daring to twitch a finger.

To nobody's surprise, it's Preston who gets the ending right.

Mine and Preston's silent exchange continues as Margot plays the next movie on our list, some melodramatic action film with shit dialogue Joe demanded we watch ironically. Despite the huge explosion that happens within five minutes of the movie starting, my attention is stolen by the feeling of Preston's hand brushing against mine as he shifts beside me.

Get a grip, Mia, Jesus Christ.

Instinct is screaming at me to nudge my hand away, even just a little, but I resist. I'm turning this into something it's not. The movie continues playing and I continue not concentrating on a single image, let alone on any of the dialogue Joe warned us about. The actors could be reciting Shakespeare for all I know.

He's being quiet too, even for him, right? Or am I overthinking it?

I can't resist any longer. I lift my gaze to glance up at Preston. The TV screen is casting a warm, orange glow on his light hair and his eyes are expertly still, as if moving them away from the screen could bring down humanity. My attention remains on him as my hand unwillingly twitches, my fingers grazing the top of his, and he swallows. I see him swallow.

I shoot my eyes back down to stare at the white duvet. Then, instead of doing the sensible thing and inching my hand from his, or even simply keeping it still, I move it closer. As if I'm no longer controlling them, my middle, ring, and pinky fingers curl around his to nest in the spaces between them, and then we're still again.

Only, the stillness lasts seconds.

'Does anyone need anything from the kitchen?' Preston questions as he jumps to his feet, and I'm suddenly mortified—the most mortified I think I've been in all my nineteen years of living.

'I'll—Yeah, I'll come with you, actually,' I blurt, and I'm praying to God nobody senses my awkwardness.

I need to squash this weirdness. Now.

Preston's surprise at my response is so mild that I wonder if I'm overreacting after all, especially when after Aiden, Margot, and Joe say they're good and we head into the kitchen, he doesn't question what the hell I did back there.

Instead of thinking it through for longer than two seconds, as the kitchen door closes behind us, I decide to approach the situation in the worst way possible.

'It's okay if you don't want to associate with me either,' I say, which makes Preston turn away from the white fridge he was approaching. 'Or Aiden, I guess.'

His brow furrows. 'You've lost me.'

I search his eyes for more, for any indication of his thoughts, feelings—anything—about what happened in the living room. Nothing. As always.

'Y'know, what you said on my first night in London, about how I shouldn't feel obliged to hang out with you if I want a fresh start or whatever.'

A pause. His eyes are locked into mine, searching them.

'I don't want that.'

Another pause.

'It seems like it,' I say quietly.

Preston clenches his jaw, then blinks slowly.

'Sometimes,' I add because no, I'm not being fair, nor am I even really talking about the living room incident anymore. 'Your reaction to Aiden's comment about that movie night at Robbie's, the way you—Y'know, well, the way you don't want to bring the past into your life here. I just mean I'm the past, obviously, so it's—I'd understand if you need distance.'

This pause is the longest yet, and despite the kitchen sink slowly dripping water, the world has never felt quieter.

'Stay,' he finally says. 'Please.'

We return to the living room with a bowl of popcorn and a bag of tortilla chips, and despite Aiden insisting he couldn't possibly eat any more after the oven pizzas we cooked, the first thing he does is jump up to shove a fistful of popcorn down his throat. We laugh and it eases whatever tension was lingering in the room, including any we might've brought with us from the kitchen, and as he grabs another handful then questions what's so funny, we laugh harder.

In the chaos of it all, I find myself returning to our duvet mountain in Aiden's place. Meanwhile, Preston takes mine, and so there's now a barrier in the form of Aiden separating Preston and me. It's probably for the best.

It's nearing five o' clock in the morning, and we're all significantly more awake than anticipated. It might have something to do with the Red Bulls we downed an hour ago to combat our increasing tiredness.

'We should do something!' Aiden exclaims as he sits upright. 'Go somewhere! It's London, baby!'

'Is he always this loud?' Joe, who's showing early signs of a sugar crash, whines as he pops his head around Margot to look at me.

'Yes,' Preston answers for me.

'Yes,' I agree.

'Hey!' Aiden complains.

'Hyde Park opens at five,' Preston offers, his tone nonchalant. 'Sunrise is at around seven.'

Aiden's grin expands, his white teeth gleaming.

'Let's do it!' he exclaims as he leaps up, which is followed by an ow! as his hip bangs into the cupboard I was pressed against earlier.

'Holy mackerel, that's a death trap.' He rubs his side as he grumbles under his breath, but is chirpy again within seconds. 'Hyde Park, yes?'

His brown eyes dart between our faces, and I'm laughing because it's such a horrible idea that we're bound to regret once our high deflates within ten minutes of leaving the house, but fuck it.

'Hyde Park!' Margot concurs as she stands, then punches the air.

'Hyde Park,' I agree as I join her and Aiden on my feet.

'Ugh, I guess,' Joe replies as he begrudgingly stands. 'I'll need another Red Bull, though.'

Margot laughs as she grabs his hand, then pulls him towards the kitchen to, I assume, grab another energy drink. I laugh behind them as the couple stumbles across the messy duvet mountain, especially when Joe nearly trips over a pillow pile.

'Have fun,' Preston announces as he stands, and it takes me a moment to realise what he's implying.

'You're not coming?' Aiden questions, or rather, screeches.

'No.'

'It was your idea,' I say slowly.

Am I missing something?

'I'd rather resist the sunrise,' he replies as if that explains his decision.

'That mean anything to you?' Aiden calls over to me from the other side of the room. 'You speak Preston, right?'

'Not a fucking word,' I confirm, which makes Preston clench his jaw to avoid smirking. 'Seriously, you're coming.'

'I don't visit often, so you have to,' Aiden argues, despite this being the second time he's visited in two weeks.

Preston sighs, and God, it's like pulling teeth.

'I'm grabbing my hoodie from the hallway, and if you've not agreed to join us by the time I'm back, we're knocking you out and dragging you there.'

With a huff, Aiden manoeuvres past the bedding on the carpeted floor, then leaves the room. I turn back to Preston with crossed arms and raised eyebrows. He responds with a challenging stare, but I don't give in. I don't let him win.

'You're coming,' I demand.

CHAPTER 6

I never thought I of all people would have to teach Preston Maddox how to live.

It's been staring me in the face, really–the reclusive persona he's adopted, his indifference towards any possibility of romance, his disengagement in casual conversation, declining his own Hyde Park at sunrise suggestion, his refusal to entertain his dad's communication attempts. He's being as nothing as possible, as if he's haunting his own life, and it's not right for someone as extraordinary as Preston to live like a ghost.

Hyde Park at sunrise is hardly groundbreaking, but it's a start.

I expected more pushback, but after my stern you're coming, Preston gave in. As he drags himself upstairs to change, Aiden pulls me aside and insists I have some kind of ethereal power over him, which I assure him I definitely do not. Shortly after Margot and Joe have gotten their shit together, Preston returns wearing a different t-shirt.

'I thought the point of you going upstairs was to change into something warmer,' Margot comments as we're leaving their townhouse, then nods towards Preston.

'Warmth has never quite fit me.'

If he insists on playing this nothing role, he should probably tone down the weirdness to match.

'He's not like other girls,' I translate for Margot.

Preston says nothing, just smirks while Aiden and Joe both laugh. I'm pleased Joe's extra Red Bull has kicked into action.

'In fairness, we can't say much, Mia; we're literally wearing pyjamas,' Aiden points out.

We catch the 137 bus to Hyde Park Corner and arrive at around five forty-five. The park is bathed in silence, and the sun is yet to show a glimmer of its face, but I don't stop searching the dark sky for it. We have no destination, nor does anyone try to determine one; we simply walk deeper and deeper into the park until our legs can no longer carry us. To my surprise, this is yet to feel like an awful idea, despite the cold nipping at my fingertips.

We find a small hill near the park's lido to sit on, and the groan Aiden releases as he plops himself onto the grass wet with dew makes it sounds like he's sprinted a marathon.

'Not like me to be dramatic,' he comments, and we all laugh.

God, I do miss him when he's not here.

After that, we sit in a silence that feels neverending. The vast lake opposite us is still, the trees, flowers, and shrubbery that frames it blowing so gently in the wind that it appears like a trick of the eye, and the sky is less black now—I'm sure the sun is coming.

The silence is eventually broken by Joe, who jumps to his feet to walk towards the lake. Margot follows closely behind, her blue hair a beacon against the park's autumnal colours, and Aiden can't resist joining them. Preston must be as transfixed by the scene in front of us as I am because neither one of us moves an inch.

'Are you glad you came?' I ask.

I don't turn my head to look at him, but I sense Preston's chest rise beside me, and it's followed by a quiet sigh.

'London asleep is a celestial phenomenon,' he murmurs.

'So... yes?'

He doesn't answer, so I turn my head to look—okay, scowl—at him. I don't shift my gaze from his offensively perfect side profile until he gives in.

'Yes, Euphemia, I'm glad I came.'

When he finally turns to me I'm grinning so hard that my cheeks might split, and he punishes me with a small eye roll.

'I know what your game is, by the way,' I say now that I've trapped his eyes in mine.

'Pray tell,' he replies, and the intensity of his gaze makes me question if it's me who's trapped.

'You're living the most uneventful, boring life possible. Intentionally.'

The corners of his mouth momentarily lift, and it's because he's been had—he knows I'm right—but the smile doesn't quite break through.

'Why would I possibly be doing that?' he counteracts.

'No idea, but you are.'

He holds my stare in silence, and the voices of Aiden, Margot, and Joe fade into the breeze blowing around us, the cold air forming goosebumps on my skin. The burning desire to turn away is impossible to ignore, but I resist.

'You are,' I repeat, and for the first time—well, ever—I win.

Preston shifts his attention back towards the lake stretching ahead, and I watch his Adam's apple bob as he swallows.

'The man who is swimming against the stream knows the strength of it,' he utters, and I have to strain to hear him. 'Woodrow Wilson.'

'Are you referencing the lake, or the conversation I'm trying to force you into?'

'There's nobody monitoring the lido,' he answers, or rather, doesn't answer because what the hell is he talking about?

Preston's eyes follow our friends as Aiden dips a tentative toe into the water, then yelps in response to the cold.

'What are you—'

'Hey!' Aiden interrupts me, and I whip my eyes from Preston to see my best friend at the bottom of our hill with his feet bare and shoes in hand. 'What are you lovebirds whispering about?'

'Firstly, shut up. Secondly, we're not even whispering,' is my response.

Preston's, however, is, 'I was just asking Mia if anyone's ever informed her that her name sounds like an STD.'

Aiden guffaws, throwing his head back. 'God, I'll never not love that.'

'I hate you both!' I yell into the sky.

'You should go for a swim,' Preston comments down to Aiden. 'There's nobody monitoring the lido.'

As Preston repeats what he told me moments earlier, Aiden blinks, then cranes his neck to look at the water as Margot and Joe stroll over to him.

'The lido's closed at this time of night—Well, day, I guess, but you get my point,' Joe pipes up.'

Preston shrugs. 'If there's nobody present to enforce a rule, does it not become a vague guideline?'

I've been so focused on Preston, Aiden, and Joe throughout their exchange that I don't realise how wide Margot's grin has grown until it's blinding. Her teeth are a bright white against her tanned skin, and her excitement is infectious.

'Fuck it, I'm convinced,' she announces.

With that, she tugs at the oversized jumper draped over her torso and shoves it over her head. I'm laughing, Aiden even more so, and I even catch a few chuckles break through Preston's lips as Aiden mirrors Margot's actions. Joe, meanwhile, stares at his girlfriend with big, wide eyes.

'It's going to be fucking freezing,' he scoffs, despite kicking his shoes off, removing his socks, then pulling his own jumper over his head.

I'm laughing even harder now. Aiden's down to his boxer shorts, Joe's quickly catching up, and Margot's in her bra and leggings. I'm in the midst of removing my shoes and socks when a loud splash snaps my head back towards the lake.

'Holy—It's fucking freezing!' Aiden yells as he resurfaces from underneath the dark water, the stillness of the lake long forgotten. 'Holy mackerel!'

'I warned you!' Joe shouts from the bank, moments before running, jumping, then cannonballing into the water.

His splash is louder, and I'm clawing at my hoodie in a clumsy attempt to remove my top layer. It's not until I'm successful and sitting in my pyjama shirt that it occurs to me that Preston, who's still sitting to my left, hasn't budged.

'Oh my God, come on,' I whine. 'Not this too.'

'I came to the park,' is his lacklustre argument. 'That's already far more than I'd planned to do toni—'

'No. Sorry, but no. Fuck off,' I reply, as poetically as ever.

I jump to my feet, then hold my hand out for him to take just as I catch another splash in the distance, I assume courtesy of Margot. Preston's green eyes inspect my palm as if it's something alien, and no matter how long I linger, he doesn't break.

'Fine.' I sigh, then drop my arm before returning to the grass. 'We'll leave it.'

As I'm reaching for my hoodie to throw back on, he grabs my arm to stop me.

'You go,' he says over a squeal from the water below, and I can't figure out if it was Aiden or Margot. 'Go, Mia. Have fun.'

'If you do, sure.'

He clenches his jaw. My blackmail isn't subtle, nor do I want it to be.

'Just this one thing,' I plead. 'Like you said, there's nobody watching. The park was your suggestion, and it was the best one.' I gesture towards our friends in the water. 'This was your suggestion, and based on their faces right now, it was an even better one.'

I'm not lying. Margot and Joe's cheeks are blushed pink from the cold water and Aiden's teeth are visibly chattering, but their smiles are the most beautiful things I've seen.

'And even if we did get caught, what would happen? Some security officer on a power trip might start yelling at us, we'd scurry out of the water—absolutely laughing our guts out, no doubt—and bolt for the park's exit while tripping back into our clothes, flag down a bus, try to contain ourselves as morning commuters wonder why there's a bunch of students with soaking wet hair riding the 137, get home, collapse into our beds, wake up at midday, and think, fuck, that was the most fun I've had all year.'

Preston's eyes are still on me, and I'm gritting my teeth to distract myself from the biting chill on my bare arms. I refuse to put my hoodie back on.

'Please,' I beg; a last ditch attempt to win the battle.

He turns back to the others with a long sigh, pauses, then relaxes his clenched jaw.

'You're paying any fines we encounter,' he grumbles, and I'm too busy trying to mediate the elation filling my body to respond.

I'm giggling hysterically as I jump to my feet, and as Preston joins me in standing, I demand he goes first because I don't trust him to jump otherwise. In classic Preston fashion, instead of adhering to social norms—or simply logic—he doesn't bother removing any clothes. Just kicks his shoes off, then darts down the hill and directly into the water.

'You're a fucking weirdo!' I scream as I chase after him, not that he hears me over the gigantic splash he makes.

By the time he resurfaces, I'm jumping in myself, although I've had the sense to remove all clothing beyond my underwear.

The water hits me like a shockwave and the world becomes a swirling, distorted version of what it was moments ago. The coldness stuns me, and when I bob my head back above water, I exhale so sharply that I'm shocked I don't pass out. It also leaves me in a vulnerable position whereby I nearly jump out of my skin when I feel arms around my waist.

'Boo!' Aiden exclaims into my ear, and I dig my elbow into his stomach behind me, which turns his boo into an, 'ow!'

'Arsehole,' I mutter.

'That was uncalled for,' he whines as he swims around to face me.

It's only now that I get a chance to drink in my surroundings, and in doing so, I'm reminded that Preston jumped into the water fully clothed. He's opposite me, positioned a little to my right while Margot and Joe are to my left, and he's smirking—no, laughing at me.

'Don't know what you're laughing at,' I snap. 'You're the one catching hypothermia in about thirty minutes.'

'She's got a point. You should take your shirt off,' Aiden chimes in.

'Subtle,' I interject.

'Sorry, my bad; not trying to be subtle. I don't care about the hypothermia,' Aiden clarifies. 'I just want to see you topless.'

In response, Preston dives towards Aiden. It's shockingly poor oversight on his part because I've got no doubt Aiden has had multiple wet dreams about this moment. The pair of them wrestle in the water as they splash each other, and I can't control my laughter—I cannot stop laughing.

'I'm enjoying this!' Aiden yells, and God, I can't breathe.

I gatecrash their faux battle and create the biggest wave I can by dragging my arm across the water, then directing it towards them. Joe and Margot follow my example, and suddenly, Aiden and Preston are bombarded by multiple tsunamis from multiple angles.

I'm still laughing as Aiden retaliates by darting towards Joe and Margot, leaving Preston to take care of me. I neglect my waves and turn to swim away, but he's too quick. His hands are on the backs of my arms, his laughter in my ear as he pulls me into him.

'Let me go!' I shriek, but my giggling is ruining the delivery. 'I'll drown you! Pull your wet t-shirt over your head, then shove you under! Watch me!'

'Graphic,' he murmurs.

My back is pressed against his firm chest while his arms are wrapped around my waist. I wriggle in his embrace, but it's hopeless—was he always this strong? He's laughing lightly, and it's the best sound I'm sure I've ever heard as his warm breath brushes the back of my neck.

It's not for another ten seconds that I notice his hands, or pay any attention to their proximity to mine. My fingers are grazing his knuckles as he holds me in place, as if making a weak attempt to remove his grip without fully committing to it. His heart is beating against my back, his warmth blanketing me from the icy water, and everything and everyone surrounding us has vanished—I'm sure of it. Flashes of the evening race through my head—tentative hands under covers and locked gazes searching for something intangible—and I'm suddenly sobered with the realisation that I'm wearing nothing but my bra and knickers right now.

With one big backwards push, I free myself from Preston's embrace. When I turn to face him, it's immediately clear that the moment I just experienced was in isolation. His gaze is light and playful; entirely void of any intensity. Despite the freezing water, I'm blushing.

'Was this not the best idea ever?' I goad him in an attempt to bury whatever the hell that just was.

'I'm rather full of them, aren't I?' he replies, which earns him another tsunami attack.

CHAPTER 7

T he trouble with avoiding something you've been dreading is that when that thing inevitably creeps up, it hits you like a frying pan to the face.

It's Dad's birthday.

A little over a month after moving to London, I'm dragging myself home to Cardiff in honour of the big event. It's not even a big event, really; he's turning forty-six, so it's not like it's a special birthday. I doubt he'd even mind if I didn't bother. The issue I have is that an inexplicable, crippling guilt will develop inside me if I don't because if I don't, no one will. And despite Dad's flaws, of which there are many, the thought of him spending his birthday entirely alone makes me feel, in short, shit.

As I force myself onto a train at Paddington with an overstuffed weekend bag, I try to focus on the pros. Pro: I'll get a chance to see Mum too. Pro: Preston's also home this weekend, so I can selfishly vent to him if needed. Pro: I can visit Aiden. Con: Dad.

Ugh. I try not to think about it as I blast my headphones up to full volume to amplify the distraction.

I'd been hoping for a lift from Cardiff Central station to Dad's house, but earlier this morning, he'd broken the news he'd be spending the afternoon at his local pub. I of all people know that mixing alcohol and driving is a terrible idea, so I was hardly going to push him on it. The concern now, however, is how drunk he'll be when he arrives home, and what time he arrives home. One thing I know for sure is that I'll be sorting out my own dinner tonight. It's his loss, really; I was going to offer I buy us both a takeaway.

Takeaway or no takeaway, we'd planned to spend the evening together, but fuck that, I guess.

I'm grumbling as soon as my feet hit Welsh soil, and I don't stop grumbling as I tap out through the train station's barriers. The only thing capable of putting a stop to my whining is the sight of Aiden, wide-eyed and bushy-tailed, standing outside the station entrance—or, well, exit in my case.

I stammer as I gape at him. 'Are you lost?'

Unsurprisingly, his response is a big, fat laugh. 'I still live here, remember? A little over a month in the big smoke and you're already forgetting us country-folk.'

He begins walking and I instinctively follow. 'You're born and bred in Cardiff, you clown, hardly country-folk!'

He's giggling as he spins on the spot, then takes my bag from my hand. Before I can thank him, he hurls an insult at me.

'Holy mackerel, Mia, you got a corpse in here?'

'Shut up.'

He starts giggling again, and only now do I realise he's leading me towards the station's car park.

'Quick one,' I say, 'why are you here and where are you taking me?'

Aiden bats the air as we walk side-by-side. 'Preston said your dad bailed, so we're acting as stand-in chauffeurs.'

As if perfectly timed, once Aiden's finished speaking, I turn to the car park up ahead and spot a familiar Vauxhall Corsa. Only, I'm used to seeing Anwen in its driving seat, not Preston.

'I'd ordinarily say I didn't need rescuing,' I declare as I step into the red car's backseat. 'But fuck me, am I grateful for the lift.'

Aiden laughs at my comment as he dumps my luggage into the boot, and he's still chuckling when he opens the passenger car door to jump in. Frankly, I don't think he's stopped laughing between when he first spotted me and now.

'He's a much better driver than you,' he says as he jerks his head towards Preston. 'Hasn't crashed and landed me in hospital once!'

'Firstly,' I snap, 'you came out of that crash unscathed. Secondly, by bringing it up, you're at risk of resurrecting seventeen-year-old trauma Mia. No one wants that.'

'Eh, she was kinda fun.'

Preston still hasn't said a word, but he's been glancing at me via the overhead mirror throughout mine and Aiden's faux bickering, a lopsided smirk plastered on his face. I give him the finger through the mirror, naturally. I still frequently scold him for taking the blame for that crash, but while it was without a doubt the wrong thing to do, I can at least see the logic behind not letting my unlicensed self own up to drunk driving a car into a bush in the middle of the Welsh countryside.

I don't say anything of the sort aloud, but Preston somehow knows I want to avoid anything Dad-related for as long as possible. Aiden tries to convince us to crash Dad's place and hang out in the inevitable free house, but Preston successfully weans him off the idea without making my horror at the prospect of it blatantly obvious. I thank him in silence; a coy smile via the overhead mirror that I hope he catches.

Instead, we just drive and talk shit. It primarily entails Aiden and me talking shit while Preston guides his mother's car around the suburbs of Cardiff, but he occasionally caves with a clever remark or observation. It's nice. It's really bloody nice. By the time we've run out of road and I have to be dropped off at Dad's, I've forgotten why I was dreading it so much.

I was on the money when I guessed how Dad would spend his Friday evening. I didn't hear him come home, so it was definitely a late one, and poorly discarded oven ready meal packaging was strewn across the kitchen, so he was definitely drunk. It's also currently eleven-thirty in the morning and he's still not emerged from his bedroom, so drunk may be an understatement.

Happy birthday to him, I guess.

I'm in the middle of making myself breakfast when the doorbell rings, and I open it to see my sister, Livvy, whose flat expression gives the impression she'd rather be shovelling shit than visiting Dad on his birthday. My face, on the other hand, must be doing something really weird because I'm stunned into silence.

'Since when did you visit Dad on his birthday?' I question after finally regaining the ability to speak.

She rolls her eyes, then moves past me to enter the house. 'I'm not totally heartless.'

Despite her sarcasm, she leans in to pull me into a long hug. She sighs as we part, and okay, fine, it's nice to see her.

'Don't let this inflate your ego, but I've missed you,' she says.

'And I don't totally hate that you're here,' I reply, and we both laugh.

'It's a bit of an oxymoron, to be totally honest,' Livvy continues as she kicks her shoes off at the bottom of the staircase. 'The only reason I came is because I knew you were here, so I wanted to be your moral support. If you'd not come home for the weekend, I wouldn't have bothered to visit.'

She glances towards the upstairs landing.

'I'm guessing he's asleep, or hungover.' She pauses. 'Probably both, actually.'

'Bingo!' I reply with fake cheer.

'You should've called if you were alone last night,' Livvy replies as I follow her into Dad's living room. 'I would've rescued you.'

I shrug. 'It's alright; some friends ended up picking me up from the station and we hung out for a bit.'

Livvy, who's now sprawled across the sofa as she twirls her blonde hair around her finger, scans my face. Her dark blue eyes narrow.

Here we go.

'Friends, or friend?' She wiggles her eyebrows. 'You better have met some rich, dashing London stranger who loves you so much he's followed you home, and you spent last night losing your v-card in a night of passion and—'

'Shut up,' I interrupt, then shove her feet off the sofa.

She yelps, then lifts her legs back up onto the chair. 'Okay, okay, I get it; no virginity jokes.' She rolls her eyes. 'In all seriousness, which friends?'

'Aiden,' I offer.

'Huh, I didn't realise he was multiple people.' She sits up with a melodramatic groan. 'I literally don't care about yours and Zack's thing. That's Dad.'

'Preston,' I correct her. 'And we're not a thing. We don't have a thing.'

'So he was there, then?'

Shit. I landed myself in that one.

I grab a cushion from underneath her legs, then throw it at her cocky little face. Her reaction is to laugh, which is a huge improvement from what would've happened if I'd done that two years ago. She would've screamed the house down. It's the small wins, right?

Dad eventually wakes up at around one o'clock, and he's as miserable as ever, but at least I have Livvy to split the frustration with. We have to wean him off visiting the pub again, and end up compromising with a promise that we'll have some drinks with him in the house.

In case it's not yet obvious, Dad has something of a drinking problem.

Livvy has gone by three o'clock, and I'm left to fend for myself in the living room while Dad watches a rugby game I have zero interest in. In my head, I'm counting down the hours until tomorrow's release. We're talking literal counting—it's five-thirty, so I've got sixteen and a half hours until Mum rescues me with a lift to her house.

Dad and I have exhausted all conversation topics, namely how uni is going and what he's been up to since I've been in London (spoiler: going to the pub), and so we've been sitting in silence for at least an hour. When he finally breaks it, I desperately wish he hadn't.

'How's your mother?'

There are a couple of ways I could approach answering this question. I could respond with an emotionless fine, or I could say I've not spoken to her yet. I could even try to change the subject and hope it won't be obvious. The trouble is that I've tried all that before, and each time, it's ended in disaster. He always finds a way to turn it into a disaster.

Ideally, I'd love to say nothing, stand up, leave the house, walk forty minutes to Cardiff Central, and catch the first train to London. Sadly, that's a total non-option.

In the end, I settle on the classic, 'fine.'

He scoffs.

Here we go.

From where I'm sitting on the long sofa at the back of the room, I can only see Dad's side profile, but it's enough. He's shaking his head, a can of cider in his hand as he rests it on his stomach. He's due a shave.

'Have you met the new neighb–'

'She still friends with that man from the school?' he interrupts, and that's the subject change option nuked.

'Yeah.'

Just friends, the same as they've been since I was a literal infant, I silently add, knowing there's no point making that definition aloud.

He scoffs again, and anyone would guess he didn't bring this situation on himself. It ceases to amaze me how men always feel so attacked by the consequences of their own actions.

'She acted so upset when things ended between us,' Dad continues as if I wasn't there at the time, and it's an interesting way of phrasing when I cheated on her. 'Wouldn't think that now, would you? It was fake. All fake.'

I bite my tongue, despite the urge to scream at him. He turns to me, and his eyes are droopy, his jaw lax. He might as well have drunk slapped across his forehead.

He juts his cider can towards me. 'She's going off with her new man like nothing happened, as if the twenty years we had together means sod all. Don't trust her, Mia.' He scoffs. Again. 'Take my word for it, okay? Your mother's a lying bitch.'

I can't do this–No, I refuse to do this.

'Oh, fuck off, Dad.'

The words have fallen from my mouth before I'm even aware of thinking them, but frankly, I'm glad. I've always kept my mouth shut when he goes on these rants, but I can't do it anymore. I won't.

'Don't speak to me like–'

'You fucked up, Dad! Accept it!' I yell, and I'm on my feet, adrenaline racing through my blood. 'This has all happened because of your affair, and the only reason you give a shit about what Mum's doing is because you don't have anyone, because the woman you cheated on her with had the sense to dump you, as has every other woman you've gone near since.'

I inhale sharply and Dad's blue eyes are darting around my face, clearly perplexed by the fact that his constant jibing has finally made me snap.

'At least they've all had a way out. You'll never not be my Dad.'

With that, I leave the room without so much as a glance back in his direction.

Chapter 8

After the mother of all teenage tantrums, I find myself angrily trudging the suburbs of Cardiff in the spitting rain at six o'clock in the evening. Despite my rage, I was thinking clearly enough to grab my hooded jacket as I left Dad's house, but not clearly enough to have a final destination in mind. This results in me following my feet, and I'm not sure if it's muscle memory or something deeper, but they walk me in the direction of Anwen's house.

It's not until I've almost arrived that I realise Preston will be there. I'm so used to it only being Anwen and Matty in their house that slotting him into the picture feels strange. When Dad's drinking was at its worst during my final school year, Anwen's house became a haven because I hardly wanted to bring Mum into the mess. In hindsight, nor did I want to bring Anwen into it, but it's a little late for hindsight.

As I'm knocking on the terraced house's front door, I realise I maybe should've called to warn of my imminent arrival. It's Matty who answers, which I conclude is probably for the best because he does so with a huge grin.

'Mia!' he exclaims, then likely upon realising I'm dripping wet, furrows his brow. 'You probably should've brought an umbrella.'

'As upfront as ever,' I say with a sincere, light laugh. 'But you're not wrong.'

Matty, who's dressed in a hoodie twice the size of him, opens his mouth to respond, but he's interrupted by the sound of footsteps barrelling down the stairs behind him. Moments later, Preston, who looks even more perplexed to see me, is standing beside him.

'Mia's here,' Matty announces.

'I can see that,' Preston replies, which gets him an elbow dig from his little brother. He returns his attention to me, and more notably, the rain crashing from the sky. 'You could've invited her in, Matt.'

Without another word, Preston gestures me inside, and it's not until the front door is closed behind me that I notice I'm shivering. I remove my soaked jacket and hang it up on the staircase's bannister, which helps, but doesn't stop Preston making a fuss. I assure him I'm fine, and make him promise to assure his mother of that when she spots me because Anwen's favourite pastime is worrying. Meanwhile, Matty gazes at us in silent awe, as if we're a figment of his imagination.

'She's due back from Tesco any minute now, so your time is limited,' Preston comments before I can decipher Matty's look. 'If it's at all reassuring, she'll probably be more horrified at me for not offering you a lift, despite my insistence that you appeared from nowhere.'

I laugh as I follow him into the family's living room. 'And I won't even try to stand up for you.'

Matty's still watching us quietly, and when my eyes meet his big, brown ones, it dawns on me. He's not seen Preston and me interact, at least not in person, since Preston was in the young offender's institute. As the realisation hits, as if on cue, the sound of Preston's voice snaps our attention back towards the living room's doorway.

'What becomes wetter the more it dries?'

Without giving us any chance to respond, he leaves Matty and me in the living room, then disappears to who knows where for who knows what.

'He's still weird,' I mutter in Matty's direction, which successfully snaps him out of his trance with a long, heavy eye roll.

'He does it on purpose,' he assures me as he plops himself onto the sofa at the back of the small room.

I instinctively begin to walk towards the sofa to join him, but decide against it because I'm still soaked. Instead, I stand as still as possible in a poor attempt to stop myself from tarnishing the carpet with rainwater.

'We should do it back,' I suggest to Matty. 'Outweird him.'

'I've tried,' Matty replies with a sigh filled with way too much despair for a kid barely in his double digits, which cracks me up. 'It's towel,' he continues. 'The riddle.'

With that, Preston reappears in the doorway with a small, blue towel in hand. He throws it to me, then winks at his brother.

'Precisely. Outsmarted by a ten-year-old, Euphemia,' he comments, and I'd hit him if doing so wouldn't splash water across the walls.

'Ugh, whatever. I knew the answer, anyway,' I argue as I begin patting myself down with the towel. 'In fact, I expect way more from you. Everyone knows that riddle.'

'You seem awfully defensive for someone claiming to be so unbothered,' he teases, but this time, I don't bite. Just smile. Really, really sarcastically.

Preston's prediction was eerily accurate—Anwen is beside herself when she walks through the front door to find me in her living room, albeit more so damp and less so drenched now. She blinks her green eyes as she freezes in the doorway, a shopping bag in hand.

'You should've given her a lift!' she snaps at her eldest son, who's leaning back against one of the sofa's arms.

He flashes me a told you so glance, and I struggle not to laugh. Anwen's voice is so soft and melodic that she could probably speak a sentence composed solely of swear words, and she'd still sound like she's paying you a compliment.

'Hand on heart, I just turned up,' I assure Anwen, despite my earlier threats to not back Preston up. 'It's my fault, honestly, it's—I shouldn't have assumed it was okay in the first place.'

Anwen's expression softens. 'Don't be silly! It's always okay! Is everything alright?'

Preston and Matty asked me the same question moments earlier, and I give Anwen the same answer I gave them.

'Yeah, totally fine! I just got a bit bored at home so thought I'd pop in to see you guys.'

Matty's got football practice at an ungodly hour tomorrow morning, and Anwen's plucked the short straw to drive him there, so she doesn't head to bed much later than him. At around ten o'clock, she announces she's calling it a night.

'You're welcome to stay over, lovely,' she says to me as she pauses in the living room doorway. 'I've got no problem with you staying in Preston's room.'

I could die. Quite happily, actually.

'Subtle,' Preston mutters from my left, apparently unfazed by his mother's comment, not that I dare to glance at him to check.

'Or,' Anwen replies, clearly aware that she's been had. 'He can offer you his room, then make up sofa bed here for himself.'

With that, she leaves the room while I silently, and desperately, attempt to dampen the heat racing towards my cheeks.

I anticipate Preston's acknowledgement of this, or of Anwen's comment, but he instead opens with, 'so why are you actually here?'

I knew it was coming, but I'm still stumped by the question. So stumped, in fact, that my response is to stare blankly without uttering a word. Eloquence personified.

'Your dad?' he offers, and God, it scares me how he always just knows.

I don't answer, but my expression must give the game away because when I turn to look at him, Preston's green eyes soften. I hold my breath in fear of the inevitable questions. What happened? What did he do? Do you want to talk about it? Only, then I remember who I'm speaking to. Preston never pushes.

'Want to go for a drive?' he offers, and God, yes. That's exactly what I'm in the mood for.

As we bundle ourselves into Anwen's cold car, it occurs to me that I've spent an impressive amount of time driving around aimlessly while I've been home. I've not been in a single car since moving to London, so I guess I'm making up for lost time. We drive slowly through the night with no plan beyond listening to the patter of rain against the windscreen.

'He just—It's the shit he spews about Mum that pisses me off,' I say after fifteen minutes of silent driving.

I try to wait for Preston to respond, but he knows the drill by now—better than I do, to be honest. Within moments, more word vomit explodes from my mouth.

'He acts so... so oblivious. As if the crappy life he's living is entirely out of his control, as if it's something Mum cursed him with when he's the one who fucked things up in the first place, and–Ugh, and God, it's so embarrassing how he so obviously wants her back but wouldn't dare say it.'

I rest my head back against the passenger seat's headrest.

'I'm just beyond relieved Mum would sooner join a travelling circus than ever go there.'

Preston laughs through his nose beside me, which is in itself an enormous win given his eerily controlled temperament.

'But then it's–God, sorry, I shouldn't–I really shouldn't complain to you of all people. My life's a literal walk in the park compared to yours, and whining about my dad is hardly appropriate with your–the situation with yours right now, I mean.'

The car falls into a silence that stretches longer than anticipated, and fuck, I shouldn't have said that. I shouldn't have brought up his dad. I'm suddenly horrified by what I just said, especially when I glance at Preston's side profile and find it even more challenging to read his expression than usual.

Eventually, he says, 'relativity is a privilege granted to people who have the energy to look outwards.'

'Is that a quote?' I ask with narrowed eyes.

'No,' he says with another light laugh, then clears his throat. 'Even if somebody else has it much worse, that doesn't really change the fact that you have what you have.'

A pause.

'That, however, was a quote. Stephen Chbosky, The Perks of Being a Wallflower.'

I shove him lightly, and any tension that was lingering is broken by light laughter. I'm now only semi-worried I traumatised him with the dad comment.

'My point is,' he says, 'don't diminish your feelings for the sake of others.'

'Well, thanks,' I reply. 'For letting me complain.'

We return to silence, one that isn't awkward, and the sound of the rain crashing against the car is soothing as we continue travelling through the darkness.

'I'm going to open it,' he says.

I blink, confused.

'The letter from my dad,' he continues, and I have to suppress a sarcastic comment about him actually elaborating for once. 'I will.'

I'm not sure if he's trying to convince me, or himself. What I do know is how crucial this moment is.

'Do you know much about him?' I try.

He sighs, then pauses before saying, 'a little based on what Mum's told me. Not much. His name—Rhys—his job, his age, the city he lives in. That kind of thing.'

'What does he do? For a job, I mean.'

'He works in academia, apparently,' he answers, and I can't resist smiling.

'You give off big academia vibes,' I reply, then fear I may have overstepped the mark again.

My fear is quickly subdued when Preston says, 'I'm going to need an explanation.'

'Well, you're a bit fucking weird,' I point out, and it makes him laugh. 'Where does he live?'

'Somewhere in England,' he responds quickly—a little too quickly, in hindsight, especially when he follows up with a total conversation deflect. 'It's getting late; we should probably head back.'

I concede with, 'yeah, we probably should.'

I wish I could've gotten more out of him from that conversation, but I got something, at least. The most he's ever given me, and it's always a game of patience with Preston. I forget that, sometimes.

'Are you okay to drop me back at my dad's?' I query. 'I can't hide forever, and he's probably asleep, anyway.'

'Of course. Are you sure?'

I nod.

As Preston's pulling up outside Dad's house, I'm suddenly regretting my decision. The porch light is on. It could easily be that he's forgotten to switch it off, but even when drunk, that would be totally out of character.

'Do you want me to come in with you?' Preston asks, interrupting my internal spiralling.

Seriously, how the hell does he always just know?

I stammer. 'No, it's—You probably shouldn't. I mean, you're not exactly my dad's favourite person, to start with, so it—'

'Come on, then,' Preston replies, ignoring me as he shuts the car engine off and opens his door.

I scramble to follow, and by the time I've left the car, he's already a few strides ahead of me.

'Okay, but be quiet,' I whisper as I hurry to catch up with him. 'We should be quiet, so it—Yeah, just sh. Sh! And no STD comments!'

'I'm getting the impression we should be quiet,' he murmurs as we stop outside the house's front door. 'And in that case, before we go in, has anyone ever told you that your name sounds like an STD.'

'Shut up!' I whisper-hiss.

The door's unlocked, an even worse sign than the porch light being left on. He's definitely awake. I lift my hand to grasp the metal handle as if it's dripping in poison, then as slowly and silently as possible, lower it to open the door. Much to my dismay, as I gently push it open, it makes a strained squeaking sound.

'Mia?' a voice calls from upstairs.

Shit.

I glance at Preston, who's behind me as I step into the hallway, but it's too late. As I turn back around, Dad's figure is at the top of the staircase like a looming shadow.

'I left the porch light on so you'd be okay—so you'd find your way back,' he rambles as he starts walking down the stairs, his sloppy movements suggesting sobering up hasn't been high on his priority list since I've been gone.

Double shit.

'It's—Yeah, thanks,' I mutter. Whatever. 'Don't worry about coming down, I'm just going to go straight to bed.'

'We should talk, it's—I'm sorry about earlier, Mia, I shouldn't have gotten so worked up.'

I resist all temptation to glance behind me because if I do, Dad will finally notice Preston standing on the porch. While my brain would kill for the telepathic ability to tell him to leave, the anxiety it's currently drowning in it wants me to beg him to stay. As Dad nears the bottom of the stairs, his blue eyes narrow to squint in my direction—most notably, towards the space behind me.

Triple shit.

In an attempt to deflect, I say, 'honestly, Dad, it's fine. Let's just go to be—'

'Why's he here?'

Fuck.

Dad's frozen on one of the bottom steps, his jaw clenched. The slack posture he'd been adopting has suddenly straightened as if the sight of Preston has drained all traces of alcohol from his veins. It's a real catch-22.

'Mia needed a lift home,' Preston replies. 'I'm not staying.'

His tone isn't argumentative, it has no sense of malice, nor is it even a little patronising. It's perfectly–and expertly–measured. Even more so than usual.

'You got in a car with him?' Dad interrogates me. 'You've not been with him this whole time, have you?'

'It's fine, Dad, please just leave it. It doesn't have to be a big—'

'I won't have a murderer in my house.'

My blood turns cold as Dad's words wash over me, but Preston doesn't flinch.

Instead, in the same calm tone as before, he says, 'I'm not staying.'

He's also not technically in the house, you prick, I think, but am wise enough not to say aloud. With clenched fists, I turn to face Preston on the porch, then nudge him back so we're both outside.

'Do you need me to stay? Or do you want to come back with me?' he whispers.

'No, it's—I'm fine, I just—God, I'm really sorry about him.'

'Mia,' Dad calls from behind me. 'You're not staying with him.'

'He's leaving!' I snap without bothering to turn and look at him, then lower my voice so only Preston can hear me. 'Seriously, I'm really sorry, I shouldn't have let you come in with me.'

Preston's bright eyes search my face, but I've got no idea what he's looking for. It takes him a moment to say anything.

'I'm capable of handling it,' he assures me, then pauses to turn his gaze from mine. 'It's not as though you can blame him.'

I scoff. 'I can, and I will. He's being a dickhead.'

Preston's lips quiver, and I think he's battling a smile. 'In my defence, I'm not suggesting he isn't being a dickhead. I just also think he has multiple legs to stand on in regards to my influence.'

'Mia! I'm not kidding anymore!' Dad's grating voice shouts from behind.

'I'm leaving!' Preston calls back before I can respond, and within moments, he's walking backwards towards Anwen's car. 'It's London, by the way; where Rhys lives.'

CHAPTER 9

I t turns out uni students do very little reading during reading week, me included. I'm not a total lost cause; since Preston assigned me my first proofreading task for Typewriter Magazine, I've become possessed by the spirits of editors past and am spending reading week devouring as many writing pieces to fix up as I can. As uncool as it is to admit, I love it.

'Yeah, it's—I'm getting ready, I swear!' I insist into my phone, which is perched on my windowsill as I swoop blush onto my cheeks.

I pause to check my reflection, then frown. I was unsure about the green eyeshadow before I even applied it; I'm worried it looks jarring against the navy colour of my eyes, but I've committed to it.

'Mia, if you ditch this party because you're marking someone's homework, I swear—'

'It's not homework! It's a short story about a Yorkshire woman who finds a penguin in her back garden and has to figure out how to get it to back to Antarctica,' I correct Margot. 'And I'm literally leaving in five—Okay, like, twenty minutes.'

Silence over the phone, then, 'a woman who—What?'

'Exactly!' I reply as I rummage through my make-up bag for my highlighter. 'You're intrigued, right?'

'Nah, that's it; I'm getting your boss.'

The phone line turns static and it sounds like Margot then throws her mobile down the stairs because there's a lot of loud banging–slamming?

'Apparently, you're abandoning the party to edit our next issue's penguin rehoming story,' Preston says in a tone so nonchalant that he makes the topic sound normal.

'Margot's being dramatic,' I argue. 'I'm finishing my make-up–nearly done, by the way–then giving the story a final once over.'

'Take a day off, Gifford.'

'Giff–What? I'm too busy to untangle your bullshit right now.'

'William Gifford,' he replies. 'Jane Austen's editor. An Oxford academic who compared her original drafts with the final manuscripts has argued a lot of credit for the final work should be given to Giff–'

'Jesus Christ, okay, I'm coming,' I reply, then mutter, 'before you bore me to death.'

If I've learned anything in the short amount of time I've lived here, it's that Preston and Margot's place is the social hub of Clapham. Ironic, really, given Margot's made it clear Preston has next to no part in that. He apparently spends most of their parties either locked away in his room, or doing his own thing in the middle of it all–reading on staircases being one of his more popular hobbies, if the last party I attended is anything to go by.

It therefore doesn't faze me when I find him reading at the bottom of the ground floor staircase when Margot welcomes me inside that night.

'You're literally a caricature of yourself. You realise that, right?' I comment to him as I'm kicking my shoes off.

While Preston blissfully ignores me, Margot snorts a laugh. She complimented my eye make-up as soon as she welcomed me in, so she's high in my good books right now. Before she can comment on my dig at Preston, Joe calls her from the living room at the back of the house. It's ideal timing because I need to state my conditions.

'You're not spending the whole night doing this,' I declare as I drop to the floor to sit opposite him. 'If you do, I'll go home.'

'I can't recall the last time we hoovered,' Preston murmurs without glancing up from the pages of his novel. 'I'd recommend avoiding the carpet, if I were you.'

'Piss off,' I scoff, then grab the opened book from his hands, and he's smirking. Of course he's smirking. I turn the book around to skim its pages. 'Please don't tell me you're reading a mafia romance because I swear to–'

'A true philistine is the one who refuses to entertain the most simple pleasures.'

'Agreed,' I reply as I return his opened book to him, and he tilts his head. Ha. Now he's intrigued. 'Like, for example, showing face at social gatherings–say, a house party. The most simple pleasure there is, right? Socialising with like-minded people.'

Preston holds my gaze, his mouth cracking into the tiniest of smiles.

'Someone shutting themselves away from something like that could even be considered rude, would you not ag–'

'Touché, Euphemia,' Preston interrupts as he slams his book shut, removes his glasses, then jumps to his feet. 'As Sophocles once said, a good man yields when he knows his course is wrong.

No books, mafia romance or otherwise.' He pauses. 'He didn't say that last bit; I added that.'

To my sincere surprise, Preston actually sticks to his promise, and Margot and Joe are beside themselves over his sudden burst of life. I frequently catch them watching him like a mirage that could disappear any moment, and those who are attending the party from Typewriter Magazine are equally as stunned. Margot keeps insisting it's all me, which is oddly invigorating—I almost want to make an awards acceptance speech.

'Don't get me wrong,' Joe calls over the music spilling in from the living room, and I have to strain to hear him because he's got his head in a fridge. 'He's still talking in riddles and giving fuck all away, but I've never seen the guy actively join in like he's doing tonight. You need to tell me your secret.'

With that, he stands upright with a supermarket-branded bottle of lemonade in his hand. I thank him as I take it, then mix it with the vodka in my, Margot, and Dana's cups on the kitchen counter to our left.

'There's no secret,' I assure him. 'I just call him out on his bullshit.'

Joe responds with a warm laugh as he runs his fingers through his auburn hair. He proceeds to shake his head as he cracks open a bottle of beer, the corners of his light eyes creased with a smile.

'Nah, he probably just fancies you,' he responds, but before I can dwell on the insinuation, adds, 'I fancy Margot so much that I'd eat shit if she asked me to.'

As we return to the living room, we find our group huddled around the large corner sofa with some overspill onto the floor. Preston's lack of hoovering comment flashes through my mind, and I stifle a laugh. The joke ends up being on me because I quickly discover the only spare spot is to Preston's left on that same floor.

'If I catch chlamydia from this thing,' I comment as I plop myself down beside him, then gesture towards the carpet. 'I'm holding you responsible.'

'You should know better than to bring up STDs around me, Euphemia, given you've yet to tell me whether anyone's passed comment on your name sounding like one.'

Dickhead.

'Besides, I warned you not to go near the carpet earlier, so relinquish all responsibility,' he whisper argues.

I whisper argue back with, 'objection. It's your house, ergo your duty to keep your guests safe. No ifs or buts.'

'No conditions? This all sounds concerningly similar to a dicta-torshi–'

Preston's interrupted by a face appearing the other side of him, and suddenly, Dana's smiling back at me as she glances between the two of us.

'Drinking game,' she says cheerily. 'You guys in?'

I don't even need to look at Preston to catch the hesitance in his eyes. The way his back stiffens is telling enough. I'm only on my third drink of the night while Preston's still on his first, so what's the harm? It's not like he ever drinks more than a few beers nowadays, anyway.

Before he can protest, I jump in with an answer. 'Yep. We're both in.'

Dana squeals with joy and her freckled face disappears from around Preston, who's watching me with a pointed look on his pretty little face.

I gasp with faux horror. 'An opportunity for even more fun? How dare I subject you to such a thing.'

'So that's a yes,' he replies in a heartbeat, and I respond with a furrowed brow. 'Someone has told you your name sounds like an STD?'

I don't satisfy him with a verbal response, and instead, elbow him in his side. He doesn't flinch, just laughs, and any fear I had that he was sincerely pissed off with me melts away.

As with all drinking games, it takes me a hot minute to figure out what the hell is going on. Dana is leading the game via an app she's inputted our names into, and it's asking people to answer embarrassing questions about themselves or others, and barking orders for specific people to do specific things. The first challenge was an order for Joe and Margot to kiss for seven seconds, so not off to the most exciting start.

Nobody has folded and taken a forfeit drink yet, and so there's an unspoken pressure bubbling away to not, under any circumstance, be that first person.

'Okay, Damien!' Dana announces, then cranes her neck around Preston to look at Typewriter Magazine's most prolific poet, who's sitting to my left. 'Let Mia post any photo on your phone to any social media of her choice.'

I flash Damien the most evil smile I can muster, and after some brief hesitation, he yields with a sigh as he hands me his phone. I resist the obvious and opt not to search for any nudes—partly because I don't want to expose myself to that, and partly because I'm not that much of an arsehole—and instead settle on a childhood picture of him with a mushroom-esque haircut. It's on his Instagram story within minutes of Dana announcing the challenge.

'Okay, okay, next!' Dana declares once we've all finished taking the piss out of Damien.

As she taps her phone screen, I swear I witness the seven stages of grief pass through her face within the course of five seconds. Only, it turns out I'm totally off the mark; she's feeling quite the opposite.

'Dana—Me,' she clarifies in case anyone was unsure, 'make out with the person to your left for at least seven seconds.'

It's the same challenge as Joe and Margot's earlier, just with a different name attached to it. I flip my head to my right—and to Dana's left—to catch a more accurate representation of the seven stages of grief pass through Preston's hilariously brooding eyes.

Resigning to his fate, he turns to Dana and allows her to do her worst. Everyone counts down from seven aloud, and before we've finished uttering the o for one, Preston pulls away. Dana doesn't notice because she's laughing, her pale face blushed red as she tries to hide it behind her blonde waves.

'You realise she's going to be fantasising over that for the rest of her life, right?' I whisper into Preston's ear.

'Kindly fuck off,' he whispers back to me, his voice so devoid of emotion that I laugh hard enough to nearly choke on my drink.

'Next—Yeah, sorry—' Dana clears her throat, and I've never seen anyone so giddy in my life. 'Next one!'

She taps her phone screen, and she starts giggling again with an overzealous eye roll.

'Well, that's our moment stolen. You'll have to give a comparative analysis at the end or something,' she jokes to Preston, then glances at me, and I'm totally lost—am I missing something? 'Preston, make out with the person to your left for at least seven seconds.'

I'm not sure the challenge processes in my mind—frankly, I can't be sure Dana even finishes announcing it before Preston speaks up.

'I'm not kissing her.'

With that, he lifts his beer bottle to his mouth and throws it back, his eyes not so much as flicking in my direction, and I'm left staring in stunned silence as if that wasn't the most embarrassing thing that's ever happened to me.

It's not subtle, either. Our group has turned silent, and those who aren't awkwardly avoiding eye contact with me are staring at Preston with confusion slapped onto their faces. I want the ground to eat me—I want this unkempt carpet to split open, the concrete below to crumble, and for me to fall deeper and deeper into the crack until the core of the earth burns me alive.

Dana, bless her, tries to come to my rescue. 'First forfeit! We should—Hey, should we have, like, an extra punishment for first forfeits?'

'Good call!' Margot agrees, and I try not to cringe at the sympathetic look she flashes me. 'Preston, down your drink.'

Preston obeys the order, and hey, I guess it's nice to know he's not totally incapable of accepting a challenge.

The moment Margot asks me if I feel like joining her for some fresh air outside, I jump. Our game ended pretty soon after my dignity was lost, and I've not uttered a word to Preston since the whole ordeal. I didn't want him to kiss me. Obviously, I didn't want that. If he'd, I don't know, made a joke out of it, maybe given me an opportunity to throw some banter in his direction before giving into a forfeit, it wouldn't have bothered me.

What bothered me was the instantaneous I'm not kissing her in front of our entire friendship group moments after he'd just kissed another girl without a second thought.

'You good?' Margot asks tentatively as we step into the cold garden.

I groan as she shuffles through her oversized denim jacket's pockets for her cigarettes, and I don't reward her with a sensical answer until she's found them.

'Was it that obvious?' I grumble. 'I didn't want to kiss him or anything, obviously.'

'No, it was—I just—' She stammers, then pauses to gather her thoughts. 'He was extremely sure. I think that's what threw me.'

As I try to gather the words to reply to her, Margot offers me a smoke, which I politely decline. She's sparking up when I finally open my mouth.

'It was like someone had asked him to eat a fucking baby,' I say, and Margot chokes a laugh.

'Sorry,' she apologises, then pauses—hesitates? 'You guys—You've definitely not had a thing in the past? I won't say a word, honestly, not even to Joe.'

I shake my head. 'No, hand on heart, we haven't. It's not the fact he forfeited—I obviously didn't want to kiss him.'

I should probably quit saying that.

'It's his baby eating-esque reaction that makes me want to throw myself off your roof,' I conclude.

'Look, it's—As much of an enigma as the guy is, I'd bet my life on him not doing that—or ever doing anything, to be honest—maliciously,' Margot soothes. 'It's probably just a misunderstanding. I bet if you go in there and speak to him, he'll explain everything.'

I respond to Margot with a strained smile that I hope I pass off as optimistic. She's right; it's not in Preston's nature to do anything with bad intentions, but she also couldn't be more wrong. If there's one thing Preston never does, it's explain. Anything.

CHAPTER 10

Despite my reservations, I take Margot's advice and brave the indoors to face Preston. Only, I can't find him, and Joe saves me from the dignity of having to ask for his whereabouts by proactively letting me know he's popped upstairs.

I try my best to engage with everyone as I await Preston's return, and I pray no one's noticing my frequent glances towards the living room door. He's been gone at least twenty minutes. Maybe I should check on him. Worry is beginning to crawl underneath my skin, and it's creating a strange amalgamation of bitterness and concern, like if someone who bought the last muffin you were eyeing up at a cafe got robbed on their way out.

In an attempt to not drive myself crazy, I resort to returning to the garden to call the worst person ever for advice.

'Mia!' Aiden screams down the phone, and he's drunk—he's off his tits, no question.

The only other people in the garden are standing at the opposite end of it, but Aiden's animalistic screech is loud enough to cast their eyes my way. I mouth an apology.

'I'm not gonna lie to you, I'm off my tits–'

See.

'–so if I start talking shit, just shout!'

'On the topic of shouting,' I say down the phone. 'Let's try five.'

'Holy mackerel, volume five?' he replies, and I'm impressed that he even understood my request. 'C'mon, at least let me have six.'

'Fine. Six. Whatever, just sh,' I mutter.

'Uh oh,' he replies in a tone not too dissimilar to a kid's TV show host. 'What's happened? Do you need me to come to London? I think the trains are still running and I'm out in Cardiff, so it's easy for me to–'

'Appreciate the love and concern, but it–No, it's not that deep, don't worry.'

'Hang on!' he shouts, and he's back to volume ten.

I mouth another apology to the garden's other occupants. Aiden's voice has been replaced with shuffling sounds, and the music that was pulsing as he was speaking is fading.

'Okay, hit me with it,' he says.

'No, it's–I'm fine, honestly; sorry I called. I won't steal you from your friends and–'

'Euphemia Evian!' he cuts in, again at volume ten.

'Sh!' I hiss through the phone, but he pays me no attention.

'I will stand in this sketchy club's smoking area and you will tell me what's wrong!'

A laugh breaks through my lips, and I'm giggling as I say, 'okay, okay! Fine, just–just sh, okay?'

'Deal,' he replies.

Finally, I spill everything. Not just tonight's events, but the other stuff–the weird stuff. How thrown I was when I bumped into Preston at Margot's first house party, the under the covers hand holding, the heat of his touch in the lake, despite the freezing temperature of the water.

For the first time in living memory, Aiden is rendered silent.

'Okay, all hands on the table and everything, Mia,' he says, finally.

'All cards on the table,' I correct him.

'Huh?'

'The saying; it's all cards on the table, not hands,' I explain.

A deafening groan echoes through the phone. 'Holy mackerel, whatever! Fine, all cards on the table,' he says slowly, 'it's the whole right person, wrong time situation, right?'

The teasing smile on my lips drops. What's he talking about?

'You and Preston. Obviously, his fate is with me, but—Hey, don't roll your eyes,' he slurs.

'How do you know I'm rolling my eyes?'

'Are you?'

'Yeah, but that's beside the point.'

We both start laughing, only Aiden's is cut short when he says, 'fuck! No, serious. I'm meant to be acting serious. Okay, let me try again.'

He draws a sharp breath.

'If—and this is a big if—but if, for example, Preston wasn't fated to be my one true love.'

That's being serious out the window.

'You guys are obviously meant for each other, and—'

'—Jesus, you are drunk, aren't you? That's so not—'

'—If feelings had gotten in the way however many years ago, any relationship you had would've imploded. You were both in really shitty places and needed each other for different reasons then, but those reasons don't exist anymore. There's no reason for you guys to not be together anymore, so the feelings are hitting you both like fucking freight trains.'

I'm lost for words. What the hell do I say to that?

I finally settle on, 'are you on something?'

'I'm right! You know I'm right!' he yells, and the small group of people I've mouthed numerous apologies to finally give in and head inside.

'No! How would that explain him reacting with literal disgust when he was challenged to kiss me?'

Aiden groans, this one the loudest yet.

'Mia, with all due respect, he's a straight man.'

'Well done,' I say with sugary sweet cheer. 'You're finally accepting that. It's only taken you three years.'

'My point is... Straight men fall into a panic so intense that it rocks their whole fucking world when confronted with their feelings.' He pauses. 'He panicked.'

'I'm not sure Preston's capable of panic,' I argue. 'The guy's in total control of every emotion—every bloody move he makes; it's eerie. We've discussed this multiple times,' I remind him.

'Well, I guess you're the exception to that.'

As dramatically as ever, Aiden hangs up, or so I think. I lower my phone to my face with a frown, only to be met with my own darkened reflection. It's dead.

When I return inside, Preston is still nowhere to be seen. I'm going to have to bite the bullet, aren't I? Ugh. I could really use a house fire right now.

Kidding—I'm just kidding.

I jog up the house's two flights of stairs until I'm faced with the attic room's closed door. I hold my breath, then knock. No response.

I press my ear against the white door, and there's sound—I can definitely hear something. Music. I can hear music. In many ways, Preston is wholly predictable. I silently pray the implicit rules of our friendship haven't changed since we first met, and with another sharp breath, I open the door and step into the room.

He's sitting on his bed—well, mattress—with crossed legs, his back against the wall and a book in his hands. His round glasses are perched on his nose, but there's not a single light on; instead, every candle in the room is set alight, unleashing a warm, autumnal scent. The music filling the space is smooth and melodic—an Arctic Monkeys song I can't place.

Preston's skin is ethereally golden in the candlelight. The ends of his light hair are curled inwards, his eyebrows quirking as he scans the pages in his hands, his eyes the deepest shade of green I've ever seen them.

'Don't worry,' he murmurs as he gestures his book towards me. 'This one's a billionaire romance. No mafia.'

I fail to swallow a laugh as I wander towards the makeshift bed, and without giving myself an opportunity to overthink it, sit into the empty space beside Preston. He removes his glasses and abandons his book when I lean back against the wall with him.

'You're a dick,' I declare without looking at him, then blindly wave my phone in his general direction. 'My phone's dead. Do you have a charger?'

He silently takes it from my hand and I hear what sounds like wires moving across wooden flooring, then a clicking sound.

'The game?' he eventually asks, and I nod while resisting the urge to glance at him.

'I didn't want to kiss you,' is my, in hindsight, unhinged response.

'Okay,' he replies.

I desperately want to turn from the worn bookcase I'm glaring at to look at him, but I stay strong. I resist. I try distracting myself with the sound of Alex Turner's voice as it bleeds from the speaker somewhere near the doorway, but it's not helping much.

'It was your reaction,' I explain, unprompted. 'You might as well have walked into the kitchen, grabbed the biggest knife you could find, then stabbed yourself in the heart. You know I'm shit at the whole making friends thing, especially when Aiden's out of the picture, so it was a bit fucking embarrassing for that happen in front of literally everyone.'

'There was no way I was going to kiss you there, like that, but I could've been more delicate about it,' he admits. 'I'm sorry.'

'Good. You should be,' I huff, then for no reason whatsoever, repeat, 'I didn't want to kiss you.'

'You mentioned that,' he replies.

'Just driving the point home.'

'I'd rather you didn't drive anything; never a good idea.'

'You fucking–'

I spin around and shove Preston's shoulder hard enough to force him into uncrossing his legs. He finds the whole thing hilarious, and it's not until after I'm glaring at his stupid face that I realise I've failed. I've looked at him. Fuck.

'You don't need Aiden,' he says as I avert my gaze. 'You underestimate yourself.'

As he finishes speaking, I give in and let my eyes find a home in his. He rests his head back against the cream wall with a sigh, and I don't think to question why my instinct is to do so, but I lower my head sideways onto his shoulder. He doesn't move me.

'Are you okay?' I say, and my voice is a little muffled by his jumper. 'You being up here, it–I probably shouldn't have been so ceaseless with the whole forcing you to socialise thing. I'm sorry if I took it too far.'

The silence that follows forces me to glance up at him. He flashes one of his infamous unreadable smiles, then shakes his head so slightly that I nearly miss it.

'It was nice–actually participating for once–so thank you. For pushing me,' he assures as I return my head to his shoulder.

'Promise?' I try.

'Promise.'

Wordlessly, he tilts his head to rest it atop mine. We stay like that for a whole song, neither one of us daring to make a sound. It's only when the next tune begins to play that Preston speaks again.

'Sometimes it all just gets a bit too loud.'

'Yeah,' I say into his chest. 'They're blasting the music down there.'

'That too.'

My heart clenches and I don't know what to do, or what to say. My eyes are on his lap, as are his hands, and he's picking at them—he's rhythmically tracing his left thumbnail alongside his right hand's index finger. The skin underneath is red, and so I lift my hand from my own lap, then lower it onto his to keep them still.

Unlike the movie night a few weeks back, he doesn't pull away, not even when I slot my fingers between his. We sit in silence as I gently stroke the patch of inflamed skin on his index finger, the melody humming from Preston's speaker melting further and further away.

'Mia,' he murmurs, and it takes me a moment to realise it's him, not the music calling my name. 'Can I ask you something?'

He lifts his head from mine and I take it as my cue to look up at him again. Our fingers remain entwined as I meet his eyes. His lips are slightly parted and his eyes flicker downwards before returning to mine, and I'm lost—transfixed by the weight of his gaze.

He wanted to ask me something. Did he want to ask me something? All sense of reality is falling away, and as I feel fingers in my hair—his fingers—tucking a thick strand behind my ear, the final string breaks and I inch forward. Enough to notice the slight citrusy scent of his aftershave, enough to brush my lips against his, and then a little more.

His lips are soft—softer than I thought possible, and I don't know if they're as warm as they feel, or if every nerve ending in my mouth is on fire. My eyes are closed but I don't remember shutting them, his hand is still in my hair, and it lasts seconds. It can't be more than two seconds when the realisation hits me, and I move—I jerk my head back, away from him, despite my body pleading with me not to.

Preston's reaction to my backwards shift is a forward one, and we're back—he's back, reigniting my senses as his lips rekindle mine. His fingers glide from my hair to trace my jawline where his hand stays, just as I begin moving my mouth against his. I sigh into him, and he's so warm—I've never felt anything so warm—and his lips taste of autumn, of winter spices, and fresh air, and—

A loud buzzing sound blasts through the room and reality crashes around me.

I jump away—jump up, I think—and there's music competing with the melody bleeding from the speaker. It's coming from somewhere to our right where—My ringtone. I can hear my ringtone. I'm talking; I'm saying things to Preston, who's now standing too, but I don't know what I'm saying as I'm saying it while I scramble over the bed to reach for my phone.

Aiden. Fuck. My phone died during our call.

'Hi!' I say into the phone, and don't mean to shout, but do anyway. 'Hey! Hi, sorry! My phone died earlier, it was—Yeah, sorry. It's fine. It's all fine.'

'Holy mackerel, I thought you'd died!' he screams, even more loudly than before. 'Nearly called the Met Police, but thought better not; they don't have the best track record with women. Or were you just pissed at what I was saying about you and–'

'It's fine!' I cut him off. 'Totally good. We've talked it through, and everything's fine! Never been more fine!'

As I reassure Aiden that I am, in fact, fine once more, I dart my eyes back towards the bed to see Preston standing above his desk. He turns his head barely an inch in my direction, and I shoot my attention back towards his bedroom window. With a hasty goodbye, I hang up on Aiden and regret doing so within seconds.

'Sorry, he—I called him earlier to—He's drunk,' I blabber as I turn back to Preston.

I can't read him. I can't interpret a single glint in his eyes, or the tiniest twitch in his expression. For once, I want to be able to read him. Just once.

'Out in Cardiff, apparently, hence the—the shouting,' I continue as I avert my gaze again. 'That's because of him being drunk, I mean, not because he's in, uh, in Cardiff. That's not why he's shouting.'

'What I wanted to ask,' Preston replies, ignoring every word I said—probably for the best—and I stare back in bewilderment.

I blink, and oh! Shit. He—Yeah, he wanted to ask me something. I nod, a little too enthusiastically and definitely too abruptly. It's not until he lifts his hand that I realise he's holding some paper—No, a letter.

'I can't open it,' he says, and there's a coyness to his voice I don't think I've heard before. 'Could you read it for me? Not now—not with me, but tomorrow, maybe. Once you're home.'

I nod, then move towards his bed. Walk around it, not over it. Stop in front of him. Take his dad's letter. Hold it in both hands. Look at it. Nod. I'm on autopilot; I'm not thinking about anything, just moving.

'Thank you,' Preston says quietly, and I hold my breath.

I don't know why.

I exhale. Clear my throat. Smile, I think.

'We should–I should head back downstairs,' I say, then clarify, 'you don't have to, obviously. I can tell everyone you feel unwell, if you want.'

'No, I'll join you,' he replies, and I stammer.

'Yeah! Cool, yeah, great!'

Be fucking normal, Mia, Jesus Christ.

He places his hands on my arms to gently nudge me aside, and I'm burning; the skin his fingers brushed against is on fire. He walks ahead and I trip after him, methodically running my finger across the top of his letter as I do so.

We remain silent as Preston snuffs out the flames of every candle, and it doesn't occur to me to help until we're plummeted into near darkness. He leans down in the far right corner of his room, presses a button on the small, black speaker there, and the music stops. I'd forgotten it was even playing. I join him as he heads for his bedroom door, and as he lifts his hand to grasp its handle, with little warning, he turns on his heel to face me.

'I'm sorry,' he says as abruptly as he turned around. 'About that just then. It's–I'm really sorry, Mia. I shouldn't have done that.'

'It's okay,' I reply quickly, and it doesn't feel like enough–I need to say something else, but I don't know what, so I just let myself speak without thinking. 'We'll pretend it didn't happen.'

CHAPTER 11

I'd convinced myself that I'd grown out of being easily influenced, but last night proved me wrong in every way imaginable. I didn't want to kiss Preston, and I stand by that. It's just that when forced into a drinking game-induced corner, and then my best friend since forever insisting that I do want that, it's only natural that it messed with my head. I was confused. Plain and simple. It means nothing, and in the spirit of it meaning nothing, I've not uttered a word to Aiden—or anyone else—about it.

Last night also has absolutely nothing to do with the lunch date I've arranged with Nick, a guy on Hinge I matched with a few days back.

Okay, maybe it does a little.

I've not exactly been making waves on the London dating scene since moving here, and if last night's kiss tells me anything, it's that I'm desperate for non-platonic human connection. I'm confident that if I had something resembling a love life going on, all of this weird stuff—this tension—with Preston wouldn't even exist. This Hinge date will no doubt fizzle into nothing, but it's a start.

Before the date, though, I've got to deal with the letter. I've not left my bed yet this morning, and I'm not allowing myself to until

I open it. I don't know what I'm afraid of; Preston's dad is hardly going to have written to say he has no interest in him whatsoever. I repeat that assumption in my head over and over again, and I continue repeating it as I unseal the letter and pull out an A4 sheet of paper.

With a deep breath, I begin to read, and I don't exhale until I've reached the bottom of the page. When I do, it's a huge sigh of relief.

'Okay,' I mutter to myself. 'Okay. Good. This is good.'

It goes without saying that Rhys wants to meet Preston. He doesn't give masses away, but he says enough to make it all seem real. He grew up in West Wales but now lives in Richmond, a fact Anwen must've already told Preston, and it was during a trip to Ynys Môn as teenagers that they met. He had no idea Preston existed until last year–shortly before he wrote this letter, by the sound of it. I'm less clear on if that's a fact Preston already knows. He doesn't have a family, nor is he married, but he has two dogs. At the bottom of the letter are his contact details.

I carefully fold the paper, then return it to its envelope before rummaging through my bed for my phone.

Hey, are you free this eve? I've read your letter (all good, don't worry!!)

He replies within minutes.

Next week? I'm in Cardiff.

Of course he'd wait until he was out of the country to ask me to read something he's been putting off reading himself for a whole year. I roll my eyes. I toy with suggesting I give him a call instead, but figure in person is best. I agree to next week, tuck the letter away into the drawers beside my bed, then refocus on the task ahead. My date.

I meet Nick, a second year History student, at Dolly's cafe. He's already there when I arrive, or at least I think it's him. That's the real peril of online dating: approaching someone you're deliberating fucking, marrying, or ideally both, only for them to tell you they have no clue who the hell you are. Thankfully, I get it right. Better yet, he's alarmingly attractive with neat, dark hair, striking brown eyes, and impeccable bone structure hidden underneath a cluster of freckles.

'I'm always scared I've got the wrong person!' I joke as I pull out the chair opposite his, then play ignorant when it makes an awful screeching sound across the floor.

Great start.

He laughs, a dimple appearing in his cheek as he does so. 'Same. I've been burned before.'

'Really? Oof, I bet that was fucking horrific.'

As any normal nineteen-year-old woman's reaction to swearing at her date within ten second of meeting him would be, my next thought is whether I should follow up with a warning that I'm a virgin. Thankfully, I have the sense not to let my intrusive thoughts win.

'Yep. Fucking horrific,' he confirms, to my great relief.

Shortly after our introductions, Nick leaves our small table to place our order and I watch him quietly as he stands in the queue, inching forward every few minutes. Seriously, he's really good looking. He's dressed in a slick, pale blue shirt with its sleeves rolled up to his elbows, and the stubble that lines his jaw is trimmed with forensic precision, his hair parted so perfectly that I suspect it would survive a hurricane. He looks nothing like Preston, not that I'm comparing the two.

I go into the date with no expectations. If anything, I assume it'll be a disaster, and so when I realise we've been sitting and chatting for nearly two hours, I have to pop to the bathroom to confirm I'm not in the middle of some grand delusion. I like him. I think I actually like him. His only flaw so far is that he's English, and hey, it's not like he can help that.

'Sorry,' I say as I return to our table. 'I didn't realise the time.'

'It's alright,' Nick replies, a small smile on his lips. 'Honestly, every date I've had since downloading dating apps has been painful, so this is a really positive change.'

A positive change. I press my lips together to hide a grin.

'Same! I don't know if it's a London thing or an app-specific thing, but it's so chaotic.'

'Well, I've always lived in London, and it's honestly always been pretty awful. The issue with dating apps is that people either want a quick fuck, or they're plain fucking weird.' He pauses, stammering a little. 'Nothing against people who want that, it's–We've all been there, right?'

I force down a cringe, just as more I'm a virgin intrusive thoughts barrel into my head.

'Just not what I'm looking for,' Nick finishes.

I mean, I wouldn't be against casual sex, I think, at least once that first time is out of the way.

Mine and Nick's date ends up lasting another thirty minutes, and it only ends because I've got a mate date with Margot that I need to go home and get ready for. Happy hour at the pub I'm meeting her at is from four until six, so it's crucial I'm not a minute late. Besides, I'm desperate to talk to someone about the miracle of this date not being a total disaster.

Once home, I quickly change out of my chunky turtleneck and into a classic jeans and a nice top combo, then pair that with my oversized faux leather jacket. I arrive at the pub dead on four o'clock, and I've not even sat down when Margot demands I spill all about my date.

I laugh as I say, 'can I at least order a drink first?'

'Already done. You've got two mojitos coming.'

'God, I want to marry you sometimes.'

Margot winces. 'Was the date that bad?'

'Actually, no,' I reply as I spot a waitress heading in our direction. 'It was weirdly good.'

A grin bursts onto her face, and the waitress must think she fucking loves rum-based cocktails as she places our drinks on our table. After thanking the waitress, Margot tucks her blue hair behind her ears as if she's prepping to listen as intently as possible to my incredibly boring story. I run through said incredibly boring story, and by the end of it, she's smiling so hard that it's amazing her cheeks haven't split open.

'And he's fit? A miracle,' is her conclusion to my tale as she looks at his dating profile on my phone.

As she swipes through his pictures, I pick at the nuts and olives Margot had ordered alongside our drinks. I quickly discover I hate olives.

'Should I have told him I'm wildly inexperienced, or is that more of a third date vibe?' I question as she hands my phone back to me.

'You tell him when you're ready, if you even want to tell him in the first place,' she says pointedly. 'Besides, you've done every-thing but the big deed, right?'

I lift my hand in a so-so gesture. 'Most things, yeah.'

I neglect to mention that these most things required hours of positive encouragement from Aiden beforehand, whose side hustle while we were travelling was convincing me that the world wouldn't implode if I gave into my NSFW thoughts about the occasional hot guy we met along the way. If it wasn't for him, I sincerely think the most experience I'd have to date would be a few kisses with Robbie Morrissey, my first boyfriend turned disaster.

'You're overthinking this whole sex thing, gal,' Margot declares. 'Honestly, if I were you, I'd just shag the next guy who gives you the opportunity, and trust me, they'll be queuing up.'

'Tempting,' I grumble. 'I'm not even, like, saving it or some archaic shit like that, I'm just... awkward.' I sigh. 'I get way too into my own head, don't feel comfortable enough with the guy, then end up not enjoying anything enough to let things go all the way.'

Margot responds by pursing her lips, then tilting her head before concluding, 'you should masturbate more.'

'Noted.'

'Or,' she tries. 'Find a boyfriend, or not even that—just someone you like enough for the whole not comfortable with the guy issue to not be a thing—and let it happen because you want to. Not because you feel like you have to.'

'What happened to shagging the next guy who gives me the opportunity?' I argue.

She brushes the air as she throws back what's left of her second drink. 'That's plan B.'

Margot's right—the finding a guy I like enough thing, not the one-off shag and masturbating thing—but it feels impossible. If I've gone nearly twenty years without liking anyone enough to make them my boyfriend, what hope do I have? The one time I did agree to the label, it was a shit show. It's like agreeing to date Robbie in college despite my blatant indifference towards him has scarred me for life. Now it's all or nothing.

I'm not far behind Margot in finishing my second mojito, and so I'm soon buying our second round. I'm standing at the bar, mesmerised by the braman going at it with a cocktail shaker when my phone vibrates in my back pocket. As if it's a sign for the gods themselves, I peek at it to see a message from Nick.

Today was fun, would love to do it again. Dinner next time, maybe? x

I'm grinning into my phone in a totally unsubtle way. Dinner. That's some serious shit. It's also less terrifying than the alternative of drinks because drinks alludes to alcohol, which alludes to end of night expectation. I don't think he was playing with me when he said he wasn't looking for a one-time thing.

The smile is still on my face as I place our order, and it doesn't waver as I return to our table.

'Looks like there's a second date on the cards,' I say as I plop back into the small booth Margot and I have occupied. 'Nick's asked me to dinner.'

'Can I be maid of honour?' she replies.

'Nah, Aiden's already bagsied that, sorry. Put in his bid years ago,' I say. 'You can take chief bridesmaid, though. My only other option is Preston, so you're the obvious choice, really. Might offend my sister, though.'

She snorts a laugh. 'I told him off for being a dick about the whole kissing dare thing before he left this morning.'

I flash a coy smile. 'You didn't need to, honestly, we talked it through. It would've been weird—we both would've found it super weird if we'd kissed—so it was just him being weirded out. Just a misunderstanding, really. A big, dumb misunderstanding.'

Was that overexplaining? It felt like overexplaining.

'You didn't go to town on him or anything, did you?' I ask.

She brushes the air. 'Nah, I was just honest about you confiding in me and saying you felt mega awkward after the whole thing. I told him it's obvious you guys are super close, so you were just worried about your friendship getting fucked up over something so insignificant.' She shrugs. 'And I told him not to pull that kind of shit again, obviously.'

I nod slowly. 'Well, thanks for defending my honour.'

'You and him are definitely okay now, right?'

I raise my hand to my chest. 'I promise. Trust me; we've been through worse.'

'Well, that sounds juicy. Is this where you finally reveal Preston's darkest secrets?'

'He has no secrets, I swear,' I lie, ignoring the guilt pressing at my chest. 'To be totally honest, I once landed him in hospital, so if anything, I'm the problem one.'

Margot's mouth drops open as her brown eyes widen. 'You can't leave me hanging like that!'

'I crashed a car he was in,' I explain as I pick at my paper straw. 'Not horribly, but enough to make seventeen-year-old me realise I needed to get my shit together.'

Margot draws a long whistle through her red lips. 'Shit, Mia. Although, that does explain the driving jokes Aiden makes in your presence.'

'He's the real arsehole,' I mutter. 'You should focus your scoldings on him.'

I return to my flat on a high, one that's only partly alcohol-induced. I should know better by now, though; nothing can stay too good for too long. I'm wolfing down a share-size packet of sweet chilli crisps when Dad's caller ID flashes on my phone screen. There are only two reasons Dad ever calls me: on my birthday, and when he's drunk. My birthday isn't until March.

Not answering doesn't pass through my mind as an option until after I've hit the green button, and even when it does, I'm only kidding myself. I'd be too anxious with what ifs if I didn't.

'Mia?' he slurs, and yep. Drunk. 'Mia? Hello?'

'Hi, Dad,' I say through gritted teeth as I sit up in bed.

'Mia?'

'Yep. Hi.'

'The boys down the pub said you don't have uni this week,' he begins, and what? How the fuck do the boys down the pub know my academic schedule? 'Dave has a son–No, a girl–a girl who goes to uni in London, and she has a week off.'

I try, and fail, to ignore his accusatory tone.

'I thought you'd come home. Why are you there if you've got a week off?'

Because the thought of spending any free time at home with you makes me want to rip off both my eyelids.

'I've got lots of work to do,' I try.

Dad scoffs. 'No, you've got a week off!'

'It's reading week. There aren't any lectures, but I've still got work to do–lots of work, actually,' I explain with a deep breath to calm myself. 'I'm using the time to get it all done. I'm working on some editorial stuff for a uni magazine too, so keeping myself bus–'

'You don't want to see me,' he slurs, ignoring everything I just said.

He's not wrong. I can't accuse him of that.

'I was home a few weeks ago, Dad,' I say, nearly pleading.

He scoffs again. 'You're as bad as your sister. At least she's not moved hundreds of miles away from me, even if she never visits. You moved there to spite me, didn't you? Like with your gallivanting around the world; all to make me feel...'

I can't deal with this bullshit right now. I refuse to. So I don't. I tear my phone from my ear, then hang up midway through Dad's rant. I shouldn't have answered. I knew I shouldn't have, but I let the worry flood in. What if something bad has happened? What if he's gotten into trouble? What if he's gotten drunk and hurt himself?

I'm starting to wish for what ifs.

CHAPTER 12

Preston's next week becomes the week after, but curiously, our plan to meet up includes a nightclub, Margot, Joe, a few of our Typewriter Magazine comrades, and Nick. I therefore don't think I'm making a bold assumption when I say he might be avoiding the contents of his dad's letter, and by default, me. There's no way I'm going to bring it up in front of everyone who knows nothing about his past, and he knows that.

I'll find a way, though. By God, I'll find a way.

If Preston had it his way, he wouldn't even be here tonight. He's still determined to play this nothing character, but I'm as equally determined not to let him. Displaying concern over his well-being is Preston's kryptonite, so after a lengthy text conversation—he refused to answer his phone when I called—I convinced him to join us on the night out via strong I'm worried about you undertones.

I meet Margot, Joe, and Preston outside Clapham South tube station, and I spend the walk there awkwardly pulling at the sparkly dress I regret picking for tonight. I didn't realise it was quite this skintight, or quite this short. It's too late for regrets now, so I lift my chin, think fuck it, and keep walking.

'You've called in the big guns for Nick,' Margot shouts, then wolf whistles as I approach the station, which naturally makes me want to die. 'If he doesn't propose to you tonight, I will.'

Mine and Nick's dinner date, which was planned for the weekend just gone, was called off after one of his flatmates set fire to his kitchen. He sent me unprompted evidence of this, and that shit looked bad, so I wasn't the least bit offended. It resulted in me inviting him to tonight because it was the only other date we could both do—or semi-do, in my case. I wasn't expecting him to say yes, but it was a welcomed surprise.

'Ew, no. Name a bigger red flag than being proposed to by a guy on your second date,' I argue as I stop in front of Margot, Joe, and Preston.

'Being proposed to on your first date,' Joe validly counteracts.

'Thoughts?' Margot chimes in, then spins on her heel to look up at Preston beside her.

Preston, who's remained characteristically silent throughout our exchange, is looking at me in—surprise, surprise—a way that's impossible to decipher. It takes him a moment to feel Margot's eyes on him, and I'm convinced he wasn't listening to a word anyone just said.

'Hm?' he queries, glancing down at Margot.

She rolls her eyes. 'Every time I think you're, like, your own species, you do something so typically guyish.' She reaches up to ruffle his hair. 'Listening skills. Work on them, P.'

'This Michael guy, it's his birthday, right?' I question the group as we begin walking into the station, and Margot and Joe nod. 'Who is he again?'

'So he's—Wait, he's a friend of the guy from that French students society you go to?' Margot muses to Joe, who nods, and she turns back to me. 'He's, like, French aristocracy or some shit and has booked the whole club. It should be a good night.'

'But we don't actually really know the guy?'

'Essentially,' Preston interjects, finally deeming our conversation worth listening to. 'What could go wrong, right?'

'Oi!' Margot shouts as she taps through a barrier, flipping her head backwards to glare at Preston. 'I preferred you when you restricted yourself to one social occasion a fortnight.'

'Mia's a dangerous influence,' he replies, then shoots me a wink I pretend to feel indifferent towards.

Our fun is cut short within ten minutes of leaving London Bridge station.

We're standing in a quiet street, and if it wasn't for the sound of heavy bass pulsing from the building we're huddled outside, I'd think we were lost. We've met up with the others, the clouds above are spitting rain, and Joe's in the midst of failing to convince a bouncer that we should be allowed in.

'No, it's—So I'm Joe. Joe Dupont,' he says slowly. 'You literally just said I'm on the list.'

'Por el amor de Dios,' the bouncer mutters under his breath, then speaks up. 'Yes, Joe Dupont and three friends. There are.' He pauses to bob his head around Joe's tall frame. 'Siete. Yes, seven—there are seven friends.'

'Gabriel, Michael's best mate, is one of my best mates,' Joe continues, and the way he says it so meekly makes me doubt him, so God help us. 'We know each other through UCL's French students society. They won't mind, I swear.'

I'd hoped Nick's introduction to my friends would be smoother than this. I flash him an apologetic look as he stands to my right, and he flashes a reassuring one back. At least he's nice about it.

'We're fucked,' I hear Dana, who's less sympathetic, grumble from behind me.

'You got any wise ideas?' I whisper to Preston, who's standing the other side of me.

'The bouncer's Spanish,' he utters, unhelpfully.

For no clear reason, the bouncer responds to Joe with, 'you don't sound French.'

This is all very Eurpoean, isn't it?

'I moved here when I was little and lost the accent,' he hits back defensively, and I can't help feeling he's making things worse. 'I'll run home and grab my passport, if you don't believe–'

'No one's grabbing any passports!' Margot interjects before shoving her boyfriend aside, which is definitely a good move.

I glance at Preston to see him chewing at his lip, his eyes unfocused. He's thinking. I can see him thinking. More importantly, I can see him resisting. What, I don't know, but I'd place a bet on it being linked to his bloody be as nothing as possible mantra. I force his green eyes to meet mine, then nod.

Whatever you're thinking of doing, do it, I think, then silently pray he somehow gets the message.

Before I can find out, the bouncer pipes up again. 'I don't like the French.'

'In fairness, nobody likes the French,' Margot replies.

'Hey!' Joe whines.

This is beyond tragic.

I'm about to wave a white flag on behalf of all of us, or most notably, on behalf of Joe's dignity, when I hear Preston clear his throat. He steps forward, nudges past Joe and Margot, and stops in front of the bouncer with a smile so naturally charming that it alone would likely be enough to get him on our side.

He opens with, 'perdóname,' and from there, all I can do is stare.

He's—Is he..? He's speaking Spanish. He speaks Spanish? Since fucking when? Joe's silently blinking at Preston and the bouncer conversing, not that I can talk because so am I.

After what can't even be a full minute, Preston turns back around to face us.

'Shall we?'

With that, he walks through the door we've been trying to get into for the past ten minutes. I follow in a semi-daze, not entirely convinced this isn't a hypothermia-induced fever dream. As we wander through a hallway illuminated with LED lights, my bubble is burst by the sound of Joe shouting from behind.

'Thanks and everything, Preston, but you couldn't have intervened before I made a twat out of myself?'

The others have coats to check in, so Preston, Nick, and I wait for them in the club's loud lobby. I'm dying to ask Preston where on earth his performance out there came from, but I should be focusing on Nick, shouldn't I?

'I'll have to buy you a drink,' Nick comments to Preston, then nods towards the entrance we walked through moments ago. 'For saving our arses out there.'

I hold my breath as I flick my eye to Preston's face. He's going to say something embarrassing, isn't he? Or weird. Probably weird.

'Not at all,' he says with a light smile. 'Save it for Mia. She's the one who convinced me to come.'

I exhale. That was... That was normal. Nice, even.

Nick announces he's popping to the bathroom while we wait for the others, and I take the opportunity to ask the question that's been hanging from my tongue since we walked in.

'You speak fluent Spanish?' I shout to Preston over the heavy dubstep, and I have to stand on my tip toes while he lowers his head to score a chance at hearing me.

'Not fluent,' he insists, standing upright. 'Just enough to charm a jilted Chilean bouncer. He loathes the French; I can't possibly stress that enough.'

I laugh into the air. 'You're literally ridiculous. I don't—When did you even have time to learn it?'

'Euphemia, I was in a young offender's institute for fifteen months,' he says plainly, and the blank look on my face must give away the need for him to spell it out. 'There's fuck all else to do.'

Within moments of looking at the nightclub's drinks menu, my heart has dropped to my stomach. Nick's offer of a drink is definitely out of the window. Their cheapest one is twenty-five pounds. I can't afford this—no one can afford this, surely? Even if I could, I've got no idea what anything is because everything appears to be some fancy cocktail with a French name.

With a frown, I turn away from the bar to search the room. Those who aren't crammed onto the dancefloor are sitting in the large, circular booths framing it, and at the edge of each booth is a huge bucket filled with champagne.

'The guy's booked out an entire club in Central London. Probably should've occurred to us that it's not a cheap place,' Dana points out as the same realisation hits me.

'Shit, I'm really sorry, guys! I assumed it'd be an open bar,' Joe says, and whew, tonight is not his night. 'And Gabriel's just messaged to say he's too ill to make it.'

We all stand in silence as a sombre mist descends upon the corner of the bar we've captured. The only person unbothered by the ordeal is Preston, who's blissfully scanning the drinks menu. He's either zoned out of the conversation and is fully immersed in his own world, which would hardly be unheard of, or he knows something we don't.

I don't have to wait long to find out.

Preston slams the black menu shut, then announces, 'when life gives you lemons, make champagne.'

I don't get a chance to question what the hell he's talking about, nor does anyone else, because he's on the move within seconds. Those who are less familiar with Preston's eccentric tendencies stay beside the bar with furrowed brows, but Margot, Joe, Dana, and I are quick to follow him.

'Joe!' Preston calls as he glances backwards, and Joe ups his pace to walk alongside him. 'I'm assuming the birthday boy is at one of these tables, no?'

'No—I mean yes. Yeah, he's...' Joe narrows his eyes to search the booths dotted around the dancefloor. He points towards one at the edge of it. 'There! The guy with the red hair.'

Preston follows Joe's eyeline until he lands on the tall, slender man being pointed at. Michael is in the midst of pouring everyone in his booth a glass of champagne, the grin on his face gleaming under the nightclub's flashing lights. Confidence bleeds from his pores, and I have to resist cringing as I watch more of the champagne he's pouring splash onto the floor than into any glasses.

Preston and Joe stop above the booth, and by the time Margot, Dana, and I have caught up, Preston's calling Michael's name.

'Happy birthday, man!' I catch him say.

Michael, who's still on his feet, turns to face him. In a gesture so casual anyone would think they've been friends since birth, Preston embraces him into one of those horrific bro hugs—the kind where two guys can't decide between a handshake and a high five, so they just hold each others' hand as they lean forward, then pat each other on the back like they're competing to uncover who can land the firmest slap.

As he pulls away, Preston introduces himself, then says, 'this thing is fucking amazing—you must've handpicked the DJ, right? Such an insane playlist.'

Michael, who definitely didn't handpick the DJ, responds with a cocky grin. It doesn't seem to have occurred to him that he has no idea who the hell Preston, or any of us, are.

'Sucks about Gabriel, right?' Preston calls over an especially loud bass drop.

'Ah, you're Gabriel's mates?' Michael replies as he inches closer.

Preston nods, and he's oozing enthusiasm—hell, even I'm starting to feel pumped. 'Yeah, Joe's one of his best mates.'

As he gestures towards Joe, who looks completely lost, Michael's grin widens. 'Shit, yeah! Joe! Good to meet you, dude. It's nice to finally put a face to the name!'

Michael reaches forward to shake Joe's hand, and then his brown eyes turn to the rest of us. We've been silent this whole time. In fact, I'm pretty sure Preston's the only one who's uttered a word, Joe included, and it doesn't look like that's changing any time soon.

'Mia, Margot, and Dana,' Preston continues, spending a few measured seconds introducing each person—enough time for Michael to drink us in. 'We did have a few others with us, but they've fucked off with the champagne.'

Preston laughs, and Michael immediately matches his energy as he shouts, 'fuckers!'

Preston brushes the air. 'Shit happens. You got any drink recommendations? The menu at this place is written in Spanish or some shit.'

Says the guy who apparently speaks fluent Spanish.

Just as I'm resisting an eye roll, I realise that's his point. He's making an inside joke.

'Nah, it's—Hey, I can hardly expect you guys to buy your own shit. Let me just—This stuff is basically on tap,' Michael says as he glances back towards the empty bottle of champagne now discarded on the floor. 'I'll get you a few bottles.'

Wait—Shit. Holy shit.

'Nah, man, don't be ridiculous!' Preston responds immediately. 'It's all good!'

Um, what? No. Abort. What the hell is he doing? Why's he declining Michael's offer?

Michael is laughing again. 'You're definitely Gabriel's mates. Way too polite!' Moments later, he catches the eye of a waiter serving the people at the booth beside ours. 'Hi! Hey, can you get these guys three bottles? Cheers!'

And just like that, our night is saved for a second time.

Five minutes later, all eight of us are getting comfortable in a booth a stone's throw away from the DJ blasting the tunes Preston feigned intense enthusiasm over. At the edge of our round sofa is a bucket filled with three bottles of champagne.

'I don't know what the fuck you're on tonight, P!' Margot, who's sitting opposite Preston and me, shouts over to him. 'But holy shit, I love you!'

His response is a small, closed-mouth smile, and the modesty of it all is just so him. As Dana is popping open a bottle of champagne, she jumps into the conversation.

'I seriously thought you'd fucked it when you declined Michael's first offer of free drinks,' she comments as she fills the glasses of the rest of our Typewriter Magazine cohort.

'Accepting his first offer might've gotten us one bottle,' he explains. 'Refusing got us three.'

Based on the way his eyes are open a little wider than usual, his lips parted slightly, it's clear he assumed this knowledge was obvious.

'This entire display,' he elaborates as he gestures around the room. 'His demeanour, the grand gesture of free alcohol—it boils down to a desperation to be loved by everyone, and he'll jump at even the slightest hint of sincerity.'

'Like someone turning down an offer of free champagne,' Nick, who's wedged beside me, concludes.

Everyone's eyes are glued to Preston, even after he's finished speaking, and as Dana reaches us to pour our drinks, I fear she's at the point of no return. She's gazing at him as if he's the answer to all her prayers, as if her life has been devoid of meaning until she met the man sitting to my left. She's down. Hard.

As I mull over Preston's words, a realisation hits me, and I'm thwarted back to college, back to my life in Wales, back to before.

'Like Robbie,' I murmur, barely processing the fact I said it aloud until after the matter.

'Like Robbie,' Preston repeats quietly enough for only me to hear.

I dart my eyes to his face, but I'm too late; Joe has snatched his attention. I watch his side profile, the DJ booth's stage lights hitting his face in a way that sharpens his jawline, not that it needed the help.

An uneasiness stirs in the pit of my stomach because that performance wasn't him, nor was the one that got us inside this club in the first place. My euphoria over Preston abandoning the nothing life he's cursed himself to, even just for a few hours, is wavering because this is a dangerous game. Even the slightest glimmer of Zack is a warning sign; I know that better than anyone.

However, my concern becomes fleeting when another realisation hits me because no, that wasn't Zack. It was a strategic play on Preston's real self, sure, but it wasn't malicious. It wasn't Zack. Zack would've just broken into the club and robbed the place.

CHAPTER 13

I 've never been champagne drunk, what with me not being a millionaire, and it's an experience like no other. I'm floating—no, flying—and the world is sparkling. There's a golden hue washed over every person, every thing, every feeling. I keep telling people this, but they don't seem to be listening.

'Nick agrees, don't you, Nick?' I say into the sky.

Nick, who's not in the sky but is strolling alongside me, laughs. We've just left the club and are making our way to London Bridge station.

'I honestly have no idea what you're on about,' he says through a chuckle.

'It's gold!' I stress, then shoot my arms out in front of me as if trying to embrace the world.

'I'd suggest copper, perhaps. Not gold,' Preston interjects.

'Ha! See! Preston gets it!'

'Oh, God,' Joe slurs from behind me. 'That's when you know something makes no sense.'

I stop in my tracks, then twirl around to point at Joe—or am I doing finger guns? I glance down at my hands. Finger guns!

'You're not wrong, Joe. You're not wrong.'

Everyone's laughing now, not just Nick, and damn, I had no idea I was so funny. I lag behind the rest of our group with Nick, whose hand is in mine, but I don't remember holding it. He's still laughing, and it's a nice laugh; deep, full, and smooth like caramel.

'Your friends are cool,' he comments, flashing his dimple as he smiles. 'I'm not even mad our one-to-one date turned into a group thing.'

'I have fantastic taste,' I beam. 'Who's your favourite?'

'Of your friends?' he asks and I nod. Then nod again. 'I wouldn't dare.'

'Wrong!' I call into the sky. 'Try again. No neutral ground allowed.'

'I honestly don't know! I've only—'

'Wrong!'

'I'm just saying I've only met them tonight, so need more time to—'

'Wrong!'

He's laughing again, practically laughing his guts out as I skip alongside him. Margot keeps flashing me backwards glances, and she's laughing too. Everyone's laughing; it's brilliant.

'Fine! Okay, okay...' Nick pauses, then turns to look down at me. 'Preston, I guess. Yeah, Preston.'

'Called it!'

Nick's polite enough not to point out that I didn't actually predict his answer once, at least not verbally.

'He's everyone's favourite,' I explain, 'and it's funny because he really tries not to be.'

I don't have any vivid memories of getting home, and it's not until I'm standing in a kitchen that isn't mine that I realise it's because I'm not home. I'm leaning back against a counter because if I don't, I think I might fall.

'Here you go,' Margot chirps as she stands opposite me, a glass of liquid in her hand.

'Champagne?' I ask as she hands it to me.

'Water,' she counteracts.

'That sucks,' I grumble, but take a big gulp anyway.

Shit, that's good. I gulp another mouthful. As I'm downing my third mouthful, I spot a figure in the corner of my eye. Preston's leaning sideways against the kitchen doorway, his arms crossed and his head tilted.

'Are you going to stand there brooding all night?' I ask.

He smirks. 'Are you going to tell me if anyone's ever passed comment on your name's resemblance to an STD?'

'Get some new material,' I heckle.

'I'll leave you guys to it,' Margot interjects with an eye roll and a badly hidden smile. 'Plus I should probably check Joe's still alive.'

'Night!' I call to her as she brushes past Preston to leave the room.

'Night!' she calls back.

'Love you!'

'Love you too!'

'And you say I'm bad at expressing affection,' I say to Preston as I yank my clutch bag from the counter, nearly spilling my water in the process.

Noticing my conundrum, Preston drags himself away from his beloved doorway and reaches to take the glass from my hand. I'm too busy scrambling through my bag to bat him away.

'I don't recall ever saying that,' he argues.

Where's my bloody key?

'And it would be a rather hypocritical statement if I had.'

It should be in here somewhere. I'm muttering under my breath as I spill the contents of my bag onto the counter. Purse, lipstick, bank card, ID... no key. Shit.

Five minutes later, or ten—I'm not sure; it could be twenty, to be honest—I'm stumbling into Preston's bedroom. I'm talking to him about syntax, or rather, I'm lecturing him about why he doesn't need to go so hard with it.

'You're really letting this editorial work go to your head,' he comments as I collapse onto his bed.

God, it's soft. It wasn't this soft before, I'm sure of it. I've shut my eyes, but I can hear his footsteps quietly approaching. Everything is echoing and so I focus on my breathing, but I keep losing track of it.

'Here,' Preston says from somewhere above. 'You can't sleep in that.'

Something soft brushes against my arms. I sit upright and open my eyes, but the softness vanishes, and—Wait, a hoodie. It's a hoodie. It slips off my lap, so I quickly grab it.

'Sorry,' I mutter to the inanimate article of clothing, then realise there's also a pair of grey tracksuit bottoms to my left.

Preston's sitting diagonally to me on the mattress, his green orbs darting around my face as if I might leap from his bed and dive out the window any second.

'Close your eyes,' I demand, in hindsight, quite aggressively.

'Don't panic, I'm leaving,' he replies as he goes to stand, but I grab his shirt's cuff to pull him back down.

'No need for the dramatics. Stay, just close your eyes!'

He raises his eyebrows. 'I was going to leave anyway, Mia, to grab you another glass of—'

'Stay! Close your eyes!'

His lips quiver but don't quite break into a smile. Finally, he humours me and shuts his eyes. In what I've got zero doubt is in an impeccably elegant manner, I wrestle my sparkly dress off my body—all while sitting down, not that I'm bragging—and reach for the clothes Preston gifted me. Forcing him to close his eyes was a good call; I'm not wearing a bra.

Pulling the tracksuit bottoms over my legs while sitting down is more challenging than removing my dress, but I prevail. The hoodie's easy. I don't even look. Just throw it over my head.

'Okay, open!' I order, then greet Preston's return to the seeing world with jazz hands.

'Jesus—take your arms out,' he responds, and he's... he's laughing at me.

Like, actually laughing. Not smirking or sniggering, or politely chuckling in response to some social cue. Crinkled eyes, hoarse voice, unapologetically laughing.

It's not until I glance down at my torso that I catch on to why. Resting on my chest is a hood. I glare at it, perplexed, and I can't—Oh, shit, I've put it on back to front. Preston's leaning forward, still laughing, and once I've wriggled my arms free he gently swivels the hoodie so that it's the right way around, and I slot my arms into the correct holes.

'I like it when you smile like that,' I say like a secret.

'Like what?' he asks, his eyes down as he begins folding my dress.

'Like you're actually happy. I like seeing you happy.'

He doesn't respond.

'It's very attractive,' I add.

'Thank you,' he deadpans.

'You know that, though.'

'Know what?'

'That you're very attractive.'

He doesn't grace me with a reply, which earns him a scowl. He's still folding my dress, and so he doesn't spot my frown until he's placed it on the floor beside him, then turned back to me.

He shakes his head with a smile. 'You're drunk, Mia.'

'You're not,' I say accusingly. 'Boring.'

'I've been advised against it by numerous psychiatrists.'

'Fuck 'em.'

He's laughing—real laughing. Again! It's a miracle!

'Nick likes you,' I reveal. 'You're his favourite. He told me so.'

'Shame. He's not really my type.'

I roll my eyes in a super dramatic, super obvious way, then reach over to smack his arm. 'You know what I mean!'

With a hmph, I wrangle with Preston's thick duvet below me until it's above me, then bury myself into it as deeply as possible. The comforting scent of aftershave and fresh linen overwhelms my senses, and I sigh into it. I shut my eyes.

'He could be the one,' I murmur.

The mattress dips beside me, and I can't be sure because my eyes are still closed, but I think Preston lies down.

'That's a confident statement to make after meeting someone twice,' he says from my left.

'No, not that one. It's not that deep. The one I lose my virginity to,' I say like it's obvious. 'At this rate, it'll be him, a one-night-stand, or that sex worker we talked about.'

'You're oozing romance right now, Euphemia.'

'Thank you,' I reply, sincerely. 'Margot says I just need to find someone I'm comfortable enough with, which could be Nick one day. Either that or I could convince someone I'm already comfortable with to do me the honour.'

Huh. I'd not even thought of that option before now. I should get champagne drunk more option—I'm full of brilliant ideas. I'm grinning into Preston's duvet, but the smile is soon wavering.

'But then my only options there would be you or Aiden, so maybe not. I think that could be traumatic for Aiden.' I sigh into the duvet. 'You can be my back up plan. Plan Z. Not Z for Zack, just to clarify. Z for the last letter of the alphabet, like, last resort.'

'On that note,' he utters. 'Bedtime. Goodnight, Mia.'

Without any further explanation, I feel him lift himself from the mattress. If it's bedtime, why is he leaving the bed? I'm rolling the conundrum around my head, and it's not until I've reached the conclusion that I must be dreaming that I realise I'm alone. I frown, and I'm about to get up—I'm definitely going to get up, but I can't remember how to, and by that point, it's too late. I'm out like a light.

I'm never getting champagne drunk again.

I'm blind. I swear to God I'm blind. Every light source hurts as if the sun's projecting laser beams into my pupils, or maybe that's just the headache.

'I hate you,' I grumble into Preston's duvet. 'And your stupid three bottles of stupid champagne.'

Preston, who's treading around his room and making way too much noise, blissfully ignores me. It's only when I'm squinting at his tall figure as he pulls his blinds further open that I realise he's not ignoring me; he's taunting me. I groan as I shove his duvet over my head as a barrier from the light. He slept on the sofa downstairs last night, which I initially felt guilty about, but that guilt is rapidly vanishing.

'I took things too far last night,' he says as I feel him sit beside me. 'Sorry.'

I scramble the duvet off my face and shoot him a squint-heavy scowl. 'Huh?'

'Getting into the club, the whole champagne thing with Michael, and–'

I interrupt him with a crude sigh. 'Oh, it was fine! Charming the buttholes off a few strangers is hardly worth toiling over.'

He opens his mouth to respond, but I get in there first.

'Seriously, Preston,' I say, this time with a softness to my voice as finally, I manage to open my eyes all the way. 'You let yourself have fun. You let yourself live. No one got hurt, and hell, you improved multiple people's nights! Ours by getting us in, Michael's by giving the poor sod an ego boost, the security guy's too, I'd bet.'

He responds by chewing the inside of his cheek, his eyes shifting towards his bedroom window with a distant look in them. I scan his side profile as he swallows, his eyelashes fluttering as he glances down at his hands, and I want to crack his head open. I want to hear his every thought. Even then, I'm not sure I'd understand him, not fully.

With my eyes still glued to him, I whisper, 'do not go gentle into that good night.'

A ghost of a smile creeps itself onto Preston's lips as he finishes the quote. 'Rage, rage against the dying of the light.'

He turns his head, and I'm grinning like an idiot as he meets my eyes.

A quiet laugh escapes his mouth. 'Did you just Uno reverse me?'

'With a Dylan Thomas quote, no less,' I reply triumphantly, then sit up as I stretch my arms into the air with a long yawn. 'Is my bag here?'

Preston nods towards his desk and I flip my head–a little too quickly because crap, that hurt–to see my velvet clutch bag sitting atop his closed laptop. Without a word, I fling the duvet off me and drag myself to my feet to grab the bag. Within seconds, I've plopped myself back onto the mattress.

Preston's watching me in a neither here nor there sort of way, but I see right through his casual demeanour. He's intrigued; he wants to know what the hell I'm doing. I don't tell him, obviously. He'd run a mile. Still without saying a word, I open my bag and unzip its inside pocket to bring out a small, white envelope.

'No, it's—We're not doing this now,' he says in a heartbeat as he attempts to stand.

I grab his wrist in a death-grip. 'Yes, we are,' I say, and as he tries to argue again, I interrupt him. 'You've been avoiding this for two weeks, and if we don't do it now, you'll avoid it for another two weeks. Or more. Probably more.'

I lift the envelope's flap, just as Preston pipes up. 'Okay! Okay, fine, but breakfast first.' He sighs. 'I'm not doing this on an empty stomach.'

I narrow my eyes at him, my hand frozen with my fingers dipped into the envelope. 'Fine.'

Preston doesn't try to make a prison breakout-style escape once I've demolished the egg and soldiers I demanded he make us. Instead, once I've swallowed my final scrap of toast, he calmly takes our plates, pops them into the dishwasher, and leads me back upstairs to his room. He didn't say a word while we were eating—literally not one; it was like living in an egg-themed hallucination. He also ate, from what I could tell, two soldiers and a quarter of an egg.

'Do you want me to give you, like, a run down?' I query as I close his bedroom door behind us. 'If you feel anxious about reading it?'

'It's okay. I'll read it.'

He's got his back to me as he answers because he's standing over his desk, but I don't complain. I'm just relieved he's regained the ability to speak. I join him as he sits down onto his bed, and as I hand him the letter, he returns to silence. He remains silent as he reads it. I watch him in anticipation once he's finished, but he doesn't bite, just starts folding the paper.

I guess it's on me, then.

'Did you know he only recently found out about you?'

He nods, still folding the paper; I'm not sure he'll stop until it becomes physically impossible.

'That's positive, right?' I try. 'Not like he got your mum pregnant, tapped out, then randomly decided to bother when it suited him twenty years later.'

'Hm.'

'He seems nice,' I try again. 'From the way he writes, I mean, and he's obviously keen to meet you. I can help you figure out what to say when you reach out, if you want. He's left his email, so if you'd rather that over a call, I'm sure that'd be–'

'I don't think I will,' he interrupts.

'Email him?' I shrug. 'I mean, hey, I'm all for a call if you'd rather do–'

'Contact him.'

CHAPTER 14

Christmas is around the corner and cracks are beginning to show in my newfound lust for a love life. Things are going well with Nick; they're slow, but there's nothing wrong. I've even been on a few other dates with guys, all of which have proved to me that I should focus on Nick. The trouble is that the snail's pace of our relationship is on me. It's been over a month since we had our first date and we remain unlabeled, and our intimacy hasn't progressed anywhere beyond a few heated kisses.

It's like there's a total mental block happening. I can feel myself drawing back as things turn increasingly serious, and it's making me want to punch myself in the face. Repeatedly. I'm home for two weeks over Christmas, and so the hope is that some breathing space and distance will kick me into getting over myself.

The only thing floundering more than my love life is convincing Preston that reaching out to his dad isn't the worst idea known to humankind. Something he'd not told me before he read the letter was that Rhys knows nothing about his past. As far as he's concerned, Preston's been living peacefully with Anwen and Matty all these years.

Preston's rented a car for the Christmas journey home because that worked out cheaper than buying return train tickets. I'm blasting a Christmas playlist via the car's bluetooth, which he's agreed to so long as I specifically play Boney M.'s Sunny every five songs. He's also refusing to close the driver's side window, despite it being under ten degrees outside. Unsurprisingly, he took my fucking weirdo accusation as a compliment.

'I'm just saying you don't have to commit to anything,' I shout over I Wish it Could be Christmas Everyday. 'You can make initial contact, then take it day by–'

He clenches his jaw, then sighs. 'How would I even attempt to approach the situation?'

'Preston, you've got nothing to be ashamed of,' I reassure him. 'I know you're intent on taking your past to your grave with you, but you don't have to. None of what you've been through is anything to be ashamed of.' I soften my eyes as he slows the car when we approach a junction. 'Just be honest with him.'

He sighs again, his clenched jaw softening, and I think I've done it. I think I've actually gotten through to him. That is, until he opens his mouth.

'Hey, Dad, I killed my little brother's father when I was thirteen, let Mum take the blame and go to prison for five years, tried to kill myself when I was eighteen, confessed to the murder–'

'–Manslaughter–'

'–and went to prison for fifteen months. Uni's fun, though.'

'Nailed it. Obviously, that's what I'm suggesting; tell him exactly like that, word for word,' I deadpan as we speed up again.

Preston's reaction to my sarcasm is to blast the music's volume up, just as Sunny starts playing for, I think, the fourteenth time.

Our first stop is Mum's house. Through barefaced lies and strategic planning, I've managed to limit my nights spent at Dad's while I'm home to two. He thinks I'm only home for five days, and he's got me from mid-afternoon on Christmas Day, so that's kept him sweet. Livvy's sworn herself to secrecy and Mum's hardly going to rat me out, so I'm spending the other twelve nights with her.

She's already at the front door, wearing her dressing gown and waving like a maniac when we pull up on the drive. My face is heating up, and as I glance at Preston to see him biting his cheeks to hold back a laugh, I'm tempted to faceplant the dashboard. I've not even unfastened my seatbelt by the time she's rushed over to the passenger door. Preston, intent on elongating my embarrassment for as long as possible, lowers my window.

'Hello!' Mum beams as she leans down to peer into the car, and she's unapologetically looking at Preston.

It's her first time seeing him in months, and her first time seeing us together since he entered the young offender's institute. While I was travelling and Preston was in his first year of uni, what started as a one-off meeting for Preston to hand over a pile of my clothes I'd left at Anwen's became the two of them catching up whenever he was in Cardiff. I figured Mum spotted an opportunity to get any potential gossip I was hiding while travelling.

'Hi, Mum, I'm here too,' I butt in as I turn to her, then lean forward to block her view of Preston.

I hear him stifle a laugh beside me as Mum rolls her eyes. I shoo her away from the car door, then fling it open to leave the vehicle before opening the backseat and grabbing my suitcase. Mum's blabbering away to Preston throughout the process, and it's a good thing he doesn't mind the cold because she's holding the whole door open now.

'Are you staying over tonight, darling?' I catch her say as I stand beside her, suitcase in hand.

Why is everyone's mothers obsessed with Preston and me staying at their houses?

'I best not,' Preston replies, and the way he's leaning over with his left hand on the steering wheel and his right arm draped over the passenger seat's headrest isn't, like, unattractive. 'I need to get back to my mum's.'

'Aw, well, if you're sure! You're welcome any time. The spare room—Euphemia's room while she's home—is a double.'

I'm starting to wish she was more on Dad's I won't have a murderer in my house level, not that I can say much after the deranged you're my plan Z comment I made to Preston while champagne drunk that I'd rather die than remind him of.

'He's going on the sofa if he stays over,' I reply, then add, 'and please don't use my full name around him.'

Upon realising the opening I've just given Preston, I slam the car door closed, then lean into the passenger car window to utter, 'don't even think about making an STD comment about my name.'

'What's in a name?' he murmurs. 'That which we call a rose by any other name would smell as sweet.'

Huh. Maybe his quote spewing urge overtook his urge to make an STD commen—

'The same can't be said about your name's resemblance to an STD, however, so please do let me know if anyone else has ever—'

'Bye, Preston,' I snap, then grab Mum's arm through her dressing gown armour.

I yank her in the direction of her house while she's waving him goodbye, somehow more manically than how she greeted us, and Preston's loving every second.

My time at home is oddly serene. The world moves more slowly outside London, and it's taken being away from home for as long as I have to realise I've actually missed it. Boredom would become the death of me if I stayed here too long, don't get me wrong, but I can at least begin to comprehend why people retire to the suburbs. Being apart from Nick has made me crave his company too, a sure sign of something positive. Maybe this will help break that intimacy barrier, after all.

On Christmas morning, I try my hardest to ignore the inevitable. I have chocolate and bucks fizz for breakfast, play party games with Mum and Livvy, stuff myself silly with the lunch Mum makes, and don't even think about Dad until it's time to leave.

'You don't have to go, you know,' Livvy says quietly from the staircase while Mum runs around looking for her car keys.

'I don't mind,' I say without meeting her eyes.

When she doesn't reply, I give in to see her pink lips down-turned, her expression soft as she exudes sympathy. I wish I had her balls. I wish I could just think fuck it and not visit Dad.

Mum drops me at Dad's place for two o'clock, and I assure her I can let myself in. The last thing I need is a Christmas Day con-frontation between my parents. Once Mum's silver car is safely out of sight, I take a sharp breath and drag myself towards Dad's front door.

I open it with a loud, 'hello!'

I'm met with silence, but don't think much of it. Dad's probably in the living room watching some shit Christmas special.

'Dad!' I try. 'Hello?'

I dump my suitcase by Dad's shoe rack, then kick my trainers off. With a sigh, I wander through the hallway and into the living room, but he's not there. I try the kitchen, and when I have no luck there, make my way upstairs. Every room is empty, including Dad's. There's not even a Christmas tree to brighten the place.

With no clue what else to do, I try his mobile. It rings out four times before I get an answer.

'Mia?' he yells down the phone, which I blame on the muffled background noise.

'Dad? Hey, Dad, I'm—Where are you? I've just gotten to yours.' I pause. 'Your door was unlocked. You know that, right?'

'You're early!' he replies, ignoring my door comment.

'No, it's—We agreed on two,' I say, then briefly lower my phone to my face to check I'm not losing it. 'Yeah, it's half past now so I'm actually—'

Dad's booming laughter cuts me off, and he shouts something to someone who isn't me. I stammer.

'Dad? Hello?'

'We said two o'clock,' he says, clearly not having listened to a word I just said.

'Yes. And it's two-thirty.'

'I'm just at the pub! I'll see you later, okay?'

I want to scream. I want to fucking scream.

'Don't bother.'

I hang up the phone, slam it down onto the sofa, grab a cushion from behind me, press it against my face, and do exactly that; scream until my throat fucking hurts.

It's not until three o'clock that I resurface into reality. I'm sitting on the sofa, pillow now discarded on the carpet, and staring into space. I'm not staying here. I don't know why exactly—in fear of worrying her, of causing an argument between my parents, or maybe just embarrassment—but I don't call Mum. I call Preston. When he answers, I don't say hello, or even let him finish saying it.

Instead, with a poorly hidden voice crack, I say, 'can you come pick me up from my dad's?'

A pause.

'I'll be fifteen minutes.'

Thirteen minutes later, Preston's rental car is rolling onto Dad's driveway. Only now does it occur to me that the drive from Anwen's to Dad's house takes twenty minutes.

'Did you speed?' I question as I'm securing my seatbelt.

'Off the record,' Preston murmurs as he reverses the car off the driveway. 'Yes.'

I blink. 'Why?'

'You sounded upset.'

I enter Anwen's house spewing apologies. It's Christmas, for fuck's sake; what was I thinking? I can't invite myself to another family's house on Christmas. Anwen, despite this, responds with endless reassurance that it's no trouble. Matty buzzes around me demanding to show off every gift he's received, and while he's doing that, Anwen's insisting I eat some of their Christmas dinner leftovers.

It's absolute chaos, and God, it makes me feel better.

Preston and I are the last ones awake. We're in his bedroom watching a shitty nineties Christmas film that I insisted on, but I'm not paying much attention. I'm too busy pretending to not give a shit about the fact I've not heard a peep from Dad since I hung up on him over eight hours ago.

My chest is tight and there's a sharp lump in my throat that I'm desperately trying to ignore as I bury myself deeper into the fluffy blanket we stole from the living room. I'm silently praying Preston's too immersed in the laptop screen between us to notice me shrivelling up as I focus on my breathing, trying to do so as slowly and deeply as I can. I squint my eyes shut, my heart beating in my ears, but it's hopeless. My cheeks are damp.

'Mia?' Preston whispers. 'What's—'

'The film's sad,' I squeak.

A beat passes.

'As much as I'd love to, I'm inclined to not believe you.'

'Why?'

'It's a comedy.'

I sniff. 'With sad undertones.'

My voice wobbles as I speak, and it'll be a miracle if he understood a word of that. I open my eyes to find him scanning my face, the light from his laptop screen illuminating his skin, and I'm fine. Without words, I try to communicate that I'm absolutely fine.

Something flickers through his green eyes—hesitance or uncertainty, or maybe both—but I can't make any attempt to figure that out because everything is turning blurry.

'Hey,' he murmurs, and it's not subtle anymore—I'm blatantly, no question about it crying. 'Hey.'

In some last ditch attempt to stifle my embarrassment, I clamp my eyes shut again, just as Preston shuffles beside me to move the laptop. I feel him lift the blanket a little, and his arms are around me, pulling me into him until my head is slotted underneath his chin.

'Your dad?' he asks quietly.

I can't speak, so I just nod into his chest. He doesn't press for more or insist everything's okay, and I've never been more grateful, even if it does result in me crying into his jumper for five minutes straight.

'I keep trying with him, but all he does is throw it back in my face,' I eventually manage to say. 'I've given him so many chances.'

'You don't have to keep trying,' Preston says into my hair.

'I do. It's not—I can't just give up. Despite everything, he's still my dad.'

I sniff as my hair falls to my face, and he gently pushes it out of my eyes to tuck it behind my ear. He keeps his hand there, his thumb stroking my cheek in a slow, rhythmic motion.

'That doesn't mean you owe him anything,' he soothes. 'You shouldn't break yourself into a million unsalvageable pieces for the sake of someone incapable of looking beyond their own destruction.'

I nestle my face deeper into his neck, my lips brushing against the smooth skin as I kiss it. I don't know why I kiss it; if it's my way of thanking him, or if it's just because I want to. He doesn't protest, and instead plants his own kiss atop my head.

'This isn't very Christmassy of me,' I whisper. 'Sorry.'

His chest vibrates with a low laugh. 'Believe me, I've had worse.'

'And I've made a mess,' I murmur as I pull back to observe the warm, damp patch just below the collar of his sage jumper. 'Sorry.'

I lift my eyes to cast him an apologetic look and find his already on me, bold and bright, despite the room's darkness. With a small smile—one I'm not sure I've seen before—he lifts his hand to my face to pat at my damp cheeks with his thumbs. I hold my breath, a heavy silence between us as I stroke the soft material of his jumper. As he removes his hands from my face, I shut my eyes and exhale, just as he plants a warm kiss onto each of my eyelids.

'Sorry,' I murmur, one final time.

'Don't be,' he whispers.

He wraps his arms around me again, and I nudge myself back into him, my breath finally returning to something more calm and measured. My head is underneath his chin, his hand smoothing the back of my hair, and we stay like that until I fall into the deepest sleep I've had since I can remember.

CHAPTER 15

The other side of Preston's bed is empty when I wake up the next morning, and I'm sobered by the light of a new day. I don't even attempt to kid myself into believing we didn't cross a line last night. We didn't kiss, let alone do anything beyond that, but what happened somehow feels more blurred. I squint at my phone to see Dad's sent me a long, apologetic text but I ignore it, and instead, head downstairs.

As I'm passing the living room, I notice a duvet hanging off the sofa. He definitely didn't sleep in the bed with me, then. That's a good thing, I think, but I'm not sure my heart is quite in it.

'Hi, lovely,' Anwen greets me as I tread into the kitchen. 'Tea? Coffee? Hot chocolate? Breakfast?'

She's filling a blue kettle with water, her head swivelled over her shoulder to smile at me from where she stands over the sink.

'I'd love a hot chocolate, thanks,' I reply as I pull up a chair at the kitchen table behind her.

Anwen shoots me a warm smile, then turns back to the sink. She's humming as she prepares two mugs and waits for the kettle to boil, although she stops at least four times to check I definitely don't want her to prepare me a three course meal. Meanwhile, I'm listening out for any sign of movement elsewhere in the house and glancing towards the kitchen doorway every few seconds.

My attention is stolen from the doorway when Anwen drops a mug of hot chocolate in front of me, and I thank her.

'He's taken Matty to Roath Park,' she says.

I sometimes forget where Preston gets his mind reading abilities from.

'Matty's teacher mentioned Boxing Day walks to him before they broke up from school, and he's been obsessed with the idea ever since.' She chuckles. 'I said we'd meet them there when you were up, if you fancied it.'

'Oh, you didn't need to wait.' I stammer. 'You should've just woken me up!'

Anwen brushes the air as she sits into the wooden chair opposite mine. 'I appreciate the peace.'

I laugh into my hot chocolate as Anwen sips at her coffee. In hindsight, the situation with Dad yesterday was a blessing. I've had a much better time with Preston, Anwen, and Matty than I would've with Dad, and after talking it through with Preston last night, I don't feel particularly guilty about admitting that. I just wish I could get through to him about his own dad.

I glance at Anwen as I contemplatively chew my lip and think, fuck it. Preston told me it was her who gave him the letter, so she's definitely aware of the situation.

'I'm trying to convince Preston that contacting his dad isn't the worst idea in the world,' I say, and a knowing look flashes through Anwen's green eyes. 'But I'm getting nowhere.'

'Mia, you've made more progress over a couple of months than I have in a year. He shuts down every time I try to float the topic.' She sighs as she cradles her mug. 'He's not said it—he never would—but I think he's frustrated with me for not trying harder with Rhys, and it's—I should've, I just—I don't know, I wasn't quite nineteen, it was a holiday romance, and I couldn't find him. I tried; of course I tried, but I should've tried harder.'

I try to interject, but Anwen stops me before I can say a word.

'Rhys came across me by chance last year, through my cousin who lives in Pembrokeshire. That was bizarre in itself; he somehow recognised her from that holiday two decades ago, and asked after me.' Her eyes shift from her mug to look at me. 'If anyone can convince Preston, it's you.'

By early afternoon on the twenty-seventh of December, I'm back in London, and home feels like an eon ago. If Aiden hadn't hitched a ride with Preston and me back to London, I'd genuinely consider the possibility that my whole time in Cardiff was a fever dream. The reason for Aiden's infringement of my seasonal London life, to nobody's surprise, boils down to a party. Margot's throwing a New Year's Eve bash at hers and Preston's house, which Aiden would've sooner died than turned down, despite him having five exams in January.

I was secretly relieved to have Aiden as a buffer during the journey home. Preston and I haven't spoken about the night I crashed his family Christmas, and I want to keep it that way. The last thing I need is more weird tension between us, nor do I want to relive the embarrassment of bawling my eyes out in front of him. That's likely the cause of our intimacy that night, anyway; me being an emotional wreck chokeholding him into it.

Preston's on Aiden babysitting duty tonight because I've got a date with Nick. The date. The date that'll make me realise our time apart has made me not only grow fonder of him, but that I'm emotionally and physically capable of being an actual person in an actual relationship-type scenatio. Or something like that.

He's cooking me dinner at his family home in South London because he's got a free house, which I'm doing a shocking job at not panicking over. I've told Aiden that his house will be empty, but telling Preston with all its insinuation felt... weird. I need to go there, act sensible and mature, and keep my head screwed on throughout because Nick is such a great guy and drawing back from him now would be a terrible move.

He greets me at his modest, detached family home with a big smile, all white teeth and dimples. It smells like heaven when I follow him into the hallway, and I laugh as he throws his hands around while describing the miso soup he's cooking.

'I know it's nothing special,' he says as we enter the kitchen, and I figure it's best I don't share how it's a miracle for me to boil an egg successfully. 'But it's perfect for a cold winter evening, right?'

Despite his attempts to be humble, the food Nick has prepared is sensational. Everything about the night is, really. We eat ice cream directly from the tub for dessert, bunch ourselves up on the sofa with blankets and cushions, and talk about our Christmases. There's nothing to complain about; nothing to criticise. Every-thing is perfect. Perfect, perfect, perfect.

And I'm trying really hard to be enthusiastic about that.

We're sitting on the plush sofa and Nick's embracing me as I rest my head on his shoulder. He says my name, I look up to peer into his deep brown eyes, and this is it. This is what the night has been leading up to, and so I do exactly what I'd planned.

I plant a kiss onto his lips and he's kissing me back within moments. We begin slow and steady, his hand at the back of my head while I slide mine underneath his t-shirt and trace circles on his stomach. Our breathing fastens, our kisses become hungrier, and I... I can't do it.

Fuck.

With no explanation, I part from Nick, and I'm suddenly on my feet as if abruptly stopping our kiss wasn't dramatic enough. He gazes up at me with something between concern and bewilderment, and God, he looks like a stressed puppy.

'I'm–It's–I'm sorry, I'm really sorry, I just...' I swallow. 'It's not you, it's me.'

It's not you, it's me. Am I taking the piss?

'Genuinely. I know that's a thing people say, but I can't stress this enough; I'm the problem. You're great.'

He blinks back silently, and Jesus Christ, this is painful.

'Amazing, even. You've literally not done a thing wrong. I've never met anyone who's done less things wrong, in fact.'

Overkill, Mia. Overkill.

I clear my throat. 'I just mean—My point is that this isn't working. I'm sorry, really.'

He blinks. Again.

'You want to stop seeing each other?' he asks quietly.

'Yes,' I answer too quickly.

He responds with a sad smile–the saddest looking smile I might've ever seen, honestly, and God, I hate myself. Why am I doing this? Why am I ruining something good?

'I just—I'm not ready, and it wouldn't be fair to string you along.'

I should shut up at that, but I don't.

'Which I know sounds super hypocritical because I've just spent the night after Boxing Day with you eating food you cooked at your family home, and we were literally making out, like, two minutes ago—'

Probably don't need to remind him of that.

'—but it's selfish to keep you tied up with me, not when I'm such a... such a... mess.'

Finally, I develop the self-awareness to close my mouth. I flash Nick another apologetic look, and like the perfect, unproblematic man he is, he proceeds to offer me a lift home. I assure him the train is fine.

The good news is that my grand exit means I can relinquish Preston of his Aiden babysitting duties early. I head straight to Preston's place from Nick's, and Aiden's reaction to seeing my face as he swings the front door open—because of course he'd answer the door to a house that isn't his—is equal part horror and equal part confusion.

'You're not supposed to be home yet,' he accuses as I step inside. 'Or at all, actually.'

'Shut up,' I grumble, then follow it up with a long, loud groan. 'I fucked it.'

I follow him through the hallway and into the house's living area to find Preston reading on the sofa as some KPop song blasts from Aiden's discarded laptop. Aiden's section of the sofa has spilled popcorn and a crumpled blanket while Preston's has a few stacked books with illegible, handwritten notes on top. I glance between the two guys; it's all very them.

Preston double takes when he spots me in the doorway, but he's looking at the opened book in his hands when he says, 'you're early.'

'Long story short, I'm incapable of developing anything resembling a fulfilling, deep emotional connection with men.'

'Same,' Aiden interjects.

'Or a physical one,' I add as I collapse onto the sofa, then reach over to hit pause on Aiden's laptop before I lose what remains of my sanity.

Aiden makes a so-so gesture. 'That... Not so much.'

He jumps between Preston and me while giggling hysterically, and as soon as I spot his brown eyes flicking towards his laptop, I snatch it away. He frowns, then mutters something about me being a buzz killer under his breath. Preston continues reading blissfully throughout our entire exchange.

'Besides, you're wrong,' Aiden offers, then gestures between him and Preston. 'You have deep emotional connections with us. We're men.'

'You don't count,' I grumble.

'Homophobe.'

I roll my eyes. 'Because I'm not romantically interested in you.'

'I'm romantically interested in Preston.'

'I know,' Preston and I say in unison, and it makes me snort a laugh.

The man himself even smirks a little; it's a post-Christmas miracle. Although, he still doesn't quite manage to draw his eyes from the pages of his book.

'Plus you two are in your friends to lovers, second chance romance era,' Aiden begins, and the scowl I shoot him is enough to scare him into following his statement up with, 'but let's not fall down that hole. My point is, Mia, don't stress yourself into thinking your love life is doomed. Things will figure themselves out.'

'It's me who needs to figure it out, though, not things. I need to not be so, I don't know, afraid of opening up to people—the good, the bad, and the ugly.'

Preston, who I didn't realise was even listening, says, 'being particular about those you divulge your darkness to is a virtue; spreading it too thinly will exhaust you.'

'For fuck's sake, he always has to one-up me,' Aiden whines, then nods towards Preston. 'He looks extra hot in glasses, though, right?'

'I think there are some critiques to be made on the style,' I suggest. 'Round frames were a good move, but maybe a little bigger.'

'Really? I don't think he could go wrong with any size so long as he sticks to wireframe; gives off hot academic vibes.'

'He's right here,' Preston interjects, finally closing his book.

I lean forward to analyse his face, then turn back to Aiden. 'Y'know what, I think you're right. Size is pretty interchangeable.'

Aiden and I are sniggering while Preston watches us, his eyebrows raised underneath his infamous glasses. Aiden proceeds to insist on trying them on, and when he does, obviously I have to. They verge on looking comically large on me, but Preston's polite about it; Aiden, on the other hand, isn't shy about informing me that I resemble a serial killer from the eighties.

'Eighties serial killers have aviator-style frames,' I point out as I reach over Aiden to return Preston's glasses to him. 'Not round.'

'Same energy,' Aiden argues.

'You're supposed to be the nice one,' I whine.

'And I still hold that title. Not once have I asked you if anyone's mentioned that your name sounds like an STD.'

Now that piques Preston's interest. I can literally feel his peepers burning my side profile as I resist all temptation to satisfy him with my attention. He doesn't care; he butts in anyway.

'Aiden has a point,' he says. 'Has anyone, by the way? Mentioned that your name resembles an STD?'

'Sorry, correction; you're both equal arseholes.'

Both of the guys start laughing, and I don't have the energy to inform them that they're the most unfunny human beings I've ever had the displeasure of knowing.

CHaPTer 16

Six hours before her New Year's party is due to kick off, I receive a call from Margot that, when I answer it, convinces me the world is imploding. It turns out their boiler is broken. It means no heating, which I assure her is no problem because the house will be too crammed with bodies later for anyone to be bothered by that, and I offer a place at my flat to shower and get ready. She reacts as if I saved her from a burning building.

'Is Nick coming?' she says into my bedroom mirror as she paints on her eyeshadow, and I suppress a cringe.

She only returned to London today, and in hindisght, I would've pre-empted her with the news of me bottling it with Nick before now, but logic has never been a redeeming quality of mine.

'No. No, we're–That's over,' I reply.

She freezes, a make-up brush in her hand as her eyes widen. 'Oh, shit. Are you okay? What happened?'

'It's fine, honestly. I ended it with him, so yeah, all good.'

'You sure? You want to talk about it?,' she says softly. 'Even if you're the dumper, it can still sting.'

I shake my head to her through the mirror. 'Totally fine, I promise. That's kind of the problem, actually. I just couldn't... I don't know, like him enough.'

Margot sits on my reply for a moment, pursing her lips. She swivels away from the mirror to look at me directly, her head tilting the tiniest amount as she narrows her eyes. It's oddly threatening.

'Is there someone else?'

'No,' I say, maybe a little hastily, so I follow it up with, 'I wish there was.'

And I do. That's not a lie or even a flourish of the truth because there isn't anyone else. It just sometimes feels like there is, and I can hardly put all of my relationship woes down to some whimsical, intangible feeling.

'What I will say, though, is that your one-off hook up suggestion has never been more tempting.'

She laughs, big and loud. 'Hey, tonight could be your night. There should be at least one hot, single guy who turns up.'

'Won't even need to be hot at this point,' I mutter. 'Although childhood trauma deems single a necessity.'

Margot's giggling as she turns back to the mirror to continue applying her make-up. A smile is breaking onto my face as I watch her, and it grows tenfold when she blasts the music on her phone all the way up and starts singing really, really badly. Maybe Preston was right; maybe I am capable of making friends without Aiden.

People start trickling into the party from around seven o'clock, and by eight, the event is in full swing. As I'd reassured Margot, the lack of heating is a total non-issue. In fact, we've got the patio doors that lead into the back garden open to let in some much-needed fresh air. I've never seen Aiden so deeply in his element; the guy's darting between people, most of them total strangers, and trapping them in long, often derailed, conversations about who knows the hell what.

No joke—I made eye contact with one of Margot's friends earlier, who was in the process of speaking with him, and was overcome with a wave of save me!

Margot has gone all out on the decor. There's bunting stuck to every wall, silver balloons bobbing around the floor, glittery confetti littered in every corner and crevice, and enough party hats to serve a stadium of people. Everyone is dressed to the nines—it's something she insisted on. We're talking literal suits and ball gowns, which while impractical, sure is fun. I've opted to recycle an emerald green dress I wore to my cousin's wedding before I went travelling last year.

The only thing missing from the party is Preston. I checked on him when Margot and I returned to their house for pre-drinks, and he gave me some spiel about how he'd join us at around eight when people started arriving, but it's nearing eight-thirty and he's not so much as popped downstairs for a glass of water. I give in at eight forty-five.

While scrunching the bottom of my satin dress into a ball to avoid tripping over the three staircases I have to climb to do so, I make my way upstairs to Preston's room. From there, we undergo our usual routine: I knock, ignoring the music playing quietly from the other side of the door, wait for a few seconds of no response, then cave and let myself in.

He's sitting at his desk, his back to me as he scribbles something into a notebook. Most importantly, given he's wearing an oversized burgundy jumper and worn blue jeans, he's very much not adhering to Margot's dress code.

'Weird interpretation of I'll join you at eightish,' I comment as I amble into the room.

He doesn't turn his chair as he says, 'Eightish is down to interpretation, no?'

I roll my eyes, then sigh. 'Come on then, what's up?'

He doesn't answer me, just keeps writing away at whatever he's writing away at. The music swirling around the room is a Florence and the Machine song, and if his private concert combined with his outfit isn't telling enough, the room's only light source are its lit candles. All very non-party joining behaviour.

'That bad?' I ask as I approach his bed.

He still says nothing. He continues to write into his notebook, and doesn't reward me with a glance in my direction as I sit down onto the head of his bed. The springs creak quietly, but his side profile remains unchanged, his eyes fixated on whatever it is he's writing.

'Hey?' I say quietly. 'What is it?'

His jaw ticks, his hand pausing before he subtly shakes his head and continues writing. He still refuses to turn to me.

'Preston?' I try—no, plead. 'Please talk to me.'

With a gentle sigh, he stops writing again, this time for good. He drops his pen as he finally gives me his attention, spinning his chair to face me. I don't know why I expect this time to be different, but his expression is void of any indication towards, well, anything.

'What would you like to talk about?' he asks as he lifts his feet to rest his heels on the mattress.

I groan. 'Something's wrong, and I'm not going to piss off until you tell me what.'

As someone incapable of talking sense for more than a full minute, Preston's response to my sincere concern is, 'having now finished the work assigned me, I retire from the great theatre of Action.'

'Jesus Christ,' I mutter under my breath, although the bastard is smirking at me, so that's a positive indication towards his mood, right?

'George Washington,' he adds. 'His address to congress when he resigned.'

'You know,' I begin. 'You think you're a lot better at avoiding my questions than you actually are.'

Our eyes meet and the temptation to look away is a burning sensation racing through my blood, but I resist. I hold his gaze, the green of his eyes like rich velvet as I try not to lose myself in them.

'I'm toning things down,' he says, breaking our spell. 'I've been engaging too much, getting too involved in things—'

'You've not; it's all been harmless and health—'

'Hyde Park, the night I got us into that club, the house parties, the amped up socialising, the situation with Rhys,' he continues, then shuts his eyes for a moment. 'I need to stop.'

'Why?' I hit back.

'It's too much.'

'It's not—I don't—' I stammer, then pause to gather my thoughts. 'None of what you've done over the past few months has been anything more than mildly daring, and it's not harmed a soul. You can't...'

As my voice trails off, Preston raises his eyebrows, and I sigh.

'You can't go back to living like you were before. I just—Don't you want more than that—than this?' I soften my eyes. 'You're not living, Preston, you're just existing.'

He shakes his head, then flashes me a look that verges on apologetic.

'Sometimes staying alive is the best I can do.'

Finally, I stop arguing with him. My lips are parted with words that I've lost; I've forgotten what they even were, and I soften my face.

'I can't go down there, Mia,' he murmurs, then swallows. 'I can't face it.'

The silence between us lasts seconds, but it's loud. Only now do I truly comprehend what he's saying, what he's actually been telling me throughout the entirety of our exchange.

'Okay, then I'll stay up here.'

He's shaking his head before I've even finished speaking.

'No, Preston, I will,' I say. 'And you can go back to becoming a huge fucking hermit, if that's what you need—for a little while, okay? For weeks, if you need it—but I won't go anywhere.'

He argues back, which I counteract. Repeatedly. There's no way in hell I'm ignoring a cry for help, certainly not one from him. I eventually convince him to let me stay with an agreement that it's temporary; that I'll head back downstairs in an hour or so. I have no intention of actually doing that, obviously.

'Oh, and you have to stop writing your angsty poetry and spend quality time with me while I'm here,' I add once I've won him over.

I nod towards the notebook Preston was writing into, which makes him crane his neck to look at it. He turns back to me with a hard look, so I grin at him—big and shameless.

'They're notes on dark matter; I'm looking into theories on their physical properties, which admittedly feels counterproductive given it's widely accepted to be invisible non-baryonic matter.'

I blink. 'So... angsty poetry, yeah?'

The way he presses his lips together suggests he's trying to hide it, but a small smile creeps onto his face.

'But yes. I'll put the notebook away, if it's that great of a deal for you,' he agrees.

'It is. Thank you.'

He rolls his eyes as he stands, then without an ounce of politeness, shoves me with his foot so that I semi-fall. I scoot myself to the other side of the bed to leave a space for him beside me, and he's lucky I don't yank the socks from his feet and shove them into his mouth.

'Well, this is fun,' he says once he's gotten comfortable.

'If you're trying to piss me off so that I leave, it's not going to work,' I scoff.

'That assumption is only fifty percent accurate.'

'Dickhead,' I mutter, swivel my body to face him, then cross my legs. 'Do you have playing cards?'

He raises his eyebrows. 'I'm intrigued to know what card games you propose we play with two people.'

'So... yes? You do.'

With another eye roll—he's going to give himself whiplash at this rate—he leans towards his desk to open one of its drawers, then pulls out a packet of playing cards. I quickly realise he sort of had a point on the whole two people game thing, so we have to resort to snap.

It's actually really fucking fun.

Preston's without a doubt using the game as a way to release his irritation over me crowbarring myself into his evening because the man's reflexes are beyond human. He literally wins every time, but he's so blasé about it—as if he's not putting a single thought into spotting a matching pair, like he knows it's coming before he or I have dealt the card.

We're taking a much needed break after our fourth game when I catch Preston double take at me. It's followed by a sigh, but of course, no explanation follows.

'Here,' he says, then lifts his oversized jumper over his head to reveal a plain white t-shirt. He gesutres it towards me, and I blink. 'You're shivering.'

I furrow my brow as he nudges the burgundy jumper in my direction again. As if by instinct, I take it, and only now does it occur to me that shit, he's right. The hairs on my arms are standing upright, and my skin feels as though it's vibrating.

'I honestly don't feel it,' I swear to him, shove his jumper over my head, then follow up with, 'I think the adrenaline of snap is keeping me warm.'

'Remind me to never take you skydiving,' he replies. 'You'd overheat.'

'Won't you be cold?' I query, but quickly shove my palm in front of his face when I realise my mistake. 'And don't recite your bullshit warmth doesn't fit me or whatever the fuck it is line.'

'I'm fine, Mia,' he says, and I narrow my eyes. 'I promise.'

Before restarting our intense snap championship, I respond to a message Aiden sent me ten or so minutes ago that has strong where the fuck are you? undertones. I explain, without intrusive detail, that I'm upstairs with Preston and promise to join him and Margot for the new year's countdown.

'You've got to come down for midnight,' I say as Preston's dealing our hands.

'Not included in our agreement,' he replies without lifting his head.

'I'll drag you by your hair.'

'I'd like to see you try.'

After another few rounds of snap, we resort to playing a word association game, then eye spy, then twenty questions, then animal, vegetable, mineral, and it's frankly the most fun I've had since I can remember. I don't even mind when every single one of

Preston's twenty questions is him asking me whether someone's ever commented on my name resembling an STD; in fact, I'm sincerely impressed he figures out a way to phrase it differently twenty times.

Although he's too proud to ever admit it, the occasional smile and laugh that slips through Preston's facade suggests he maybe doesn't feel as awful as he did when I first crashed his party of one. My hypothesis is proven when, as it's approaching midnight and I'm getting ready to brave whatever awaits downstairs, Preston stands. Without a word—I'm afraid he'll realise what he's doing if I make a sound—he follows me as we leave his room, and the time it takes us to walk down the three flights of stairs isn't enough for me to question why I've held his hand throughout the journey.

'You're alive!' Aiden screeches within literal seconds of us entering the living area, and I instinctively yank my hand from Preston's.

He bounces towards us, shoving people aside with zero hesitation as he does so, then embraces me with a big, fat hug, lifting me from the floor to spin in a circle. I'm cackling the whole time, and when I'm finally returned to solid ground, I glance to my left to catch Preston with a lopsided smile on his face. I should've thought of this earlier; if anyone can lift a mood, it's Aiden.

'As much as I'd love to greet you like that,' Aiden says to Preston once he's done with me. 'I don't have the upper body strength.' He pauses. 'Nor would I trust my body to respond appropriately.'

'You're gross,' I whine, then playfully shove him.

He giggles, then takes both of our hands to force us through the path he created moments earlier. I steal a glance towards Preston and find no obvious sign of intense regret in his eyes, which is always reassuring. We follow Aiden into the house's back garden, at which point, I spot Margot and Joe standing in a huddle with few others towards the bottom of it.

'Preston!' Margot yells as soon as she spots him.

She greets him with a hug, which I'm sure he hates, then graces me with an even tighter, longer one.

As she's releasing me, she whispers, 'I'm glad he's alright,' into my ear.

I wasn't the only one worried, then.

We've got about ten minutes until midnight hits and we spend it chatting excitedly about the new year. Preston's quiet, even for him, and I don't move from his side for a second. As Aiden's rambling about oysters, as one does on new year's eve in a Clapham back garden, I catch Preston flash the tiniest smile, and it's enough–it's more than enough.

In my relief, and likely aided by Aiden's infectious enthusiasm, I lean into Preston to lightly rest my cheek on his shoulder. I await the inevitable shrug to ease me off, but it never comes. He lets me stay there.

CHAPTER 17

It feels like we've been standing in Margot and Preston's back garden for no time at all when the threat of midnight arrives.

'Three minutes!' Joe shouts over the group.

Naturally, this sends Aiden into a frenzy.

'Fuck, okay—Holy mackerel, right!' he declares, his dark, brown eyes darting between every face in the small circle we've created. They land on me as he says, 'okay, Mia! We're kissing, obviously. Tradition and all that.'

'I appreciate my say in the matter,' I reply.

He ignores me.

Aiden and I have been each other's new year's kiss since the dawn of time, and I've got no plans to change that, but I like to at least pretend to keep him on his toes.

'Margot and Joe, I assume you guys are doing your thing.'

Margot responds to Aiden with a salute.

'Not getting many participation vibes from you,' he continues, spinning on the spot to face Preston.

'Correct,' Preston confirms.

'Trick question. Participation is mandatory,' he hits back, and I figure it's best I don't point out that no question was asked.

'You can either give me a small one, or make out with everyone here—including me, to clarify.'

'This is all very totalitarian,' Joe points out, accurately.

'You don't have to make your decision now,' Aiden continues, ignoring Joe in the same way he ignored me. 'You've got...'

'One minute, forty seconds,' Joe finishes for him.

'One minute, thirty-nine seconds to decide,' Aiden concludes, then turns back to the rest of us. 'If I see one person not locking lips when midnight hits, I will cast you out. Indefinitely.'

'I feel mildly threatened,' Margot murmurs from my right.

'He doesn't intend it to be mild,' I whisper back.

Those who aren't in a relationship with someone in our circle, or who haven't been claimed by Aiden, flash coy glances at one another.

'I'm kidding,' Aiden announces to the group, then pauses contemplatively. 'Well, semi-kidding.'

'He's definitely kidding,' I interject. 'Ignore at least eighty percent of everything he says. Generally, that is—not just now.'

'One minute!' Joe yells.

Before we know it, one minute becomes thirty seconds, which becomes twenty, which becomes ten.

'...Nine! Eight! Seven! Six! Five! Four! Three! Two! One!'

Joe's one is like a klaxon, and he's quickly silenced by Margot, who jumps to wrap her legs around him as they begin, rather aggressively, making out. Aiden breaks our circle to dart towards me, and I'm laughing as he plants a big, wet kiss on my lips, his hands on either side of my face as he pulls me into him. He licks my cheek once he's finished, which is a new development in our tradition.

'Gross,' I whine as I rub my cold skin.

Aiden's so busy snorting in amusement that it takes him longer than it should to catch Preston, who I'm sincerely surprised hasn't tried to make a run for it, watching us.

'Having carefully analysed my options, I'd rather not make out with everyone,' he calls over the yelling surrounding us, his eyes on Aiden. 'Just a small one?'

'No tongues,' Aiden confirms, and I've never seen the man's eyes light up so quickly.

'The fact you said that means you definitely thought about it,' I mutter, not that he hears me.

Before I've said more than a few words, Aiden seizes his opportunity, leans over me and towards Preston, grabs his face, then plants an equally passionate kiss on his mouth as he did on mine moments earlier. I guess I should be flattered that mine had equal enthusiasm.

'Definitely putting that in the bank for later,' Aiden concludes once he's released Preston.

Despite our encouragement, Preston insists on returning upstairs once the hype of the new year countdown has worn off. I concede in the knowledge that him being downstairs was a big step in the first place, although I demand our agreement remains; I'm not leaving his side. As a result, by twelve-thirty, Preston and I are alone in his room again.

'This is the part where you tell me how amazing your time downstairs was,' I say as we collapse onto his mattress. 'Wow, Mia, that was so much fun. I'm so pumped I followed–Wait, no, fuck off would you ever say pumped.'

I jolt forward to sit upright, then bend my elbow to point at the ceiling as a sort of warning sign in case he contemplates interrupting me.

After clearing my throat, I continue with, 'Euphemia, your company has been a pleasure, as has that of our chums, and I cannot thank you enough for encouraging my participation.'

I flip my head around to look down at Preston, who's still lying on his bed, his eyes closed but an undeniable, albeit tiny, smile on his angular face.

'Are you quite finished?' He tries to sound accusatory, but frankly, he sounds like he's never loved me as much as he does in this moment.

'For now,' I conclude, then fall back into a lying position.

'Chums,' he mutters. 'You think I'd say chums?'

'You heard me.'

'You're a fucking clown.'

In the best way possible, what he just said is probably the most un-Preston thing to ever leave his mouth, and I'm laughing—deliriously busting my gut with laughter over a situation that barely scrapes the funny barrel.

When I've gathered myself, I release a long sigh—admittedly with a few giggles breaking through—then turn my head to look at Preston. His eyes are open, finally, and he's wearing a look I'm not sure I've seen before. His eyelids are ever so slightly drooped and the barely there smile from earlier hasn't wavered, only he's not trying to hide it anymore; I'm sure he's not. I think it's contentment.

'Have I ever told you how impossible you are to read?' I say without thinking.

'No, but everyone else has,' he offers, pauses, then says, 'you're better at it than most—than anyone.'

I laugh. Loudly. In hindsight, not my best move considering our faces are inches apart.

'I'm so not.'

He doesn't reply, just twitches his lips in amusement. Despite being buried underneath Preston's woollen jumper and the blanket I've bundled myself into, I suddenly feel naked, as if he's cracked me open.

'I'm not,' I repeat, avoiding his gaze.

He doesn't reply for a while—a whole minute, at least—and so when he does, I grasp onto every word.

'Me included.' He exhales quietly. 'I've never understood myself.'

Words are lost on me—again. He's got it all wrong; he underestimates the degree to which I have no idea what to think, say, or do around him. The words I settle on, the actions I resort to are all executed in some blind fight or flight response to his own words and actions.

In something of an awkward panic, I say, 'in your defence, you talk so much fucking shit. I'd be in a state of confusion twenty-four-seven if I had to live inside your head. I mean, God, imagine what your thoughts are like.'

With that, he's laughing—that proper laughter again, teeth and all. He turns to lie on his back, but doesn't stop laughing, just directs it into the air.

As we fall deeper into the night, we talk about nothing for ages, not so much as blinking in recognition at the sound of party guests trickling out of the house. We don't even bother to turn on a lamp or light any of the room's candles—we instead sit in the moonlight peeping through the room's single window. Our spell is briefly broken when Aiden tentatively knocks on Preston's door—I had no idea he had tentative in him—then announces he's crashing in one of the unoccupied rooms on the second floor. It results in him demanding a full room tour, which Preston humours him with.

Once Aiden's gone, we continue with whatever the hell we were talking about as if he never interrupted, and it's not until it's veering towards two o'clock that we wave the white flag. Preston shuffles through one of his drawers to find me some tracksuit bottoms—the same grey pair he gave me the night I got champagne drunk—and then pops downstairs to grant me privacy. On his return, I'm burrowing myself back into his thick duvet and my dress is draped over his desk chair.

'I can find you a hanger,' he says as he stops above the mattress, then leans down to hand me a glass of water.

'Nah, it's fine, thanks,' I reply, batting the air. 'Although I appreciate the five star service.'

He laughs lightly, and within seconds of him turning away, I stop him.

'Sleep here,' I say, and as he turns back to me, I try to explain it with, 'I'm not allowed to leave you, remember.'

'Technically, I'm leaving you.'

'Even worse.'

His hesitation isn't subtle as he glances towards his bedroom door, then back to me.

'Please,' I try, not bothering to formulate some flimsy excuse this time.

His eyes scan my face as he otherwise remains frozen. He swallows, and then without a word, he surrenders. Instead of continuing to walk towards the door at the back of the room, he walks around his mattress, places his glass of water on the wooden floor beside it, then shuffles into the empty space beside me.

We remain silent, the sound of our slow, measured breathing acting as the sole reminder that we're both here. The cold is nipping at my toes, but I stay as still as I can, as if I'm afraid the smallest shiver could be the catalyst that changes Preston's mind.

My eyes are closed but I know he's lying with his back to me so I take the opportunity to, as carefully as I can, wrap as much of the duvet around me as possible. It doesn't help.

'You're cold,' I hear him murmur moments later, and I open my eyes to see he's lying on his back.

When did he turn around?

Just as I'm about to assure him I'm the perfect temperature–in fact, I couldn't be warmer–a horribly timed shiver runs down my spine. The sheets I'm wrapped in vibrate, just as he turns his head to look at me. He takes a deep breath, his chest rising slowly, then releases a long sigh.

Our silence continues as he turns his body towards me, and there's no thought process behind it; I unravel the duvet enough to inch towards him, enough for the warmth of his body to toy with me, but too much to resist giving in. I move closer again, but he doesn't stop me as I nestle into him, my face in his neck, my chest pressed against his. He wordlessly takes my left hand to nudge it under his t-shirt, and the heat of his chest sends a shockwave through my skin. He wraps his right arm around me, his hand at the nape of my neck, his thumb gently stroking the spot where my hair begins to grow.

'Better,' I whisper. 'Thank you.'

He doesn't reply, at least not verbally; he just continues rubbing my neck, then plants a kiss–the smallest, blink and you'll miss it kiss–on my forehead. He doesn't stop me when I wrap my leg around his, or when I trace my fingertips along the skin underneath his t-shirt, or when I lift my head to look at him, or even when I press my lips onto his. In fact, he kisses me back.

Only, it's different to before.

I don't jolt away in the grand realisation of what's happening, of what it means or could mean if we don't stop. I'm done with caring, and I figure so is he, because we just keep kissing. I sigh into him as he manoeuvres me onto my back with a delicacy that implies anything too abrupt could break me in two. Still without words, I guide his hand under my jumper–his jumper that I'm wearing–in frantic desperation. It's like he can't get close enough, like we should be one person, not two.

My breath is turning shorter, my kisses hungrier as I use every slither of will power to resist digging my fingernails into his back. Then, with no warning, he tears his mouth from mine. Before I can question it, his lips begin tracing my jawline with sporadic kisses, and they continue moving downwards until they reach my neck.

I'm not thinking straight, or really thinking at all, when I take his hand again–the one underneath my jumper–and nudge it higher, refusing to let go until we reach my chest. He's still kissing my neck, now with increased urgency as his thumb teases my nipple, and I'm not breathing anymore. I'm so focused on containing a gratified sigh, of maintaining whatever composure I can, to allow myself to breathe.

I'm lightheaded as Preston's lips return to mine, and I'm fisting his shirt in some kind of satisfied anguish, as if I'm trying to ground myself as waves of pleasure shoot through my bloodstream from the circles his thumb is tracing around my nipple. I can't remember giving in, but I'm breathing again. It's quick and heavy, and not remotely subtle, but I don't care anymore.

I release his t-shirt to move my hand back underneath it, but the heat of his skin isn't enough–nothing feels like it's enough. I move my hand from where it's pressed against his chest, lowering it until the soft material of his boxers graces my fingertips.

And that's where I fuck up.

Preston pulls away—his lips, his body, his hands. Everything. It's only now that I realise his breath is as short as mine, and before he can move even further away, I grasp his shirt again.

'We could do it,' I whisper in a hurry, my eyes closed. I know I don't have much time. 'What I suggested the night I got champagne drunk.'

'No,' he says, instantly. 'No, it wouldn't be fair; I can never be anything more to you than what we are right now.'

'I know,' I say, pressing my forehead against his. 'It wouldn't be that. Just once. Just this one time.'

'You've not—You're not thinking clearly,' he argues. 'You don't want this.'

'If it's not you, it's going to be some—I don't know, some random guy I meet once, then never see again. It'll be meaningless and disappointing, and I'll just be glad I got it over with.' I take a sharp breath, still not daring to open my eyes. 'That's what I don't want.'

He's going to argue again; I know he is, so I keep going.

'You're the person I'm most comfortable with, the only person I ever really feel like myself around. I thought I was—I kept thinking there was something wrong with me, with the way I shut down around people—around guys I'm sure I've liked enough to want it, but I never have.' I swallow. 'But it's—I do now. I'm practically suffocating under the want of it because I've never wanted it more than I do now, with you.' With an uneven breath, I slowly open my eyes and find his. 'I want it to be you.'

It's silent again, and that's good—it has to be better than him point-blank refusing.

'Just for tonight,' I whisper. 'Once tonight is over, we can forget it even happened, if you want.'

He still doesn't respond, but I catch his jaw twitch under the room's faint lighting. Only then do I realise my massive mistake, my grand misjudgment. I'm assuming he has any desire to do this, that without the complications of our friendship, he'd even want to.

'If it's because—If you're not attracted to me; if you're not into it, I mean, that's obviously okay.'

'It's not that,' he replies, even more quickly than his initial no.

The abruptness of his words makes me stammer, and the pause in our conversation makes me realise our bodies are closer than before.

'If one of us changes our mind, or it feels too weird, or—or whatever it is, we'll stop. We don't have to commit to anything,' I murmur. 'We can just try.'

I silently pray I've said enough as I close my eyes and nudge my face forward, brushing his lips so lightly that I'm not sure he'll even feel it. He does, though. After a few seconds, he cups my cheek, and I plant another soft kiss on his lips.

'Is this okay?' I whisper.

He doesn't say anything back. Instead, he responds by slowly—much more slowly than before—moving his mouth against mine. I place my hand back on his chest, this time over his shirt, but fail to keep still for more than a few seconds as I tug at the bottom of it. He helps me pull it over his head, the only downside being a halt in our kisses.

With the threat of having to part a second time looming, I take the opportunity to remove his jumper from my torso, and then we're kissing again. The coldness that brought us together is gone as I press my chest against his, our bodies in rhythm as we move against each other.

My breath is short again, and I'm so focused on trying to stop a pleasured sigh escaping my mouth that I nearly miss the one leaving his. The sound stirs something within me, somewhere deep in my gut, and I give in; to every feeling, sensation, desire.

'If you need to slow down or stop completely, tell me, okay?' he says into my ear, then plants a kiss behind it. 'At any point, if anything's uncomfortable, or hurts, or—just anything—you tell me immediately, okay?'

'Mhm,' is all I can manage as his lips move to my neck.

He moves his body between my legs as his kisses shift downwards, to my shoulders, my collarbone, my chest, my stomach. All the while, my ability to think is decreasing by the second. This isn't new; I've gone this far before with other people, but this feels like a different experience altogether. My head is clear—the clearest it's ever been—as Preston's kisses dip below my stomach, my breath catching in my throat as the final thread snaps and I let go—fully, this time.

CHAPTER 18

To say I'm surprised by Preston's presence beside me when I wake up would be an understatement. Not because I forgot what happened last night—the opposite, really. I was sure he was going to have so intensely regretted the whole thing that he'd run, but no; he's sitting above the covers with a pillow behind his back, his glasses perched on his nose, and his left leg bent to prop up the notebook I banned him from yesterday.

That's why, in my half-asleep state, the first thing I utter aloud is, 'you're still here.'

A beat passes.

'Should I not be?' he replies into his notebook.

'No, it's good; it's a good thing,' I clarify. 'I just didn't think—It's—Ignore me.'

He turns to me then, his eyebrows raised. As our eyes meet, above all else, I'm hit with the realisation that this isn't... weird. This doesn't feel weird. At least, it doesn't until I realise that despite not wearing a shirt, Preston's bottom half is covered while my clothes—well, the clothes he lent me—remain a crumpled heap on the floor beside me.

'I thought you'd wake up and freak out,' I confess as I gather them. 'And then, y'know, fuck off to never be seen again.'

My comment earns me an unexpected smirk as he turns back to whatever he was writing, and I use the opportunity to throw his jumper over my torso. It's oversized enough to reach the top of my knees, so don't bother with the tracksuit bottoms.

He's still smirking into his notebook when I'm finished dressing, so I narrow my eyes. 'What?'

'I almost did,' he explains as he turns back to me, and before my inevitable spiral, continues with, 'but I quickly concluded how dreadful of a person that would make me.'

'It would,' I grumble. 'It'd make you a massive bellend, actually.'

He laughs through his nose, and I watch silently as he returns his attention to his notebook. I try to hold my tongue, but I've never been very good at that.

'Do you regret it?'

His silence is telling, and he knows that—he must know that.

'You do, don't you?' I say quietly.

'I don't,' he replies, pauses, then continues. 'I'm just not sure it was a good idea.'

I don't understand how that's any different, but I don't want to press the issue, especially not when he lifts his arm for me to shuffle closer and rest my head on his chest. He wasn't lying about the notebook last night; it's filled with nonsensical equations and illegible notes.

'You need to work on your handwriting,' I comment as I squint to read it.

'The extent of your kindness never ceases to amaze me.'

With that, he shuts his notebook, drops it onto the floor beside him, then places his glasses neatly on top of it. I'm still looking up at him when he leans his head back against the wall and shuts his eyes.

'I don't, if that makes any difference.' I say as I lower my head back to his chest. 'Regret it, I mean.'

'You might feel differently tomorrow.'

'I won't.'

When he doesn't respond, I worry I might've been a little short with him.

'It could be a good thing for you,' I say in an attempt to rectify any snappiness. 'Get you back in the game.'

'The game?'

'Yeah, the game. You know, get you out of your however many months of the self-inflicted dry spell you've had, give you a nudge to get back on the dating horse, terrorise the women of Clapham, etcetera.'

'I say this with love, Euphemia,' he replies without a flicker of emotion in his voice. 'But please stop talking.'

'I'm just saying you should put yourself out there,' I reason. 'I bet you have no trouble on the London dating scene.'

'I wouldn't know.'

'It won't have changed that much from when you were in first year.'

'I didn't date in first year.'

I frown. 'Seriously? You must have at least had, like, a one-night stand with someone.'

'No.'

I pause as I read between the lines. He has to be fucking with me.

'If you've literally not—You're telling me you've not been with anyone since...' I rack my brain. 'Since, God, your Zack phase? So for, like, two and a half years?'

A pause.

'I presumed you knew. Is it that surprising?'

'It's—I mean, I suppose not, thinking about it, but it's—I mean, I wouldn't have guessed that from last night, is what I'm saying. I thought—Huh. I mean, I guess it's like riding a bike, right? Maybe? Not really something you'd forget.'

'You know,' he murmurs, 'the more you talk, the more I understand how you got yourself into this situation in the first place.'

I sit up to smack his chest. 'You're making me wish you had fucked off this morning.'

With a hmph, I jump to my feet and, out of spite, don't tell him where I'm going as I head towards his bedroom door. Not that he seems to care; when I fail to resist a glance in his direction before leaving, he's back on his notebook hype. He's smirking, though; a clear sign that his lack of questioning is very much intentional, and very much because he knows it'll annoy me.

It's not particularly early—about nine-thirty—but the silence filling the house suggests Preston and I are the only ones awake. The private world we've carved out for ourselves suddenly feels neverending, as if this is our new reality; a fate I should probably reject more than I do. As I enter the second floor bathroom, its tiles feel like ice under my feet and I yelp at the shock of it.

I may have made a little more sound than I realised because as I leave the bathroom, I'm met with the grinning face of my best friend.

'Mia!' he exclaims.

'Aiden!' I reply with matching enthusiasm.

'Perfect timing. Holy mackerel, do I need to talk to you about this guy last night,' he begins, and in predicting what I know will ensue, I stop him before he can go off on one.

'Hold that thought. I forgot how freezing this house is without heating, so let me grab some bottoms and we can debrief in your room—Well, the room you squatted in overnight.' I pause as I take in the empty hallway. 'Have you been waiting outside the bathroom door this whole time?'

He nods enthusiastically.

'What if it wasn't me?'

'I can sniff you out from a mile away.' He shrugs. 'Honestly, I thought the Cardiff dating scene was ropey, but this guy was—'

I palm his face, then nudge past him to head back upstairs. 'One minute!'

I'm laughing to myself as I return to Preston's bedroom, and it's the strangest thing; I keep wanting to laugh this morning, as if some delirious joy has infected my body.

'I've promised Aiden a debrief,' I begin as I wander towards Preston, who's now sitting cross-legged on the mattress with his notebook, then catch myself when I realise how that sentence could be interpreted. 'As in—I mean, he's got some outlandish story to tell me, not as in me telling him about last night—as in us last—'

'You sound like you're malfunctioning,' Preston interrupts, probably for the best. 'Tell him, if you want. I don't mind.'

I purse my lips in contemplation as I reach for the grey tracksuit bottoms on my side of the bed. Telling someone about last night hadn't yet passed through my mind, let alone who that someone might be. If anyone, though, it would be Aiden.

'I don't know,' I think aloud. 'Maybe.'

'Here,' Preston says, and I look up to see him with a pair of thick, white socks bundled together in his hands.

He gestures them towards me and I narrow my eyes.

'Seriously, how do you always know? It's creepy,' I mutter as I take the socks from him, as opposed to saying, I don't know, thank you.

I've barely finished my first knock on Aiden's door when it bursts open, and then he's in front of me, manically gesturing me inside. I follow him towards the bed in the corner of the room, and as Aiden begins talking, I can't help noticing it looks as if a bomb has exploded.

His suitcase has been left open in the middle of the room with clothes bursting from it, and the crumpled wrapper of a family-size packet of crisps lies beside it. If the amount of crisps scattered across the bed is anything to go by, I'm not sure any have actually been eaten, and a green blanket I'm used to seeing on Preston and Margot's downstairs sofa is dumped in a big heap in front of the doorway—a heap I have to jump over to keep up with Aiden.

'You realise you've not moved in, right?' I question as he falls onto the bed with dramatic grandeur.

'I'll clean it before I leave,' he says, brushing his hand in the air.

'You're a menace.' I laugh, then jump onto the bed to join him—Well, I jump on him, really.

He catches me with perfect precision, as if we've rehearsed this a million times over, and I embrace him into a hug that resembles a spider entrapping its prey. I keep my arms around him as he awkwardly yanks at the duvet to pull it over us, and we draw a collective shiver before immersing ourselves as deeply into it as possible.

'Pretty fucking stupid idea on our part; sleeping at a house with no heating in peak winter,' Aiden mumbles into my hair, which makes me giggle. 'Not that you seem put off—you're all smiles this morning.'

'If only I lived somewhere with heating that was a ten minute walk away.'

'Imagine. What a concept.'

At that, we're both giggling, which inevitably becomes deranged laughter that lasts a full five minutes.

Aiden wasn't bullshitting me about his story of loss and love because it's absolute chaos.

'So let me get this straight,' I say, gathering my thoughts. 'Literally no one knew who he was, or where he came from?'

'Nope.'

'Or saw him enter the house?'

'Nope.'

'Or leave?'

'As Shakespeare once put it, nope.'

'Yet he knew everything about Joe?'

'Yep.'

Well, shit.

The guy in question appeared some time after midnight, apparently—hence why he's a total mystery to me. As he is to everyone, by the sound of it. By one o'clock, he was making out with Aiden, but he kept talking about Joe. Naturally, Aiden interpreted this as the guy being madly in love with Margot's very much heterosexual boyfriend, so cut things short. Only, the guy apparently started crying, disappeared into a bathroom, then disappeared for good.

'Margot's convinced he climbed out the window,' Aiden explains, 'but have you seen the size of that window downstairs? He was skinny, don't get me wrong, but not that skinny. Joe's also now terrified, which is understandable.'

I laugh at the idea, then laugh harder in the knowledge of Joe being nervous about the best of times. The poor guy can't catch a break.

'Any fun tidbits from your VIP party with Preston?' Aiden asks, perfectly innocently. 'I was disappointed to not find you viciously making out when I popped up for my room tour, just to add.'

Before I can catch myself, I physically cringe, my body contorting as if trying to make itself as small as possible. Instead of reacting as any sound-minded person would by gathering my thoughts, then deciding on carefully shutting down the conversation or maturely explaining what happened, I instead clamp my mouth shut and dig myself deeper into the bed.

'What?' I hear Aiden's muffled voice from above. 'What is it?'

I try to pull the duvet over my head, but it's wrapped around us too tightly. I shut my eyes and say nothing, which obviously, is a great alternative.

'What are you... Wait, did you kiss? Holy mackerel, you kissed, didn't you?'

Oh, boy.

The laugh I make sounds more like a bark.

'So, I mean, technically yes...' I say as I slowly emerge from the duvet to confront the inevitable.

I'm met with Aiden's wide brown eyes, something between wonder and celebration slapped across his face. I'm not sure I've ever seen the guy look so happy, which is a pretty sensational statement to make about him. He's nodding enthusiastically, willing me on, but I can't formulate the words. His eyes dart around my face, searching for clues when suddenly, his expression drops. Then, the euphoric look he was flashing me moments ago reappears, this time on acid, and he jumps into a sitting position like an explosion.

'Oh my God, you fu–'

I smack my hand over his mouth with a loud, panicked, 'sh!'

His response is to continue trying to say—or rather scream—something into my palm, which makes me immediately relieved to have kept it there. I don't move my hand away until I'm without a doubt confident he's finished. I slowly sit upright, place my free index finger over my lips in a sh motion, then carefully slide my hand from his mouth to find an enormous smile underneath.

'You were sitting on that?' he whisper-hisses. 'You let me ramble some pointless story about a stranger for, like, twenty minutes straight while you were sitting on that?'

'I wasn't sure I was going to tell you,' I reason.

'Uh, rude,' he scoffs, but the grin on his face says otherwise. 'I can't believe—Holy mackerel, I—No, holy fucking shit, I can't believe it. Explains why you're so chirpy this morning; you just needed a good, hard—'

'And I'm stopping you there.'

'Did you use contraception?'

'Yes, Dad.'

'More importantly, was it good?'

Before I can even try to respond, he's talking again.

'Duh. Hence the spring in your step.'

I try to shoot him a glare, but my face doesn't listen. Instead, my cheeks flush as my eyes shy away from his.

He lets out a long whistle 'That good?'

'I don't exactly have anything to compare it to.' I shrug awkwardly, turning back to him. 'I do feel ridiculous for getting so in my head over it before, though. It didn't even hurt.'

'Not exactly the master of female anatomy or anything here, but I'm pretty sure that just means you were into it,' Aiden muses.

He starts giggling as he reaches towards a cream pillow at the end of the bed, only to inexplicably pull a half-opened packet of sweet chilli crisps–a different packet to the one that's exploded over his suitcase–from underneath it.

'Outstanding. Incredible. Random, but also not? How did it even happen?' he asks as he juts the packet under my nose, and I take one. 'Actually, I know what it was. After you saw him kiss me at midnight, you realised what you were missing out on. It's all on me; I made this happen and will forever take full credit.'

I roll my eyes. 'We'd kissed before, but it–'

'What?' he yells, his mouth full of crisps. 'You–When? Why didn't you tell me?'

I lift my palms up in defence. 'It was literally once and wasn't even–It wasn't a big deal.'

Aiden swallows what's left in his mouth, then slowly shakes his head.

'Holy mackerel, this is, like, way faster than my plan–I've been trying to make a plan of action for you both, and sex doesn't happen until at least year two in that–'

'You've made an action plan for mine and Preston's non-existent relationship?'

'Don't get me wrong, it's in its early stages–a first draft at best–but it was going to be a five year plan. Fuck me, we can clearly skip way ahead, though. Are you going to keep it on the down low for a bit? Or just go in all guns blazing, social media official and every–'

'Whoa, slow down,' I interrupt. 'No, it's–That's not–You've got the wrong idea.'

Aiden turns silent, then stares at me with a furrowed brow, his hand frozen inside his crisp packet.

'It was...' I pause to find the right word. 'He did it as a favour.'

Aiden still says nothing, just blinks. If anything, he looks more confused.

'It was a one time, no strings attached situation so that I could get the whole virginity thing over with,' I elaborate. 'We're not getting together, or anything serious like that. Just a favour.'

'A favour,' Aiden repeats as though the word is alien.

'What?' I poke.

'Why?'

'Well, you know, I've just been so uptight about the whole sex thing that I thought—'

'No, why aren't you considering anything more serious?'

I stammer. 'It would be beyond weird—we'd never work—and that's not even accounting for Preston abiding by this zero relationships, like, ever mantra. It's not even—we don't like each other in that way, and I want to be single, have fun, see what's out there.'

With every word I say, Aiden's looking less and less convinced. I shake my head.

'Just trust me; it's for the best.' I say. 'I know what I'm doing. I've got it under control, and—'

'Okay, okay, if you're sure,' he concludes, giving in, moments before a familiar grin grows on his face. 'Remind me to ask Preston for a favour later, will you?'

CHAPTER 19

It quickly becomes clear that Aiden's concerns were unfounded. A fortnight has passed since New Year's Eve, and mine and Preston's relationship hasn't spiralled into some awkward, misshapen mess, nor are we suffering intense bursts of desire when in each other's presence. If anything, that night has resolved whatever weird tension had been simmering between us since reuniting in September. He's seemed better as well; he's been doing better, so much so that he casually dropped the fact he's finally reached out to Rhys into conversation a few days back.

That night was exactly what I needed, too. I went back to a guy's place after a party a few days back, and the experience was fine. Nothing groundbreaking, but I hardly expected that from a one night stand with a stranger. I'm even back in touch with Nick, so by all accounts, my love life is thriving. With January exams to deal with, lectures restarting, socialising, and everything in-between, there's not been any space for things to turn awkward between Preston and me, even if the universe wanted it to.

Sure, I think about that night with him a lot, but I figure that's healthy and normal.

I'm on my way to the first Typewriter Magazine meeting of the year, which is being held at Preston's place because it's doubling up as a semi-social, which to my delight, was his idea. Despite his crisis over it at Christmas, I think I've actually convinced him that enjoying life won't kill him, not that I'm getting complacent; I know him too well to get complacent.

I'm turning up at his house early to help organise things before everyone else arrives, which he assured me was unnecessary, but I assured him it was. Within moments of being ushered into his house, I'm proven right.

'You can't invite a bunch of people over and not have any snacks!' I exclaim while gesturing around his very empty kitchen.

'There's a corner shop five minutes away if anyone's that ravenous,' he argues as I continue flapping.

'Perfect. C'mon, then.'

Without any further explanation, I return to his living room to grab my coat from the sofa, then throw it back on. He doesn't bother with a jacket of his own as he follows me out of the house, but nor does he complain at me, so I choose not to fight that battle. He silently guides me in the direction of the infamous corner shop, and in hindsight, a lack of snacks probably isn't that big of a deal. I just have this urge to make everything perfect, as if one tiny error could ruin the evening, and in turn, Preston's revived sociability.

I flash the shopkeeper a warm smile as we enter, but don't let his response of a grunt deter me. We roam the aisles while I grab multipacks of savoury treats and chocolate, then shove them into Preston's hands.

'I'm not sure inflicting diabetes on the entirety of our society is the wisest move,' he comments as I'm reaching for a huge bag of sugary sweets.

I spin around to glare at him, but upon scanning the huge pile of food in his arms—he's resorted to having to carry it like a baby—I realise he may have a point. As I surrender and go to take the food from him to pay for it, he stops me.

'It's alright,' he says, 'I'll get them.'

Before I can argue, he's heading back towards the front of the shop. I'm about to chase after him when I spot something green in the corner of my eye, and I'm struck by the best idea.

'I'm just going to grab something!' I call back to Preston. 'I'll meet you outside!'

I exit the shop a few minutes later with an even bigger grin than when I entered, and I find him waiting with his back to me, which is perfect. I reach up to tap his shoulder, then shove the small Swiss cheese plant in his face as he turns to me.

'Merry Christmas!' I declare, which earns me literally no response—not even a blink.

After a beat, he says, 'it's the thirteenth of January.'

'Merry late Christmas, then. Whatever,' I say with an eye roll, then gesture the plant towards him again. 'It's a Swiss cheese plant.'

'Or Adanson's monstera,' he murmurs.

Jesus Christ, of course he knows its scientific name.

When he doesn't take the plant a second time, I move the brown pot into my left hand to free my right one, then use that to snatch the plastic bag filled with snacks from him. He falls right into my trap. With a sigh, he grabs the plant from my struggling left hand, then scans it as if the concept of nature is foreign to him.

'Something for you to take care of,' I explain as we walk. 'You know, to nurture and love and stuff.'

'Is this your method of gently informing me that I'm cold and emotionless?'

'No!' I stammer. 'No, it's—That's not—I just think it'll be good for you to have something you need to, you know... keep alive.'

A moment of silence interrupts our conversation.

'You have the subtlety of a foghorn.'

'You could just say thank you.' I clear my throat. 'Why, Mia, what a thoughtful gift you've bequeathed on me. I may even honour it with your namesake.'

'I'm not sure how I feel about your recent habit of mimicking me with dreadful accuracy,' he mutters.

'And I don't like how you always ask if anyone's ever told me my name sounds like an STD, so I guess we're even.'

'Have they? Out of interest.'

'Ugh, shut up! That wasn't supposed to be an opening!'

He fails to fight back a smirk, then analyses the plant in his hands. 'It would be bequeathed to me, by the way, not bequeathed on me.'

Ordinarily, I'd hit him, but I don't want to hurt the plant.

While Preston heads up to his bedroom to find a suitable home for his gift, I tackle the mission of pouring snacks into bowls. On my sixth bowl, I admit to myself that I did go a bit hard on the whole food thing, so I put the rest of it aside as a just in case. I'm in the process of transporting two bowls of crisps and a plate of breadsticks into the living room when Preston emerges, and within twenty minutes of him grabbing the rest of the food from the kitchen, people start arriving.

We get the magazine-related stuff out of the way pretty quickly. The idea was that we'd figure out a plan for the new semester, but as always, Preston's already got it covered with eerie precision. The meeting's essentially just a tickbox exercise of people signing off on his plan. Since my accidental sign up four months ago, I've somehow convinced people that I'm competent at editorial.

Preston doesn't even have to pass people's poetry and stories on to me anymore; he's been relegated to being CC'd in emails sent directly to me.

Combined with feeling like I won't fail my January exams, my newfound ability to make friends without Aiden, and something resembling a love life, it's almost like I'm a functioning adult in my own right.

Margot, who has nothing to do with Typewriter Magazine whatsoever, joins the meeting with wide-eyed wonder, and I've never witnessed someone listen so intently to something they have no ties to. Her time to shine comes after the meeting as murmurings of drink and music start to fill the room, at which point she declares she'll get everyone the first round, then hires me as her second in command.

'Is he always that organised?' she queries once we're alone in the kitchen, and she doesn't have to refer to Preston by name for me to know she's talking about him.

I snort. 'Yep.'

She's laughing under her breath as she scans the alcohol on the small kitchen table, and I reel off whose is whose using the notes I frantically typed into my phone a few minutes ago.

Margot's measuring out some whisky when she says, 'Dana fancies him so much it's almost offensive.'

I sigh. 'I know, right?'

'Is he interested?' she asks. 'Or do you reckon there's potential for him to be?'

'Ugh, I don't know, he's... he's set himself this no dating rule that I'm trying to knock out of him. Don't get me wrong, I've got nothing against people staying single, I just don't think he's doing it for the right reasons,' I explain, poorly.

Before I can apologise for the vagueness, Margot flashes me a reassuring smile. Despite her Preston's darkest secrets comment when we first met, she's never actually pushed me for anything.

'I wish he'd at least give her a shot,' I continue. 'She's really sweet.'

'You're speaking with Nick again, aren't you?' Margot questions, seemingly from nowhere, then halts her pouring.

I nod, which cracks her smile into a huge grin. 'Wait here!'

Without further explanation, she grabs a couple of the drinks she's finished pouring, then nudges past me to shimmy out of the room. A minute or so later, she's bursting back into the room with Dana in tow.

'Double date!' she announces after closing the door behind them.

Dana's response to Margot's exclamation is a furrowed brow, which tells me she's been given zero context into why she's been kidnapped into the kitchen. I stammer as I glance between them, and I'm silently pleading my expression isn't reflective of the circus rolling around my mind. Call me sensitive, but I'm not sure a double date with someone I dumped one day and someone I slept with literal days afterwards is the wisest idea. For a moment, I'm thrown because God, why would Margot suggest this?

The trouble is, Margot has no idea about what happened between Preston and me on New Year's Eve.

Despite all of the above, I slap a smile onto my face and with as much enthusiasm as I can muster, then say, 'Oh my God, yes!'

Dana, who's been left hanging throughout this, glances between us with a tinge of concern on her soft face.

I double check the kitchen door is closed, then say, 'you, me, Nick, and Preston.'

I'm sincerely impressed by my own faux enthusiasm. Screw the editing, I should look into an acting career. Dana's freckled cheeks flush lightly, but the way her hazel eyes brighten reassures me that this might not be an awful idea, after all. I just need to convince Preston of that.

My method of making Preston agree to a double date isn't entirely ethical, and look, it's not that I lie to him as such; I just don't divulge every single detail. At the end of the night, once everyone's left, I casually suggest we hang out with Dana the following Wednesday, which he agrees to. I neglect to mention that I have a date with Nick that same day, and instead frame Nick joining us a few days later as a casual, friendly why not.

It's not until I'm waiting at one of UCL's student pubs for Nick on the Monday before our double date that I realise he has to agree to the whole thing too. It's not exactly a stress I wanted to add to our first in-person meet up since I told him I wasn't interested, then ran away from his family home literal days after Christmas.

He looks the same as ever when I spot him walking past the bar near the pub's entrance, his dark hair neatly styled as he approaches with an effortlessly casual demeanour, a contrast that just works with the smart navy shirt and lightly checked trousers he's wearing. I don't know why this surprises me; I think, in part, it's because I feel so different to the last time we saw each other. I've changed, so he must have too, and his exterior should reflect that. Only, there's no reason for him to be any different, nor for him to look any different, even if he was.

I wonder if he can see it in me, if the way I'm sitting, the way I'm breathing him in as he flashes me a coy smile feels unfamiliar in any way. I suspect not, partly because I'm sure it's all in my head and, in reality, this put together persona I've adopted recently isn't the big deal I think it is.

'I feel underdressed,' I joke as he leans in for a hug before sitting into the wooden chair opposite mine.

His response is a shy laugh. 'Sorry, it's—I never know how to dress for pubs.'

'Inconsistent vibes,' I concur. 'Sometimes formal, sometimes a messy piss up.'

I'm off to a great start, aren't I? My joke may be bad, embarrassing, and cringeworthy, but Nick laughs anyway.

A silence creeps between us, one that's undeniably awkward, so I naturally fill it in the worst way possible.

'I'm really sorry about Christmas,' I blurt.

'It's okay,' Nick replies quietly.

'No, it's—I let myself get way too inside my own head, and I think I just got scared by how serious we were getting, so it—'

'Mia, honestly, it's fine,' he assures me, then smiles. 'You needed some space; that's normal. No pressure form here onwards, okay?'

'Ugh, do you have to be so nice?' I mumble, then follow up with a more upbeat, 'first drinks are on me.'

Nick tries to stop me, but I refuse to give in. Shortly after, I'm battling my way back to our table with two glasses of wine in hand, and elbowing anyone who dares cross my path in the process. It's a stark reminder of why I don't spend too much time in student pubs and bars, regardless of the cheap drinks.

'Question,' I begin as I plop back into my chair, then pass Nick his drink. 'Have you ever been on a double date?'

Nick raises his eyebrows. 'Is this an opening? I can't say I have.'

'It is,' I reply. 'If you hate the idea, just say, but I told Dana—you remember Dana, right?—that I'd try to set up a double date for her with Preston, and I may or may not have commandeered our date on Wednesday to become that, and by may or may not have, I mean definitely have.'

I'm speaking so quickly that I have to take a big gulp of air once I've finished, and it takes Nick a solid ten seconds to unravel what I just told him. When he does eventually open his mouth, I cut him short.

'Also, Preston doesn't know it's a double date.' I pause. 'I'm working on that.'

Nick shrugs. 'Sounds fun. Dana seemed nice from what I remember, and as established one drunken night, Preston's my favourite friend of yours.'

I'm sure the awkwardness suddenly fogging the room is actually contained within my head, but the mist still feels heavy. I flash a tight smile, which verges on painful as Nick continues talking.

'Any particular reason he's being hoodwinked into romance?'

'It's complicated,' I try to say in a blasé fashion, but I'm not sure I sell the delivery of it.

I pretend to be oblivious of the disappointment that falls onto Nick's tanned face when he realises I'm not going to elaborate.

CHAPTER 20

For better or for worse, I don't reveal the true intentions of our double date to Preston until it would be morally questionable for him to back out. When I spill the beans the morning of, he's unnervingly unfazed. I soon discover why.

'Huh. I should give you more credit,' he murmurs from the other side of the phone—a text felt cruel; face to face felt too intense. 'I wasn't anticipating a confession.'

I frown into my phone. 'What?'

'I know it's a date; you're extremely unsubtle.'

I jump from my bed. 'Wait, are you—You knew this whole time?'

I can hear the smirk in his voice—literally hear it—as he replies with, 'yes, Mia.'

'How?' I yell.

'Well, to your credit, I initially interpreted it as us genuinely hanging out with Dana. Then I thought about it for approximately five minutes.'

'Come on, it wasn't that obvious.'

'It was. The addition of Nick a few days later was essentially just verification.'

What he's saying is that I've been toiling over this for days when not only did he see right through me, but he's seemingly unbothered by the whole thing.

'Are you still going to come?' I ask hopefully.

'Yes.' He sighs. 'But I'll clarify the situation to Dana.'

I harshly shake my head, not that he can see me.

'You don't have to! If you hate every second, that's fine, and you can be totally honest with her and say you just want to be friends.' I lower my voice, make it as warm and smooth as possible. 'Just try, Preston. Please? For me?'

He sighs through the phone again, his silence implying at least some degree of contemplation. After another minute or so—a long, painful minute—I hear him take a breath.

'Fine.'

Preston and I are meeting Nick and Dana at the uni pub I broke the double date news to Nick at, our logic being that it's always quieter on Wednesday evenings because it's the uni's big club night so everyone is out elsewhere. Having successfully wrangled Preston into agreeing to treating the night as a date, I use the journey there to lay out my terms.

'You have to actually try, like, put actual effort in,' I begin. 'None of your silent, mysterious bullshit.'

'I'll alter my personality accordingly. Noted.'

'You know that's not what I mean!' I argue. 'If you go into the date with the attitude of it being hopeless, then it will be. Besides, you like Dana, right? She's pretty, super nice, easy to talk to.'

'Am I her intended date, or are you?'

'I'm ignoring you because I know you're trying to piss me off.' I wave my hands in the air. 'It won't kill you to flirt a little, that's all I'm saying.'

'Hm,' he utters as we enter the tube station, but doesn't elaborate until we've passed the ticket barriers. 'What's the protocol on sex on the first date nowadays? Yay or nay?'

I trip over a stutter, then blurt, 'it's—I—I mean, fine, I guess. No problem if that's what you both want, but—Well, no, not but in a negative way—I'm not trying to be negative—I just mean I don't think that's what Dana's looking for with—'

'Euphemia,' he interrupts as we step onto an escalator. 'I'm fucking with you.'

It goes without saying that I spend the entire tube journey glaring at him. Frankly, the only reason I stop when we reach the pub is because I notice Dana sitting at a booth at the back of the room, and the last thing I need is having to explain my glaring.

'You look amazing!' I squeal as she stands, then lean in to hug her.

I'm not just being nice, either. Her blonde hair is styled into loose waves, complimenting her soft features, and she's wearing a red dress that hugs her in all the right places.

After parting from Dana, I conspicuously poke Preston's thigh in what, in hindsight, is an extremely unclear instruction. He somehow catches my drift and proceeds to greet Dana with a hug, albeit a quick one. I nudge him into the space beside her once she sits back down, then take a spot on the opposite bench. Nick arrives shortly after us, and he one ups Preston with a longer hug and a peck on my cheek. As he's greeting Dana with a more platonic hug, I flash Preston a pointed look of follow his lead, but he's too busy watching Nick to notice.

After saying hello to Preston, Nick shuffles into the space beside me, effortlessly taking my hand to give it a squeeze atop the table.

He's gently stroking my thumb as he turns to the rest of the group with, 'drinks?'

'I'll give you a hand,' Preston replies before I can blink.

As the guys make their way towards the bar, I turn back to Dana with a smile. Her enthusiasm hasn't weaned since we first greeted her, and as I glance away to see Preston's back disappear into the crowds at the bar, a pang of guilt tears through me. I really do hope he gives this thing a chance; I don't want to get Dana's hopes up, only for them to crash and burn.

On the bright side, my anxiety over Preston putting in lacklustre effort is proving to be a great distraction from the I've had sex with the other person's date shaped elephant in the room.

Thankfully, that thought has little time to fester because within moments of it popping into my head, Nick and Preston are returning to the table with drinks in hand. As Preston sits into the space beside Dana, he slides his arm over the back of their booth.

Good. This is good.

I'm so distracted by Preston's body language that I barely notice Nick taking my hand to hold it atop the table again. I flash him a warm smile when I do, and in that moment, I've never felt like more of an idiot for almost ruining things with him at Christmas.

Having convinced myself that I'd have to lead our four-way conversation this evening, to say I'm stunned by Preston's sudden extroversion would be an understatement. In hindsight, I shouldn't be shocked; I know better than anyone how capable he is of surfacing different versions of his personality on request. Crucially, as with my infamous champagne drunk night, he's not taking it too far.

A discussion on library all-nighters led to the question of who holds the record for staying awake the longest amount of time, and Preston's bold claim of sixty-seven hours was immediately met with scoffs of disbelief. Within five minutes, though, somehow all three of us are falling for his story.

'My intention was seventy-two, of course, but I overestimated myself,' he's saying as his audience watches, silently transfixed. 'I was delirious by the time the sixtieth hour hit, so I try not to beat myself up over it.'

Dana's leaning sideways into him, their intimacy aided by the way his arm has moved from the back of their booth to her shoulders. He's gently grazing his knuckles across the side of her arm, and I'm hypnotised by the movement, his low, deep voice seeping into my ears like a song.

'Mia, as our resident English literature student, you must know Keats' To Sleep, no?'

The sound of my name makes me blink in quick succession, and I realise I'm slouching. I straighten my back, then stare back at Preston as my mouth falls open with a stutter.

'John Keats,' he elaborates, then quotes, 'o soft embalmer of the still midnight.'

'Oh! The poem, it's–Yeah, it's–Yeah, I did that at A-Level, actually.'

Preston responds with a smile, one filled with so much warmth and reassurance that I feel ridiculous for getting embarrassed over being caught off guard.

'I had a fascination with the poem so wanted to emulate the narrative weaved throughout it–get into that headspace, basically.' He laughs lightly. 'Disgustingly pretentious, I know, but forgive me; I was eighteen.'

The rest of us remain silent, and there's no way he's not spinning some fictional yarn. I know this–we must all know he didn't actually stay awake for nearly three full days without so much as a nap in-between, but I believe him. Every single word. Judging by the wide-eyed expressions on Dana and Nick's faces, I'm not the only one.

'On that note,' he suddenly chirps, and everyone jolts a little as if the collective spell Preston had us under has broken. 'I believe it's my round.'

Dana follows him to the bar, and I watch them in silence as he hovers his hand over the small of her back, bending down to say something into her ear. She starts laughing, her bright eyes boring into his as she looks up at him.

'So... yes?'

Nick's voice snaps me back to the present, and I tear my attention from Preston and Dana to be met with his warm face. His eyebrows are raised, a dimple on his cheek as he wrestles with a smile, and I'm stammering.

'God, I–Sorry, I was just–I was in my own world then, sorry.' I shake my head. 'What did you say?'

He gives into a laugh. 'I asked if Preston's always been this captivating. I'm convinced the guy could talk to me about toilet paper and I'd get invested.'

It definitely wasn't just me, then.

I resist another glance in Preston and Dana's direction as I reply with, 'basically, yeah.'

As Nick chews over his response, there's an unquestionable hesitancy passing through his brown eyes. My gut churns with the question I know is coming, but I'm left with no time to practice any potential answers.

'Not a loaded question, I promise, but have you and him ever been more than friends?' he asks, and I resist a flinch.

'We're friends,' I reply, maybe a little too abruptly. 'Always just friends.'

It's not technically a lie.

'We're close–too close, really, to ever become anything else, you know?' I explain, unnecessarily. 'He probably knows me better than anyone, so it's–Yeah, even if we hypothetically, I don't know, fancied each other or whatever–hypothetically–it would be too jarring. Does that make sense?'

I swear to God, Mia, stop talking.

Despite my scrambled words, Nick nods slowly. 'I get what you mean. I've got a girl mate–from school–who I love to death and all that, but would never go there.'

That bullet was more of a cannonball, so frankly, dodging it feels like I just performed a miracle.

The rest of our evening continues in the same vein; Preston spouting whimsical stories that we all eat up, Dana inching ever so closer, him embracing her that little bit more each time.

The double date has been perfect; everything I'd hoped for, and then some. Preston's been impossibly charming from start to finish, he's shown nothing but genuine interest in Dana–hell, he's gone as far as flirting wit her–and the awkwardness I feared has barely reared its ugly head. Perfect.

The only dampener is the nauseous feeling that just won't budge, not even with the glasses of water I'm ordering with every alcoholic drink. Frankly, if I wasn't currently on my period, I'd be concerned.

I pop to the bathroom before we leave, and when I return to our table to collect my things, Nick is the only one still there. Preston and Dana are waiting for us outside, he tells me, which makes sense; despite it being a Wednesday, it's busy enough for the large space to feel stuffy. Part of the reason I briefly visited the bathroom was to earn a moment of peace, so yeah, it makes sense. If it didn't, I probably wouldn't be so thrown by what I stumble across as I leave the building with Nick a few steps behind.

I catch the kiss for what can't be more than a second, but a second is all I need. At the sound of the pub door swishing open,

Preston and Dana part, and it all happens so quickly that the image of them together feels like a hallucination.

'You're Euston, right, Dana?' Nick says from behind me, oblivious to what we're interrupting.

Dana turns on her heel to meet us with a beaming smile, her hand in Preston's, as she says, 'yes! Victoria line.'

'We can go via Euston too,' I offer, but it sounds more like I'm insisting. 'Goodge Street is just closer, is all. We can walk with you.'

Dana turns back to Preston, a look of pure admiration in her hazel eyes, and he shrugs with a, 'sure.'

Preston and I don't utter a word to each other during the walk to Euston station, not intentionally; we're just distracted by our dates. The fragility of that excuse is made apparent when we part from Nick and Dana because as we make our way to the Northern line platform, we still don't say anything. Our silence continues as we board the train, speed through the underground, and emerge from Clapham South station.

Is it me? Am I making things awkward?

As we stop at the crossing outside the station, I take a deep breath and give in.

'I'm impressed,' I say, but my voice feels strange, so I cough to clear my throat. 'You went above and beyond tonight.'

I brave a glance at his side profile, my posture relaxing when I spot an easy smile on his face. As the green man flashes on the crossing, we begin walking and he cranes his neck to look down at me.

'I'm not too proud to admit I wound up enjoying the evening,' he murmurs. 'I should listen to you more often.'

'Frankly, the fact it's taken you years to have this revelation is a little insulting.'

He laughs, the tension from our journey rapidly easing, and God, I'm relieved—so relieved that my nausea feels lighter.

'And you'll give Dana a chance?' I query, but I'm not quite able to meet his eyes.

The same appears to be the case for him because he turns away as he says, 'tentatively, yes.'

I nod and we fall into silence, the nausea returning in a violent wave as the strangeness that engulfed our journey home creeps back in.

'You and Nick seem to have picked things back up nicely,' Preston murmurs after a few minutes, but it does little to budge the tension.

I nod, then say, 'yeah, for sure. He's been really good about it—really understanding, you know?'

Silence returns, and I'm suddenly acutely aware of Preston's presence beside me, as if his energy is seeping into my skin like an unbearable itch that no amount of scratching can soothe. I could scratch down to the bone and it would still burn. The quiet is suffocating, and it's not just me—I refuse to believe this feeling is isolated.

'I feel a bit sick.'

I don't know why I say it, and when I do, it's more like a choking sound.

Preston halts in the street, resulting in some curses thrown from the people behind us. I stumble to a stop beside him while apologising to no one in particular, and his hands are on my arms—grounding me—as he leads me out of the way of passers by.

'Do you need to sit down?' he's asking, his eyes scanning my face, and I can't find the words. 'Mia? Hey?'

I shake my head. 'No. No, I'm being silly, it's—I'm fine, honestly. God, sorry, I don't even know why I said that.'

I laugh, but it can't be remotely convincing because Preston lowers himself to my level, his face in front of mine, his voice a low, even whisper.

'Here,' he murmurs, his hands not parting from my arms as he gently guides me to sit on the narrow staircase of a stranger's house. 'Shut your eyes for a moment. Deep breaths, okay?'

I obey without question, and the concrete is freezing against the back of my legs, a cooling relief as I take a long, deep breath. I feel ridiculous—I must look ridiculous—but I push any embarrassment aside to focus on my breathing. When I finally open my eyes again, I'm met with the deep green of Preston's. He's crouching in front of me, his hands still at the side of my arms, keeping me upright.

I've never felt such desperation to hug somebody, but I fight it. I clamp my eyes shut and dig my nails into my palms to dampen the urge because it's not the right time, or place, or situation—not anymore, possibly not ever again.

Then, out of nowhere, a quiet, 'do you want a hug?'

I ping my eyes open and he's still there, his sharp features appearing unusually soft under the streetlights, and I'm nodding—timidly, mechanically nodding, but nodding nonetheless. Preston pulls me into him and his chest smells of ember, of the fire that was blazing in the student pub and the coldness of the late January air.

'We're allowed to physically interact, Mia,' he soothes into my ear.

'You hate hugs,' I say weakly.

'With a passion,' he concurs, his voice void of emotion, and God, it makes me laugh.

Despite his comment, he doesn't let go, and instead laughs alongside me as I lift my arms to pull him closer. We stay like that for what somehow feels like forever but no time at all, and when we part, I jump to my feet as I shake out whatever's left of the ache that was pressing on my chest earlier.

I brace myself for the questioning I'm sure is inevitable, but to my grand relief, it doesn't come. He doesn't demand an explanation.

Instead, as we begin walking again, Preston says, 'do you know what I find most shocking about tonight?'

I respond with an inquisitive rise of my eyebrows.

'Not one person said anything.'

I slow my pace with a frown. 'About what?'

'About how your name sounds like an STD.'

With no consideration for anyone sharing the pavement with us, I shove Preston sideways, and he's lucky there's not a double-decker bus speeding past. The sight of one would urge me to push that bit harder.

'You make it far too easy, Euphemia!' he calls into the sky as he rebalances himself, earning us some judgemental glances, not that he or I care.

'And you're a prick,' I hiss, storming ahead. As his footsteps speed up behind me, I resist the temptation to look back at him as I say, 'that sleep story was bullshit, wasn't it?'

When he doesn't respond, I give in and glance back to see him snickering at the ground. He shakes his head, still without providing me with anything resembling an answer.

'Wasn't it?' I try again, slowing my pace so that we're walking side by side.

Without so much as a glance in my direction, he utters, 'turn the key deftly in the oiled wards, and seal the hushed Casket of my Soul.'

CHAPTER 21

'..So you got jealous?'

'No!' I exclaim, really putting the work in to draw out the offence in my voice.

The phone line goes quiet, and I worry I might've done what I once thought to be impossible by rendering Aiden silent. In my brief panic, I try to elaborate.

'Not, it's—You don't understand,' I groan. 'It was horrible; a deep, sharp physical pain that made me feel like I could be sick one minute and suffocate the next.' I sigh, shaking my head. 'My stomach didn't agree with something in my drink, probably.'

Another moment of silence, then, 'so, like, super jealous.'

'Ugh, it's pointless talking to you.'

With that, and despite his muffled apologies from the other end, I snatch my phone from my ear and slam the end call button. I turn onto my stomach, faceplant my bed's plump pillow, then release a long, loud groan that would earn me a visit from emergency services if my flatmates could hear it.

Once I've calmed myself, I return to my back to stare at the ceiling with a long sigh. Nearly three weeks have passed since the night of our double date, and I'd withheld going into detail with

Aiden about it for this exact reason. Without bothering to move my head, I scramble around my duvet to feel for my phone, then lift it to my face to find an onslaught of messages.

I'm sorryyyyyyy!! Pls forgive me! :(xxx

Miaaaaaaaaa

That was mean of me, I'm sorry. Your concerns are legit! Make a doc appointment maybe? You might be allergic to something

Helllooooo

I'm a terrible person I'm sorry

With a sigh, I give in. He's too difficult to stay mad at.

Forgiven. You're lucky I love you

Aiden replies within seconds.

You know this isn't Preston, right?

I walked right into that one.

I don't have time to stay grumpy, so I suck it up, perk up, and embark on getting ready for the day. My call with Aiden was a thinly veiled distraction as it is because after taking over a year to finally respond to his letter, Preston is meeting up with Rhys, and he's asked me to join him. I'm not sure I've ever been more anxious over something in my life.

I take so long deciding what to wear that I have to skip breakfast and leave my hair unstyled, resulting in my usual brown waves looking less beachy, more wind tunnel. Five minutes after I'm supposed to have left, I instinctively grab my denim jacket despite it not matching the outfit I wasted a literal hour deciding on.

As I'm leaving my flat five minutes late, I've got to run for the bus that'll take us to Clapham Junction station, which I've got no doubt is worsening my disheveled appearance by the second. I catch the bus by the skin of my teeth, and I'm spouting apologies the second I spot Preston leaning against the bus stop with his eyes down as he scrolls through his phone, seemingly without a care in the world.

He looks great–effortlessly put-together with an outfit I've got no doubt he threw on without a second thought, his light, wavy hair styled a little more neatly than usual being the only hint towards the abnormailty of the day ahead. He's wearing a brown suede jacket I recognise from when we first met, an olive green jumper hidden underneath it, and I'm half-tempted to ask if we can switch. My outfit would look way better with that jacket.

I jog up the steps to the top deck of the bus, and he follows without having to exert nearly as much energy given our height difference. By the time we capture a row towards the back, my chest is heaving as if I just sprinted the length of the Thames. I even direct Preston towards the window so I can have an extra few seconds to catch my breath, then fall into the aisle seat with a loud sigh.

'Your hair is different,' he says as the bus starts moving.

I groan, then faux headbutt the seat in front of me. 'God, is it that obvious?'

I've still got my head pressed against the plastic headrest when I hear him say, 'it's nice.'

His voice is soft and light, the sincerity in his words undeniable, and it throws me so much that I stare silently at him for a questionable amount of time before thinking to say thank you.

It's only when Preston turns to peer out of the window, his shoulders relaxed, his legs casually stretched out under the empty row in front of us that it occurs to me he seems perfectly fine. There's not even the tiniest hint of anything beyond indifference in his manner.

Surely, I can't be more nervous about today than he is?

'Dare I ask?' he questions without shifting his attention from outside.

'There's something wrong with you,' I mutter.

'Yes, that's medically documented. Multiple things, actually,' he replies, turning to look at me with a smirk. 'I can acquire a list for you, if you're interested.'

I roll my eyes. 'What I mean is you seem eerily calm about...'

I vaguely gesture into thin air, his green eyes lazily following my movement before returning to meet my gaze.

'Hm,' he replies, and I assume that's it until he continues with, 'we'll see.'

On that ambiguous note, he turns back to the window. Our journey to Richmond primarily consists of me talking shit as a result of my ceaseless, crippling anxiety while Preston humous said shit. As we're boarding the train at Clapham Junction, we find ourselves on a near empty carriage, which amplifies my apparent desire to not allow a moment of silence.

The conversation I had with Aiden this morning is biting me in the arse because as we get comfortable, there's a quiet voice in my head pushing me to ask about Dana because I'm not sure if they've seemed friendlier during the past two Typewriter Magazine meetings, or if that's just my imagination.

I eventually give in with, 'how are things going with Dana?'

Straight to the point, I guess.

Preston, who's only received a restbite of about five seconds following a conversation I trapped him into while we were waiting on the platform about the history of the railway–something it turns out he has disturbingly extensive knowledge on–responds with a nonchalant shrug.

'Well.'

Well. The word is so simple–four letters, one syllable, neither here nor there–but it feels seismic. That's good; that's really good. I thought he'd run as soon as he'd fulfilled his double dating duty, but this is a sign he's actually showing interest in women, in a love life he refused to even acknowledge as a possibility when we first spoke about it in September.

I nod. 'Have you met up with her much? Outside of magazine meetings, I mean.'

'A few times, yes.'

'Wow, I better get a wedding invite,' I joke. 'I'll be first choice for best man, right?'

God, why did I say that?

He doesn't provide me with an answer; a kind gesture to prevent me embarrassing myself further, I figure. Instead, he shakes his head with a weak laugh, then turns to look straight ahead.

'You can tell Dana, by the way. About us, I mean.'

Why am I still talking?

'If she asks, or just generally if you want to,' I continue. 'Don't feel like you have to lie for my sake, I mean.'

He doesn't say anything back, just nods.

'How are you and Nick?' he asks a few minutes later.

'Yeah, good,' I reply.

It's not a lie; for every time Preston has met up with Dana, I suspect I've met up with Nick twice. We've still not had sex, but I don't think that'll be the case for much longer.

'It feels way more natural this time around, like, no overthinking, or pressure, or anything like that,' I explain, then apparently have an anneurism because I deem it perfectly normal to follow up with, 'your favour has worked miracles; first that club night hook up I had and now I'll probably have sex with Nick soon.

That'll be three guys in, like, two months. There's clearly no stopping me.'

Why in God's name I thought that was something worth saying aloud, I don't know. I at least have the sense to resist my next intrusive thought, a question of if he and Dana have hit that milestone yet. It would be pointless asking anyway because even if he said no, I've already decided in my head that they have.

In the midst of my inner turmoil, Preston watches me in silence. Eventually, just like before, he turns away, biting his cheeks in a feeble attempt to stop himself from laughing at me.

'You really are anxious about today, aren't you?' he comments.

'Fuck off.'

Preston's calm disposition doesn't waver as we arrive at Richmond, not even when we leave the station, or pull up Google Maps to find the cafe we're meeting Rhys at, or even when we begin walking in the direction of it.

Then, out of nowhere, he stops abruptly in the street, spins around, walks about two steps in the direction we came, then turns back around and stops again. I nearly get whiplash just from watching him.

'I'm going to leave it,' he announces without actually looking at me, then turns around again to start walking towards Richmond station.

I trip after him, grabbing the sleeve of his oversized jacket to bring him to a halt.

'Whoa, wait! Hang on,' I say through a stammer. 'Don't—Okay, look, let's sit down.'

I nod towards a bench up ahead—in the direction of the cafe we're supposed to be on our way to—and while Preston doesn't refuse, he doesn't agree to it either.

'Just for a minute, okay?' I try, and he takes a deep breath before nodding.

He doesn't say another word, and nor do I, as we walk over to the wooden bench. It's situatied on the edge of Richmond Green and is overlooking the park, which I hope will instill some sense of calm. It's my first time ever visiting the London suburb, and what we've seen so far doesn't feel too dissimilar from home because while it's busy, the pace feels slower than that of Central London. The familiarity is a comfort, at least to me, despite the cloudy sky and chill in the air.

We sit onto the bench with collective sighs, and as soon as I spot Preston's leg bouncing, I place my hand on his knee. He stops.

I take a risk, knowing I'm essentially giving him a green light to run, and open with, 'firstly, you don't have to do anything you don't want to. If you're not ready, that's okay; we can turn back around. Try again next week, or next month, or next year if we have to.'

I pause to gauge his reaction, and although it's slight, he frowns. I determine it to be a good thing, a sign that the prospect of waiting another year to meet his father is the last thing he wants. His knee is twitching again, so I keep my hand on it, gently stroking my thumb against the rough denim of his jeans.

'Secondly, if we do go ahead with this, you don't have to share anything you don't want to. You can tell him nothing about your past, if that's what you want. I have zero expectation for you to tell him anything, let alone everything, and it's easy to avoid. Just focus on the now, and your plans for the future.'

Preston's frown deepens, which prompts me to bite down on my lip. Shit. As panic over the possibility of having said something wrong begins to seep in, I'm distracted by the feeling of something warm on my hand. His fingers slide between mine, and I instinctively curl my own around them. I give his hand a squeeze.

'Hell, spend the whole time discussing the history of the railway, if you want,' I try, which finally earns me a quiet laugh. 'Seriously, I'm not even kidding; that was eerily engaging earlier.'

I sigh as I scan his side profile, and as he leans back against the bench to gaze into the grey sky, I inch closer to him. He doesn't stop me, not even when I lower my head to his shoulder, my hand still in his. I may be overstepping the mark—it's not that I don't know this as I do so—but I do it anyway. Within moments, I feel his head rest atop mine, so I decide the risk was worth it.

'My point is,' I continue, my voice quiet. 'This can be whatever you want it to be. The power is entirely in your hands, and frankly, I'm sure Rhys would be made up from just having an opportunity to say hi to you.'

'Hm,' he replies, the word dissolving into the cold February air.

I anticipate some rebuke, or at the very least, a question, but he says nothing. We don't move from the bench, or from each other, as minutes tick by. I'm in the midst of contemplating what to say next when I feel Preston's chest rise.

'Okay,' he says, finally.

He lifts his head from mine, releases my hand, clears his throat, then stands. I follow with wide-eyed anticipation and no idea which way the coin has landed.

'We'll meet him,' he declares, releasing me.

I fail to fight back a smile, and it must be a goofier one than intended because as Preston glances down at me, he rolls his eyes. I jump from the bench with unapologetic enthusiasm, then follow as he begins walking.

I don't take my attention off Preston as we restart our journey to the cafe. He must feel the weight of my gaze, but he doesn't say anything. I initially put his silence down to the nerves he must be busy stifling, but there's something else hidden in his expression. He's focused straight ahead, but there's a distant, glazed look in his eyes, as if he's existing in a different world.

'Throw me a bone,' I say, in part to distract him from the sight of our destination now moments away. 'Just this once. What are you thinking?'

He shakes his head as he looks at the ground. It's followed by a short laugh, but it doesn't sound like a particularly joyous one.

'What you said earlier—about plans for the future,' he murmurs, pauses, then says, 'I've never had enough confidence in having one to make any plans.'

CHAPTER 22

I'm not rewarded with any time to respond to Preston's comment on his future because we've reached the cafe. I quickly learn that the extensive Facebook stalking I did has paid off; I spot Rhys immediately. He's sitting in one of the cafe's far corners, a book in his hands and a navy mug on the table in front of him.

Preston is indisputedly the spitting image of his mother, and so I wasn't surprised when I struggled to draw comparisons between him and Rhys via the few photos I've seen of him. Where Preston is fair, Rhys's features are dark, but seeing him in person—a distant look in his brown eyes, the way he's rhythmically tapping his foot, his posture—is stirring a sense of jarring familiarity. I can't explain it; it's nothing aesthetic, but they're so glaringly related that it's giving me vertigo.

I'm so hypnotised by Rhys's presence that it takes the sound of Preston's voice to draw me back into reality.

'Drinks are on you, I presume?'

My face falls into a frown, and I spin on the spot to find him gazing at the menu behind the coffee bar. I'd bet my life that he's not so much as glanced in the direction of the cafe's sitting area.

'What with me being forced here against my will,' he continues.

'I know you're only trying to be funny because you're anxious, so I'm going to let that slide.'

'Am I that transparent?'

He's still staring at the menu.

'Yes.'

'I'll reference this the next time you accuse me of being unreadable.'

'Shut up.'

He smirks.

I glance back towards Rhys, who as far as I can tell, hasn't spotted us because he's doing exactly what he was doing when we entered the cafe. I turn back to Preston, who's also doing exactly what he's been doing since we entered, and I have to swallow a laugh.

'Sorry to pull you away from such an engaging read,' I say, nodding at the cafe menu. 'But let's talk game plan.'

Finally, Preston gives in and turns to look at me, his eyebrows raised and his gaze notably not daring to shift in the direction of the seating area.

'We've got three options,' I begin. 'I buy the drinks while you head over to Rhys.'

He physically flinches at the notion.

'You buy them, and I head over to break the ice or whatever, or whoever buys the drinks and we head over together.'

'We should go together,' he replies in a heartbeat, clearly not contemplating option one for a second.

I'm not especially convinced he's keen on the together option either.

I nod. 'Okay, I'll go. Get me a hot chocolate, please. Oat milk, if they have it.'

He stammers—Preston Maddox stammers like an actual human being—then grabs my arm before I can move an inch.

'We should go together.'

'This isn't about what we should do, not that we should do anything; there's no right answer,' I argue. 'But anyway, my point is that you obviously want me to head over first, so that's what we'll do.'

To my genuine surprise, he doesn't argue again. He swallows, nods, mutters what I decipher as a thank you, then effortlessly flips on the charm as if our entire conversation was in my head as he turns towards the barista waiting to take our order.

In the knowledge that I'll be the one making a run for it if I do, I don't allow myself a second to think before turning away from the coffee bar and treading in Rhys's direction. I'm internally swearing my ass off as I approach his table—seriously, I'm on the verge of turning myself inside out with nerves—and I take a sharp breath as my approaching presence forces Rhys to look up from the pages of his book.

Our eyes meet, his lips parting slightly, and it's—I was wrong. I was wrong aout them sharing no physical similarities. Their mouths. They have the same mouth. I'm so distracted by the revelation that I don't realise I've been silently staring at him long enough for it to turn really fucking weird.

For some reason, I judge the next best step to be me blurting, 'God, sorry! Hi!' in his face.

No explanation or indication towards who I am. Just a needlessly aggressive hi!

After another moment of silence, and with a subtle tilt of his head, Rhys says, 'Mia?'

'Yes! Sorry, hi,' I repeat, then make things worse with, 'I do have more words in my vocabulary than sorry and hi, by the way.'

On the bright side, Preston will almost seem normal compared to me at this rate. It's not until Rhys is on his feet and gesturing for me to sit opposite him that I realise I've got no idea how he knows who I am.

He must sense this somehow because once I've gotten comfortable, and once he's returned to his own seat, he says, 'Preston mentioned you might be coming.'

His accent is distinctively Welsh, and while his voice is quiet, it somehow has no trouble competing with the chatter bouncing around the cafe. I'm dying to ask what else Preston's said about me, if anything, but I hold my tongue. Rhys is smiling, but it's one that doesn't quite reach his eyes, and his shoulders have deflated.

Only now does it occur to me that he's assumed the worst; that Preston chickened out, and I've rocked up to apologise on his behalf. Maybe I'm just searching for comparisons, but it feels like a very Preston-esque assumption.

'Oh! No, it's—He's just grabbing our drinks. Preston, I mean. Did you want another one?' I ask as the thought suddenly occurs to me, despite a quick glance at his mug revealing his drink to be untouched. 'Or a cake or something? I can grab one quickly if—'

'I'm fine, thank you,' he reassures me, smiling again, this time with his eyes.

The confirmation of Preston's presence triggers Rhys's foot tapping again, despite his blatant relief, and it's sweet. It's really sweet, actually.

'What are you reading?' I ask, then nod towards his book, which is now facedown on the table between us.

He combs his fingers through his wavy hair with a nervous laugh, hesitates, meets my eyes, then says, 'Honestly, I have no idea.'

I start laughing with him as he continues.

'I picked it up before I left—didn't even think; just plucked it from my bookshelf, and all I've done is stare blankly at its opening page.'

With that, he leans forward to take the book, then scans its cover before flashing me a view of it.

'A Tale of Two Cities,' I read aloud.

'Apparently so,' Rhys murmurs, scanning the cover again before returning it to the table.

'It was the best of times, it was the worst of times,' I quote, which earns me another smile. 'I'm studying English, so Dickens is basically my gospel. Between you and me, I don't love the classics, but he's my favourite—Sorry, totally irrelevant.' I shake my head. 'And probably the last thing an academic wants to talk about on their day off. Ignore me.'

'No, please don't reign it in for my sake. Physics is my field, so no work overlap, don't worry.'

I fight back a smile. Of course it's physics.

I'm so wrapped up in Rhys and our increasingly relaxed conversation that my initial reaction to a familiar presence behind me is confusion.

'Sorry I took so long,' Preston says as I swivel in my armchair to see him holding a drinks tray topped with two mugs. 'The queue was endless and they've only got one person serving.'

He was already being served when we parted and they had multiple people behind the counter. I've therefore got zero doubt Preston's claim is him covering for the fact he probably spent at least five minutes panic-staring at the coffee station with our drinks in hand before actually making his way over to us. He's lucky I'm too nice to expose him.

Rhys enthusiastically assures him it's not a problem—too enthusiastically, but in the best way—and stands to offer Preston some help with the tray he's carrying. Given all that's on it are two mugs, Preston politely declines the offer, which prompts Rhys to glance between his seat and the tray multiple times. The guy clearly has no idea what to do but is desperate to do the right thing, despite there being no right thing, and the whole awkward interaction is probably the sweetest thing ever.

I take my hot chocolate from the tray Preston's placed onto the table as he sits into the armchair beside mine, and as he gets comfortable, I catch him scratching at the side of his index finger. I resist reaching out to place my hand over his, but flash him a look of what I hope reads it's okay.

'Thanks for coming,' Rhys, whose foot tapping has sped up, says to Preston as I take a sip of hot chocolate. 'I appreciate it. I really appreciate it.'

Preston, who's renowned for his open, expressive disposition, shrugs. He bloody shrugs. I, of course, know that's not a sign of indifference but one of his tendency to shut down when faced with difficult situations, but Rhys doesn't know that. I subtly shift my eyes towards Preston, this time with a glare of say something! while praying he catches it.

He either does, or his logic overrides his anxiety.

'It's—Yeah, no, it's fine,' he says, and my shoulders relax as I sigh with relief. 'Sorry I took so long to write to you.'

Rhys is aggressively shaking his head, but his voice is soft. 'No, please don't apologise.'

Okay, good. This is good. Awkward, which was inevitable, but good. Preston's hands are still fidgeting, but they're calmer, and Rhys's foot tapping has slowed down. They might progress to eye contact by the end of today at this rate.

It turns out Preston's anxiety over revealing his past to Rhys was unfounded. While Rhys asks him questions—a lot of questions–they're all focused on the present and future. When he does veer towards past territory, Preston effortlessly steers the conversation away from it. Doing so has become second nature to him, I guess; he's been busy perfecting it since he moved to London.

It's subtle–far more subtle than the way he's avoiding any talk of his past–but he's not particularly warm about the topic of his future, either. He finishes off every future-related discussion with a maybe or perhaps or possibly, and the comment he made to me before we entered the cafe rings louder in my head each time. I try not to let it eat away at me too much, especially when as our conversation is coming to an end, Preston agrees to Rhys's suggestion of a future meet up soon.

As the three of us part ways outside the cafe, I can practically sense Rhys twitching with the desire to reach out and touch Preston; to embrace him, to land an affectionate tap on his arm, to just touch him in some capacity. He resists, which in hindsight, is for the best because I've got no doubt that would be all too much all at once for Preston.

As Preston and I are strolling back towards Richmond station, I'm grinning as if I've been struck with some sudden delerium. It takes him about half a second to notice.

'Was there caffeine in that hot chocolate or something?' he mutters from my left without looking at me.

'That went well!' is my chirpy response. 'I don't know if you noticed, but he was looking at you like you were the best thing he's ever–Oh, God.'

I bring myself to a halt, which forces Preston to stop just as abruptly.

'You're not freaking out are you? Y'know, doing the whole something went well so now I've got to sabotage it thing, right?'

'I have no idea what you're talking about,' he replies, and is there...?

There is. There's a jovial tone to his voice as he starts walking again, and I have to jog to catch up with him. He's being playful. He's not freaking out. My delerius grin grows wider, and as he glances at me as we're entering Richmond station, Preston's lips quiver with a badly hidden smirk.

'No, Euphemia, I'm not spiralling.'

'Personal growth!' I yell after him as he taps through a barrier. 'Before you know it, you'll be asking Rhys if he thinks my name sounds like an STD!'

He's snorting a laugh as we start walking side by side again. 'I think that's more of a fourth meeting enquiry.'

'You asked me it the literal first time we met—Well, met as you, not Zack, I mean.'

He shurgs. 'And that's where I went wrong.'

'Huh?'

'You've never answered. I evidently jumped the gun.'

I roll my eyes.

'Unless you were waiting for the right moment, and now happens to be that right moment. In which case, has anyone ever told you that your name—'

'Fuck off.'

I storm ahead as his laughter echos behind me, and I've never been so irritated yet so thrilled at the same time.

By the time we bundle onto the train, any annoyance has dwindled into nothing. I'd been so anxious about today that I felt physically ill, and when Preston freaked out moments before meeting Rhys, I thought that was it. I was so sure he wouldn't go through with it. As I watch him fall into the seat beside me with closed eyes and a long sigh, above all else, I feel really fucking proud of him.

An overwhelming desire to hug Preston floods my body, but unlike Rhys, I don't have the willpower to resist. His eyes are still closed as I lean into him, then wrap my arms around his waist and press the side of my head into his chest. His back stiffens, and I've got zero doubt that he'd probably shove me to the floor if such a thing was socially acceptable, but I don't care.

'Hugs give you hives, I know. Sorry,' I say. 'But ten seconds?'

His body relaxes, but he doesn't agree to my terms and instead murmurs, 'five.'

'Eight.'

'Five.'

'Seven and a half.'

'Four.'

'You can't go down!'

'And that's time.'

With that, Preston carefully wraps his fingers around my wrists, then nudges my arms from him. I at least appreciate the delicacy.

'That wasn't five seconds,' I grumble as I turn to frown at the window, then cross my arms.

'That was more than five,' I hear him argue. 'Besides, I agreed to four.'

I'm still glaring at the passing scenery outside the train, but I fail to stop myself laughing. It kind of ruins the faux angry thing I've got going on. When I hear Preston chuckling to my left, I'm a gonner—my laughter grows, but I balance it out by calling him a dickhead.

We're about halfway to Clapham, my eyes still focused outside the window, when I can no longer resist asking him what I've been trying not to since we entered the cafe.

'Preston?' I say, my voice quiet.

'Hm?'

'You don't feel like that anymore, do you? What you said about not having a future?'

He doesn't respond to me for a while, each second of silence feeling no different to what I imagine having my heart grabbed, twisted, and squeezed would.

'Sometimes,' he says, finally, and my stomach drops as I turn from the window to meet his gaze. 'I don't think it'll ever not be sometimes.'

I try to speak, but he stops me.

'But mostly, no,' he adds. 'Actively planning a future is still... difficult, but the concept of having one feels less precarious than it used to. Only on occasion does it still feel that way.' He pauses again, his eyes shifting away for a moment. 'When it does, I just talk to you.'

I scoff. 'No, you don't. You've never told me this.'

A ghost of a smile flickers onto his face, but I'm not in on the joke.

'I don't tell you,' he explains. 'I just talk to you. Generally, I mean. About anything.'

I tilt my head, then narrow my eyes until the penny drops, at which point I stutter, then say, 'oh.'

I frown.

'Oh, okay. Well, that's good, I think.' Another pause. 'Although now I'm going to be paranoid every single time you talk to me—which is very often, can I add—so thanks for that.'

'"The spoken word is silver but the unspoken is golden".'

'That's recycled!' I accuse, poniting my finger in his face. 'From that house party in Cathays, remember? The one where my sister got shitfaced! You said that quote to me there—from War and

Peace, right?' I turn away, shaking my head. 'I expect better from you.'

'I'm acknowledging the parralels,' he explains—a clear attempt to redeem himself.

I start tutting as I shake my head. 'Can't believe you thought you'd get away with that. Recycling a quote.' I scoff again. 'Honestly.'

<h1 style="text-align:center">CHAPTER 23</h1>

At the beginning of the academic year's second reading week, Aiden hits us with the best idea. A trip.

He initially demands somewhere in mainland Europe, which everyone immediately shuts down because we're all skint, but a compromise quickly develops and we agree on the less glamorous Brighton. It's super easy to get to from London, and with it being the LGBTQ+ capital of the UK, Aiden is willing to compromise.

Over the course of three days, we organise trains and book an Airbnb big enough to house eight—Preston, Dana, Margot, Joe, Aiden, Aiden's self-declared love of his life, Nick, and me. I'm optimistic but don't get carried away at the prospect of Aiden's companion, Caleb, because Aiden claims every guy he meets to be the love of his life at least once. The only person to maintain the title for longer than a few weeks is Preston, which on balance, isn't working out too great given he and Dana are still going strong.

Preston, to no great surprise, had to be convinced into joining us on the trip—no doubt due to his I'm not allowed to enjoy life policy. I called him out on exactly that—albeit via a private chat—when he responded with a pass to Aiden's group chat message. It took a nearly two hour phone call to persuade him to agree, but I wouldn't have come close to convincing him at the start of the academic year. Progress is progress.

We meet Aiden and Caleb, who are both travelling from Cardiff, when we switch trains at East Croyden, and within an hour and a half we're bursting through our Airbnb's front door and claiming our rooms as if it's an Olympic sport. It's through the ensuing chaos that I discover Nick was a literal track star at school because he singlehandedly nabs us the biggest room in the place.

The bed is at least a queen size, and there's an impressive dressing table propped against the room's window overlooking the coastal city. If you sit at the right angle, maybe crane your neck a little, you can even catch a glimpse of the distant ocean. There's more than enough wardrobe space at the other side of the room, so much that we should probably offer it as spare storage for the others.

'I should've guessed,' I say through laughter as Nick stands on our bed with his fists in the air, triumphant. 'You've got popular-boy-next-door-star-athlete written all over you.'

Nick halts his celebration to frown. 'Is that an insult? Why does that feel like an insult?'

I lift my hands up defensively. 'I'm saying nothing.'

He jumps off the bed, his dark eyebrows raised, and I have no more than a split second to try and evade his hands as he darts towards me. I'm laughing again as he pulls me into him, and we collapse onto the plush bed in an entangled mess.

'Thanks for inviting me here,' he murmurs, then kisses the top of my head. 'It's going to be fun.'

I smile into the duvet with closed eyes. 'Thanks for snatching the best room.'

I'm glad I've got my back to him because moments after speaking, I cringe. Probably not the best thing to say to a guy after he expresses enthusiasm over spending a weekend with you. I shuffle myself around to face him on the bed, then press my mouth against his, my lips lingering as an implicit apology for being such a loser.

'Seriously,' he says into my ear once we've parted, my face nuzzled into his neck. 'Do I really give popular-boy-next-door-star-athlete vibes?'

'One-hundred percent, without a doubt yes.'

I'm still giggling over mine and Nick's interaction as I amble into the beach house's huge living space, and I find the one person who wasn't remotely interested in competing for the best room.

'Oh, to be so altruistic!' I sing as I manoeuvre around the long corner sofa in the centre of the open-plan room and skip towards Preston, who's slid the patio doors open and is leaning against the balcony they lead onto.

He doesn't reward me with much of a response, or even bother to turn his head as I step onto the glass balcony—he just flashes his signature lopsided smile as he stares towards the calm sea. I instinctively want to comment on how harsh the ocean breeze is and how freezing he must be in nothing but a t-shirt, but I know better than to question it.

'Saying that,' I continue. 'Leaving Dana to fight for the biggest room alone is extremely inconsiderate.'

'Space I can recover. Time, never,' he replies, then turns to me. 'Napoleon.'

I resist an eye roll, but give in to raised eyebrows.

'I've intentionally gotten us the smallest bedroom,' Preston elaborates. 'It's still a comfortable size, has a sea view, and is the only one separated from the rest. Complete privacy and the sound of the ocean. There's no better way to spend time, wouldn't you agree?'

With that, he shoots me a wink, then strolls back into the house with his hands in his trouser pockets. I glance in the direction of all the rooms–mine included–then towards the room Preston's claimed. Fuck. He's right. There's a small bathroom next door to his and Dana's room too. They've practically got an en suite.

Despite travelling four hours versus our measly one hour to get here, it's Aiden and Caleb who lead the charge for our night out. Nobody else has any say in it, not that I mind; nobody plans a night out quite like Aiden, and as I'm rapidly discovering, or like Caleb. They've not even been seeing each other a month, and they're like some extroverted, hive-minded power couple. It's incredible.

I can't believe I'm saying this–I really cannot stress how much I never thought I'd say this–but Aiden's finally met his match.

Caleb's also six foot four, muscly but not to the extent of any vein-popping, dresses like he's just walked out of a Vogue magazine, smells amazing, has the most incredible dark, curly hair, and is extremely good-looking, so I totally understand Aiden's fixation.

'No, you're not–Okay, so this club is literally a restaurant!' Caleb's waving his hands around as he paces back and forth in front of the sofa, and he clicks his fingers as he points at Joe, who's dared to question his and Aiden's logic. 'They do food. That's the whole point–it's a club for people who want food, but don't want to compromise with a boring as shit sit down meal, to then walk miles to find a good party spot, but also not have to deal with shitty club food. It's good food at a good club!' He pauses. 'A gay club, obviously, but you're all couples so you can't morally complain about that.'

My instinctive response is an acknowledgement that only Margot and Joe are an official couple. I trip over that thought and fall into a realisation that I'm not even contemplating this in the context of Nick and me, but Preston and Dana, as if their relationship is more significant to my life than my own.

Joe's staring, wide-eyed as he mutters, 'it sounds... loud.'

Margot groans beside him. 'Babe, yes, it's a club.'

'But also a restaurant...' he replies quietly.

'Yes!' Caleb and Aiden scream in unison, which makes the rest of us burst out laughing.

Hell, even Preston, who's opted not to sit on the sofa with the rest of us to instead lean sideways against the patio doors, laughs. He likes those doors, doesn't he?

Everyone is happy to roll with the club-restaurant hybrid, even Joe once he gets his head around the concept, although Aiden and Caleb's condition is that we pre-drink at the beach house. Preston takes it as his opportunity to really lean into his self-inflicted caricature by trying to read—sorry, reread, as he corrected me—Homer's fucking Odyssey at the kitchen island while the rest of us drink on the sofas in the opposite side of the room.

'No chance,' I say with a scoff when I spot him sitting alone, then storm towards the kitchen area to pluck the open book from his hands. 'I thought you were fucking with me earlier when you said you'd skip pres for this. In hindsight, extremely naive of me.'

He responds by leaning back in the black barstool, his arms crossed. 'It's in your name, no?'

I place his book out of reach on the island as I replay his comment in my head. As I turn back to him, if anything, I'm more perplexed. I'm not drunk enough for his riddles.

'Just try to make sense, like, once. Please?' I whine.

'Mia,' he says slowly. 'Your surname backwards literally spells naive.'

I frown. 'Huh? It doesn't—Shit, it... it does. How have—How the fuck have I never noticed that?'

My face must be a picture because Preston's snickering, all the while I'm in the midst of an identity crisis.

'I'm surprised my dad didn't try spinning that as an excuse for his multiple fuck ups,' I conclude as I plop myself into the seat beside Preston's, then badly mimic Dad's voice. 'It's not my fault I cheated on your mum and then cheated on the woman I cheated with. I was too naive to realise what I was doing. Poor me.'

'Can we save trauma dumping for later? Once I've had a few drinks?' Preston rudely replies as he attempts to reach for The Odyssey.

I slap his hand away. 'Nope. Also, you're T-total nowadays, so double nope.'

'I'm not T-total; I just don't get extraordinarily drunk. As per the–'

'–advice from multiple psychiatrists,' I finish for him, and my Preston impression is even worse than that of Dad, but it's too late to back down now. 'I therefore must perch upon the kitchen stool–'

'–Is this a stool? Not sure I'd call it a stool–'

'–and read my literature while my fellow cohort enjoy the festivities of Bright–'

'Hey,' a voice interrupts, and I flip my head around to find Dana standing at the other side of the kitchen island.

I flash her a smile, and she's smiling, so I keep smiling, but is this awkward? Or is that just my general existence?

'Please tell me you've convinced him to join us,' she asks me before nodding towards Preston.

'I'm joining,' he replies. 'Technically thanks to Mia, but only because I want her to stop talking.'

I resist a playful shoulder shove, although I'm not sure why, and instead shrug. A win is a win. Dana responds with a light laugh, then moves around the island to stand beside Preston.

She's stroking the back of his neck as she asks, 'want me to grab you a beer?'

He jumps from the stool, then says, 'not yet, thanks. I'll have a Coke or something first.'

Dana nods, and it's stupid—I know it's childish, but a sense of achievement—pride, maybe? I don't know—overwhelms me because as the conversation Dana just missed signifies, I know Preston never starts a night with alcohol. I know him. Better than she does.

Jesus, I need to get over myself.

'Is everything alright in the father department, by the way?' Preston queries, pulling me from the whole internal toxic narrative I've got going on. 'I was kidding earlier, about the trauma dump thing. Sorry, I shouldn't have said that.'

I blink at him, then glance towards the sofa at the other end of the room to see that Dana has returned there. She, Joe, and Nick are in the midst of being enthusiastically hand-waved at by Aiden.

I shift my eyes back to Preston, whose head is tilted as he watches me. 'Oh, it's—Yeah! God, yeah, it's whatever. Well, the same as usual, really.'

'So not alright?'

I shake my head and use the pause to gather my thoughts. 'No, it's fine. Genuinely. Your pep talk over Christmas helped a lot, actually. It's not that I've stopped caring, or even necessarily stopped trying with him, but I've stopped taking his fuck ups personally.'

'Hm,' he says thoughtfully as I jump off my stool. 'I'll accept that.'

I roll my eyes. 'Thanks for your approval. On the topic of fathers, is everything still on with Rhys next week?'

He's nodding as he starts walking towards the others, and I follow silently. 'You don't have to come again, honestly.'

I brush the air. 'I want to. He's cool, and I feel like it being a second meeting gives me some leeway to complain about you. A good rant opportunity, y'know? No secret revealing, don't worry.'

We've reached the others by now, so Preston doesn't reply verbally. Just elbows my side with a sickeningly charming smirk as he catches Aiden's eye. It's a strategic move on his part—I'll not get a word in edgeways with Aiden in the picture, so I can't pester Preston any further with father-related topics.

With two drinks down—or in Preston's case, none—we decide to head out to our pre-drink bar at nine o' clock. The bar is another one of Aiden and Caleb's suggestions, so while I'm not surprised it's a gay bar, I wasn't expecting the nautical theme. The bar is shaped like a goddamn pirate ship.

'Gay pirates,' Caleb shouts into my ear as we enter, I assume in response to my perplexed expression.

'Obviously,' I reply.

While Nick, Preston, and Margot order our first round of drinks, the rest of us secure a large table—shaped like a giant barrel because of course it is—near the bar's entrance.

'This place is making me feel like I've literally ingested acid,' Nick says over the nautical music, something I never even knew was a genre.

'Good!' Aiden replies.

'Embrace it!' Caleb concurs.

Okay, I kind of love him.

By the time Nick, Preston, and Margot are returning with our drinks, utterances of a drinking game are in motion. As if I wasn't still scarred from last time, we settle on the same game that led to my total humiliation after Preston refused to kiss me. I don't bring the topic up, partly because I don't want to relive the pain and partly because Nick's sitting to my left.

I silently sip at my mojito as Dana inputs our names into her phone's app, and it's not until we're four questions and two dares in that I begin to relax. I think the aggressively upbeat nautical music and general nautical atmosphere is helping. We agreed to skip any non-couple kissing dares before we started, so theoretically, I should be good.

Or so I thought. Because this game fucking hates me.

It's Caleb's turn, and he clears his throat as he reads from Dana's phone. 'Who in the group are soulmates.' He pauses to snort a laugh. 'Soulmates. Who says soulmates in the twenty-first century? I mean, we're all couples, so do I skip?'

Margot answers from my left before anyone else can. 'Nah, we can make it work. Regardless of couples—you can say two people in a couple if you think that, obviously—but regardless of our couples, just say who you think are soulmates.'

'Oh, sure, makes sense,' Caleb replies, and he's pointing at Preston but his light brown eyes are on me, and it's not until he says, 'you two, obviously,' that I realise his other hand is gesturing towards me.

He says it like it's nothing and without any indication of a second of thought. I laugh, and Jesus Christ is it an awkward one, but thank every god known to humankind because Aiden jumps in when I've never been more desperate for him to.

He scoffs, then turns to Caleb and says, 'um, hello? I'm right here,' to which Caleb blinks, and Aiden rolls his eyes. 'Me and Preston, duh.'

I flash Aiden, who's sitting directly opposite me, a thank you glance to find his dark eyes already on me. He smiles softly with a subtle shoulder lift, and I'm not sure I've ever loved him more than I do in this moment.

'Second round?' Nick suddenly pipes up, and I'm not sure if he's oblivious to what just unfolded, or if he needs an escape route.

CHAPTER 24

'I literally gave him a cop out!' Margot exclaims, a cigarette teetering between her fingers. 'I told him he was free to pick an existing couple if he wanted. I didn't hallucinate that, right? Wouldn't surprise me given this place.'

'Not hallucinating,' I confirm.

You two, obviously.

Caleb's voice is ringing through my head, big and loud. It's like a record on repeat, and not even the nautical soundtrack blasting from the bar can drown it out. Obviously. That's what got me. Obviously. What does that even mean?

Margot brushes the air as a puff of smoke escapes her lips. 'Nick seems alright about it, at least from what I can tell.'

He responded with a clipped it's fine when I asked if Caleb's comment had bothered him as he and I grabbed a second round at the bar, so I'm not sure Margot's quite on the mark there. Caleb, who'd evidently been scolded by Aiden moments earlier appeared midway through our drink ordering and kept apologising to us, which somehow made the ordering process equal parts funny and tragic. My life summarised, essentially.

'I'll talk with him and Dana tonight to make sure they're okay,' I comment in a half-hearted attempt to avoid admitting any awkwardness between Nick and me. To avoid that eventuality, I change the topic of conversation with, 'who would you have said? On the soulmates question?'

Margot glances at the concrete below with a coy smile, but doesn't answer.

'Ask me later,' she says, lifting her head before taking one final drag. 'When I'm too drunk to keep my inhibitions.'

On that cryptic note, Margot stubs out her cigarette, then turns back towards the club. Only, as she does so, she momentarily halts, says something into the doorway, then turns to flash me a smile—a sympathetic one, I'm sure of it—and disappears into the bright yellow building. The strange exchange is explained almost immediately because as Margot vanishes, Dana appears.

'Hey!' she beams at me with a wave, and God, why is she so nice?

'Dana, hey!' I reply with what I hope is matching enthusiasm.

I've got no idea what to do with my hands as she stops opposite me. I settle on clasping them in front of me as I stand stiffly upright, as if I'm a doctor about to break some tragic news.

Dana opens her mouth, then blurts, 'I just wanted to make sure you know I'm totally cool about that whole drinking game situation in there.'

Seriously, being this inexplicably nice can't be legal.

'Oh, it's—Yeah, that's good. I was going to pull you aside to make sure you were cool, so that's—Yeah, that's really good.'

She responds with a smile, and God, she's lying. She's so obviously lying to save face, or worst case scenario, to avoid making me feel bad. Caleb's comment—mine and Preston's relationship—makes her uneasy. I know it does.

'It's cool, if you're not. Cool with it—with Preston and me, I mean,' I begin, and Dana tries to argue, but I stop her with, 'I know he and I are close and it's kind of, I don't know, intimidating for lack of a better word. I just—Yeah, please don't worry about us doing anything behind your back. I promise I'd never hurt you—or anyone—like that, and nor would he.'

I probably don't need to keep going, but I do.

'I don't know if I've ever said, or maybe Preston has, but my parents had a messy divorce because my dad cheated, so it's—Yeah, I'd never do what he did to anyone, or play any part in causing hurt like that, y'know?'

Dana smiles again, and this one has a glimmer of sincerity, so I'm satisfied the unnecessary deep dive into my personal life has helped.

She opens her mouth, hesitates, then eventually says, 'I asked Preston if you guys had ever... I mean—What I mean is I know you guys have...'

I'm momentarily confused by her vagueness.

'Oh! It—Well, yeah, no—It—I mean, yeah,' I ramble, and try to save it with, 'we have, once. Just once.'

She nods, and the way she's pressing her pink lips together suggests she's still holding back. I give her the space and silence to get whatever's on her mind out.

'I trust you. Genuinely, I do, and him. I just...'

She sighs, and I brace myself for whatever's next.

She glances at her hands, then lifts her blonde head to meet my eyes as she says, 'he's really guarded, isn't he?'

It's totally not what I expected, but is in some ways, worse.

'I don't think I know any more about him now than I did before we started going out. I know nothing about his life outside uni, about his family, or even what films, books, or music he's into, and just... Yeah, that kind of thing, you know? I like him a lot. More than he likes me,' she continues, and cuts me short the moment I try to interrupt. 'It's fine, seriously. I knew that going into it, but I didn't realise he'd be so hard to... get to know, I guess.'

I relax my shoulders, and give her what I hope is a reassuring smile.

'Don't take it personally,' I say softly. 'He just needs time to open up—More time than most people, but he'll get there.'

Dana is nodding. 'Thanks, Mia. You're probably right. I mean, we get along really well, the sex is great, we're comfortable in each other's company, and besides, it's still early days, right? There's nothing wrong, not really. I just need to be patient with him.'

On the bright side, Caleb's you two, obviously echoing through my head has been abruptly replaced with the sex is great. I grit my teeth together and force my lips into a strained smile.

Thankfully, the rest of the night progresses without any further instances that make me want to gouge out my own eyeballs. I'm not sure if it's due to our rocky start, or due to something I ate, but there's a nauseous sensation in the pit of my stomach that won't budge. It results in me not drinking much, which I don't mind because it's not like I'm alone in that.

Speaking of Preston, from what I can tell, he's had fun—like, actual fun. He's gotten involved in every conversation, asked questions with genuine interest, embraced the restaurant-club with his whole heart, and hasn't threatened to head home early once. Hell, he was the only one to actually partake in the restaurant aspect of the club because everyone else was too full of alcohol—or in my case, nausea— by the time we reached it.

I figure it's the nausea that's making me squeamish with Nick. He's shut down my every attempt to talk to him about what happened, and I'm trying not to overthink it. Outside his refusal to talk things through, he's not saying or doing anything wrong, but the perfectly reasonable comments he's making are irritating me, his jokes feeling flat despite others laughing, his touch, no matter how loving or gentle, making my skin itch, and I'm just finding it all a little... annoying.

That's why when we arrive home and fall into bed, I don't decline his advances. Intimacy will help, I figure–knock me into my senses–so I kiss him back, peel his clothes from his body, let him pull my dress over my head, press myself against him as he moves against me, our breaths heavy.

The trouble is that afterwards, I don't feel any better. I don't feel worse, I guess, but I'm not sure a state of passive nausea is the best reaction to sex with your nearly boyfriend. Nick falls asleep within minutes of us finishing–not hugely unusual for him, and I take the opportunity to escape the room I'm sure is rapidly shrinking while trying to ignore the way my eyes are watering, and the way I'm struggling to breathe.

Approximately two seconds after exiting the bedroom, I get the fright of my life.

'Holy–Fucking hell!'

Preston, who's standing in the kitchen area in complete darkness, looks over his shoulder to smirk at me. After a beat, I realise the microwave perched on a counter in the far corner is on because what else would he be doing at two in the morning beyond cooking himself a meal, right?

It's only when he turns to face me, his expression changing–darkening–that I realise I'm shivering, that the dampness from my eyes has slipped down to my cheeks, and that my breathing is ragged as I stand frozen wearing Nick's oversized band t-shirt.

'Are...' Preston says slowly. 'Is everything okay?'

His jaw hardens, his green eyes glancing towards my bedroom door, which I'm only now realising is adjacent to the kitchen area. The area I'm convinced Preston has been in for a while, for longer than the amount of time Nick's been asleep, and God. I don't need to do the math.

'No!' I reply quickly. 'God, no, it's not—Nothing like that. Fully consensual,' I assure him, then immediately regret adding that detail. 'Sorry, it's—I feel a bit nauseous, that's all, so wanted some air.'

He glances between me and my bedroom door again, and fucking hell, he definitely overheard.

'Are you sure?' he murmurs, and there's something in his voice I've not heard before; his tone is somehow as soft as it is firm, and I'm suddenly certain that if he asked me to unveil my deepest, darkest secrets in that same voice, I'd not so much as hesitate.

'I promise,' I reassure him.

After one final glance between the bedroom and me, he nods slowly. I wrap my arms around myself, partly for warmth and partly in an attempt to calm my breathing.

'Why are you creeping around the kitchen in total darkness at two in the morning like some seaside ghoul, anyway?'

My attempt at humour eases the sharpness in the air because it steals a laugh from Preston. He shrugs as the microwave pings, then ambles towards it, still without bothering to turn a light on.

'Strawberries,' he answers as he opens the microwave, then pulls a bowl from it.

'You eat strawberries warmed up?' I exclaim, nearly gagging at the thought.

'Not quite,' he replies. 'Although I'm intrigued by the suggestion. Next time, perhaps.'

I'm frowning at him as he grabs another bowl—a bigger one—from the kitchen island and approaches me. I'm not in the right headspace for his bullshit right now, so I reach for the kitchen light. Preston stops in front of me as it switches on, and I spot a bowl of strawberries in his left hand, and a bowl of melted chocolate in his right.

'Huh,' I mutter. 'Way more normal than expected. You must be evolving.'

As I'm wrapping the beach house's complimentary living room blanket around me and stepping onto the balcony with Preston, I notice my stomach has stopped churning. The blanket is big, pink, and fluffy, so my shivering has relaxed too, despite the cool February air.

'Feeling any better?' he asks as he lowers himself to the balcony floor, crossing his legs as he sits.

'Stop reading my mind for, like, five seconds,' I grumble in response as I join him. 'But yes.'

He gestures his bowl of strawberries towards me, and I grab one to dip into the melted chocolate. It takes one measly bite for my earlier nausea to feel like a total joke. I forgot how good this stuff tastes, so I steal another, then another, then another, and it takes the sound of Preston's laughter to make me realise how unhinged I must seem right now.

'Thanks for twisting my arm to come on this trip,' he says after a minute or so. 'I'm glad I did.'

I turn to him with a smile, and I suspect melted chocolate slathered over my mouth. 'Hey, this one was basically all you. You've made fantastic progress since I uncovered your zero fun aloud pact.'

'A pact requires multiple people or parties.'

'Literally how do you have friends?'

'It must be my dashing good looks and intelligent wit.'

'Yes, because your name sounds like an STD is peak intelligent humour.' I pause as I grab another strawberry, then mutter, 'prick,' under my breath.

'That's an extremely serious endeavour of mine, not a joke. I'm genuinely curious to know whether anyone–'

'Fuck off.'

He starts chuckling, and the sound of it fills my body with more warmth than a fluffy pink blanket ever could. He's been doing that a lot recently–laughing and smiling the most I think he ever has, at least since I've known him.

'I spoke with Dana about the drinking game situation,' I say tentatively. 'You shouldn't be afraid to open up a little more to her. Not the big stuff—I understand you need way more time for that, obviously, but maybe mention Matty, or listen to the music with her that you listen to with me.' I shrug. 'Start small.'

'Hm,' he replies, unhelpfully, and I'm about to demand more of an answer when he continues with, 'I think I should end things with her.'

I nearly choke mid-strawberry. I cough, only to start stammering as I try to find the right words, and I know he shouldn't. He can't end things with Dana because he's self-sabotaging–I know this is him self-sabataging, and I have to tell him that. I know I should tell him that, but the words are stuck in my throat like black treacle.

'We're never going to work as anything serious, and I know that's what she wants so–'

'No!' I exclaim, finally finding my words–the words I know I should say, and I reel off the script. 'You'll say that with any girl you get remotely close with–I know you will–and you can't go through life like that, Preston. You can't do that to yourself.'

He rests his head back against the patio door behind us, then utters, 'I've done worse.'

I soften my gaze as I scan his side profile, the sound of the distant ocean lapping the shore filling the quiet between us. He closes his eyes with a sigh, then speaks so softly that it's almost a whisper.

'Why are you so desperate for me to be with someone?'

I blink.

'I'm not—It's not that. I just...' I sigh. 'I just want you to be happy.'

'Happy,' he repeats in the same quiet voice, the word sounding like a question. 'Do you know what Mark Twain said about happiness?'

'Nope, but I'd bet you're about to tell me.'

'Correct,' he murmurs. 'Sanity and happiness are an impossible combination.'

A pause before my response of, 'Mark Twain can fuck off.'

A smile cracks onto Preston's lips as he opens his eyes, and it lingers as he watches the ocean. I'm picking at a strawberry as I turn my own gaze towards the water.

'Dana mentioned that you told her about us,' I say, although I'm not really sure why.

I feel his eyes on me, but I don't look away from the ocean as he replies with, 'sorry. She asked me outright and I didn't want to lie.'

'No, it's—Sorry, I didn't mean it like that. It's totally fine. I told you to be honest if she asked. I genuinely wouldn't have minded if you'd told her unprompted.'

Another pause.

'You would've,' he argues.

'Yeah. Yeah, you're right, but I'd have pretended not to.'

We both laugh quietly, and I'm twirling a strawberry stalk between my fingers.

'I think...' I begin, but my voice trails off, so I force the words out. 'I think we should maybe take a step back. From each other, I mean.'

When I turn to him, he's slowly nodding. 'Probably.'

'Not, like, stop being friends or anything crazy like that, but set some boundaries, maybe just as a temporary thing,' I muse. 'Even if Nick and Dana were out of the picture, I think it would be a good idea. I'll still come with you to meet Rhys, obviously, and generally be around if you need to talk, so–'

'You don't have to.'

'No.' I shake my head. 'No, I want to. I just think giving each other space generally could be a good thing, and it'll–I don't know, give us the energy to focus on our other relationships, do our own thing and all that good stuff because it's–We–Things are–'

'It's not healthy to be so reliant on each other.'

I swallow. 'Yeah.'

The urge to turn to him, to wrap my arms around him, or even just rest my head on his shoulder is nearly suffocating, but I can't. That's the whole point; it's why we're doing this, why we said what we just said. I can't. I dig my fingernails into my palms with a deep breath.

'To kick things off,' Preston says, his tone light. 'No more strawberry privileges.'

He jumps to his feet, wishes me goodnight, and just like that, he's gone. Only then does it occur to me that he didn't eat a single piece of fruit.

Ten minutes after Preston leaves, I return inside to find Margot sitting on a kitchen counter with a mug in hand. I quickly gather myself to hide any indication towards an internal crisis. Her blue hair is pulled into a messy bun with too many flyaways to count, her cheeks flushed red, I figure from the alcohol.

'If you're looking for strawberries,' I say, 'that's my bad, sorry.'

She blinks, momentarily confused as she sways lightly–a sign that she's still pretty drunk.

'Nope! Way too healthy,' she says as she gestures her mug towards me. 'Coffee.'

I laugh. 'Each to their own.'

She responds with a wide, proud grin, and as I begin to walk towards my bedroom, she stops me.

'I would've said the same,' she says, giggling.

I halt and narrow my eyes, searching her face for elaboration. 'You've lost me.'

She rolls her eyes, the brown in them partially hidden under hooded eyelids, and for a moment, I don't think she's going to answer me. Hell, I'm convinced she's forgotten what we were talking about.

Only, as she jumps up with her mug in hand and scurries in the direction of her bedroom, she glances over her shoulder to call back to me.

'The soulmates question! My answer would've been the same.'

CHAPTER 25

All things considered, mine and Preston's new arrangement is working well. We've switched from speaking every day to speaking a handful of times a week, and we're seeing each other less—once, maybe twice a week, always in a group context. His second meeting with Rhys was the only exception, and even then, we were only alone together for the journey to Richmond and back. By most people's standards, that's still a significant amount of time to spend in someone's company. For us, it's kind of weird, sure, but that's the point. Our new normal needs to match everyone else's regular normal.

It's been working as hoped too. I've been seeing Nick more often, and I assume the same goes for him and Dana. Our romantic relationships have sort of become an implicit no-go topic when we do catch up. So yeah. The space Preston and I have carved between us is working as we'd hoped.

And it's made me realise I need to break up with Nick. For good, this time.

Without Preston as a distraction, I've realised he was never the problem, not really. Nick's lovely; an absolute sweetheart who I couldn't fault if I tried, and any girl would be beyond blessed to have him. Just not me. There's nothing to really pinpoint, and it's nothing he's done. I'm just... not that into him. I feel like such a shitty person for fucking him about after everything that went down over Christmas, but the cruelest thing for me to do would be to keep pretending.

I need to be the bad guy, one last time.

'Are you sure this is okay?' I ask into my long mirror, locking my eyes with Margot's as she sits cross-legged in front of it. 'I'm worried it's too lazy looking, like I'm giving a message of I'm ending things and I literally couldn't care less.'

'You know,' Margot replies, then pauses as she runs a straightener through her hair. 'I don't think I've ever known someone to get so stressed over what to wear to dump someone.'

'Ugh, I know. I never cared this much about what I wore to our dates, for Christ's sake.'

Margot flashes me a sympathetic look, then shrugs. 'Probably a sign you're doing the right thing.'

True.

'Okay, I'm—Fuck it, I'm going,' I declare as I reach down to grab my pink shoulder bag from my bed. 'In theory, I shouldn't be long, so I'll be back in, like, an hour?'

As I'm moving towards my bedroom door, Margot says, 'keep me updated, and if you need a fake family emergency phone call, I'm your gal.'

'This is why I love you!' I shout back to her, then leave my room with a deep breath.

I meet Nick at Dolly's cafe, which I only realise is our first date location as I'm stepping through its doors. It's somewhere we frequent pretty regularly, so its significance never occurred to me, and now I feel like an even bigger asshole than before. So that's great.

Nick's already sitting at a table when I arrive, so with the bravest face I can muster, I approach the window seat he's left free for me.

'Hi!' I say, probably a little too enthusiastically.

'Hey, Mia,' he says in a notably more normal tone.

He's dressed as cleanly as ever without a hair our of place as he stands to give me a hug, and I can't untangle whether there's an awkwardness between us, or if I'm imagining one as a result of what I know is coming. Nick's already bought our drinks, so I thank him, then wrap my hands around my mug of hot chocolate.

God, this is going to be horrible. I hate this. I'm going to really bloody hate—

'I bumped into Dana on campus the other day,' Nick pipes up, seemingly out of nowhere.

He—What? I stammer. Where can this possibly be going?

My instinct is to freeze, but I fight it and ask in a causal tone, 'oh, really?

'Yeah.'

'Talk about anything interesting?' I pry because I'm desperate to get this exchange over with.

He releases a short laugh as he glances down at his coffee mug, and I'm staring at his perfectly neat, dark hair, confused. He's tracing his thumb up and down his mug's red handle, and I'm mesmerised by the action as he finally answers my question.

'You lied to me about you and Preston.'

My stomach drops. No. Fuck. Of course that's what they talked about. Of course it is. I'm shaking my head so quickly that it's making me dizzy, and I resist a stutter.

'Dana assumed I knew, I think,' Nick continues. 'So it was a bit fucking awkward when she mentioned it, to be honest.'

I'm still shaking my head as I say, 'it's—I didn't lie. You never asked.'

The words sound even more flimsy aloud than they did in my head.

'I did. On our double date, I asked if you and him had always just been friends.'

He finally looks up to meet my gaze, but I wish he hadn't because his deep, brown eyes are filled with strain, as if he can't decide whether he wants to yell or cry. I squirm. God, I'm literally squirming like some cartoon villain.

'And that's one-hundred percent the truth. We've always just been friends, I swear. It wasn't–It was one time.'

Nick starts tracing his mug's handle again, his lips pursed in what I assume is contemplation until he sighs, then shrugs.

'I'm not sure that's really the point,' he argues. 'I figured it might've occurred to you to mention that you'd fucked him.'

The bluntness of his words sting, and if my drink was deep enough, I'd not give drowning myself in it a second thought. I apologise, but Nick's shaking his head and muttering something under his breath. I try apologising again, and again, but he still says nothing to me.

Then, without warning, he snaps his head back up to meet my eyes and say, 'I think we should end things.'

I almost laugh. Despite knowing it would be the worst possible idea, I want to tell him that's the whole point of us meeting. That's why I turned up today–to break things off. Instead of trying to one-up him, I just nod, then apologise again. Only, I'm not sure that's the right response either because he's laughing again, this time with a sharp edge to his voice.

'See,' he says like it's obvious. 'You're not even trying to fight our case.'

He's right. I know he's right, and he knows he's right, and everything is such a mess. With a long sigh, he lifts his drink to his mouth, finishing it off with one final gulp.

'Look, it's–' He stands, then sighs again. 'There are no hard feelings, honestly. I've obviously just walked into something bigger than me, and it–Just yeah, I'm sorry to end things, I really am, but it's for the best.'

He shrugs his long, camel jacket on, hesitates, then says, 'at least you and Preston don't have any obstacles now, right?'

Again, I deem it best not to overstep the mark and point out that Dana's technically still an obstacle.

I somehow feel even more terrible over messing Nick around by the time I arrive home. Margot still has no idea about Preston and me, so I claim some general he didn't think it was working excuse when she asks how he ended up being the one who did the dumping, a lie that makes me feel even more awful.

For reasons I'm too chronically tired to untangle, the end of whatever Nick and I had drives me further from Preston. Maybe it's the guilt over the Nick situation, or maybe it's my way of avoiding slipping back into old habits and consequently fucking things up for Preston and Dana, but I start only ever really seeing him during Typewriter meetings. I still check up on him over text, but I don't let our conversations run too long.

It's the end of March, deadlines are finally out of the way, and our second semester at uni is drawing to a close. As there was no Typewirter meeting this week and I was too hungover after an impromptu night out to attend the last one, I've not seen Preston for over two weeks. It's nothing. In the grand scheme of things, two weeks is nothing, especially when I consider I didn't see him for an entire year, but it feels like a lifetime.

That's why when I knock on his and Margot's front door wearing a little red dress after she essentially blackmailed me into joining what she's claiming to be my celebratory birthday night out, my reaction to Preston appearing is a blank, silent stare. The only saving grace is that he does exactly the same thing.

'Oh, hey,' I say through a stutter as I take in his semi-formal overshirt. 'I thought you said you were going to pass on tonight.'

Margot's head suddenly appears from around him. 'He's actually incredibly easy to blackmail. Told him it was your birthday thing, and that was it.'

'It's not my birthday thing!' I shout, but she's already skipping back into the house while cackling.

'Seriously,' I say, turning back to Preston. 'It's not. You don't have to come.'

He's smiling, and it's nice. God, I love seeing him smile.

'I was admittedly a bit offended you didn't invite me to your birthday celebrations,' he replies, 'so it's reassuring to know that Margot was bullshitting.'

I smile back at him, and we fall into silence as he gestures me inside. I have so many things I want to say to him, to ask him, but I don't know where to begin and I've suddenly forgotten how to even talk to him as we walk through the downstairs hallway.

'Is Nick meeting us at the–'

'Mia!' a deep voice interrupts Preston, and I turn from him to see Joe barrelling towards us with open arms. 'Happy birthday!'

I groan as Preston steps aside for Joe to embrace me, practically squeezing the life from me.

'My birthday's tomorrow,' I reply once my lung capacity returns.

'Is it?' he questions, visibly confused as we wander into the living area.

'I'm literally going to kill your girlfriend,' I grumble, which makes both guys laugh at my expense.

When Margot and I combine our blackmailing abilities, we can perform outright miracles because we somehow convince Preston to drink more than two beers. Despite claiming otherwise at the beginning of the night, I'm now fully rolling with the whole birthday celebrations thing, and so use that as my main ammunition to convince him to let loose more than usual.

While walking to our first Clapham bar of the night, I quietly assured him that he doesn't actually have to drink, but he shrugged it off.

'Once a year won't kill me,' he said with a wink that made me feel freshly resurrected.

Joe orders everyone a round of shots at the first place, which can't be easy on his wallet because there are nine of us. However, I quickly conclude he must really fucking hate me because they're tequila, my arch nemesis (excluding myself). It's at this venue that Preston miraculously returns from ordering our second round with a giant birthday badge.

'Please don't tell me you found this in a pile of sick outside or something!' I call to him over our table while waving the badge in the air.

He shakes his head. 'While I wish I'd thought of that, alas not. I asked the barman if they had any, which led to my discovery that they had multiple. Lost and found, I presume.'

'Ah,' Margot chimes in from my right. 'So for all we know, could've originated in a pile of sick.'

I contemplate Margot's point for half a second, shrug, then pin the badge onto my tight dress, somehow without stabbing myself in the boob.

'I'm sure they cleaned it,' I conclude, snapping my head back up.

My comment—at least I hope it's my comment, not my boob stabbing—earns me a laugh from the table. There are some Typewriter Magazine members in attendance, alongside a few of Preston's housemates, and I'm praying Dana's omission doesn't boil down to me.

The night's final destination is a sticky-floored club in the middle of Clapham, and as Preston and I are the only ones without any jackets to check-in, we find ourselves alone for the first time since he answered the door to me earlier. The first time in about a month, excluding then.

We're waiting in the windowless red lobby, the soundproofing flimsy at best because the stairs leading down to the club can't be more than ten feet away. I'm looking anywhere that isn't in Preston's general direction while silently cursing myself for not getting more drunk. I'm heavily tipsy at most.

I can hardly bear it, and the pulsing club music is too weak of a distraction, so I give in and swivel around to face him. He's already looking at me—I don't think he ever wasn't.

'You should've invited Dana,' I offer because I hate myself, apparently.

His eyebrows briefly knit together as he shifts his attention towards the staircase opposite us, then shrugs.

'I ended things with her, so I imagine that might've been rather awkward.'

I blink. No, he can't have; I would've noticed. At a Typewriter meeting, or—Well, I guess I missed the last two, and come to think of it, Dana and Preston didn't interact much at the other two meetings post-Brighton. I put that down to a privacy thing, though. I mean, Preston's hardly renowned for his PDA.

I don't know what to think, let alone say, so as always, I decide to make an ass of myself.

'Oh, that's—Wow, sorry. That's such a shame. What happened? How long—When did you end things?'

He scratches the back of his head, tugging at a few light strands on his neck, but keeps his eyes forward.

'When we got back from Brighton.'

What? Wait, what? Brighton was nearly a month ago. I stare at him, mouth open and eyes wide.

'You didn't... Why didn't you say anything?'

'You were so enthusiastic about us,' he murmurs, granting me a brief glance and a shrug before turning back to the stairway. 'I didn't want to disappoint you or distract you from Nick when you and he are doing so well.'

Suddenly, I'm laughing. Hysterically. Frankly, anyone walking past us to hit the dancefloor downstairs must think I'm either in the middle of a breakdown, or am ten times drunker than I actually am. When I finally gather myself, Preston's watching me with raised eyebrows and crossed arms, and above all else, I'm thrilled in the knowledge that I've rendered him utterly and painfully confused.

'Nick and I have broken up,' I explain, meeting his eyes.

Preston's response is unreadable. Not just typical Preston un-readable, but the-meaning-of-life-and-the-universe unreadable. It throws me. The smile that remained from my laughter wavers, and I'm lost in the green of his eyes as heavy dubstep music drowns anything resembling my ability to think straight. Naturally, I resist the feeling with more bullshit.

'Which is actually a depressingly funny story because I met up with him intending to end things, but he beat me to it, so that's karma, I guess.' I comedically roll my eyes as if I'm auditioning for some daytime sitcom. 'But it's—Yeah, no, my point is ditto.

We broke up. Not seeing him anymore, or anyone generally, but it–Yeah.' I cough. 'I'll stop talking now, sorry.'

A beat passes.

'Right,' he says, his eyes moving across my face as if analysing every last detail.

'Yep,' I concur.

Another beat passes.

'Cool.'

CHAPTER 26

C ool.

Cool.

Since when did Preston Maddox say cool? Before I have a chance to question his sudden vocabulary switch-up, I spot some familiar faces from our group approaching, so welcome them with one big wave. I try to catch Preston's eye as we make our way down the stairs, but he's already way ahead.

Once downstairs, my first stop is the bar. Margot and a few others join me while the rest of our group, including Preston, head straight to the dancefloor. It seems silly in hindsight because the guy's not some alcohol-induced werewolf, but I was holding onto this fear that Preston having more than a few drinks would lead to the re-emergence of Zack. That he'd not be able to stop, that he'd go too far or revert to a version of himself that would make him feel like a stranger. Tonight has buried that fear for good—buried Zack for good.

It's nearly midnight and Joe's reverted to his role as timekeeper, this time for my birthday. We're huddled in a tight circle as he's yelling his countdown into the questionably musky air, and as the clock strikes twelve, I figure I best not mention I wasn't actually born until two in the morning. Margot's screaming happy birth-days into my ear as she wraps her arms around me, then lifts me from the dancefloor to spin in circles.

'Welcome to non-teenage life!' she shouts in my ear.

Everyone's throwing happy birthdays at me, total strangers included, and I'm so distracted by the chaos that I forget I'm supposed to be avoiding Preston. I've not glanced at him since I stepped onto the black and white dancefloor because after our revelation upstairs, I've got no idea what I'd say to him, or how to even look at him.

He's standing directly opposite me in our circle, the club's neon blue lights turning his eyes a deep teal colour, and they're on me. His gaze is so focused, so direct that I'd bet everything I have on him watching me the entire time I've been trying to avoid watching him.

I'm so sure the music has stopped—that the world has stopped—because his, 'penblwydd hapus,' is the clearest, smoothest sound I've heard all night.

Only, when Joe loudly interjects with, 'is that Welsh? Does it mean happy birthday?' I realise I was wrong.

I trip back into reality with a laugh, then answer him with, 'yep!'

Margot says something, but I don't hear what. I smile in the hope that it'll do, and it does—she turns to Joe to start speaking with him while my eyes are pulled back towards Preston. From that moment on, he's all I can look at. Every movement, every quirk of his lips, every hand gesture, every nod of his head, every laugh. Every single thing.

I can't stop looking.

I don't say anything to him. We don't say a single word to each other after his penblwydd hapus, but I can't stop looking. We both can't stop looking, from quick glances between dancing bodies to lingering stares over strangers' shoulders.

It's one-thirty and Preston's gone. He's only momentarily left for the bar with Margot and Joe, but if my accelerating heartbeat is anything to go by, my body hasn't quite gotten the message that he's returning. It's as if I've lost all ability for logic—as if my body doesn't know what to do, doesn't know how to react to the loss of his presence. It's ridiculous, but I don't know where to look. I went so long trying not to look at him, but now he's gone, I've forgotten how not to.

I feel his hand before I hear his voice. He brushes it across the back of my arm with such delicacy that I question if I imagined it, his thumb lingering on my elbow. I don't know how I know it's him, but I do, and my assumption is confirmed when he murmurs into my ear.

'Upstairs.'

By the time I've turned around, he's gone. I glance back to the rest of the group, briefly frozen before shouting something about heading outside. My legs carry me across the dancefloor and towards the red stairway until I'm walking up it, until I reach the top of it.

He's there, as promised.

He's gazing at the floor, his hands in his trouser pockets and a faraway look in his eyes as he leans back against the empty lobby's wall. If he notices me, he doesn't show it, at least from what I can tell through my view of his side profile. The music from downstairs is more muffled than when we were here before, although the sound of my blood pumping in my head probably has something to do with that. I keep walking.

'Hey,' I say as I approach, and he lifts his head.

'Hi,' he replies, standing upright as he turns his body to face me.

We don't say anything else; we don't need to.

I reach for Preston's hand as he reaches for mine, and I'm not sure if he pulls me into him or if I push myself forward, or maybe it's both. I don't know. I don't know, or really care because I'm kissing him as if it's all I'm capable of doing, as if I need it to stay alive.

He releases my hand to cup my cheek, but I have to touch him—I need to know he's real—so I press my palm to his chest until I can feel his heart hammering underneath his shirt. He tastes of the sweet alcohol he's been steadily drinking throughout the night, and everything about him is warm—his body, his touch, his presence. I can hardly bear it; I need him closer. I lift my arms to wrap them around his neck and brush my fingers across the back of it, his hair as soft as silk as he places his other hand on the small of my back.

'I'm going to—I need to...' he murmurs, but continues kissing me moments later. 'I need to head home before...'

More kisses, this time dotted along my jaw, then my lips again until finally, he stops. He pulls away ever so slighlty, and although my eyes are still closed, I feel him swallow.

'Sorry.'

He lowers his hand from my face, but not before stealing one final kiss on my temple. I open my eyes as he steps back-wards—steps away from me—and he's turning around. He's turning towards the lobby's exit, but I want to demand that he stays. I'd beg; I'm so desperate for him not to leave that I'd be willing to beg, and I don't care how pathetic it'll look. I will.

Only, instead of pleading with him to stay as he starts treading towads the exit, I say, 'I'll come with you.'

He hesitates without turning to look at me, and I don't know what he's thinking—I never know—but if I had to guess, his instinct is to tell me not to. His instinct is to order me back downstairs, but he can't find the words—he can't find any words because he doesn't say anything. Still without turning around, he nods, and when I follow him outside he doesn't stop me.

He doesn't stop me when we pass my flat on the way to his, either. We keep walking—walk straight past it—without saying a word to one another, nor do we utter a thing during the ten minute journey to his house. He's always a few steps ahead. Enough to notice any sudden absence of mine, but with a purposeful space between us as if he's afraid of something. He's flexing his left hand—the one he used to cup my face at the club—and I can't stop noticing it, can't stop staring at his hand.

We keep walking and Preston still doesn't stop me, not even when I ascend the steps leading to his house as he unlocks his front door, not even when I follow him upstairs. By the time we reach his bedroom, the journey to it feels like a dream. The whole night feels like fiction, and I'm suddenly so sure that nothing else in this world is real outside this room.

The door hasn't fully shut when we start kissing again. My back is against the wall, centimetres from the doorway, and my hands are in his hair while his steady my waist. Something vibrates—his phone—Preston's phone vibrates, thwarting me back into reality as he releases my mouth to remove it from his pocket. With a quirk of his lips—lips I desperately need back on mine—he flips it around for me to read. It's exactly two o'clock.

'Penblwydd hapus,' he whispers with a kiss behind my ear.

I'm giggling as I guide his mouth back to mine, then take his phone to place it on the bookshelf beside us. I don't know if it's the alcohol or sheer impatience, but I'm tugging at the hem of his shirt, willing it off him. He follows my lead to pull it over his head, and I use the opportunity to yank down the zip at the side of my dress so that it falls to my ankles.

His lips are on mine again, and within moments, he's dotting kisses along my cheekbone, my chin, my neck. I move from the wall and tug at his belt to guide him deeper into the room, unable to stop myself despite being terrified by the prospect of moving too quickly, of him finally putting an end to everything, but he doesn't. He doesn't stop me.

Without a break between kisses, he slides his hands down my back, and I wordlessly lift myself up so that I'm straddling him, my legs wrapped around his waist. I can feel his heartbeat again, this time through my own chest as I press it against his warm skin, and it's loud, quick, erratic. He's alive—he's never felt more alive.

He walks me to his bed before gently lowering me to it, my back hitting the mattress so softly that I barely feel it. I pull him down so that he's leaning over me before he can contemplate hesitating, and as we begin kissing again, I unfasten my bra, my fingernails nearly piercing my skin with urgency.

He moves his mouth downwards again, but doesn't get any further than my neck before he tears it from my skin. He lifts his head and his green eyes meet mine, searching them, and I panic. It's dawned on him; he's realising what's happening—what we're doing—and he's going to stop it. His lips part, but I'm already speaking before he can make a sound.

'I want to.'

He swallows, and I don't think about it—I'm not really sure why I do it—but I inch forward to kiss his Adam's apple. When I return my head to the pillow, his eyes are piercing into mine as if examining them for a lie, as if there's any doubt what I said isn't the indisputable truth.

'Please,' I try again.

He remains still, and only now do I notice how heavy his breath his, how heavy mine is, and how perfectly in-sync they are. My body is screaming for his lips as his eyes flick downwards, then return to my face.

'I really want to,' I whisper.

He shifts his eyes down again, then lowers his head to press his lips to my neck, exactly where I kissed him moments earlier. My skin is buzzing as he pulls away, only this time, it's so that he can return his attention to my mouth.

'I do too,' he murmurs with a kiss.

I wake up to an unfamiliar song—an eighties one, I think, with an energetic beat but a jarringly haunting melody. That, and some shuffling, paper rustling, and a muttering sound—a voice. I open my eyes, only to squint at the sunlight pouring in through the opened window at the other side of the bedroom.

'Have you seen my physics book?'

Preston's voice is different. Off-kilter. As I pull myself up and my eyes adjust to the light, I spot him sitting on the wooden floor at the end of the mattress, his back to me, and I don't think to question how he knows I'm awake because moments after noticing him, I notice the mess. His books, usually in carefully organised piles or slotted into his bookshelf, are strewn across the floor as he mumbles under his breath, his words undecipherable. Despite my half asleep state, what's happening immediately dawns on me.

He's panicking.

'Preston. Hey, Preston, it's—' I say, suddenly wide awake as I reach for the first item of clothing I see; a burnt orange jumper draped over his desk chair. 'It's okay. Preston, hey.'

He doesn't hear me, or doesn't listen.

'It's here somewhere—I know it's here, but I can't find it. I've seen it. I had it. I know I had it.'

With the jumper now tossed over my torso, I shuffle to the end of the bed and reach for him. I'm careful–I know I need to be careful–so I keep my touch light, my fingers barely grazing the fabric of the hoodie he's wearing as I move my hand across his back and rest it on the side of his arm.

It's at this point I notice the blood.

His right hand's index finger is wet with blood. He's scratched it. I know he's scratched it because I've seen him do it before, in that exact spot. Some of the pages of his opened books have drops of red on them, and my chest is tightening, my throat closing up.

'Preston,' I repeat, trying desperately to keep my voice even. 'Listen to me. Please. It's okay.'

He doesn't turn to look at me, just keeps shuffling through the opened books in front of him as he says, 'you saw it. When you first came here in October. Blue–It's–it's blue with–'

'Preston.'

My voice is firm this time, and while he stops rambling about the book, he resorts to muttering under his breath again. With no idea what else to do, I dart my eyes around the room because he's right–despite being aware that his search is a thinly veiled distraction, I know the one he's looking for.

His desk. It was on his desk, and so I spin around to find it untouched. Despite the books thrown across the rest of the room, his desk is perfectly organised and the book is there. It's exactly where it was six months ago.

'It's on your desk,' I say, 'It's okay. It's on your desk.'

He's shaking his head again, still refusing to turn around as he mutters, 'it's not.'

I don't move my eyes from him as I stand to quickly tread towards his desk, not even when I reach for the book. I'm grasping it tightly, my knuckles white, as I return to my knees at the end of the bed.

'Here,' I say, gently but directly placing it into his hands. 'It's okay. It's here.'

Finally, he stops searching through the books, stops rambling to himself, stops doing anything beyond staring at the book in his hands. We sit with the quiet for a minute. My hands are twitching with desperation to reach for his injured finger, but I know he needs a minute.

Finally, he turns his head to look at me, his gaze briefly vacant until he blinks. I keep his eyes locked into mine as I lower my hand to his, then brush my finger along the side of his, careful not to touch the wound.

'Can I fix this for you?' I whisper, and after a brief pause, he nods.

CHAPTER 27

I t's not until we're sitting opposite each other on the mattress once I've finished cleaning, disinfecting, and bandaging Preston's cut that he says anything to me. What he says is probably the least surprising thing he ever has, his voice barely audible.

'I'm sorry, Mia.'

'What for?' I question, despite knowing the answer moments after waking up this morning.

'I didn't think.' He's shaking his head with a frown, his eyes darting down to his hands. 'I wasn't thinking straight and maybe I had too much to drink, I don't know, but I shouldn't have–Last night was my fault, and I'm really sorry, but it's–Fuck. Fuck, it's your birthday, and I've ruined–'

'It's okay,' I interrupt, but he's shaking his head harder.

'I've ruined your day and I've fucked everything up between us because I can't–We can't ever be anything, and I shouldn't have–I can't lose you. I don't want to lose–'

'Preston, listen to me,' I interrupt in the most commanding voice I can muster up. 'It's okay. You've not ruined anything, and it's okay.'

I reach for his hand and gesuture my head downwards to force his eyes into mine.

'We're okay,' I say slowly, 'I promise we're okay.'

He doesn't argue this time, but his chest is rising and falling at an unnaturally quick rate. I keep his hand in mine as I take a deep breath, then exhale slowly: a wordless instruction he knows to follow as he repeats the action.

'Nothing's changed. Nothing has to change,' I continue, then repeat, 'we're okay.'

'I'm sorry,' he repeats as he releases my hand, his voice quiet.

'Don't be,' I murmur. 'It was nice.'

He looks down again, his brow furrowed as he plays with his hands. I can practically see his mind racing, but I've got no idea of what he's thinking. I give him time to gather his thoughts, to line them up and make sense of them. A minute passes, maybe two.

'What if it happens again?'

He doesn't lift his head as he speaks, just continues looking at his hands. I know what the right answer is. I know I should tell him it won't happen again, that we won't let it, that we'll be more careful from now on. I know that's the right answer.

What I say, though, is 'then it happens again. And we'll be okay again, just like we are now, and just like we were the first time.'

His expression hardens as he clenches and unclenches his jaw. I anticipate his rebuttal—another shake of his head, maybe even some kind of stunned accusation. Instead, he returns his eyes to mine, then as small as it is quick, nods.

'Although, caveat,' I say lightly, then gesture my head towards his bandaged finger before waving my arms in the general direction of his room's mess. 'You can't do this next time it happens.'

My quip earns me a twitch—not quite a smile and definitely not a laugh, but the left corner of Preston's lips twitch upwards. Neither of us draws any attention to the fact that I didn't say if it happens, and I'm not sure it's accidental.

I was so sure we'd have to confess to Margot and Joe. Preston and I disappeared from the club at the same time with zero explanation, and for me to then wake up in their house the next morning, the evidence felt pretty glaring. Except it turns out Preston's intention was to leave regardless—he'd told them as much when they were at the bar together. When he briefly returned to instruct me to meet him upstairs, the others interpreted whatever it was I shouted over to them afterwards as my own leaving announcement. We tripped into the lie, really, and didn't correct anyone's interpretation of it.

I deem it best not to say anything to Aiden either. He took the aftermath of last time as a personal loss, and given mine and Preston's relationship is staying exactly the same, I want to avoid disappointing him a second time. The day after my birthday, Preston and I travel back to Cardiff for the Easter holidays, and I'm convinced Aiden will see through us. He'll take one glance in our direction and know what happened between us.

When he and Caleb meet us at Cardiff Central station without so much as a funny look, I realise my paranoia was for nothing. We hang out at his place for hours without inflicting any suspicion, not even when Caleb rambles an apology—his fourth, I think—over his soulmates comment when we visited Brighton. I imagine it has more to do with Preston's eerily stern poker face than my own acting abilities, though. At the end of the night, I head back to Mum's and Preston heads back to Anwen's without Aiden being any the wiser.

We've gotten away with it.

I'm in Cardiff for five days in total, but only spend one with Dad—something I would've been riddled with guilt over in the past. Livvy visits that same day, something I admittedly had to talk her into, but the time the three of us spend together is actually kind of... nice. Dad apologised to me about what happened over Christmas, and he's doing better with his drinking; he genuinely seems to be trying, which is more than he's ever done before. Maybe sometimes you've got to step away from something so that it can begin to mend itself.

I split the rest of my time at home between Mum and Anwen's house. I wouldn't usually spend the night at Anwen's, just visit in the day, but the wobble Preston had on my birthday has made me wary. When questioned about his bandaged finger, he told Anwen that he'd sliced it while cooking, a lie I wasn't particularly comfortable bolstering, but I understand. He doesn't want to worry her, and nor do I.

She knew something was off, though; mothers always do. That's why when she casually–too casually–asks me how he's seemed recently while Preston's showering that evening, I'm aware she's trying to get out of me what she knows she'll never get out of her son. I'm honest. I tell her he's doing well because he is, overall. He's seemed better than he has for a long time, possibly since I've known him. He's interested in things, he's not shutting himself away, he's spending time with friends. He's participating in life.

He has moments, yes–and I tell Anwen that–but he's finally letting himself live.

Once I've answered her question, I anticipate some relief, and ideally some reassurance that what I've said has eased her mind. I get more than that, though. I don't know if it's what I said or the way I said it, or if she's maybe just feeling extra sentimental this evening, but she responds by pulling me into a long hug.

'Thank you, Mia,' she says into my ear. 'So much.'

As she removes her arms from around me, I spin around at the sound of the kitchen door swishing open.

'Ti 'di gweld fy nghrys-t? Yr un gyda–'

Preston is standing in the doorway without a shirt on, his hair wet and eyebrows raised.

'Dare I ask?' he questions, switching to English.

'None of your business,' I reply without hesitation.

I'm making a conscious effort to look at his face, not his chest, and I've got no idea why I'm struggling so much because it's not like I haven't seen it before. Multiple times by now, actually.

Thankfully, Anwen drags my thoughts out of the gutter with, 'what t-shirt are you looking for?'

'I think I left it here last time I was home,' Preston answers. 'The front is plain white, but it has a continuous line drawing of a–'

'Oh, that one's in the bottom drawer of your wardrobe at uni. I remember seeing it before we left,' I say without thinking.

I glance sideways at Anwen. Shit. That sounds suspicous, doesn't it? Like I know the intimate details of his room, his clothes, his day to day life. I mean, I guess I sort of do, but for perfectly innocent reasons. Anwen, who was already smiling at my none of your business quip, widens her grin, her green eyes brightening.

If Preston has any anxiety over me badly toeing the just friends line in full view of his mother, as expertly as ever, he doesn't show it.

Instead, he furrows his brow and asks, 'is it?'

'Ugh, you're useless,' I reply. 'Yeah, I noticed it the morning after your end of term party, when I was looking for a spare shirt for Aiden.'

Smooth save, Mia. Practically genius. Preston and I share a look, and dare I say he appears to be remotely impressed. See, I think. I'm not always shit at improvising, just most of the time.

'Hm, okay,' Preston mutters, then combs his hand through his damp hair. 'No worries. Thanks.'

He begins to tread back towards the kitchen door, but Anwen interjects before he gets very far.

'Oh, before I forget! I didn't realise Mia was staying, so the spare duvet needs a clean. Do you need me to give it a quick wash and tumble for tonight, or will you both just sleep in Preston's bed?'

Without hesitance, Preston answers on our behalf. 'Separate beds. I'll sort out the washing, don't worry.'

With that, he leaves the room, and I try to kid myself into being happy with his response.

Within a week of my birthday, Preston and I have returned to London. I spent most of the journey toiling over how delusional I was about our time at home. It wasn't that I assumed something would happen between us again, and it's a good thing it didn't—a great thing, obviously—but I might've let my imagination run away with the possibility. I figure getting back to London, and back to reality, can only be a good thing.

'Are you heading straight home?' Preston asks me as we're leaving Clapham Common station.

I'm making a shitshow of trying to adjust my bag more securely onto my back, so with a mocking laugh, he takes it from me to throw over his own shoulder.

'The laugh was unnecessary, but thank you,' I mumble, then click my tongue. 'I might come to yours for a bit, if that's alright? Say hi to Margot.'

He shrugs. 'Sure. No skin off my teeth.'

'Please, control your enthusiasm.'

I can't see his face because he's storming ahead, but I can hear him snickering into the air. Asshole.

When we arrive at Preston's house, there's no sign of Margot. When I'd spoken with her about Easter plans, she said she wasn't heading home until the second half of the holiday, and that Joe was away for the whole of it. I figure she must be out with friends or something, so Preston shoots her a message to ask when she'll be home.

In the meantime, I dump my bags in the corner of Preston's living room and collapse onto his sofa to aimlessly scroll through TV channels.

'She's gone home with Joe, apparently.'

I sit up on the sofa, then turn around to see Preston entering the room behind me, his head down as he types into his phone.

'Margot, that is,' he says, looking up. 'She's going to spend a week or so with him, then a week with her family.'

'Oh! Oh, cool. So they're both away?' I ask, and he nods. 'Is anyone else home?'

I'm not entirely sure why—I guess because there's no reason for me to stay now—but I stand up. I'm suddenly unsure of what to do with my hands, so I don't really do anything with them. Sort of just let them dangle awkwardly by my side without stepping forward, or stepping anywhere, for that matter.

'Just us,' Preston replies quietly.

Just us.

'It's—I guess I should head back to mine then,' I continue.

Preston's nodding. 'I suppose.'

He's not moved either. He's holding his phone in front of him, but looking at me while standing just inside the room. As I take a step towards my pile of bags beside the TV, he's suddenly talking again.

'You're welcome to—You can stay if you'd like; we could do something, maybe,' he says quickly. 'Watch a film or something.'

'Yeah!' I reply, then realise I should probably tone down my enthusiasm. 'That'd be cool.'

There's no reason we can't watch a film in his living room. It's a smart TV, it links to Netflix, and it's a Friday night so there are probably a few non-terrible films on regular TV. As previously established, it's not like there's anyone else in the house who might want to use the living room.

Despite all of this, we head upstairs.

We do as discussed. I change into some comfortable sweatpants in the privacy of a bathroom while Preston finds us something to watch, and he does; he finds some indie Irish film I've never heard of. By the time I meet him in his bedroom, he's got it set up and ready to play on his laptop while he changes his shirt. I try not to stare as I get comfortable on his bed and prop the laptop atop a pillow. It's like we've rehearsed every action, like we're performing a script until we're sitting side-by-side on his mattress as the film's opening credits play.

We last about thirty seconds, maybe less.

I turn my head to say something, but I lean in a little closer than I should, inch a bit too far forward, and forget the words–forget myself–when I feel his gaze on me. Instead of saying whatever it was I was planning to say, I close my eyes and plant a light kiss on his lips. I intend to leave it at that, but as I pull away, Preston inches closer; close enough to kiss me. And I kiss him back.

The film is still playing but we've shoved the laptop aside, although I don't especially remember either of us doing it. My back is flat against the mattress, my shirt long forgotten as Preston leans over me, his lips decorating mine with kisses. I'm melting into his touch; the feeling of his body pressed against mine, his skin shooting electricity through my own, his hand in my hair when his index finger–the one I plastered up a week earlier–grazes my cheekbone.

'Hey,' I whisper as I pull away, then find his eyes in the dim lighting. 'We don't have to–We can stop if it's too much.'

I lift my hand to place it over his, over the plaster covering his wound. He blinks, his attention briefly shifting to what I'm referring to before returning it to me.

'It's okay,' he murmurs after a moment, then nods, I think to himself more so than me. 'I'm okay.'

I take his words at face value and nudge my head closer, reigniting his lips with mine. My hands are pressed against his chest, as if what remains of the logical side of me is making some feeble attempt to slow him down. Not because I want him to, but because I think it's the right thing for me to do. I quickly abandon my attempts as he lowers his kisses to my neck, drawing a pleasured sigh from my mouth

'If you change your mind, that's okay,' I say with another sigh. 'We can stop if you need to, okay? Just say when.'

I'm echoing his own words back to him; the words he told me on New Year's Eve, and the first time we found ourselves in this entanglement. He pauses his kisses to look at me again, and the moonlight hitting his face makes his skin appear as if it's glowing, his cheekbones sharper and green eyes brighter than ever.

'Okay,' he whispers, then even more quietly, 'thank you.'

'Just say when,' I repeat, then seal my promise with a gentle kiss.

Only, Preston's when never comes.

CHAPTER 28

I spend the night at Preston's house, and the next one, and the one after that. In fact, at no point do I go home, nor plan to, and Preston's not exactly pushy about it. I only return to my place briefly to grab some fresh clothes, and it's a passing visit; I'm back at his within the hour. None of Preston's other housemates are due to return any earlier than Margot, so we've got the place to ourselves for the whole two weeks or so.

We've both got exams to grapple with shortly after the Easter holidays, so we spend most days revising at cafes and campus libraries. We tried studying from Preston's place but wound up getting distracted by each other and the potential that comes with an empty house, so the libraries and occasional cafe visits were a compromise.

It was during one of these cafe visits that we temporarily returned to the world outside the private one we'd curated together. We were taking a break from revising, which in Preston terms, equated to reading a textbook on Russian history because as well-established by now, he's certified deranged. His arm was around my waist, his hand on my thigh, and I was absentmindedly playing with it as I rested my head on his shoulder. I wasn't really doing anything beyond that, just watching him turn the pages of his book with his free hand.

Then suddenly, Preston's back stiffened as he sat upright, pulling his arm from around me and forcing me to lift my head, at which point I spotted Damien, Typewriter Magazine's poetry contributor, entering the cafe. Within seconds of Preston's posture switch, Damien glanced in our direction with a double-take. He smiled, then started ambling towards us.

'Hey!' he said cheerily, and with what I hoped was total ignorance, as he stopped at our table. 'I didn't realise you guys were still around.'

'We spent the first week or so at home,' I reply, maybe a little too quickly. 'So yeah, back now. For good!'

He was nodding, a grin still on his face. 'Nice. I'm heading home in a few days. We should do something before then!'

I nodded back with matching enthusiasm, despite my niggling sense of irritation over an arbitrary feeling that Damien was infringing on us, interrupting mine and Preston's imaginary world. I didn't need to worry; Damien didn't end up messaging either of us to do anything, I definitely didn't message him, and I doubt Preston made any efforts to either.

Damien's cafe appearance was the first shock to our system. We both knew that what we were doing wasn't our forever, but I think it was the first time we consciously acknowledged it. For the rest of the day, Preston pulled back. He gently nudged me off his shoulder when I tried returning my head to it, moved to sit opposite instead of beside me, stayed at the cafe for a few hours after I left. Slept on his sofa that night.

By nine o'clock the next morning, though, we were back in bed together.

We stay up for hours some nights, often just talking about nothing but somehow everything. I don't think there's a topic we don't cover, at least excluding what it is we're doing; we never talk about that. For the first few days, I kept count of how often we had sex, but I gave up pretty quickly. At no point is there a repeat of what happened after we slept together on my birthday, and every time we do, I assure him we can stop at any time. He never asks to.

It's not that I disliked sex with Nick, or even with the one-night stand I had in January, but it wasn't this. It wasn't anything like this. There was always something in the background with them. A little bit of fear, maybe anxiety, or some amalgamation of both that made it feel more like going through the motions. I never really communicated with Nick during sex; we sort of just did it, and it was fine—nice, even—but it's instinctive with Preston. I don't get embarrassed about asking to try something new, or telling him what feels good, not that I ever really need to. It's like he implicitly knows me; knows my mind, my body. Everything.

After Damien's unexpected appearance, we have moments of uncertainty, but they're always brief. I see a wariness in Preston's eyes sometimes, usually in the early mornings when the quiet sobers us into remembering that our time is running out. He'll say something to me on occasion; nothing explicit, but something to remind me—to remind us both, I think—that we don't have forever. He'll suggest a night out with everyone once exams are over, check that I've got everything sorted for when I return to my flat, or ask when my flatmates are back in London. Just small reminders.

It's eleven o'clock on a lazy Sunday morning, and Margot's due back tomorrow. We're in Preston's bed, where we've stayed for the past sixteen hours, and he's reading something while I listen to his heartbeat, my ear pressed against his bare chest and my arm draped over his torso. I crane my neck to look up at him, and he's holding his physics book, his brow furrowed behind his round glasses as he subtly mouths the words he's reading.

God, he's such a fucking nerd.

The image is in such stark contrast to what we were doing—what he was doing to me—barely ten minutes ago that I have to turn away to stop myself from giggling. I lower my ear back to his chest to listen to his steady heartbeat, a small smile breaking onto my lips as I shut my eyes. I'm on the brink of dosing, my eyelids fluttering closed when I feel him take a breath.

'There's a guy on my course I think you'd like,' he murmurs out of nowhere, and I return my attention to his face. 'I can send you his socials, if you're interested.'

He says it like an afterthought, just a passing comment without so much as sparing me a glance. I know not to take it personally. I know it's his way of reminding me that this thing between us is purely physical, that from tomorrow, our real life restarts. I know it's his way of protecting me—protecting us—from getting hurt, but that knowledge doesn't stop the sudden feeling of being underwater.

'Maybe,' I say, and I keep my eyes on him for long enough to notice his jaw twitch, then return my head to his chest. 'Yeah, send me his socials.'

The quiet that follows is suffocating, as if something is clawing at me, pulling me out of this world we've created and forcing a chasm of space between us.

But then Preston murmurs, 'I'll forewarn him about your name; politely ask him not to pass comment on its resemblance to an STD,' and everything, even if it's temporary, feels okay again.

I'm at Preston's house when Margot returns the following morning. Preston's making a late breakfast while I watch TV in the living area, and she bursts through the door with a big smile and an even bigger hug, and that's it, I figure. The past two weeks are over, our time has drawn to a close, and we can shut the curtains on the things Preston and I did together–draw a line in the sand and put an official stop to everything.

It doesn't stop, though.

It becomes more difficult and less frequent, but it doesn't stop. I finally return to my flat, we no longer spend every minute of the day together, and from everyone else's perspective, we're no different to what we were pre-Easter. I spend a few evenings a week at Preston and Margot's, just like I did before, and so long as Preston sleeps on the sofa, nobody questions anything. Once the rest of the house is asleep, I'll pop downstairs to invite him upstairs. We just need to be careful we don't fall asleep afterwards, which has only happened once, but he woke up early enough the next morning to cover our tracks.

Preston's encouragement to put myself out there continues, as does mine with him. If anything, it amplifies, even though we keep sleeping together. We see other people, and we agree that if either of us starts something serious with someone, we'll stop. I want to show him that I'm totally open to that, that I'm dating people, so I meet up with the guy from his course. He's attractive and we get along, so I go back to his after our dinner date and we have sex, which is fine. I don't see him again.

Once exam season is over, Preston and I head back to Cardiff for summer, and continuing things becomes even more difficult and infrequent.

But it still doesn't stop.

Preston doesn't want to risk us getting caught by Anwen and for her to get the wrong impression of what we are, so the nights I stay over his, he sleeps on the sofa. Mum's place is too risky, her house too small, and I'd rather she didn't get the wrong impression either. Dad's house is an obvious no-go. We find ways, though. If I've got a free house, or if he does, we'll let each other know.

Even on the days physical intimacy is impossible, nothing feels lost or wasted; the fear that spiralled Preston into a panic the morning of my birthday never materialises because our friendship is stronger than ever. We waste hours doing nothing of any real significance. Just talking, reading, listening to music, watching films—even spending time in silence together feels like something magnificent. It's probably the best summer I've ever had, honestly.

It's not until the day before we're due to return to Lonodon that we fuck up. Not with our parents, thank God, but with someone I could argue is worse.

Aiden's birthday lands on the last day of August, and since he's been of legal age, he's demanded we celebrate it by going on an absolute bender. The usual routine for these nights is that we end up in bed together—not like that, obviously—but we'll sleep in whoever's bed is closest together. This year, though, Aiden has Caleb. Instead of collapsing into bed together at the end of the night, I take one of his absent housemate's bedrooms while Preston is relegated to the sofa.

I, knowing that the poor man has spent half his summer on sofas, feel bad about the eventuality. It results in me, in my slightly drunk state, creeping into the living room at four in the morning to convince Preston into swapping. He point-blank refuses, and possibly because of his own slightly drunken state, we compromise with him sharing the spare bed with me under the agreement that nothing will happen. Just sleep. Except we don't just sleep, obviously.

Traditionally, on the nights Aiden and I don't share a bed on his birthday, he'll appear at some undisclosed time the next morning for a debrief. I knew this—I hadn't forgotten, not even as I was drifting off to sleep after inviting Preston into my bedroom for the night—but Aiden's debriefs are never before ten o'clock. Until this morning, apparently.

I'm stirred awake by the sound of knocking against wood. By the time I've come to my senses and realise that Preston is still beside me, the bedroom door is opening. I could try to brush it off; say nothing happened, that we both woke up early and are just hanging out. The trouble is explaining why I'm not wearing any clothes.

Aiden appears in the opened doorway with Caleb, mouth open as if he was in the middle of saying something—which wouldn't surprise me; he probably started talking before he even opened the door—but he clamps it shut within seconds, his eyes widening. I yank the duvet up to my shoulders in a last-ditch attempt to avert suspicion, but I don't know why I bother; I'm not kidding anyone.

'I maybe should've texted first,' Aiden says slowly, then a pause, and God, can they at least close the door? 'Noted for next time.'

Caleb, on the other hand, exclaims, 'ha! Called it!'

Aiden does eventually have the courtesy to close the door, at which point I jump out of bed and scramble my pyjamas back on while swearing, maybe a little excessively, under my breath.

'His debriefs are never before ten!' I whisper-hiss to Preston

He's sitting up in bed with raised eyebrows, his lips quirked upwards. How is he so calm? Hell, he looks like he wants to laugh. I aggressively button up my pyjama shirt with one hand while shoving my phone in his face with the other.

'It's not even quarter-past nine!'

He opts to ignore my rant, and insted, tilts his head with, 'would you like me to speak with him?'

'No, it's—No, I should. I will. I'm just not sure—What do I tell him?'

'Whatever you feel comfortable telling him,' Preston soothes. 'You're in control of the narrative.'

'Do you think I should lie?'

Preston's response is a measured expression, and while it doesn't indicate anything on any kind of surface level, that in itself gives me his answer. I shouldn't lie.

'I'll support whatever you decide to do,' he continues. 'Truth, half-truth, or lie.'

I shake my head. 'I'll be honest.'

I can't lie, not to Aiden.

Fifteen minutes later, when Preston is in the shower and Caleb is doing something upstairs, I wander into Aiden's living room to find him sitting on the sofa shoveling dry cereal into his mouth as he watches, from what I can tell, a shark documentary.

'Hey,' I say awkwardly as I stop in the doorway.

He turns from the TV to look at me, a mouth full of food and eyes wide. I nearly flinch at what will inevitably follow; an accusation of me keeping something so big from him, and worst case scenario, an assumption that Preston are I are something we're not.

Instead, what Aiden says is, 'I'm sorry.'

I blink, perplexed. He swallows the last of his cereal.

'I shouldn't have—I need to stop, like, barging into things. Rooms, your life, etcetera,' he elaborates.

I'm shaking my head as I wrap my arms around myself. 'No, that's—barge. Please barge.'

He gives me a close-mouthed smile, which makes my stomach flip. Aiden's grins are big and toothy, not coy—not like this one.

'I'm always invading London, and when you're here, I practically dictate that you see me and tell me everything, do everything with me, and it's—You're allowed some privacy, is what I'm saying. I shouldn't just assume—'

'Whoa, slow down,' I interrupt him, then tread over to the blue sofa to join him on it. 'Aiden, I invite you to London. I want to do everything with you. I like seeing you.'

'It's okay if you don't, or if I'm too much with it, too much with everything because I know I can be, so—'

'Aiden, listen to me. You're never too much, and don't ever let anyone ever make you think otherwise.' I pause as I lock his big, brown eyes into mine. 'Promise me that?'

He nods, but I need to hear him say it.

'Promise?'

'Ugh, yes, promise,' he grumbles, then mutters, 'holy mackerel, you're scary when you want to be.'

I respond with a smirk, and finally, Aiden smiles—actually smiles, teeth and all.

'I just—I feel really bad,' he says. 'Obviously last night's kind of a huge deal for you both, and I fucking barge in unannounced, waking you up before you've even had a chance to speak to each other about it. I totally ruined your moment and probably made things way more awkward between you both when—'

Shit, he thinks last night is the first time Preston and I have hooked up since my birthday.

'No, it's—That wasn't... unusual,' I say, cutting him short. 'For us, I mean.'

Aiden, whose mouth is still open from his rambling, narrows his eyes.

'We've been...'

God, what do I even call what Preston and I have been doing for the past few months?

'We're not—Before you get the wrong idea, we're not in a relationship or anything. Everyone left London over Easter and we started just, I don't know, spending lots of time together, and we were—We kind of started sleeping together, like, casually with a plan—Well, more of an assumption than a literal plan, I guess—but with an assumption that we'd stop once Easter was over, except we... didn't. It's casual, though; that's the main thing I'm trying to get at.'

He blinks, silent. Aiden. Silent.

'So, like, friends with benefits?'

'Uh, it's—I don't know if—' I stammer. 'I mean, technically, I guess, but like, not in an unhealthy way.'

Silence. Again. Have I entered some parallel universe or something?

I'm watching him in anticipation, bracing myself for whatever scolding he's about to throw in my direction, but then his arms are around me. I nestle into him, hugging him back like I'm grasping onto dear life because I'm suddenly scared; terrified by the enormity of what Preston and I are doing, of what could happen if everything goes wrong.

'Just be careful,' Aiden murmurs into my hair. 'For both of your sakes.'

CHAPTER 29

By the time my second year of university kickstarts, summer feels like a blink in time. It's near impossible to believe that a whole year has passed since I stumbled across Margot in Dolly's cafe, and it terrifies me a little, honestly. Is time just going to move increasingly quickly until I'm suddenly eighty years old with a lifetime behind me?

For the first time in a long time, things are good. Really good. I passed first year with an upper second-class, Mum's living her best life now that she's not got the responsibility of Livvy or me living with her full-time, Dad's promise to relax his drinking has stayed firm—he's following advice from his doctor and has even attended some AA meetings—I'm officially second in editorial command at Typewriter Magazine, and I've got a close group of friends who, as far as I'm aware, actually like me.

Better yet, for the four or so years he's been in my life, I don't think I've ever known Preston to be as content as he is right now. He breezed through his second year with a first-class, Anwen and Matty are thriving in Cardiff, he meets up with Rhys at least once a month, he's actively engaging with people and enjoying things, and every now and then, when his guard is down, I catch him talking about the future.

Despite Aiden's reservations, Preston and I are still sleeping together. We're abiding by the same rules—what we're doing isn't permanent, we're making efforts to meet other people, and the moment anything begins feeling remotely precarious between us, we'll stop. And we will. Eventually, we'll stop.

It's the third week of our first semester, and I'm on my way to my Monday lecture when I realise I left the book we're reading for that class at Preston's. I was there on Friday for a film night Margot hosted, and in hindsight, bringing the book was pointless because I didn't read a word of it. I know exactly where it is—on Preston's desk—so I make a quick detour to his house before catching the tube.

It's Joe who answers the door, and despite it being nearly ten-thirty, the way he squints at me, his hair jutting up in all directions, makes it pretty clear he's not been awake longer than five minutes.

'Margot or Preston?' he mumbles, still squinting.

'The latter,' I reply as I fight a laugh.

Joe replies with something totally unintelligible because he's yawning as he speaks, but Margot comes to my rescue as I'm stepping into their hallway.

'I've told him not to answer the door when he's just woken up,' she says with an eye roll as her boyfriend ambles back into the house, then gestures towards the staircase beside us. 'He should be upstairs. Think he's got a guest staying over, though. Some guy I briefly saw last night—kind of cute, actually, so hey, there could be potential there for you.'

I frown. Since when did Preston have guests, let alone guests who stay the night? I thank Margot, then begin my journey up the three sets of stairs leading to Preston's room. I'd usually pause at his closed door, maybe listen out for any music. As I've got a book to grab, a tube to catch, and a lecture to attend, though, I don't.

I knock, and the second I hear a yeah! I push the door open without giving much thought to the fact that Preston always says yes. Never yeah.

'Hey! Sorry, I think I left my–'

The word book catches in my throat, turning it into a strangled sound as I freeze on the spot, Preston's bedroom door slamming shut behind me. My stomach churns as I blink, then blink again as if doing so will clear my head–clear reality–of the image in front of me.

Sitting at the head of Preston's bed wearing a baggy hoodie, his back against the wall and a phone in his hand, is Robbie Morrissey.

If I thought I was hallucinating when I bumped into Preston last year, I must be downright losing my mind now. I'm blinking again. Preston's standing at his desk, to Robbie's left, leaning back against it with crossed arms and a look that's impossible to even attempt to untangle. The only thing I can decipher is that it's not good. Whatever's running through his head is not good.

'Hey, Mia.' Robbie lifts his arm in a short wave, then returns his attention to his phone

Hey. Hey. Is that all he has to say?

'What the hell are you doing here?' I try.

While Preston sighs, uncrossing his arms to rub his hand across the side of his face, Robbie looks back up with blue eyes wide.

He shrugs. 'I needed somewhere to stay.'

'Don't you have a house or something? In Cardiff?'

The last time I checked, his parents had kicked him out of their house for letting it burn down–literally–but he was renting a place in the city while working in event management.

'Not anymore,' Robbie responds, but he's looking at his phone, not me, as he speaks.

I turn back to Preston, my eyes wild in hope of something resembling an explanation. He lightly shakes his head before turning towards his bedroom window, his jaw clenched. Everything about him is... off. His posture is stiff, his hands are fidgeting, his face pale, his eyes sunken, his body tense. I glance back at Robbie, who seemingly hasn't got a care in the world as he starts shuffling through a duffel bag on the floor beside him, then back to Preston. For whatever reason Preston—or rather, Zack's—former best friend is here, it's killing him. It looks like it's literally killing him.

'There's clearly some weird tension going on here, so I'll take the hint,' Robbie interrupts my thoughts as he jumps up with a towel in hand, then waves it towards Preston. 'There's a shower on the floor below, right?'

'Yes,' Preston replies without looking at him.

'Nice. Cheers.'

I watch in silence as Robbie brushes past me, leaving the smell of an aftershave that was once so familiar behind him. With Robbie gone, I turn back around to meet Preston's eyes, but he beats me to it.

'He lost his job and his parents won't even talk to him,' he explains. 'He doesn't have anywhere else to go.'

'Okay, sucks for him. That's his problem,' I retort as I close the space between us, then stop in front of him. 'Why didn't you tell me?'

Preston glances towards his window again. 'He just turned up last night.'

My eyes widen. 'He just turned up? What do you—As in, he literally just knocked on your door unannounced with zero warning? I doubt—'

'Yes,' he cuts in, then ticks his jaw. 'Quite literally.'

I'm missing something. I have to be missing something.

'I didn't even—I had no idea you guys were still friends, let alone still spoke. I just... Why on earth would you keep in touch with him when he's so... connected to before?'

Despite my ambiguity, I don't doubt Preston knows exactly what I'm referring to, what before means. When he was doubling as Zack, intentionally driving his life off a cliff as self-inflicted punishment for letting Anwen take the blame for killing Matty's father.

'It's complex, Mia,' he begins with a sigh. 'He was my closest friend for years, a time I spent the entirety of lying to his face about my life, my family, my name, all the while dragging him down to my level.' I try to interrupt, but he continues. 'And we barely speak, honestly; I've not sent him a message, let alone uttered a word to him, since February.'

Since February? They've not spoken for seven months, but Robbie deemed it perfectly normal to show up unannounced demanding a place to sleep?

'He knows nobody here is aware of my life before London,' Preston continues, 'and he's promised not to say anything.'

Preston might trust his word on that, but I sure as hell don't.

'How long is he staying?' I snap.

I know I shouldn't be short with him, but I'm annoyed. I'm angry—at Preston for letting Robbie take advantage of him like this, at Robbie for knowing Preston would feel too guilty over before to say no.

He looks towards the window again as he utters, 'I don't know.'

I scoff, but Preston pays me no attention, not out of rudeness, but out of something I fear is far worse. His arms are crossed again, one hand scratching at the the fold in his elbow so harshly that the soft skin is turning angry and red. This isn't just about guilt or favours. Robbie being here is a glaring reminder—a symbol—of everything Preston has spent three years trying to move on from, and the past two years refusing to let intrude the life he's built in London.

Robbie being here is going to kill him from the inside.

'You have to kick him out,' I say gently as I reach out to unfold his arms, to stop him hurting himself.

'Mia, I can't just–'

'Yes, you can. You can tell him to fuck off, and next time, not turn up to a city he doesn't live in and just assume someone he knew three years ago will be happy and willing to house him for free until who fucking knows when.'

Preston's clenching his jaw again, and his gaze is still fixated on the window. When he speaks, his voice is barely a murmur.

'I want to help him.'

Despite me insisting he doesn't owe anyone anything, Preston doesn't kick Robbie out. In fact, the two become inseparable. At no point do I see Preston without Robbie lingering like some annoying fly, not even at Tuesday's Typewriter Magazine meeting. I figure Robbie must know about Preston and Dana's history, or at least have some vague idea of it, because he spends the entirety of it flirting with her. I guess some things never change; Robbie will always want what Preston has, or has had.

It's at this meeting that I hear Robbie refer to Preston as Zack for the first time.

In his defence, I don't think it's intentional; he corrects himself within seconds, and nobody but me overhears, but that's not the point. Preston visibly flinches at the sound of his former nick-name, and I doubt hearing it coming from Robbie's mouth helps matters. He's stuck to his promise by not uttering a word about Preston's past to anyone, but I'm nervous—one slip up could ruin everything.

And Preston knows that.

As each day passes, and not one goes by without me finding some excuse to check in on him—on them both—he becomes increasingly drawn into himself. He stops engaging in group coversations, barely even looks at people, becomes worse and worse at responding to my messages, ignores my attempts to call him, and frankly, if it wasn't for Robbie opening it on his behalf, he'd probably not open his bedroom door to me whenever I check in as a result of an ignored phone call.

It's written all over his face, too. He's not sleeping. I know he's not because his eyes are more hooded than usual, the shadows under them dulling their usual bright green. He's restless; he's never not fidgeting, he's always on his feet as if he's in perpetual fight or flight, and I don't think I've ever seen his jaw clenched so often. His gaze is increasingly empty, his smiles feel forced, and by Friday, he's stopped bothering to even fake them.

It's as if all of the progress he's made over the past year or so is rapidly reversing in real time, and I have no idea how to stop it.

What I do know—what I knew from the second I saw him—is that Robbie has to go.

As he does most weekends, Preston spends the one following Robbie's jumpscare of an appearance in Cardiff. Robbie doesn't join him, which is a blessing wrapped in a curse because while it means Preston gets a break from him, it also means Robbie's swanning around his London townhouse like he owns the place. I don't like the thought of him alone in Preston's room, filling its four walls with his presence, shuffling through Preston's things, leaving his trace in every corner of his personal space.

As getting Robbie alone has been impossible with Preston in London, what with his leech-like qualities, I jump at my first opportunity to do so. I wasn't kidding when I said the guy seems to think he owns the place because when I knock on Preston's front door, bright and early at nine o'clock on Saturday, Robbie is the one who answers.

'Hey,' he says with a smirk, his brown hair lazily styled off his face like he doesn't have a care in the world. 'You know he's in Cardiff for the weekend, right?'

'I came to talk to you,' I reply, shoving myself past him to enter the house.

'Why do I feel like you're pissed at me?' he complains as he follows me into the open-plan living area.

If I didn't know any better, I'd think he sounds sincerely per-plexed.

Given nobody in this house except for Preston ever wakes up before ten, rarely even for nine AM lectures, the space is empty, and there's no sign of any movement elsewhere. I contemplate sitting onto the sofa, but my body's too full of energy, is itching too much to keep still, so I stay standing as Robbie ambles into the room.

'You want a drink or anything? I was just gonna make breakfast, if you want–'

'Robbie, you need to leave,' I interrupt.

Robbie's response is to freeze on the spot with an empty stare, as if what I just said was out of the blue, as if I've not spent the past week or so glaring at his face, his side profile, the back of his head–whatever the situation called for. His blue eyes are wide, his thin lips pulled into a frown as he watches me.

'I mean, I know we're technically exes and everything, but I kinda thought you were over that.'

'I literally couldn't care less about that.'

'Brutal.'

'For Preston's sake,' I say, ignoring him. 'You being here is fucking with him.'

He frowns again. 'He said it was cool for me to stay so long as I don't bring up shit from the past with anyone.'

Again, his tanned face is plastered with confusion. If it wasn't for the gravity of the situation, it'd almost be funny how reading him is like reading a kid's picture book compared to Preston. I wait a few moments, wait for him to admit he knows what he's doing—that he knows as well as I do that him merely being here is skyrocketing Preston's anxiety.

Except, he doesn't. His expression turns from puzzled to entirely lost, and he's suddenly transported back to the boy who was desperate for me to like him, who was so fixated on being loved—by me, by his peers, by his parents—that he shaped himself in the image of someone who wasn't even real. He knew Zack for longer than I've known Preston, so despite everything, he was real. To Robbie, he was real.

I exhale with a long, heavy sigh, the tension in my body slipping away as I momentarily shut my eyes. I lower myself to the sofa, then gesture to the empty space beside me. After some hesitation, Robbie follows my instruction and sits beside me.

'Look,' I mutter, my voice turning soft. 'Things are obviously a bit shit for you right now, and it's—I don't think you're intentionally trying to hurt anyone, but it's hurting him.'

He shrugs, but it's an awkward one, like his skin isn't his own and he's trying to shed it. While I'm stressing over the progress

Preston's made over the past three years being obliterated, Robbie might not have made any to reverse in the first place.

Ugh, I feel bad for him. For fuck's sake.

'You're trying to find somewhere in Cardiff, right?' I try, and Robbie flashes me a coy glance, then nods. 'Aiden's still there and he knows everyone–literally, it's scary. He's bound to know someone looking for a flatmate, so I'll reach out.'

'Oh, that's–Yeah, that would be helpful. Thanks.' Robbie's looking at his hands as he speaks. 'It's the–I don't really–I'm kinda out of money too. Since the bar I was managing went bust, I mean, so rent is kinda tricky. To pay, I mean.'

I bite my cheeks to mask my instinctive irritation.

Keeping my voice gentle, I say, 'I know things aren't great with your parents, but they surely didn't just tell you to fuck off when they found out you were essentially going to be homeless. With all due respect, they have more than enough cash to cover you until you get a new job.'

His cheeks flush as he fidgets, still avoiding my gaze. God, he's like a wounded animal.

'I've not exactly told them,' he mumbles. 'I called my mum when I was made redundant, just y'know, asking if they'd loan me some money for some stuff, but I didn't really–I didn't say what for, or that I'd lost my job, or that I couldn't afford to keep paying the rent at the place I was living in at the time.'

A pause.

'So they have no idea you've got no job and nowhere to live? They just think you want money?'

'Yeah, kinda.'

I groan, and God, I want to slam his head into the coffee table.

'It's embarrassing, Mia,' he adds before I can muster a response, his eyes finally on me. 'They never fucking liked me in the first place, then after the fire, they finally had an actual reason not to and kept telling me how much of a fuck up I was. I can't prove them right.'

'You won't be proving anyone right,' I argue. 'Just be honest with them, Robbie. Please? At times like these, you've just got to swallow your pride and–'

'I'll be gone by the end of next week,' he interrupts, standing. 'I'm not gonna spill any of Preston's dirty secrets, so you don't need to worry about me poisoning his new perfect fucking life with my shitty one because that's all you actually care about here, isn't it?'

I groan. Of course that's what this comes back to. It's what it always comes back to with him, isn't it?

'Your idea of the perfect life is wildly twisted, but yes, I came here out of concern for Preston,' I hit back, then continue the second I hear him scoff. 'But now that you've actually shed the bullshit and been honest with me, I genuienly want to help. I'll speak with Aiden, and you need to speak to your parents because they owe you, Robbie. They can't treat you like some commodity to throw money at for eighteen years, then the second you fuck up, drop you like dead weight. The least they can do is pay your rent for a few bloody months.'

I take a sharp breath as the space between us is filled with silence, my blood pumping in my ears as Robbie scans my face. Slowly, his shoulders relax and he averts his gaze to look towards the kitchen area.

'What if they say no?' he utters. 'What if I tell them everything, and they care so fucking little for me that they still say no?'

I want to tell him they won't–they can't–but it's a promise I'm in no place to make. Instead soften my eyes and offer him a reassuring smile, all the while silently praying that he abandons his ego for long enough to find out.

CHAPTER 30

I don't know how the hell I did it, or what the hell I said that got through to him, but on Tuesday the following week, Robbie is yelling down the phone to let me know that he spoke with his parents. Better yet, they've transferred ten thousand pounds into his bank account.

Ten thousand fucking pounds. Jesus wept.

I'm almost regretting encouraging him to open up to them. I forgot how offensively loaded they were. Seriously, for the most fleeting of moments, part of me regrets breaking up with him and shutting the door to a life of immense generational wealth. I quickly realise how horrific of a fate that would be, of course, but Jesus.

Robbie is demanding a night out with everyone in celebration of his newfound wealth, which while I acknowledge is an unmeasurably dreadful idea, it's going to happen regardless of my input. I'd rather be there to prevent any of Robbie's potential drunken slip ups about Preston's past. Besides, maybe I'm overreacting; sure, a night out with Robbie and Zack three years ago was total chaos, but Zack no longer exists, and Robbie has to have matured over the past three years.

It takes being in Preston's house barely a minute for me to realise how horrifically naive of an assumption that is.

I'm standing frozen in Preston's bedroom, the door clicking shut as I watch the scene unfolding in front of me. Preston's sitting in his desk chair, and he's tapping his foot with so much ferocity that he's on the verge of burning a hole through the floor while he chews at his fingernails. Robbie, on the other hand, is sitting on Preston's bed, his legs crossed and a rolled up bank note in his right hand. There's a closed textbook on the mattress in front of him, atop which is a credit card and a transparent packet of white powder.

'What the fuck are you doing?'

I don't address him directly, but I think it's pretty clear to Robbie that he's the target of my question. He's rubbing his nose with the back of his wrist as he looks up at me with that gratingly innocent look in his eyes. He sniffs, then rubs his nose again.

'I take it you don't want any then,' he says with a laugh like this is funny or something.

I flicker my eyes to Preston, but before I can even try to force his green eyes to meet mine, Robbie must notice me trying to do so.

'God, Mia, lighten up. It's fine! He didn't use—You used paracetamol or some shit, right? Not coke or anything like that,' he asks, glancing at Preston, then rounds the shitshow up with, 'when you tried to kill yourself, I mean.'

I stare at Robbie in stunned silence. Is he fucking stupid? Can he hear himself? Does he have any idea what the hell he even just said?

'Are you actually this fucking dull?'

'Mia, it's fine. Don't—'

'No, Preston, it's not. It's not fine. He needs to leave your house—he needs to leave London. Now.'

Robbie's watching us, wide-eyed. Or maybe that's just the cocaine.

He stammers. 'Sorry, it's—I didn't mean to be offensive. I just meant this won't, like, trigger him or anything, right? Because it's not got anything to do with—'

'I swear to god, Robbie, shut up before I call the police.'

'No one's calling the police,' Preston utters, but still doesn't look at me.

'See. It's cool,' Robbie concludes, and Jesus Christ, this boy couldn't read between the lines if he drew them himself.

I wanted to so badly believe that he had his shit together. That, sure, he'd lost his job and wound up without a place to live, but he was trying to be better. Instead, he opts to throw Preston's grossly unnecessary generosity back in his face the second he no longer needs him.

Robbie nods sideways at Preston. 'He's not taken any, if that's what you're worried about,' he says, then lowers his voice to mutter, 'used to do it all the time, but he's too good for it now.'

Exactly! I want to scream. He used to do it when he was in a really dark place! That's the point! Robbie's glaringly insensitive comment regarding Preston's suicide attempt aside, I refuse to believe he's not clever enough to realise doing a class A drug in front of Preston is something that might be bad for his mental health.

I turn back to Preston, who finally meets my eyes, and my heart clenches as my stomach drops. He looks the worst he has since Robbie showed up, and I'm angry. I'm so fucking angry. This was meant to be good—Robbie getting the money to return to Cardiff and get the hell out of Preston's life was meant to be good, and this night is supposed to be a drunken mess at worst. Not this.

I want Preston to stand up for himself, to tell Robbie to get the hell out of his bedroom, out of his house, but one glance is enough to tell me why he doesn't. Why he hasn't. His eyes are glassy, as if there's an invisible barrier between us and him—between the rest of the world and him. He's disassociating.

'Robbie, can you give us five minutes, please?' I say, my attention still on Preston.

I try to keep my voice measured to stop him arguing, which works, but the lack of urgency in my tone must make him think there's no rush because he doesn't move an inch.

'Now, please,' I say through gritted teeth, then glance at him.

He lifts his hands defensively, mutters something under his breath, then grabs his cocaine—God forbid he forgets that—before jumping up to shove past me and leave the room. The second the door closes, I say Preston's name, but receive no response, so I tentatively tread towards him. Once I reach him, I bend down so that our faces are level, but he continues staring into space.

'Preston?' I try, but still nothing. 'Hey, let's go back to mine. Robbie can do whatever the fuck he wants to do tonight, and we'll just hang out at mine. Okay?'

Suddenly, Preston's shaking his head. 'No. No, I need to—I don't want him to say anything about Zack.'

'He won't,' I soothe, but I'm not convincing myself, let alone him. 'I really don't think going out is a good idea.'

'It's fine. I'm fine,' he replies, finally looking at me, and despite the distant gaze vanishing from his eyes, I've never believed anything less in my life.

I open my mouth to offer that I head out to keep an eye on Robbie while Preston stays home, but that alternative feels worse.

I scan Preston's pale face, his hooded eyes, his downturned lips. No, I can't leave him alone. There's no way I'm leaving him alone in this house tonight.

I sigh. 'Fine. We both go, but you don't leave my side.'

He doesn't answer me.

'Promise me, Preston,' I push.

Again, he doesn't answer, at least not verbally. Instead, he nudges his hand towards me and I take his signal to reach for it. With my fingers entwined in his, he squeezes—a silent promise.

As we join Robbie downstairs for pre-drinks, everything is eerily calm. Robbie's a little twitchy and won't shut up, I assume due to the class A drug swirling around his system, but he's sticking to his promise by not saying anything about Preston's past. It's quite impressive, in a roundabout sort of way. I'm not drinking, and nor is Preston, despite Robbie's insistence.

Preston sticks to his own promise, although I free him to use the bathroom; that would be a bit much. It's during his first bathroom visit that Margot approaches me while I'm downing a glass of water in the kitchen.

'Hey, so FYI,' she says as she stops to lean against the counter opposite me. 'Your ex just offered me cocaine.'

Ugh, he's like a fungus.

I faux bash my head backwards against a kitchen cabinet. 'Firstly, sorry. Secondly, can we remove that label and disassociate him from me completely?'

Margot laughs. 'Not my thing, but I think a few people have taken him up on the offer. Nice of him to hand it out for free, I guess.'

'Nice isn't quite how I'd put it,' I grumble. 'I'm really sorry about him staying here.'

'Eh. He's been fine, and besides, hardly your fault; he's Preston's guest,' she argues, then shrugs. 'And Preston did ask us if it was cool before letting him stay, although I'm getting the impression you would've preferred it if we'd said no.'

'Abso-fucking-lutely.'

Margot laughs, lifting her head to look at the ceiling as she does so.

'Is he alright, by the way?' she questions, glancing at the empty doorway, her voice quiet. 'Preston, I mean. It's just that he's see med... I don't know, stressed recently.'

How do I even try to answer that? I clearly don't answer quickly enough because Margot's talking again.

'Listen, it's—I know Preston's a super private person and every-thing, and there's obviously something not quite right between him and Robbie, and I just—If you or he ever need someone to talk to, I'm here, yeah?'

I flash her an apologetic look, then nod. 'I know. I know, and thank you.'

'But he's okay, yeah?' she tries again. 'Preston?'

I don't want to lie, so with another glance towards the kitchen doorway, I say, 'I've got everything handled, don't worry.'

I keep everything handled for the remainder of our pre-drinks, and keep handling things as we progress to the tube, and then to the club. Preston sticks to me the whole night, but I'm not sure he says more than a couple of words to anyone. I've got my uber social face on to try and distract anyone from realising that, but my smiles are wearing thin, my laughs turning more hollow with each one I force.

Through what I imagine is an entirely non-coincidental occur-rence, within five minutes of us entering the club, Robbie bumped into Dana. We've been here nearly half an hour, and he's spent the entirety of it dancing with her and talking into her ear. I'm at the bar for another glass of water with Preston in tow, and I take the opportunity to scope out his take on the whole thing.

'Does that bother you?' I shout over the music, then subtly point towards Robbie and Dana across the dancefloor.

'Does what bother me?' Preston asks without even pretending to look at where I'm pointing.

'Robbie and Dana.'

I gesture towards them again, but it's like Preston's running on a delay. He stares at my hand for a moment, then slowly turns to search the crowds.

'Oh,' he mutters, then shrugs.

I'm not sure he realises he still hasn't answered my question.

'So it doesn't?' I try.

'Them?' he asks as if he's only now joined our conversation, but I don't point that out—I just nod. He shrugs again. 'No. I hadn't noticed.'

I can't resist a short laugh. 'Don't tell him that; I'm pretty sure he's only doing it as some kind of show for you. I'm going to pull Dana aside to warn her at some—'

'Small world!'

I spin around at the sound of a familiar voice, my lips instinctively curving with a smile, only for that smile to fall flat when I realise who's now standing in front of me.

God, not now. Why is this happening now?

'I've literally never been to this place before! How weird is it that the one time I am, you guys are here?' Nick says with a laugh and possibly some malice, but frankly, I'm too exhausted to figure that out.

'Hey!' I reply with what I hope is matching enthusiasm. 'Yeah, pretty weird! We're just grabbing some drinks—Well, water because we're not drinking—but yeah.'

Preston says nothing. I glance up at him beside me, and I'm not convinced he even knows who Nick is.

'You celebrating anything in particular, or?' Nick continues. 'I guess not if you're on the H20.'

Celebrating Robbie Morrissey getting the fuck out of London, I think, but don't say.

'Just a night out,' I reply, brushing the air.

'Oh, nice. Cool.'

Holy shit, this is painful. Nick glances from me to Preston, and I'm praying—practically begging—for something to click in Preston's head to spur him into saying something. Just hello. Hi. Something.

'What about you?' I ask because I apparently want to elongate the pain.

'Mate's birthday,' he replies. 'No one you know, but yeah, it's his twenty-first so a bit of a mad one.'

'Sounds fun!'

'Yeah. Yeah, it's a good night so far.'

I'm going to smash a full bottle of vodka over my head. I swear to God, I'm going to jump over the bar, grab an unopened litre bottle of vodka, and slam it across my skull.

'Well, it's—Yeah, it was good to see you guys.'

He glances at Preston again, but nope. Still nothing.

'Yeah, good to see you, but yeah, it's—I better head back,' he continues. 'See you around!'

'Yeah, you too! Have a good rest of your night!' I say with a wave as he goes to turn away.

'Happy birthday to your friend,' Preston says, at last, and again, on an apparent ten second delay.

Nick pauses, glances between us one final time, then gives Preston a thanks before disappearing towards the dancefloor.

'You know, I'm starting to think this is my version of A Christmas Carol. Granted, I never thought it'd be set in a sweaty club in Clapham, but pretty sure that's all my ghosts of Christmas past cover–'

'I need the bathroom.'

My mouth is still open, the rest of my sentence hanging in the air as Preston turns away, and then he's suddenly walking with purpose in the direction of the club toilets. I nearly go after him, nearly call his name, but no. I need to chill out. The guy's allowed to use a bathroom.

I keep my eyes locked to the back of the room where the bathrooms are as I continue queuing for my water, only turning away briefly to order it. I didn't get a chance to ask Preston if he wanted one, but I order another in case he does, and turn back towards the bathrooms the second I've finished asking. I glance away from it one last time to grab the two cups of water, then move to the edge of the bar to wait for Preston.

The trouble is, Preston never appears.

CHAPTER 31

I don't understand how it's happened. I was watching the bathroom door the whole time. My back can't have been turned for longer than ten seconds while I was getting our drinks.

But then, it only takes ten seconds.

'Fuck,' I mutter as I place the plastic cups of water on the bar, then scramble through my small shoulder bag to fish out my phone. 'Fuck, fuck, fuck.'

I hit the call button on Preston's contact, but it rings out. I try again, and again, and again. Maybe he's with the others; he might not have realised I'd moved to the edge of the bar, might not have been able to spot me and returned to the others as a result. I lift myself onto my tip toes to scan the crowds packed onto the dancefloor, my eyes landing on Margot's blue hair after ten seconds or so.

Margot, Joe, Dana, Robbie...

I keep listing names, keep scanning faces, but he's not there. Preston is nowhere near anyone.

'Fuck,' I mutter again.

I try calling him one more time, and when I have no luck, I send a message questioning his whereabouts. I abandon the cups of water and force myself through dancing bodies to reach my friends–and Robbie–on the dancefloor.

'Have you seen Preston?' I call into Margot's ear, and she turns to me, her brow furrowed.

She's shaking her head. Fuck. No.

Without another word, I go to turn around, but Margot grabs my arm.

'Is everything okay?' she asks.

I don't know, I want to say. I really don't know.

Instead, I reply with, 'yeah! Totally cool! He said he was going to check if you guys wanted anything from the bar before going to the bathroom, but he must've gone straight there!'

I don't even know why I'm lying, if it's me clinging onto the final shreds of my ability to protect Preston's privacy, or if it's just some shoddy attempt to kid myself into believing what I'm saying is true.

As I go to leave the dancefloor, there's a hand on my arm again. I turn around expecting Margot, but it's Robbie's blue eyes that I meet.

'Not now!' I yell, yanking my arm away.

I push through groups of people singing and dancing, but he follows me.

'Mia! Wait!'

'What?' I snap, turning to face him in the middle of the dance-floor.

'I saw him leave!'

'Preston? You saw him go towards the exit?'

Robbie's nodding, but before I can dart towards the door leading to the club's lobby, he's shouting over the music again.

'He's obviously gone home; it's no big deal! It's not gonna kill you to spend five minutes apart from each other!'

'You don't get it, do you? You've got no fucking clue.'

I'm not sure I say it loudly enough for him to hear, but I don't care. I'm not even sure I wanted him to hear. I turn back towards the exit, then keep wrestling through the crowds until I reach the club's lobby. A quick scan of it tells me he's not here, so I move towards the only other direction he could've gone and leave the building.

The cold air hits me like a shockwave, and I wrap my arms around myself as I begin walking. Given I'm wearing a short, thin dress, it doesn't help. If I was capable of logic right now, I would've grabbed my jacket from the coat check on the way out.

'Preston!' I call into the crowded street.

I can barely hear my own voice among the drunken shouting and pulsing music of Clapham's high street, so if he's anywhere close, he's got no chance. I dart my head around in all directions, but it's so busy. It's too busy. He'd hate this—the crowds, the music, the shouting. I shut my eyes and take a deep breath.

Okay. He'd hate this, so where would he go?

Somewhere quiet. Somewhere that's out of the way. I turn back towards the club I just left and notice an alleyway beside it, one I'd walked past without noticing. It's a long shot, but Preston's still not responding to my calls or messages, and I've got no idea what else to try.

I spot him immediately. In hindsight, I don't know how I'm so certain it's him because it's dark, but I don't doubt for a second. He's sitting on the ground, his forehead resting on his knees, his hands in his hair, and his back against the wall of the club.

'Fuck,' I utter, then raise my voice as I hurry towards him. 'Preston!'

He doesn't even spare me a glance, and as I reach him, I realise he doesn't just have his hands in his hair. He's pulling at it, tugging harshly as if he's trying to tear it from his scalp.

It's much quieter here. While I can hear distant shouts echoing from people walking past the alleyway, we're deep enough into it to ignore them, and the music from the club is more of a thumping beat. I'm shivering, but I don't know if it's the cold or what I've stumbled into.

'Preston? Preston, hey.' I bend down in front of him, but he doesn't react, just keeps tugging his hair, his breath short and body shaking. 'I'm here, okay? I'm here.'

He's muttering, but I can't understand a word of it. I don't even know if he can hear me, if he's processing any of what I'm saying. Maybe it's fruitless, but I keep trying regardless.

'Can I help? Tell me what I can do to help.'

He starts shaking his head, but doesn't lift it from his knees or say anything beyond whatever he's mumbling under his breath. I don't know if me being here is making things worse, and maybe Robbie was right—maybe I should just learn to give him space.

But then I hear a strained, quiet 'please don't go.'

My heart lurches to my throat, but I try not to show it—try to keep my voice calm.

'I'm not going anywhere,' I promise.

He's shaking his head again, but he lowers his left hand from his hair, some strands of which are between his fingers, and inches it towards me. I take it, and he squeezes tightly, his body still shuddering but his breathing a little less erratic. He squeezes my hand so hard that it hurts, but I don't ask him to stop.

'I'm here,' I repeat. 'I'm here, and you're safe, okay?'

I keep promising him that I'm here, that I'm not going anywhere, but I've got no idea if it's helping. At the very least, it can't be making things worse because after another few minutes, Preston's breathing evens out, his grip on my hand eases, and his shaking has become more of a light trembling.

Finally, he lifts his head from his knees to rest it back against the bricks behind him, his eyes closed.

'Sorry,' he murmurs.

I'm shaking my head as I instinctively lean forward, but cut myself short in fear of overwhelming him. His response is to reach his arm out to pull me in, and he's so warm that it's a shock to my system, making me realise how cold I am. We sit together for a few minutes in silence, our arms wrapped around each other, my head on his chest as his heart races underneath it.

'Let's go home,' I murmur into his shirt, and I feel him nod above me.

I check that Preston's okay to stand, then check again, then again, by which point he's already on his feet. His light hair is dishevelled from where he was yanking at it, so I wordlessly reach up to smooth it down. I keep asking him questions—probably too many questions—about whether there's anything I can get him, or if he needs something to drink, or if he needs to stop for a minute, but he says no each time.

As we begin walking along the busy street, he takes my hand, gently stroking my thumb with his. I look up to see him watching our interlocked fingers, his lips slightly parted.

'Did I hurt you?' he asks quietly.

'No,' I assure him. 'No, I'm—'

'Hey! Guys!'

Oh, fuck off.

I release Preston's hand to spin on the spot, forcing a group of girls in short dresses to weave around me, throwing curses in my direction. I barely notice; I'm too busy shooting Robbie the harshest glare I can muster up as he jogs towards us. Preston has turned too, but his expression indicates nothing beyond indifference.

'Piss off, Robbie!' I hiss as he comes to a stop.

'I was just checking you found him,' he argues, nodding at Preston.

'Great. I did. Bye.'

With that, I turn back around, then take Preston's hand to continue walking in the direction of my flat and Preston's house. I'm convinced there's absolutely nothing Robbie can say that'll make me give him a slither more of my attention, but I should know better than to underestimate the extent of his bullshit.

'I know you guys are fucking!'

I turn back around to stare at him, and his pupils are wide, his straight hair styled out of place as he glares right back at me. I want to respond with, we haven't for about two weeks thanks to you, but I resist. He's approaching us again, and the strangers walking by are casting us intrigued glances. I'd rather not give Robbie's show an audience, so I grab his arm and yank him aside.

'Doesn't bother me,' he says once we're out of the way. 'But just an FYI. I know, so no need act all secretive for my sake. It's pretty fucking obvious.'

I continue glaring as I wrap my arms around myself again, but it doesn't stop the goosebumps springing up. I run through every retort in my head, every insult I could throw, every denial. Only, Preston beats me to it.

'Are you done?'

His voice is loud, but he's not shouting, and it brings both Robbie and me to a stark silence. I can feel my pulse in my ears, my body still shivering with cold despite the adrenaline. Robbie stammers, then clamps his mouth shut. He opens it again, his gaze suddenly coy as he looks his feet.

Finally, he mutters, 'yeah. Sorry.'

'Good,' Preston replies, then looks at me with a double-take before murmuring, 'your jacket.'

Before I can question him, he's walking back towards the club. I hurry after him, but for the second time tonight, I'm stopped by Robbie's hand on my arm. I swivel around to face him, my teeth gritted, a hiss to demand he lets go on the tip of my tongue when he cuts in first.

'He's in love with you. You know that, right?'

Within the blink of an eye, my glare becomes a blank stare, and I'm stammering.

'That's not—No, we're—Look, you're right, okay? Congrats. We've been sleeping together, but that's it. It's not—It's nothing like that between us.'

'You might wannna tell him that.'

I don't even know where to begin with a response, so I just stare at him. Again.

He releases dry laugh. 'He's gotten further with you than I ever did, so good for him, I guess. It's how it's always been, right? He's always been at least one step above me, right?'

God, this is petty. This is so fucking petty. Does he hear himself?

'If you seriously think he has it easy—has ever had it easy—then you're actually delirious.'

'I'm just saying,' he argues. 'Zack's always been better than me, so I might as well stop—'

'Preston,' I snap back.

'Fucking hell. Whatever!'

'He didn't just change his name for a laugh, you know,' I point out. 'He was so traumatised after killing Matty's father and lying about it for years that he tried to kill himself, Robbie. He willingly chose prison over maintaining the charade. Can you please try—just try—to comprehend that for more than ten seconds?'

Robbie's hardened jaw relaxes, and he looks at the floor again. 'I didn't come here to fuck with him, alright?' He lifts his head back up. 'I just—I needed somewhere to stay, and for years, he was—I thought he was my best friend. We did everything together, and I told him shit I've never told anyone else. That was all bullshit—our entire friendship wasn't real; I get that now, okay? And I'm not gonna stand here and pretend that didn't fuck with me, but I didn't know where else to go.'

I sigh, closing my eyes for a moment. He should've gone to his parents first; it never should've come to this, but I get it. I do get it.

'This isn't good for either of you,' I reply as I glance over Robbie's shoulder to see Preston returning with my jacket, so before he reaches us, I add, 'for what it's worth, he genuinely cared about you back then. He does genuinely care about you.'

Robbie's nodding, his blue eyes refusing to meet mine, as Preston stops to my right and hands me my jacket. I thank him as I pull it on, and as we're about to turn away, Robbie stops us.

'I'm sorry,' he says, and he's looking at Preston. 'Really, I am.'

I flicker my eyes up to Preston's face with no real idea of what to expect, but I don't know why I bother—as always, I can't read him.

Then, in a quiet voice—timid even—he says, 'I am too.'

Robbie offers him a small smile, one that almost looks sad, then turns away to walk in the direction of the club until he disappears into the crowds.

CHAPTER 32

I find out through Margot.

She doesn't even say hello when I answer her call two days after Robbie's club night, just, 'you've heard, right?'

The tone of her voice is completely off. Wrong. I stand from my desk chair, abandoning the assignment that I was working on.

'Heard what?'

Silence over the phone.

'Heard what?' I repeat.

'I assumed—Shit, sorry, I should've called last night when Joe asked me about it. I just—I dismissed it, thinking it was some weird rumour or something, but it—Preston confirmed it, all of it, when I asked him just now.'

I still have zero context, no real indication towards what Margot is talking about, but I know. Somehow, I know exactly what she's talking about. Exactly what's happened.

'His life before London,' I murmur, more so to myself.

Another pause, then a soft, quiet, 'yeah.'

'How?'

I give as little context as she did, but Margot also somehow knows what I'm asking.

'I've got no idea. Joe overheard some girls talking about it in one of his seminars, but I don't know how they found out. Joe's sure they don't even know Preston, and then in my lectures today, people were talking about it. He's on our course, right, so not as weird, I guess, but yeah, anyway, I asked Preston when I got home—he didn't show up to any classes today,' she rambles. 'And he—Yeah, he said it was all true.'

'He just said it outright? Like, casually, or what?'

'Yeah, super casually.' She lowers her voice. 'Honestly, he's been acting weird since Robbie left. That's why I called; I really don't think he's, I don't know... coping, I guess.'

Since Robbie left.

I'm going to kill him. I'm going to fucking kill him. After what we talked about, after Preston housed him, after everything, he does this? I take a deep breath because if I don't, I'll scream.

'Acting weird?' I question. 'In what way.'

Margot hesitates again.

'Honestly, kind of like a dick.'

No. No, no, no. This is bad. This is really bad.

I'm not entirely sure what I expect when I turn up to Preston's house fifteen minutes later. I had an idea; I assumed Preston would be locked away in his room, that maybe Joe, Margot and I would spend time speaking in hushed whispers with me maybe answering any questions they have. Either way, I thought I'd have to spend at least ten minutes outside Preston's door trying to convince him to let me in.

However, when Margot walks me into their living area, he's there. Standing over a kitchen counter blasting music, a beer in front of him as he types into his phone while Joe cooks on the hob to his right.

'For what do I owe the pleasure?' Preston asks as I enter, but barely looks at me.

He doesn't avoid meeting my eyes in a coy way; more like he doesn't want to exert the effort. He's talking normally, at least. Like Preston. That's a good sign, right?

'I wanted to talk to you,' I reply, then add, 'in private.'

'Ominous,' he says with a snorted laugh.

Why is he making this difficult? I glance at Margot, who shrugs awkwardly. Preston, however, remains reeking of indifference.

'Preston?' I try, and this time he turns to face me, his eyebrows raised expectantly as he leans sideways against the counter with crossed arms.

I try to tell him with my eyes, try to plead with him to stop whatever the hell this is and follow me upstairs. He sees it; he must be able to read me because he always knows what I'm thinking, but he gives nothing of the sort away. Not immediately, at least.

'I take it this is about the murder, suicide, prison etcetera public broadcast, no?' he says, his expression void of emotion.

I catch Joe's eyes widen via his side profile, and I start stuttering.

'Either that,' Preston continues, 'or you're here for another fuck, but I suspect that's unlikely based on the vibe you're giving off.'

'P, c'mon, don't be a dick,' Margot interjects, but Preston just turns back to the counter with a laugh.

I feel sick. I feel physically sick. Why would he say that? Why would he reveal what's been happening between us in front of everyone? Why would he–

Fuck.

Robbie told everyone about us, didn't he? Spilling the details of Preston's past just wasn't enough for him. He had to go all the way. My throat is closing up, my face flushing hot, my hands turning clammy.

No, I'm not going to let Preston do this. I'm not going to let him fall back down a hole he worked so hard to close.

'Upstairs,' I say–No, demand this time. 'Now.'

Instead of laughing or smirking, this time, he rolls his eyes, grabs his beer, then storms out of the kitchen.

'Come on, then,' he mutters as he shoves past me.

I flash Margot and Joe an apologetic look, then follow him upstairs and into his bedroom.

'I know this is horrible, and I know you're hurting, but you need to stop this,' I say as his bedroom door closes behind us. 'I'm not letting this happen.'

'I didn't realise you were so omnipresent,' he replies as he drops into his desk chair. 'Or influential, for that matter.'

'Preston, stop.'

I await another retort, but Preston just watches me as he leans back in his chair, then stretches his legs out. He's sipping at his beer bottle, his eyes vacant of any shred of vulnerability, his posture lax. Above all else, he looks bored.

'We can deal with this, okay? We'll figure it out,' I say gently. 'You can't resort to Zack, not after everything.'

He scoffs. 'I'm not doing that.'

'In all but name, you are.'

He's staring at me again, challenging me with his deep, green eyes that are usually so comforting, but now feel unnervingly unfamiliar.

'You're drinking, you're acting rude, you're being totally inconsiderate of anyone's feelings, and you're swanning around like you couldn't give a single fuck about anything,' I list. 'It has Zack written all over it.'

'You're being paranoid,' he says with an eye roll, then tilts his head. 'Is that all? I'm heading out soon and you're really killing the mood.'

I frown. 'Heading out? Where?'

'Some girl's flat party in Battersea.'

'Some girl? Who?'

He shrugs. 'Someone I met last night.'

I furrow my brow. 'Last night? Where?'

'Jesus, why the twenty questions? At a club.'

I blink.

'You were out last night? Like, drinking? And you're going out again tonight?'

'Yes, Mia.'

'No.'

'No?' He shakes his head, laughing. 'You're funny; I'll give you that. Feel free to join, by the way. You seem like you need it.'

I don't want to join. The last thing I want to do is spend a night with a bunch of strangers while I watch Preston spiral further into the hell he's self-inflicting. I chew the inside of my cheeks. The issue is that if I don't go, there won't be anyone to stop him doing something stupid.

I lift my chin, then with a shrug, say, 'sure. Sounds good.'

For the first time since I walked into his house, Preston cracks. It's brief, so brief that I nearly miss it, but his jaw momentarily hardens. Within seconds, he's smirking, but it's too little too late. I've already caught him.

He didn't think I'd accept his offer.

Ten minutes later, we're leaving, and Preston's expertly maintaining his careless facade. He's downed another beer, and has spent the entire time blasting offensively loud drum and bass music. He shuts down all of my attempts to talk seriously about what's happened, usually with some comment akin to loosen up.

I can see right through him. It's astounding, actually, how easily I can read him when he's like this. He's trying to wind me up, to piss me off so that I leave, to stop me from joining him at this stupid party. To make me give up on him.

I don't even question him when, on the way to our bus stop, he stops at a corner shop to buy a packet of cigarettes. Our bus is six minutes away, so he lights one up as we wait.

'Want one?' he asks, gesturing the packet towards me.

I want to strangle you, I think, but say, 'I'm good, thanks.'

He shrugs, then returns the packet to his pocket before taking a long drag. I watch with gritted teeth as he exhales, a burst of smoke filling the space between us.

'Have you spoken to Robbie about why the fuck he did this?' I ask.

I expect another loosen up, but Preston surprises me with, 'he said it wasn't him.'

I scoff. 'And you just believed him?'

He responds with a shrug as he stares at the road opposite us, then murmurs, 'what difference does it make? It's happened. It doesn't matter.'

I stare at Preston's side profile in disbelief as I shake my head. 'I'm not going to let him off that easily.'

Preston's lips twitch upwards as he brings his cigarette to them, and by the time he's blowing out the smoke, he's doing it through laughter. Nothing's funny–none of what's happening is funny–but he keeps laughing. He glances at me, and something about my face must be really bloody hilarious because he laughs harder.

I don't satisfy him with a response, just hold my breath in an attempt to avoid his secondhand smoke. It's not until our bus is slowing to a stop that he says anything to me, and when he does, it's irrelevant.

'You're familiar with the playwright, George Bernard Shaw, I presume?'

With that, he steps forward and hops onto the bus without waiting for my answer. I never give him one, not even once we've found two seats because I'm not playing his games, not tonight. Within an hour of entering the party, which is a flat located on the tenth floor of a high-rise, I discover Preston isn't just testing me. He's trying to drive me towards committing arson.

I'm sitting on a sofa at the back of the large, crowded living room as some irritating, mulleted modern art student spouts shit into my ears about the Renaissance or whatever. Preston, on the other hand, disappeared into a girl's bedroom—the girl who invited him here, I assume, or certainly hope—about twenty minutes ago.

'Who do you know here?' Renaissance guy asks, and I wish he'd shut up.

'No one,' I reply, my voice devoid of emotion. 'I came with a friend.'

'Oh, cool. Which friend? I might know her,' he replies, then clearly fishing, adds, 'or him.'

'You won't.'

Please fuck off.

'What's their name?'

'Preston.'

The dark-haired stranger, whose name he either hasn't given me or I wasn't paying attention when he did, widens his eyes. I stare at him expectantly, daring him to say something.

It's not even a good mullet. A total hack job.

'That third year student who, like, murdered his dad, then had to take two years out of uni to go to prison? That's–'

'Who told you about that?' I interrupt.

Rumors have legs, and of course people are flourishing the truth as they see fit. I'm digging my fingernails into my palms, my blood boiling with something between rage and despair.

'Some guy on my course,' Renaissance guy replies, then asks, 'is it true?'

Some guy on your course needs to mind his own business.

'He was thirteen. It wasn't his dad, it was a young offender's institute, and it was manslaughter, not murder. Convicted murderers don't get out of prison after two years, you fucking idiot.'

Without waiting for a response, I stand abruptly and shove my way through a group of people standing above the sofa.

I find the girl before I find Preston. I've been free from Renaissance guy for about ten minutes, and she's leaving the bathroom as I'm waiting to go in. Her top is inside out.

'You top,' I say, nodding towards the label at the bottom of it, and she stops in her tracks.

She glances down, then throws her head back with a laugh as she thanks me. Then, with zero warning, she grabs my hand and pulls me into the small bathroom with her. Within moments, and without locking the door, she's pulling her tight tank top over her brunette head.

'Mia, right?' she asks me, now topless and braless.

I'm trying to keep my eyes on her face as I sigh, then say, 'yeah.'

'I'm Sophie,' she beams.

I just want to pee.

She's flipped her top around so that it's no longer inside out, and she's shoving it over her head as she continues chatting.

'You and Preston aren't some serious thing, right?' she asks once she's done. 'He said you're not, but I wanted to make sure.'

That's nice of her, I figure. I also figure she's familiar with the Preston and me hooking up part of his recently revealed history.

'Nope.'

She's nodding. 'Phew, good! He's a great fuck, right?'

Yep. Definitely heard that part of the rumour.

'I've got a thing for bad boys, but they're all talk, no action ninety-nine percent of the time, right? Usually shit in bed.'

Please stop talking.

She's laughing again as she combs her fingers through her curled hair, then checks the bathroom mirror to wipe some mascara from underneath her eyes.

'Can I be honest with you?'

I want to beg her not to be, but I concede with a, 'sure.'

'You're hot.'

Admittedly not what I was expecting. Oddly complimentary, though.

She meets my eyes in the mirror as she continues. 'If you're into this kind of thing, I think the three of us could have a lot of fun.'

I have to physically strain myself into swallowing a laugh—a sort of deranged, hopeless laugh. Instead of laughing, I politely decline Sophie's offer.

'We'll probably be in my bedroom for most of the night, so if you change your mind, just knock.'

After that perfectly normal conversation, Sophie leaves and I lock the door behind her.

Preston and I don't leave the party until four in the morning. One thing Zack never did was stay overnight at a girl's place, so at least this new version of him is consistent. I've got no doubt Preston staying so late was another failed attempt to force me into surrendering, to give up on him.

As we're leaving the high-rise, I say, 'Sophie asked me for a threesome with you.'

He snorts beside me. 'You should've said yes.'

'I'd have sooner thrown myself out of one of those tenth floor windows.'

He shrugs. 'Speak for yourself.'

'Can you drop the act, please? For five minutes,' I interject before he's even finished spouting his bullshit. 'You're trying to piss me off so that I give up on you, and it's getting old.'

'I'm not doing anything,' he hits back, just as quickly.

We're upping our pace as we stride along the Thames, as if we're racing each other, trying to force the other to fold first.

'Right. Okay. So if I'd enthusiastically responded to Sophie with a sure! I'd love to! Sign me up! and then just appeared with her raring and ready to go, you would've been all for it?'

'Yes.'

'I don't believe you.'

'Is this your way of telling me you don't want to fuck when we get back?'

'You're being ridiculous!' I snap, coming to a sudden halt.

I spin around to face him, and he's close—he's standing directly in front of me, barely inches between us, and it's horrible. It's so fucking horrible because despite everything, despite what's happened, the way he's behaving, the crude conversation we've tripped into, I have an insatiable urge to kiss him. It's like I'm begging for him—the real him, not whoever this is—to break through the surface.

He holds my gaze, his lips quirking into a smirk. He's challenging me again; all he's done tonight is challenge me—dared me to break.

'Talk to me, Preston,' I whisper. 'Stop playing this character and talk to me.'

Realising he's been unsuccessful once again, Preston turns away. He doesn't glance back at me as he starts walking along the river, but he's laughing. That dry, empty laugh. I drag my feet after him as he pulls a cigarette from his pocket and lights it, the flame briefly illuminating his face with an orange glow. He's still laughing, still well ahead of me.

'It is a curious sensation!' he calls into the black sky, then turns on his heel to jut his cigarette towards me. 'The sort of pain that goes mercifully beyond our powers of feeling. When your heart is broken, your boats are burned: nothing matters any more.'

'Preston, what are you–'

'It is the end of happiness and the beginning of peace!' He lifts his head to the sky again, then lowers it to meet my eyes. 'George Bernard Shaw.'

CHAPTER 33

It's been over a week since the story of Preston's past spread through UCL like a virus, and in a lot of ways, it's old news. Most of the rumour spreading has occurred online, and it's mainly been constrained to other third year students. People are finally starting to move on, but the damage has been done. Preston's still behaving like some evolved version of Zack.

I've been out with him another two times—both to night-clubs—and he's spent the entirety of those times testing me like he did with the flat party. If he wasn't so intent on pissing me off to the point of no return, I doubt I'd see so much as an invitation to these nights out. According to Margot, he's spent every other night out of their house, not returning until the early hours of the morning. I guess I wasn't invited to those ones.

The first thing I did the morning after the flat party was call Aiden. He couldn't help—I knew there was no way he could fix everything—but I didn't know what else to do. He tried reaching out to Preston, but wasn't even honoured with a response. He's travelled to London for the weekend, and we're in my bedroom with Margot trying to set out a plan for some kind of Preston-based intervention.

It still feels like nothing short of a miracle that Margot didn't tell me—and Preston, for that matter—to fuck off after everything came out, let alone that she's being so understanding about it all. She'd asked me multiple times if he and I were a thing since that first house party, and I always assured her we weren't. She could've easily been pissed at me for not telling her about that changing over Easter and summer, but she wasn't—she isn't. She just desperately wants to help.

The trouble is that I was hoping our meeting would inspire hope, that talking things through with Aiden and Margot would make me realise that we can fix this. If anything, it's making a solution seem impossible. Every resolution offered, every suggestion, every seed of an idea feels too small.

They don't realise how complex of a thing this is to navigate—how complex Preston is to navigate—not even Aiden, not really. Given one of his suggestions was for me to corner Preston after sleeping with him in, quote, a sneak attack at his most vulnerable, I'm not exactly sure Aiden's our idea guy anyway. Even if that wasn't a dreadful suggestion, mine and Preston's relationship has been entirely platonic since Robbie showed up, so it wouldn't be an option.

While Margot's sitting on my bed, Aiden's slowly spinning on my desk chair—it helps his thinking process, apparently—and I'm sitting on my floor between them, my back against my bedroom wall.

'It just—It feels hopeless,' I interrupt them mid-conversation, and they pause to look at me inquisitively. 'He won't listen. He won't even try to.'

'If we literally lock him in a room, he won't have any choice,' Aiden argues, but I'm already shaking my head.

'He'll ignore us.' I sigh. 'Maybe it's just time. Maybe he needs to get this out of his system and–'

I'm cut short by a knock on my bedroom door. With a grunt–my flatmates know I'm busy–I jump to my feet and answer it, poised and ready to ask whichever one of them it is to go away. Only, it's not a flatmate.

'Nick?'

It's like I'm questioning his existence, not just his sudden appearance at my place. I stare at Nick in my doorway, as well-dressed and as clean as always, and I'm sure he's a mirage. I glance back into the room to see Margot and Aiden looking equally as perplexed, then turn back to Nick standing in my doorway.

Not now. Whatever the hell it is, not now.

'Sorry, it's–This isn't a good ti–'

'I just need five minutes,' he interrupts, his tone verging on pleading.

'We're in the middle of some–'

'It's about Preston.'

Within five minutes, Aiden and Margot have been relegated to the kitchen while I sit on my bed as Nick stands above me. I did offer him a seat, but he refused. He's fidgeting–frequently running his fingers through his dark hair–so I figure he's too full of energy to keep still.

'If you're about to ask me if the rumors are true,' I begin, not bothering to hide the dryness in my tone. 'Tell me which version you've heard and I'll–'

'I did it,' he blurts.

I frown. 'Did what?'

'Told people. I told people about it–about Preston's past.'

I laugh. Has he lost his mind? That's literally impossible. Does he mean he heard it from someone else, then spread the rumour further? Because I sure as hell never told him a thing about Preston's history, nor does he have any way of knowing we started sleeping together after he and I broke up.

'I didn't tell you about any of that,' I point out.

He scratches the back of his head as he grimaces. 'No, it's–I overheard it. Eavesdropped, if I'm being totally honest because you weren't being loud or anything. The night–Remember that night I bumped into you guys in Clapham?'

I nod, my eyes narrowed.

'I was waiting outside the club for some mates, and you–I saw you talking to someone. Some guy you know from home, I'm assuming by his accent, but yeah, not important. I Googled it–what I overheard–and found stuff online about Preston. An article, some old social media posts–that kind of thing.'

'What?' I say, my voice barely audible.

'I feel bad–I've felt really bad about it because that's really personal stuff, obviously, and in hindsight, I was just being bitter. I didn't think it would spread that much. I only told a few people–some of the people I saw you guys with, and some I was with, but it–I don't know, it became much bigger...'

Nick keeps talking. I know he keeps talking because his mouth is moving, but I can't hear him over the buzzing in my head that's getting louder by the second.

It wasn't Robbie.

Not just generally throughout that night, but during the conversation Robbie and I had outside the club, he didn't say anything explicit about Preston's past. I did. This–all of this–isn't Robbie's fault. It's not even Nick's.

It's mine.

Preston is no longer talking to me.

He's not replying to my messages or answering my calls, and all of my attempts to visit him in person have failed. He's rarely home anymore according to Margot, and when he is, he locks himself in his room, sometimes by himself, sometimes with people—usually girls—she doesn't recognise. She only ever sees him leaving for and returning from lectures when he actually bothers to go, and always declines her offers to sit together at said lectures.

It goes without saying that he's dropped off the face of the earth when it comes to Typewriter Magazine. Dana approached me about it—about the rumors—at the first meeting without him, and I thought she was going to be angry. With him, maybe, for not telling her anything about his past. At me, or maybe at both of us, for jumping into bed together. She wasn't angry; she was just worried.

Preston's not ignoring me because of what I've done; he still doesn't know this is all my fault. I don't want to tell him over a text message—I can't tell him something like that over a cold, digital screen—and he's not given me any chances to tell him in person, or even over the phone. I can only assume the radio silence is a result of him realising that there's no way I'm going to give up on him, no matter how many shitty things he says or does in my presence.

It's not just me who's fallen victim to Preston's avoidance tactics, either. Rhys has reached out asking me if everything is okay with Preston because he's not responded to any of the recent messages he sent him. I didn't know what to tell him, so ended up apologising on Preston's behalf with a vague he can get like this sometimes. Anwen's checked in with me too. Preston's not visited home since everything kicked off, and the excuse he's given is being busy with uni, but she doesn't believe him.

I couldn't lie to Anwen, but I couldn't reveal what's happened when Preston would clearly rather her not know. I wound up striking an awkward balance of vaguely admitting to her that he's having a difficult time, but essentially begged her to please not worry. That in itself felt like a lie; maybe she should be worrying. I am.

I know this is all going to come to a head, that it's going to get worse before it gets better, that he can't keep this act up forever. He's going to crash, but when he does, I'll be here.

It happens sooner than I'd expected, honestly.

It's early December, and the Zackification of Preston has been going on for about five weeks when I get another call from Margot. I don't know how I know—it's like there's something intrinsic swirling around my bloodstream that alerts me to every move Preston makes—but I immediately know what she's about to say.

'He's started isolating himself, hasn't he?' I say.

'It's been three days,' she confirms, then stammers as she rambles an elaboration. 'He's not left his room for three days. He's not even bringing strangers around anymore. I know he's in there—in his room—because I've heard him moving around and he's playing music, but he won't open his door to me.'

My chest is starting to feel tight, my legs becoming shaky, and before I'm consciously aware of myself doing it, I start searching my room for a jacket.

'He's not answering my texts either. He's not turned up to any lectures this week, and it's—I don't know what he's eating. His shelf in the fridge is empty, and his cupboard stuff hasn't been touched all week. I don't know how he's eating.'

He's not, I think as I shove my shoes on. Moments later, I'm leaving my flat.

When I arrive at Preston's house, what I find is exactly as Margot described. There's no sign of Preston's presence anywhere in the communal areas; it's as if he doesn't live here, as if he's never lived here. There are no personal items, no clothes, no shoes—nothing that belongs to him.

Margot's picking at her acrylic nails as I ascend the staircase leading to Preston's bedroom. She's staying at the bottom of it to give us—give him—space. She was right about the music too. It's quiet, but the sound of classical music is seeping from his door. I take a sharp breath as I stop outside it, then give it a light knock.

'Preston?' I try.

Nothing.

I glance down at Margot, who's chewing on her lip.

'Preston, it's Mia,' I try again.

Still nothing. In fact, I'm sure I hear the music's volume creep up. It doesn't deter me. I knock again, and again, and again. I wait for so long, knocking and calling his name, that Margot eventually retreats to the ground floor.

An hour after my first knock, I'm sitting on the carpet outside his bedroom, my back against the wall and his door to my right.

'I'm not going anywhere until you answer me,' I call through the wood, then sigh. 'I just need to know that you're okay. You don't have to open the door or even say anything—just text, if you want. But I'm not leaving until you tell me you're okay.'

I wait. Still nothing. I wait longer—another hour—and still nothing. Margot has brought me a serving of her dinner, alongside a gentle suggestion to concede and join her downstairs, but I decline the offer. I eat the food outside Preston's door, then wait another hour, and another, and another.

It's creeping close to eleven o'clock, and I'm practically falling asleep, my head resting sideways against Preston's door as I knock it. I'm knocking out of habit by this point, as if I've been pro-grammed to do it and this is my default setting. Margot's practi-cally begged me to give up, or at least take a break, but I won't.

I don't realise I'm dosing until my leg vibrates. I startle awake to scramble for my phone in the pocket of my jeans, and I squint at my screen. It's a text message from Preston, and all it contains is a single comma.

I take a deep breath, then exhale the most enormous sigh of relief I think I ever have. I reply immediately, demanding that he text me the same thing every single morning so that I know he's okay, and I've got no idea if he will because he doesn't send anything back. At eight o'clock the next morning, however, I re-ceive another message from him containing nothing but a comma. I receive that same text message at the same time every day that follows, give or take a few minutes.

Until one Tuesday morning, I don't.

CHAPTER 34

I arrive at Preston's house at twenty past eight, and maybe I'm overreacting. Only ten minutes had passed without his text message before I left my flat, but it's never that late; he's never sent it later than three minutes past the hour. It sure as hell is never twenty minutes late.

I don't realise that my knocking has woken Margot until she's already ushered me into the house. I'm asking her when the last time she heard anything from Preston was, and she's squinting back at me as she yawns between words, her blue hair yanked into a dishevelled ponytail. I apologise for waking her, or at least I think I do—I definitely intend to—before racing up the three flights of stairs to reach Preston's room.

There's no music. There's always music.

I'm knocking like my life depends on it, but it's to no avail. I try calling him, but he doesn't pick up the phone. As eight-thirty approaches, I stop being polite and just try to open the door, but it's locked. Margot's watching me from the bottom of the stairs, now fully alert as she picks at her nails.

I don't know what to do. What the hell do I do?

'Preston,' I say through the door, and I'm trying to hide the panic in my voice, but I can't imagine it's very convincing. 'If you don't let me in within the next five minutes, I'm going to call emergency services.'

It takes barely ten seconds for my phone to vibrate with a message.

Fine go away

I blink at Preston's message. No. No, there's something wrong. He doesn't text like that. Not in incomplete sentences with awkward grammar and no punctuation. It's like he rushed it, or had no energy to exert anything very sensical—just the bare minimum to get me to stop.

I take a deep breath, then shut my eyes as I say, 'you need to talk to me, okay? You don't have to let me in, if you don't want, but you need to talk to me.'

I glance down at Margot, whose eyes are wide as she whispers, 'is he okay? Did he message you?'

Okay feels too uncertain, so I reply with, 'yeah, he messaged.'

Relief visibly flashes through Margot's face, and I wish the level of my own relief could match hers. She remains at the bottom of the stairs as I knock again.

'I'm going to call emergency services otherwise, okay?'

It got a text message out of him the first time, so I figure a second threat might prompt him into speaking. I's not an empty threat, either. I will call them. I wait a few seconds, but nothing, then another few. Still no sound from him.

Just as I'm about to call through the door again, there's a click. It takes me a moment to realise what it is, or maybe I just don't believe what my ears tell me. But no, he's unlocked the door. I stare at the white wood for a few seconds, then reach for the handle before hesitating.

'Can I come in?'

Silence. I wait a minute.

'I'm coming in, okay?'

I lower Preston's bedroom door handle as I glance back to Margot one last time, and she responds with a small, encouraging smile. In a lot of ways, what I open the door to find is what I expected.

The blinds are drawn and there aren't any lights on, nor are any of the candles illuminated. Once my eyes adjust to the darkness, I can see that the room's a mess. Preston's books are strewn across the floor, similar to the morning of my birthday, and there are clothes discarded in a similarly chaotic fashion. There are some empty food cartons dotted around, but not enough—nowhere near enough for nearly two weeks. The air feels heavy—it's stuffy—and I suspect the window hasn't been cracked open once throughout the time he's locked himself in here.

He's lying in his bed with the duvet bundled around him, his back to me, and he doesn't turn around at the sound of me entering the room. The bedding is too bunched up for me to catch a glimpse of his face, but I know he's awake because he unlocked his door barely two minutes ago.

'Preston?' I try as I tentatively approach him, manoeuvring around the mess on the floor.

He ignores me.

As his face comes into view, I can see that his eyes are open lazily, as if he's exerting all his effort into not letting them close. I don't know what he's looking at because the only thing in his direct field of vision is a washing basket piled full of unwashed clothes. I'm not sure he's looking at anything at all, not really. I've never seen him with this much facial hair either. It's darker than I imagined it would be.

'Hey,' I say gently.

I get nothing back, not even a glance, or a flicker of an eyelid.

I keep walking until I'm standing over him, then lower myself to the floor to sit beside his head. At that, finally, Preston rewards me with a reaction—the reaction being him closing his eyes, but it's something.

'You didn't message me,' I murmur.

I don't know why of all things I could say, that's what I choose to go with. Even if I'd said something else, I don't think his response would've been any different.

'You've seen I'm fine. You can leave now,' he mutters, his eyes still closed.

'I think we have very different definitions of fine.'

His jaw ticks. He can act as annoyed as he wants; I'm not going.

'You're not eating,' I say, and he grunts.

Again, I'm not sure why that's what I say.

'Are you taking your medication?'

'I'm fine, Mia.'

That's a no, then.

He doesn't even sound angry anymore, just tired. He's holding the duvet just below his chin, and I don't know what, nor do I really know how I know, but he's hiding something. Upon realising I'm clearly not leaving, Preston opens his eyes. I offer him my hand, but he just stares at it. I don't move it away, though.

As I glance down at my hand, I notice a speck—the tiniest, misshapen circle of a speck—on a section of the cream sheet not covered by the duvet. Its reddish-brown colour tells me every-thing I need to know. My stomach drops, my chest tightens, and my head is suddenly spinning, but I force my expression to remain even.

'Preston, let me see your arms.'

'It's fine.'

It's not fine. None of this is fine, and he knows it's not. The tightness in my chest has spread to my throat, so much so that every breath I take aches.

'I'm still not beyond calling emergency services,' I threaten for the third time.

He doesn't even bother with a response this time, just sighs. To make it as clear as possible that I'm not fucking with him, I reach into my jeans pocket to pull out my phone. That does the trick.

'Don't.'

I expect him to be short, for his voice to be filled with irritation, but it's not. It sounds strained, like he's begging.

He sighs again, closing his eyes as he murmurs, 'it looks worse than it is.'

Before I can question his claim or try to argue, he shuffles on the mattress. I watch silently as he shrugs the duvet off his shoulders—not too much, just enough for him to slide his right hand into my view. More dark splotches have appeared on the mattress, and there's a slither of relief when I realise there are no big pools of anything, although some are still wet.

'I had a difficult night, that's all,' he mumbles.

I take his hand, take it so gently that I'd swear it was made of china, and ease his arm towards me. He doesn't resist. He just lets me, his eyes unfocused but facing the general direction of his washing basket again.

I try not to react, but it's not easy.

There's a deep gash on the underside of his wrist, and it's too wet with fresh blood to make out if he used something to create it, or if he's just clawed at his skin that severely. The rest of his arm is covered in thin scratches, some red and angry, some scabbed over. Some have existed long enough to have healed. I don't even think–I just reach for his other hand and pull it towards me. There's no gash on this one, but it's otherwise a similar story.

I try to keep my breath even, despite the anxiety-induced nausea swirling in the pit of my stomach.

'Is this–Have you done anything else? Have you taken anything?' I try not to ask the last question with urgency, but fail miserably.

'No.'

'Promise me.'

He sighs. 'I promise.'

I watch him carefully, in part hoping that if he's lying to me, the silence might draw a confession.

He must sense my uncertainty because this time, with conviction, he repeats, 'I promise, Mia.'

I nod slowly, and only just about manage to stop my voice from breaking as I say, 'I'm going to get something to clean this up, okay?'

He gives me the smallest nod back, his eyes remaining distant.

As I stand and begin treading towards his doorway, I hesitate. What if he locks the door behind me? What if he does something to himself–something worse–once my back is turned? I can't leave this room. I open his door to glance outside, and okay. Good. Margot's still at the bottom of the stairs, and she jumps to her feet once she spots me.

'Hey, is he–'

'Can you get me some–some tissues, or a clean cloth or something? Whatever you have. Please,' I interrupt her. 'And fill a bowl with some water? It's–He's got a cut that needs cleaning up.'

I don't give further context because I've already aired enough of his life for the world to see, but I imagine it's fairly obvious.

Margot's nodding, but as she's midway through turning around, she stops to look back to me.

'We've got a first aid kit, if that would be better,' she offers, and I nod enthusiastically.

Two minutes later, and after spending the whole time with one foot in Preston's room and the other outside it, Margot returns with a green zip-up bag, an unopened packet of cloths, and a large mixing bowl of water.

'I thought it would be good to cover all bases,' she explains as she awkwardly hands them over to me.

I thank her, then return fully into Preston's room. I was watching him the whole time Margot was grabbing the supplies, but honestly doubt I needed to. He didn't move. I didn't see him so much as twitch once.

'Hey,' I whisper as I return to sit on the floor by his head.

He doesn't acknowledge me, just keeps gazing into the distance.

'Is this okay?' I ask quietly as I take his right hand.

He gives another slight nod.

He doesn't react much as I get to work, at least not beyond a few light flinches as I'm carefully cleaning the wound on his wrist with some antiseptic wipes. By the time I'm finished, I realise he wasn't completely bullshitting me; it did look worse than it is. I've bandaged the larger, deeper cut on his wrist, and some of the scratches on his arms have warranted plasters.

Preston's eyelids are still drooping, still fluttering, especially now that I've stopped prodding his arms. He keeps fighting them open, blinking harshly every minute or so as if trying to shock himself awake.

'Let yourself sleep,' I whisper.

He shakes his head, but doesn't look at me as he murmurs, 'nightmares.'

My heart aches, and I don't know how much more it can take. Without a word, I uncross my legs to stretch them out, then shuffle myself into a lying position on the floor so that I'm on my side, facing him. I reach out–lift my arm over him but under the covers, and nudge myself closer. I inch closer again. I keep inching forward until I physically can't anymore because I've hit the side of the mattress. I crane my neck so that my head is under his chin, my face buried into his shoulder.

I don't mean to, but I start to cry.

Not a loud, inconsolable sobbing, but a small, quiet sniffling. I close my eyes to try and stop the tears, try not to let my shoulders jerk, try to stop my body from shaking because it's not fair–I can't put this on him to deal with, not now–but I'm not as successful as I'd hoped.

A blanket of warmth engulfs me, and it takes me a moment to realise it's the duvet being thrown over my body. Preston's arm is behind me–around me–and his hand is at the back of my head, his fingers in my hair as he strokes it. We stay like that for a while, silent, and I don't think it's for too long–it doesn't feel like an especially long time. Only, as I feel Preston's breathing turn deeper, his chest rising and falling more slowly, I feel for my phone in my pocket and see that nearly an hour has passed.

Carefully, I lift his arm from around me and ease myself back into a sitting position, my eyes not leaving his face for a second. He's fast asleep. I manoeuvre the bedding so that it's covering him fully again, leaning in to press my lips to his temple as I do so, then stand. I look around the room, taking in every discarded book, every clothes pile, every empty food carton, and I start to clean.

He's still asleep by the time I've returned every item to its correct place, and so now all that's left to do is clear the rubbish. The surfaces and carpet are in need of a general clean, but I'll deal with that later. I've held onto anything sharp I came across while tidying up, and checked everywhere else I could think of, so deem the risk of leaving low enough to take the rubbish downstairs.

I find Margot sitting in the living room as I enter it with a black bin bag filled with stuff from Preston's bedroom, and she greets me with a tentative smile. I can see that she wants to ask questions–probably a million of them–but she holds her tongue.

'He'll be okay,' I say, which I hope answers most of them.

I don't know if that's true, not really, but I believe it enough to not feel like I'm blatantly lying. Margot nods back at me, the relief on her face apparent. I carry the bin bag through the living room and into the kitchen, then return to sit on the arm of the sofa Margot's occupying.

'Do you want anything?' she asks me. 'To eat or drink? Or any-thing–Just, yeah, anything else?'

'No, thanks,' I reply as I tuck my hair behind my ears, then take a long, deep breath. 'I think...' I chew my lip. 'I think I'm going to stay here for a while. Is that okay? I'll head to mine to get a bag together, and just–Yeah, for a few days, I mean.'

'Of course,' Margot replies without hesitation. 'I can go over and grab your stuff now, if that would be helpful? If you'd rather stay here and keep an eye on things.'

I glance towards the ceiling as if I expect to be able to see through it, then turn my eyes back to Margot's warm face.

'Are you sure? It–Yeah, that would be helpful. Thank you.'

Margot's already on her feet, nodding. I compile a list of things I need off the top of my head, no doubt missing the most crucial bits, then hand Margot my flat keys and she's on her way. While she's out, I return to Preston's bedroom to find him still fast asleep. Assured, I jog lightly back down to the ground floor to find some cleaning supplies in the kitchen, then return upstairs.

Cleaning is helping me not think; it's probably why I'm so intent on doing it all now. To not think about what's happening, or how it's all my fault. I obsessed so much over the threat of Robbie spilling Preston's secrets, was so intent on controlling him that I neglected to consider the risk of me fucking things up. I was so busy being angry at Robbie for something he never ended up doing that I wound up igniting the fire myself.

I'm wiping Preston's desk clean when Margot returns. I can see from the dates on his medication and the number of pills left that my earlier assumption was accurate. He's not been taking them, likely for weeks. I make a mental note to check in with his doctor, if that's even a thing I can do, and with his lecturers and personal tutor.

I open Preston's bedroom door to receive my bag from Margot, and it's not until I'm unpacking it that I realise I forgot to add my toothbrush to the list I gave her. Thankfully, she thought of that. I find an unopened duo packet of toothbrushes down the side of my backpack, alongside a note scribbled on lined paper.

Wasn't sure which toothbrush was yours, so popped into a corner shop on the way back to buy new ones. Also chocolate! x

I peer into the bottom of my bag to find a family-sized packet of chocolate buttons. It's such a small thing—a silly thing, really—but I nearly cry.

chapter 35

A few days turn into a few weeks, and in hindsight, I was naive to think they wouldn't.

I as good as move into Preston's bedroom, only returning to my flat for brief intervals, and only really leaving his house for lectures and Typewriter Magazine meetings, of which I'm now primary editor. On the days I feel confident enough in Preston being alone for an hour or two, Margot and I will do something together, even if it's just heading to Dolly's for hot chocolate.

The first few days are the most difficult. Preston barely talks to me, not out of stubbornness; his brain is so foggy that he can't string words into coherent sentences. When he eventually woke up the day I moved myself in, he didn't know why I was there—couldn't remember me tending to him a few hours prior, not initially. I'm itching to replace his bed sheets, to get him a change of clothes—a shower, ideally—to make him call his mum, to speak with his doctor, but I resist the urge to overwhelm him.

He continues not sleeping very much, and when he does, his nightmares comment begins to make sense. He only suffered with the occasional one during the nights we spent together over Easter and summer, and he was always dismissive of them. The most I could ever get out of him was a non-descriptive PTSD remark. I'm not sure he'll ever tell me more than that, so all I can do is my best—try to ground him afterwards, ask if he needs anything, reassure him.

During those first few days, one of the few coherent conversations we have begins with him saying, 'sorry.'

'What for?' I query, simply relieved he's saying anything at all.

We're lying in bed as dusk is creeping in, the natural light spilling into his bedroom and casting a warm orange glow over everything. Preston responds to my question with a slow blink, and I've lost him—I'm convinced he's lost track again—when he answers me.

'The plant.'

I furrow my brow, clueless. I'm scanning his face in search of an explanation when it hits me. He's talking about the Swiss cheese plant—the one I bought him the night he hosted a Typewriter meeting at his house.

'What do you mean?' I try.

He hesitates, blinking again. 'What are we—Sorry, I can't remember what we were...'

'The Swiss cheese plant,' I gently remind him. 'You apologised, but I don't know what for.'

'Oh,' he says, then adds, 'I killed it. I'm sorry.'

I'm shaking my head. 'No. No, it's here—there. Look, it's there. It's fine.'

I point behind him and in the direction of his windowsill where the plant lives, perfectly green and alive. Preston doesn't exert the energy—or rather, doesn't have the energy—to turn and look at where I'm pointing.

'It's alive,' I assure him.

It wasn't in the best state when I first arrived, no, but it wasn't dead. Given the circumstances, it should've been nothing but a withered stalk trapped in dry, cracked soil.

He frowns. 'I don't–Are you sure? I was–I think–I kept trying to water it, but I'd forget if I already had and I didn't want to drown it, but it–If nothing else, I always tried to water the plant, but I couldn't–It was rotting. Its leaves had fallen off and it had turned black, so it–I had dreams of it doing that, so maybe I'm confusing–' He takes a sharp breath. 'Are you sure it's alive?'

'I'm looking at it right now, okay?' I reply as I lift my eyes above his shoulder one more time. 'The plant is alive.'

His tense expression eases, a sign that he finally believes me. At the very least, that he's beginning to. I'm careful to not get too comfortable with the more positive current state of things. I do, however, allow myself a private celebration because despite everything, I'm realising he kept his promise. He didn't let it die.

It's also the longest conversation he's managed to hold with me, even if it wasn't entirely sensical, which in itself feels like a miracle.

On the fifth day, he seems better. He gets out of bed, to start with. While that's not unusual in itself–he's been using the bathroom, albeit infrequently as he's not drinking or eating as much as he should be–this time is different. He stays up. He sits at his desk, reads for a little bit, talks to me without much trouble.

He's reading at his desk when I sense an opportunity. I'm standing over his bed, taking in the view of his crumpled sheets and the faded red-brown stains on them.

'I'm going to give these a wash,' I announce.

Before Preston can think of objecting, I'm tearing the pillowcases from his pillows. I can feel his eyes on me, but he doesn't say anything, at least not until I'm balling the fitted sheet into a heap.

'Thanks.' A pause. 'I'm going to take a shower.'

In an attempt to dampen my grin, I end up flashing a sort of deranged smirk at Preston's mattress. He stands from his desk, then grabs his towel from the back of the door where it's been hanging untouched since I turned up.

I've already put fresh sheets on Preston's bed, and the old ones are in the wash by the time he returns. I try not to visibly react to how much weight he's lost, now clearly evident as he stands with a towel around his waist.

'My shaving stuff was in the bathroom cabinet,' he says as he searches through his wardrobe, his back to me, and I freeze. 'The shaving foam is still there, but the razors have mysteriously vanished.'

Do I tell him I hid them? It'll be glaringly obvious why. I'm pretty sure what he's said is a not-so-subtle hint that he's already guessed. As he turns to face me, a plain white t in his hand, the suspicious look in his green eyes makes it blatantly obvious that he sees right through me. Fuck.

We're in a Mexican standoff. I don't want to tell him where I've hidden his razors, nor do I want to leave him alone with anything sharp. He, reasonably, wants to get rid of the facial hair he's been uncomfortably scratching since I got here. We settle on a compromise—I'll hand him a razor from an undisclosed location so long as he lets me watch him shave.

'Do you have to stare?' he mutters into the bathroom mirror as he lathers shaving cream onto his face.

'Yes,' I say from the toilet—lid closed and jeans on, obviously.

'It's unnerving.'

'Good.'

He shoots me a sideways glare, so I grin back at him, big and proud. He rolls his eyes, then turns back to the sink below him to grab the razor I placed there five minutes earlier. He holds it using his hand with the bandaged wrist, and he's running his thumb along its rubber handle. I'm about to ask him if he's okay when he turns to me.

'Could you do it?'

His voice is higher than normal–the difference barely noticeable, and I'm sure nobody but me would even catch it–but it's definitely higher. I stand from the toilet to approach him slowly.

'Yeah. Yeah, sure.'

'It's stupid,' he continues, 'I'm being stupid, I'm not–I wouldn't do anything–I just don't–I feel–'

'Preston, it's okay. I'll do it. Here,' I say as I grab a blue towel–I've got no idea whose it is–then spread it across the tiled floor between us. 'Sit down.'

I assume he knows I've never shaved anyone's face before, but I still deem it sensible to give him a heads-up as we sit opposite each other on the towel, a small bowl of water to my left. He assures me I'll be fine, but it's his face I'm more concerned for.

With the razor in one hand, I lift my other to his face, then delicately hold the bottom of his chin to keep him steady. His hand is on my knee as I dip the razor into the water beside me, then slowly swipe down from the top of his ear until the blade is level with the tip of his nose.

'Did I cut you?' I ask–okay, semi-shriek–as I pull the razor away.

His lip twitches as if there's a smile trying to break through, but not quite. 'No, Mia. You can be firmer. Longer swipes are fine, too.'

I'm shaking my head. No way. Too risky. I continue as I started, making small, gentle progress across the lower half of Preston's face, dipping the razor into the water between each swipe. His hand is on my knee the whole time, his fingers playing with the seam of my jeans.

My extremely cautious approach makes the task take at least twice as long as it should, and it still results in three small cuts, which I frankly blame on Preston because one is on his cheekbone and the other two on his jaw. If they weren't so abnormally sharp, we wouldn't have this problem.

'I'm sorry,' I murmur, the razor now discarded into the water bowl as I cup his clean-shaven cheek.

I trace my thumb along the underside of his right cheekbone, just below the cut I made as I inch my face forward, lightly pressing my lips against the red mark. As I do, Preston reaches his arm around me, pulling me closer so that I can rest my head against his chest.

'Thank you,' he whispers into my hair.

I shouldn't be—I know it's not fair—but when Preston wakes up the following morning in the same hole I found him in, I'm angry. He was so much better yesterday; he let me change the bed sheets, he showered, he let me shave his face, he was talking to me. Doing things. Now I can't even get him to look at me.

I take a moment to step outside. I don't go anywhere, just stand outside his bedroom for five minutes and take slow, deep breaths. It's not him I'm angry at, it's this situation—it's my desperation for him to be okay again, but I should know better. I know the path to okay isn't linear, and yesterday was still progress, even if today isn't.

The following day is better—not by much, but still better. He's talking to me, and for the most part, he's making sense. He picks at some of the food I make him. He doesn't leave the bed and he's still not sleeping, but he lets me gently brush his hair and wash his face with a soapy, wet flannel. I get him to sit up for ten seconds, then use the short window to change his shirt because he's been wearing the same one since his shower a few days prior.

As evening becomes night, he starts regressing. I'm trying to talk to him, but he's ignoring me, or possibly worse—he's not processing what I'm saying. I keep talking, anyway, my face inches from his as we lie side by side in a bed that feels like it's swallowing us.

It's during a pause in my rambling that finally, Preston says something.

'I'm doing it again, aren't I?' he whispers, his eyes meeting mine for the first time in hours.

I try to smile, then whisper back with, 'it's okay.'

He blinks slowly.

'I'm sorry I'm like this.'

I instinctively reach for him as I shake my head, searching for his hand under the covers until I find it and slot my fingers between his. I bring the back of his hand to my mouth with a soft kiss. I keep it there, my lips centimetres from his skin until we both fall asleep.

For the most part, from there, things get better. There are still bad days, but he's starting to eat again. He's showering more often, changing his clothes most days, holding conversations more easily, and rarely spends the entire day in bed. He's even taking his medication again, so long as I remind him.

He's still not ventured downstairs and won't let anyone but me into his room, but we're getting there. Slowly, we're getting there.

On the tenth day, I convince myself I have to be honest with him. He's had an overall good couple of days, any hiccups minimal enough to remain convinced that he won't fall back into the hole I found him in. It feels like the right time to tell him this is all my fault, or at least as right as something like that ever can be.

I'm toiling over how to approach the topic as I take an unnecessarily long time to water Preston's Swiss cheese plant, and I don't dare turn to face him.

'You need to name it,' I say, clearly desperate to avoid the inevitable.

After mustering up the courage to do so, I spin around to find him watching me from the bed. He's lying on his side, a notebook on the floor beside his mattress filled with doodles. He's been absentmindedly scribbling in it all morning. He continues doodling as he watches me.

'I'd planned to name it after you, but concluded that would be rather dark if it did end up dying.'

I hope for some jest in his eyes, but nothing of the kind breaks through. They remain a little distant, as if wanting to commit fully to real life, but not quite managing to.

'I don't mind.' I shrug. 'Mia, though. Not Euphemia.'

He wants to smile. God, I can feel his want to smile tugging at the space between us, but his expression remains placid, his eyes somewhere else. I'm being ridiculous—I know he's in no place right now to crack some predictable joke I equal parts love and hate, but that knowledge doesn't make me feel better. I push down the lump in my throat, then clear it with a sharp cough.

Maybe now isn't the right time for a confession.

In a sudden panic, the whole point of this conversation I started now lost because I've changed my mind, I instead stumble through a, 'hey, I was wondering—I wanted to ask, what made you stop? The drinking, going out, smoking etcetera, I mean.'

I wince at my own words. I was careful not to make any direct reference to Zack, but it still feels like too much—too direct of a question. I'm about to apologise when Preston stops tracing a pen along his notebook, his hand freezing on the spot. His eyes remain on its lined pages as he speaks, but he doesn't start drawing again.

'I'm not sure it's wise to tell you.'

I laugh, and it's notably awkward. 'Cryptic.'

He's still gazing at his notebook as he takes a slow, deep breath, then holds it for a few seconds. As he exhales, he lifts his green eyes back to me.

'You'll take it the wrong way.'

'If this is your attempt to not make me worry, you're kind of making it worse,' I tease, but I'm not sure I've made the jovial tone in my voice obvious enough, so add, 'I'm joking!'

Again, I can feel his want to smile. Again, that want fails to translate to his lips.

'I was at Oxford Circus,' he says as he turns back to his notebook, and I'm not sure I'm following. 'The station, that is. I don't remember the date or time, or frankly anything about that night beyond suddenly being alone on the platform. I was drunk. Just drunk, I think, nothing else—not that night, anyway, and I was looking at the board; the tube schedule, I mean, but I couldn't read it. Too drunk, probably.' He shrugs. 'I'm not sure, but it's—I digress. I was looking at that when I heard the electricity of the tracks sparking, the tunnel rumbling, the wind increasing. I knew the train was coming, and I just... I thought about it.' He pauses. 'No, that's not quite right. Thought about it sounds too intentional. It's more accurate to say the thought entered my head.'

He's not explicitly said anything, but he doesn't need to. What he's implying is as clear as day. He takes another long breath, then turns to look at me once again, I think to reassure me.

'I would never have done it, but I didn't want to get to the point where I would.' His next sentence is quiet, almost meek. 'It scared me, so I stopped.'

CHAPTER 36

Two weeks have passed since Preston first let me into his room, and it's one of his better days. I'm sitting on his mattress, typing away at a uni assignment that's due in a week while Preston reads a fantasy novel beside me. I'm so immersed in my work that I don't notice him close the book, then place it on his lap.

'I had the most peculiar dream last night,' he murmurs, and I turn to him.

'A nightmare?' I ask as I try to remember if he woke me up with one.

He shakes his head. 'Not really. I was in a house—an empty house, entirely void of furniture, of people, of things. Just walls and floors, and there was nothing outside, either. The windows showed nothing more than black. Not darkness, just... black.'

He glances down at his book, then turns back to me with a furrowed brow.

'I started ripping up the floorboards with my hands. I've got no idea what I was trying to achieve, or what I was trying to reach, but I kept ripping the wood. My fingers were bleeding, my hands bruised and searing in pain, but I just kept ripping.'

'What was underneath?'

A pause, then, 'nothing.'

'That sounds pretty nightmare-ish,' I point out.

He flashes me something between a grimace and a smile, a look I didn't even think was possible for someone to muster.

'Nightmares are far worse than that,' he says matter-of-factly, then out of nowhere, adds, 'I'm sorry for the way I treated you after Robbie visited.'

I frown. 'It's okay. You were just trying to cope.'

He's shaking his head as he clenches his jaw. 'It's not okay. It's not fair for me to treat you like that just because I'm having a difficult time.'

I swallow, my mouth turning dry. No. No, he doesn't understand. It's my fault. This whole thing is my fault. None of this would've happened if I'd been able to keep my mouth shut. I scan his face, and knowing this is one of his better days, I realise it's time. Some honesty is long overdue.

'Preston, I...' I close my eyes for a moment, taking a deep breath. 'It's my fault. What happened.'

I open my eyes and I know he's about to argue, so I interject before he can.

'On Robbie's last night here, when you headed back into the club to get my jacket, Robbie and I were—We were semi-arguing, I guess, and it's—I mentioned things. Out loud. I didn't think—I thought I was quiet enough, but it—Someone overheard.'

There's a choking sound, and I don't realise it's me until my vision begins to blur. I wipe at the tear that's racing down my check as I try to steady my breathing.

'Someone overheard me, and they told people,' I croak. 'If I hadn't said anything, none of this would've happened.'

My eyes are so full of tears that I don't see Preston lean into me. He nudges my laptop aside, wrapping his arms around my torso as he pulls me into him. He's warm, the cotton of his hoodie soft against my damp cheek.

'This is all quite melodramatic,' he murmurs from above as I press my face into his chest, and he's... He sounds like he's trying to joke with me.

Did he even hear what I said?

'You don't understand,' I say through a sob. 'I was the source of it. I'm the reason everyone found out about your past.'

'I don't care.'

'But it's my fault. People found out because of me.'

'Mia, I don't care,' he repeats, his thumb stroking the back of my neck. 'I don't care that it was you someone overheard, or even who overheard it. I don't care, okay?'

He's missing something. He must not be understanding what I'm saying. I open my mouth to try again, to make him understand, but he speaks before I can.

'I'm just really grateful you're here.'

During my third week at Preston's, I wake up one morning to find myself alone. The panic is immediate. I call his name as if I expect him to appear from underneath his desk or something, and I'm still half-asleep as I hurry out of his room. I check the bathroom. Nothing. I call his name again, but get no response. I barrel down to the first floor to check the bathroom there, but still nothing.

I've already started talking as I rush into the living room where Margot is watching something on her laptop.

'Have you–'

The words catch in my throat as I glance towards the kitchen area. He's there. Preston's there. Just, like, standing there as if it's perfectly normal, holding the fridge door open.

'Hi...' I say like a question.

He shifts his attention from the inside of the fridge to me, a packet of red grapes in his hand.

'Hey, are these mine?' he asks like it's nothing. 'Or yours, more accurately. I presume so because they're on my shelf.'

'I wasn't sure, but I said he can have them either way,' Margot interjects.

She must notice the what the fuck? expression slapped across my face because with her head turned away from Preston, she mouths, I'm trying really hard to act normal. I stifle a laugh. I'm euphoric. I literally want to cackle.

This is the first time he's left his bedroom in nearly a month.

'It's—Yeah, they're ours,' I reply with an overzealous nod.

'I'll pay you back for all the food and stuff, obviously,' Preston says as he enters the living area with the fruit in hand.

Given he's barely eaten any of the food he's referencing, like hell is he paying me a thing. I don't tell him that; I don't want to say anything that could threaten the possibility of him disappearing upstairs. I just smile.

The three of us sit on the sofa together, Preston with an open book as he snacks on grapes, Margot and I trying not to watch the whole time. I only know she's resisting staring because whenever I catch myself doing it, I glance at her to find her fighting the same battle.

Preston returns upstairs once he's finished eating, and he can't have spent more than fifteen minutes in the living room, but I'm thrilled. I'm evidently doing a shit job at hiding my happy-verging-on-deranged state because he asks me why I'm acting like I'm running on one brain cell.

'That's such a mean comment!' I whine as I drop to the mattress, which he's now sitting on, and give him a harsh shove. 'I'm happy. Sue me!'

For a moment, I worry the playful nudge overstepped the mark, but then I catch his lips twitch. It's a smile. He's smiling. The unfiltered joy racing through my bloodstream is clearly messing with my capacity to think rationally because I'm suddenly diving forward, my arms around him.

He can't have seen it coming because he falls backwards onto the bed, and he's laughing. Laughing! Not that he exactly has a choice because I'm literally pinning him down, but he doesn't shove me off. He mirrors my gesture, wrapping his arms around my back as his chest vibrates with another laugh.

I lift my head to peer down at him.

'Done?' he asks, his voice deep and smooth.

'Nope,' I reply, then lower my head to nestle it in the space between his neck and shoulder.

His skin smells like soap, and I realise he must've already showered. It means he was awake for a little while before I found him downstairs. At least half an hour, I'd guess. He was awake for half an hour, entirely alone and okay. He was okay. I need some way to expel the energy electrifying my body, so I squeeze him, then sporadically kiss his neck—not with any kind of romantic flare, but more so annoying, uncoordinated platonic affection.

He slides one of his hands up my back to stroke my hair, and as he combs his fingers through it, I peck his neck again. He's not even trying to get me off, and with the hand that isn't on my head, he traces circles on my lower back where my shirt has ridden up.

He's so warm. I kiss his neck again, this time gently, just as he kisses my temple.

I kiss him again, and again, and again until I'm lifting my head to kiss his lips.

He kisses me back, a sigh escaping my mouth as if I've been waiting a lifetime for this moment. His tongue is sweet from the grapes he was eating, and there's a hint of mint from the toothpaste he must've used earlier this morning. Our kisses become less delicate, our breaths heavier as I adjust myself so that my palms are pressed against the mattress, his hands on my waist, the flimsy material of my pyjama shorts grazing his fingertips.

Before I realise he's doing it, Preston flips me onto my back, our kisses intensifying as I tug at his t-shirt. He follows my cue to pull it over his head while I fumble at the flyer of his jeans as if suddenly possessed, or maybe out of pure desperation for him—for us—and it's as if I'm incapable of thought, nor of logic, or anything close to it. I'm barely breathing as I pull him closer, and there's no rush; there's nowhere we need to be or anything we need to do, but I'm impatient. Far too impatient to bother with my own clothes, or any more of his.

The feeling of him inside me stirs, above all else, an overwhelming sense of relief. It's as if every good thing I've ever felt is hitting me all at once, as if it's been years, not months since we last did this. I have a sudden urge to cry, not in a bad way—not even close—but I fight it as I tug at the back of his hair with desperation while simultaneously pulling him as close as physically possible.

His breath is hot in my ear as he kisses the space behind it, and everything is familiar—he's so familiar that the lump in my throat is becoming so sharp that I'm sure it's going to pierce my skin. I need him. I've never needed anyone or anything more, and I'm telling him this. Between sighs of pleasure, I keep telling him I need him, not caring how pathetic it probably sounds as our bodies follow each other's rhythm.

I'm not sure what it is that triggers the recollection of where I am, of where I've been for nearly four weeks, but it hits Preston at the same time. It's been mere minutes since we started kissing, but he's abruptly tearing himself away from me; he's pushing me aside, and I can tell he's about to stand as he readjusts his flyer, so I reach for his hand to keep him sitting, to force him to look at me.

'Sorry. I'm really sorry.' He's speaking so quickly that I can only just make out the words. 'I shouldn't have—I didn't mean to—'

'No, it's—My fault,' I say, just as quickly. 'I kissed you. It's my fault.'

What the hell was I thinking? Seriously, what the fuck is wrong with me?

I was so terrified of freaking him out downstairs that I rehearsed every glance, every word, every syllable, only to go and do this? I might not always be the most emotionally switched-on person, but this is beyond that. This is grossly irresponsible.

Preston's looking down at his hands, shaking his head.

'And summer, and over Easter,' he continues. 'I shouldn't—I never should've let that happen in the first place, let alone let it continue for as long as it did.'

I stammer. I want to tell him that I'm grateful for that time, that it was probably the happiest time of my life, but I can't. I shouldn't. That's not how I should feel.

Instead, in a gentle voice, I say, 'it's okay. We're okay.'

At that, Preston lifts his eyes to meet mine, his forehead creased with concern as he clenches and unclenches his jaw.

'We're okay,' I repeat, and finally, his face relaxes. 'I promise.'

CHAPTER 37

Christmas break lands at the perfect time. While I'd not go as far as saying that Preston is back to normal, he's well enough to spend time at home in Cardiff–something he's desperately needed since things went awry. He's eating again, he's sleeping without much trouble, he's leaving his house, he's reconnected with Rhys, and he's finally accepting external help through his doctor. He's not been back to uni, but his first semester deadlines have been postponed until after Christmas through extenuating circumstances.

New Year's Eve proves to be a lot less eventful than last year's, but in the best way. Aiden, Caleb, Margot, Joe, Preston, and I spend it in the cosy confines of Aiden's otherwise empty flat, playing board games, drinking wine, and eating pizza like we're actual adults or something. None of us get very drunk, not even Aiden, and my heart is so full by midnight that I literally cry, and the six-way hug Caleb instigates in an attempt to comfort me just makes me cry harder.

Before I know it, it's the first of January, and I enter the new year with unrelenting optimism. After everything, maybe it's misplaced, but I'd rather run into the future with hopeful naivety than spend every moment crippled with uncertainty-induced anxiety. Naivety is in my name, after all.

By the time Preston and I are returning to London a week or so later, he's well enough for me to move back into my own flat. It's weird at first. My flatmates from first year and I renewed our tenancy for the same place, so it's not like I'm living with strangers or anything, but a loneliness haunts the space. I'm so used to Preston's company, so familiar with his presence, that it feels like a part of me is missing.

Within minutes of me returning to my flat, I want to visit him, but I resist. I can't. We've been living on top of each other for nearly two months, and we need to give each other space. We need to get back to normal, to where we were before summer—before Easter—and we can't do that if we're together twenty-four-seven. So long as I know he's safe and okay, that's all that matters. That's what I have to be content with.

It's not easy, but I get there—we get there. Lectures kickstart again, Preston works on his postponed assignments, I get back on the dating scene, and we keep things strictly platonic between us. Preston gradually returns to Typewriter Magazine meetings, and he starts socialising beyond Margot, Joe, and me. He and Dana even seem to be hitting it off again, which is great. Obviously, that's a great thing.

He still has days—he won't ever not have days—where it takes him longer to get out of bed, where he doesn't see anyone, where he doesn't eat as much as he should. But everything, especially given how horrifically things could've gone after Robbie's visit, is as close to perfect as it could ever be.

And I'm fine. It's fine. We're fine.

It's mid-February, Aiden's in London for the weekend, and it's not until we've been sitting in Dolly's cafe with Margot for a whole fifteen minutes that I notice the glances. Aiden's sitting opposite me while Margot's to my left. I'll be in the middle of saying something, and they'll just flash each other a nondescript look, their lips twitching as if I'm interrupting some private conversation.

'This is honestly kind of painful,' I declare, finally giving in. 'What is it?'

They turn to me, their eyes wide and innocent as if they're not clearly conspiring something.

I sit back in my chair, my arms crossed. 'You have ten seconds to tell me why you're treating this like an intervention, and not like three friends meeting up for coffee.'

'Actually, funny you should say that,' Margot begins, giving me nothing. 'I guess this is an intervention. Sort of.'

So there is something.

'I mean, obviously, we do also want to hang out, but Aiden and I figured now was a good opportunity to get you cornered–No, not cornered. That sounds bad. I just mean... Shit. Okay, so basically...'

Is she malfunctioning?

'We think!' Aiden suddenly blurts.

'You think?' I ask, turning to him. 'Congrats, I guess.'

'Shut up,' he grumbles, then clears his throat after one more glance in Margot's direction. 'We think that you should speak with Preston.'

I narrow my eyes. 'I speak with Preston, like, every day.'

'Exactly,' Margot mutters under her breath, eyebrows raised as she stares at her empty coffee mug.

Before I can question her, Aiden's talking again. 'Come on, Mia, you know what I mean.'

'No, I really don't.'

They glance at each other again, so I naturally contemplate throwing my glass of water at them.

'You do!' Aiden argues, unhelpfully. 'You should speak with him about how you feel—properly speak with him. None of you guys' weird tip-toeing around the topic, or competing to see who can be the most sensible bullshit because holy mackerel, that makes me want to throttle you.'

I blink slowly. What is he even—

Margot interjects with a loud groan, then turns to look me dead in the eye. 'You need to tell him that you love him.'

I trip from a stammer into a laugh. They've lost it. They've certified lost their minds.

'I'm—' I sigh, then raise my hands defensively. 'Yeah, I love him. I assumed that was a given, and I've probably said as much aloud to you both, but I'm not in love with him.'

They fucking glance at each other again.

'I'm not!' I snap.

I knew Aiden was living this fantasy, but Margot too? They're ridiculous. They're actually ridiculous. They've hoodwinked me out of my flat under the pretence of a cute friendship coffee date, only for them to hold me at metaphorical gunpoint until I confess the non-existent romantic love I have for someone I'm terrified beyond comprehension of losing.

'Didn't you spend the entirety of Easter and most of summer, like, in a relationship, just without actually calling it that?' Margot questions.

Before I can argue, Aiden jumps in.

'And didn't you tell me it was literally the best summer ever?' He scoffs. 'Pretty bloody clear why now I know you spent it ridi—'

'Don't be gross,' I interrupt.

'Gross, but he has a point,' Margot defends Aiden. 'No offence, Mia, but it's been really obvious since that first flat party at ours. Like, we're talking blinding.'

'And Nick could see it,' Aiden interjects. 'And Caleb.'

'Exactly! Plus both of you guys' other relationships have crashed and burned because you're so hopelessly in love with each other. It's tragic.'

Now they're just being rude.

'Ugh, tell me about it,' Aiden grumbles, then turns to me. 'Plus seeing Preston and Dana on that first double date made you feel physically ill. Hardly normal.'

I open my mouth to tell them to stop, to put an end to this low-budget, borderline offensive intervention, but instead, I squeak, 'I can't!"

It shuts them up, at least. They're watching me, their brows furrowed, mouths hanging open slightly.

'I can't feel that way about him,' I say, nearly whispering.

'But you do?' Margot hits back, and the look I flash her must give me away because she sighs, her eyes softening. 'Tell him, Mia, because while I'd bet my left tit that Preston feels the same, he's too terrified to ever tell you first.'

'Heh. Left tit. I'm going to start using that.' Aiden giggles.

I ignore Aiden's comment and shake my head. 'It's not that simple, and it's—Besides, I'm pretty sure he and Dana are starting things again.'

'Has he told you that?' Margot replies.

She's responding too quickly for me to keep my guard up.

'He's—I'm—' I stammer. 'No, but y'know, I can tell by the way they are at Typewriter meetings and stuff.'

'Okay, well, all the more reason to do it ASAP.' Margot shrugs. 'Before anything gets too serious between the two of them.'

God, why is she making sense? It's so unfair.

I glance between Margot and Aiden, speechless beyond a few stutters escaping my lips. They don't understand. If I tell him—if

I so much as insinuate that my feelings are deeper than something platonic sprinkled with some physical attraction—and Preston feels differently, how would we come back from that? We'd have to distance ourselves, possibly forever, and I can't bear the thought. Do I even know how I feel? Everything between us is so complicated that I could just be getting carried away, or confused.

Maybe I should speak with him, if not just to squash any uncertainty about what there is, or isn't, between us. That's sensible, right? Yeah, that's the sensible thing to do. It wouldn't be me making a grand gesture in some delusional hope that he might have feelings for me. I'd just be talking to him. Sensibly.

'I'm not—I'll talk to him,' I state as I take my phone from where it's sitting face down on the table, not looking at Margot or Aiden as I do so. 'Just to make sure we're on the same page. No love confessions. Absolutely nothing like that.'

'Right...' they say slowly, and in unison, like a pair of clones.

I'm opening my message thread with Preston as Aiden adds, 'but you'll have an actual conversation about feelings and stuff?'

'Sure,' I grumble as I begin typing without allowing myself to think about what I'm doing.

Hey, are you free now?

It's not until after I've sent the message that I realise what now means, that I've asked him to talk now. Like, right now. Before I can send some panicked second message to clarify it doesn't have to be today, or frankly ever, he's already replied. Fuck.

Free until two. I'm at the student centre, if you're close.

Why's he there? That's barely ten minutes away. Why isn't he busy, either? Shouldn't he have like, a lecture? Or be working on an assignment or something? Two o'clock is nearly a whole hour away, so there's zero reason for him to be on campus this early.

Upon sharing Preston's response with Margot and Aiden, they react in the most offensive way possible. Instead of approving my draft response of I'm somewhere really far away and can't get to you before two, sorry! they refuse to back down on their deranged intervention until I reply to Preston to say I'm on my way. Frankly, it's a miracle they don't demand they join me on the walk to the student centre.

It's a good thing they don't because I spend the journey talking to myself.

'Sensible,' I mutter under my breath as I swerve the crowds of students. 'You're being sensible, and it's just a chat. You chat all the time.'

It goes without saying that there are a few questioning glances thrown my way, but I ignore them. I've got my earphones in to drown out the increasingly panicked thoughts screaming at me, so I'm sure it just looks like I'm on the phone with someone. I'm sure the pale, flustered expression I can feel my face is twisted into the entire time looks totally normal. It's also raining pretty heavily, so the umbrella I'm using probably masks most of it. Probably.

I take five once I reach the entrance of the student centre, in part to settle the nausea that's developed in the pit of my stomach, but also to fix my appearance in the reflection of the building's large, glass windows. Not that it matters what I look like because this is just a normal, sensible chat. I'm not trying to, like, impress him. Obviously.

My phone vibrates in my pocket, and I nearly throw up.

Are you there yet??

Oh my God, they've made a group chat. Margot and Aiden have literally created a group chat exclusively for this purpose. I ignore Margot's message and return to my preening, only for another one to come through less than a minute later.

We can see you've read the message

It's Aiden this time. His message is quickly followed by three snake emojis.

I'm here, shut up

With a huff, I shove my phone back into my pocket, yank my umbrella down, and scurry into the student centre. It's not until I'm inside that I realise I don't actually know where Preston is specifically, and this is hardly a small building. We hang out together here every now and then, stealing the same seating area in one of the ground floor's far corners, so logic tells me to check there.

Naturally, that's where I look last.

With bated breath, I approach the area with slow, deliberate steps. It's fine. It'll be fine, I try to kid myself. It's just a chat.

Jokes aside, I might be sick.

I'm so lost in my own head that I don't spot her at first; not until I'm too close for there to be any doubt, not until it's too late for me to realise I'm staring. It's Dana. I can only see the back of her blonde head because Preston's the one facing me throughout their hug, but that's all I need to recognise it as her.

They're hugging. Preston hates hugs. He doesn't hug anyone.

It's enough. The sight is enough for the penny to drop, and it's one I can't witness any longer. My legs are carrying me—they're walking back in the direction I came—before I even realise I'm moving. In fact, I'm nearly jogging. By the time I've reached the middle of the floor, I am jogging. Hell, I'm practically sprinting through UCL's student centre as if that's a perfectly normal thing to do, and people are staring, but I don't care enough to slow down.

I exit the student centre, at which point I should probably slow down, but I don't. I need to get as far away as possible, and it's still raining, but I don't have time to put up my umbrella. I don't even know where I'm going.

This was stupid. This was so fucking stupid. What was I thinking? Why had I let Margot and Aiden convince me into doing something so ridiculous? Not just ridiculous, but reckless. It's not fair for me to be so selfish, to even contemplate putting Preston in a position where our friendship could be at risk for feelings I'm not even sure of myself.

'Mia!'

Fuck.

I trip to a halt at the sound of Preston's voice, but I don't turn around. I can't bear turning around.

'What are you—Mia!' he calls again.

I start moving again—walking, this time, thank God—as I shout back to him.

'It's okay; I'm going! It's nothing!'

Whether he hears me over the rain and the crowds clogging the pavement is debatable, but I don't stop to find out.

'Mia!'

As I'm entering a large, square garden just off campus—I've got no idea what possessed me into thinking a gated garden is the ideal escape location—there's a hand on my arm, and finally, I turn around and come to a stop.

Preston's green eyes are wide as they dart around my face, and his hair is dark and wet from the rain—he's wet, his face dotted with raindrops as his white t-shirt sticks to his chest, and he looks confused. No, he looks concerned. Deeply concerned. Why I think what I say next is the best next course of action is beyond me.

'You're wet,' I rasp, highlighting the extremely obvious, and only now do I understand the alarm in his eyes.

Oh, God, I'm crying.

CHAPTER 38

'I'm literally so fine,' I say through sniffles as Preston takes my hand, then ushers me deeper into the garden.

We walk until the rain stops, and I don't understand. I don't understand why I'm crying, or how he's controlling the clouds, or what's even happen—We're under a huge tree. The rain hasn't stopped; we're just under cover, and I'm still crying. At this rate, it would be kindest if someone just took me out.

'What is it? Mia, what's wrong?' Preston's hands are on my arms as he glances down, his brow furrowing as he catches sight of the umbrella I'm grasping so tightly that my knuckles have turned white.

'I forgot to use it,' I reply like an idiot.

'What's wrong?' he repeats.

He's evidently not as interested in my pink umbrella as I'd assumed, so I shove it into my jacket pocket as I mumble, 'nothing.'

I don't even try to sell the lie, not that I catch much of his response through my blurred vision. Not crying would be a great start.

Preston's mouth is open again, but whatever he's thinking of saying, he decides against it. Instead, he silently pulls me into him until my head is pressed against his chest, his hands lightly stroking my back. After what I stumbled across moments earlier, a hug from him right now feels like some kind of fucked up irony. Despite this, I don't move. We stay with our arms around each other until I regain control of my breathing and my tears dry up.

'I'm sorry,' I say as I force myself out of his embrace, and I'm shaking my head, my face no doubt blushed beyond a natural colour. 'I'm really sorry. I just—I saw you and Dana, and I shouldn't have—I knew I never should've even—You hate hugs, and I know you don't just hug anyone, so obviously you guys are rekindling things, and that's great! That's so great!'

'I don't... Mia, what are you talking about?'

'In there, just now,' I try. 'I saw you hugging Dana, so obviously, you guys are trying again, which is—'

'I just hugged you,' he says, his face no less perplexed, even after my explanation.

'Yeah, but that's different,' I argue. 'You've developed a tolerance with me.'

His brow furrows again, and then he's... His lips are twitching. They're twitching as if he wants to laugh. Is he a sadist or something?

'You're going to have to explain to me how that relates to any of this,' he murmurs, implicitly referring to the fact I just sprinted a whole street to try and get away from him while hysterically crying.

Only, I can't. That's the whole point. I can't tell him anything, not now—not after seeing him and Dana. It's not appropriate, nor will it ever—

'I'm not rekindling anything with Dana, by the way, in case that's yet to make itself obvious.'

I blink, and my thoughts stop. They vanish. My head literally empties itself.

'You are,' I whisper, and he laughs.

He's laughing.

'I'd like to think I'd have a degree of say in the matter, in which case I can assure you I'm not.'

My expression remains blank, which is why I imagine he elaborates without any prompting.

'We'd not really spoken since... everything, and it was–Frankly, it was a little patronising because she said she was sorry about my past, but also clearly didn't want to specify any details in case of instigating a breakdown or something, or at least that's the impression I got based on her deeply sympathetic, verging on fearful stare throughout the whole conversation.'

He takes a breath, then shrugs.

'But yes, my point is that she ended the conversation with a hug, and I was hardly going to tell her to fuck off.' He pauses. 'I hated it, to clarify. The hug. The conversation, too.'

God, yeah, it sounds like his worst nightmare.

'She didn't ask to get back together?' I ask, lifting my eyes to peer into his as if to check he's not lying–as if he ever would. 'You don't want want to get back together?'

'No, I'm not interested in her.'

'You should be,' I respond because apparently, I'm the sadist.

'Noted,' he replies with an eye roll, then pauses as he scans me. 'You've not answered my question about...'

He gestures vaguely towards me, which in hindsight, is kind of him. I'd rather he didn't reference my crying and sprinting-related breakdown with words.

As the realisation of what's happening–of the reason I'm here in the first place dawns on me–I feel sick again. This was supposed to be a sensible chat, for Christ's sake. A calm, totally normal, mature chat about our situation. How can this possibly be anything like that after my performance?

I should tell him it's nothing. I should say I'm just in a weird mood, or that I'm stressed over some uni work, or maybe even fabricate some lie about Dad doing something to upset me. I should back down while I can. I should do that—I know I should just bow out, but if my reaction to seeing him and Dana has proved anything, it's that I can't kid myself any longer. I can't lie to him any longer.

'I like you,' I declare.

Great start, Mia.

'You're so important to me,' I continue, which isn't much better. 'You know that, obviously, but it's more than that. When I saw you just now—When I thought you and Dana were getting back together, I honestly thought I was about to die, and that sounds fucking insane—I know how melodramatic that sounds, but it literally felt like someone had clawed through my chest, grabbed my heart, and squeezed it.' I take a breath because I'll suffocate if I don't. 'And that's not normal. Obviously, that's really not a normal reaction to seeing your friend possibly rekindle a relationship with someone you think would be good for them, so I think that's—The issue is that, is what I'm saying. Us being friends. Just friends, I mean.'

I'm not sure why I deem that the most appropriate place to stop speaking because God, do I leave so many lines to read between and hurdles to jump through, but I leave it there anyway. I guess I'm just lucky Preston never fails to make complete sense of the shit I spout.

'You don't... I thought you didn't want our friendship to get fucked up over something insignificant, that anything between us would be awkward,' he says out of nowhere.

I twist my face in utter confusion. 'What? I've—No, I don't think anything between us is insignificant. I'd never think that. Or awkward.'

'You said it.' He frowns, then speaks slowly as he analyses my features. 'You said it to Margot. After our first kiss.'

I blink in quick succession as if it'll stir the memory, but come up short. Is he—Wait, is he referring to that silly kissing dare situation? When Margot spoke with Preston the following morning to tell him his reaction wasn't cool?

'No, it was your reaction to the dare she was talking about. The dare was awkward and insignificant, not our kiss—not you.' I shake my head. 'I never told Margot about the kiss.'

A pause, then, 'oh.'

I frown. 'I don't—Even if that was the case, that was over a year ago, and so much has happened between us since. You don't—You wouldn't have thought it might've changed?'

Preston's wide-eyed reaction answers my question without him uttering a word. He's dead serious. I'm shaking my head, but Preston is speaking again before I can say another word.

'The way I was before Christmas isn't—That wasn't just a one-off, Mia.' He steps back, only a little—barely an inch—but it feels like a mile. 'Do you understand what I'm saying?'

Before I can even think of nodding, he continues.

'I'm never not going to be like this,' he says, his voice cracking ever so slightly. 'And that's not... It's not fair on you. On anyone, but especially not you. I can't do that to you.'

I'm shaking my head with determination. 'I don't want you to be someone else.'

'I know you think that now, but you won't—you wouldn't think that forever. It would become too much. I'd become too much for you.'

'Preston, it doesn't make a difference whether we're just friends or something else; I'll always be here. I'm going to have to deal with whatever you go through whenever you go through it be-cause I'm not going anywhere—I'm never going anywhere, so fuck it, we might as well try.' I cross my arms, then huff. 'Frankly, I'd like to think me sitting outside your bedroom door for, like, six hours while you blatantly ignored me would've gotten that message across.'

He's turned silent again, and the only sound to be heard is the quiet pattering of rain falling onto the leaves of the tree we're shaded under. His eyes are on me, scanning my face as if it's a code he can't crack.

Finally, he finds his words and they're quiet; unassuming. 'What if things don't work out? I couldn't—I can't lose you.'

He sounds young—younger than he's ever sounded before, and it makes me want to curl my arms around him to shield him from the cool air, the rain, the world. Instead, I swallow, then take a long, deep breath.

'Then they don't work out.' I take a step forward, closing the space he created between us minutes earlier as I tentatively take his hand. 'And that's okay. We'll figure things out; we'll be okay. We're always okay, and I'm always here. For as long as you'll want me, I'll always be here.'

His jaw ticks and I can see him fighting. His thoughts or his words, I'm not sure, but he's fighting something. Logic, proba-bly. That's what I've been doing since I kicked off this whole exchange.

'I just...' he tries, then shuts his eyes for a moment. 'I don't know if this is a good idea.'

Despite the resistance in his words, he doesn't release my hand from his.

'Maybe it's not,' I admit, 'but I can't keep living like this, like we're between something and nothing; obsessing over what could be. I know you're more careful than I am, so maybe it's different for you, but living like this feels like a worse fate than us never trying.'

He glances down at our hands, our fingers entwined, then looks back up to meet my eyes. 'I'm in love with you, Mia; I have been for a long time, and you know that.'

I blink, a stammer falling between my lips as my head explodes and my soul bursts from my body, so frankly, it's a miracle I stay upright.

'I don't,' I manage to squeak. 'I didn't know that.'

Silence hangs in the air between us for a moment that feels like forever.

'Oh,' he replies, then pauses before saying, 'I presumed it was obvious.'

'Right. Okay, well, I think it's well established by now that nothing you do, say, think, or feel is ever obvious. The literal opposite, actually,' I ramble, my voice turning higher by the second.

Another, 'oh', then, 'sorry.'

The man looks confused—genuinely perplexed—as if he had this idea in his head that he was some open book or something. It's so ridiculous that I nearly laugh.

'Is that—' he begins, then glances away before returning his attention to me. 'Is that enough, though? When I've got so much bullshit that you'll have to deal with, I'm just not sure—I don't know if that's enough of a reason for us to do this.' He sighs as he uses his free hand to run his fingers through his wet hair. 'I'm difficult; you know that better than anyone. I'm difficult to understand, to live with, to get through to. In every way, I'm just... difficult.

'You're easy to love,' I hit back. 'Loving you is the easiest thing I've ever done.'

I anticipate a retort, but instead find Preston's eyes boring into mine as if I've just declared some grand revelation.

'And I know you don't believe that, and nothing I can say here will probably convince you of the fact, but I'll prove it to you. Give me a chance to show you how true that is; that's all I'm asking. A chance, for us.'

In the split second between me waiting for his response and leaning closer, it occurs to me that what I'm about to do might be the most terrible idea I've ever had—and I've had many. A split second, however, isn't enough to stop me.

I lift my arms to wrap them around his neck, and his hands are suddenly on my waist as I brush my lips against his. My logic, finally catching up with me, stops me from moving again; stops me from breathing, thinking, existing.

But then he kisses me, and I'm alive again.

I kiss him back like it's the first time, and I don't know what this means. If it's him agreeing to give me—give us—a chance, if it's a lapse in judgment, or if it's a goodbye, but I don't dare stop kissing him. The air is cold and wet, and the rain is falling between leaves and splashing against my head, but I've never felt as warm as I do right now.

Preston draws his lips from mine, but he doesn't leave. His forehead is pressed against mine as the rain turns heavier, the sound of it battering the tree above us nothing short of a symphony. My eyes remain closed from our kiss and I'm intoxicated, my head light and my breath short as I sense him draw a breath.

'Are you sure you want this?' he whispers.

'I've never been more sure.'

He responds with another kiss, this one slower and deeper as I fall into his touch, all sense of reality slipping away until I'm delirious. I must be delirious because I'm smiling until it hurts, but don't dare tear my lips from his, not even when my smile becomes a gleeful laugh.

'On one condition,' I murmur, pulling away, but reigniting my lips with his within moments.

It's him who breaks us apart this time. 'Dare I ask?'

I inch away to meet his gaze, then say, 'stop with the fucking STD gags.'

He's laughing now, and the sound of it illuminates the entire garden, so much so that I can't even fake annoyance.

'You've never answered me,' he replies instead of just agreeing to the damn thing. 'Every single time I've asked, you've never answered the question.'

I glare back at him. 'What does that have to do with anything?'

'That's all I've been waiting for,' he says, leaning into me again. 'To stop me from asking. An answer.'

I try to maintain an aura of irritation, but with his lips so close to mine, it's impossible.

'You're telling me that if I'd answered yes or no that very first time you asked the question, you never would've asked it again?'

'Correct.'

I'm stammering and he's laughing once more, so lightly that his breath on my lips feels like a phantom kiss.

'I–You can't be serious, it's–I–Well, you have asked it. Multiple times. Nobody ever had before you started berating me with it, so I guess to answer the original question, no. All the questions since, though–yes. You.'

'Hm...' he murmurs thoughtfully, teasing my lips with his, and it's torture. I can barely breathe from the want of it. 'See? Was that so difficult?'

With that, he presses his mouth to mine again, and I'm laughing. We're laughing. Just kissing and laughing in the middle of a garden in central London as the rain beats down, and the prospect of any future moment feeling better than this one seems impossible. But with Preston, I'd bet on it happening anyway.

EPILOGUE

1 8 months later

Graduating from university, as it turns out, is as terrifying as it is exhilarating. Sure, the world is my oyster and all that shit, but I also have no idea in hell what I'm supposed to do next, and despite begging multiple people for an answer, everyone keeps insisting that's for me to decide. Frankly, it's way too much pressure for a twenty-two-year-old teenager like me.

If my dress would stop riding up for more than ten seconds, that would probably help.

I awkwardly yank it down as I wait in the neverending queue of UCL English department graduates, all the while feeling eternally grateful that I opted for a longer skirt. If this thing had a miniskirt, it'd probably be up to my belly button by now. I'm never taking Aiden's fashion advice again; the man is cursed. The line shuffles forward as graduate's names are called out one-by-one, and I take a deep breath as I eye up the stage ahead.

'It'll be over in seconds,' I whisper to the black laminate floor. 'Just jump up, grab the diploma, shake a hand, then get the fuck off the stage.'

Unsurprisingly, my pep talk is doing little to reassure me. Dad's in the crowd, hidden somewhere among the rows of seats facing the theatre's stage, as is Mum. Together. Not together together obviously, but the two free guest tickets I was provided with for my graduation are for adjacent seats. Whoever organised the seating plan has clearly failed to account for the UK's forty-two percent divorce rate. On the bright side, five years ago–hell, two years ago–I would've dropped dead at the thought of my parents being seated together, but things are okay now; better between them, even if it is solely for my benefit. Mum's very good at ignoring Dad's bullshit, and Dad's bullshit isn't as bad as it used to be.

Neither one of them has been any help whatsoever in my what the hell do I do with my life from here? conundrum, though. Mum's always insisted she doesn't care what I do so long as I'm happy, and Dad's mellowed at the worst possible time to wind up saying the exact same thing. I almost wish he was still a monumental prick. The only person who's so much as alluded to what they think my next move should be is Aiden, but I'm not sure dolphin trainer is a viable career for an English grad, despite his and Margot's claims otherwise.

The worst person by far, though, is Preston. Where my parents and friends–excluding Aiden's marine-centric advice–are diplomatic and gentle, Preston's approach to the whole thing is simply don't. Don't make a plan, don't worry, don't think. My response every time is a demand that he gets a new therapist because the man's clearly unhinged. He's here too, only not in the audience, but in a queue similar to mine as his master's graduation has coincidentally landed directly after mine.

I've scanned the backstage area several times over for his economics cohort, but have come up short every time. As the stage curtain grows closer and closer and my line shortens further and further, I swallow a stone. I hate this shit. I'm tugging at my red dress again, all the while thanking the graduation gods that my robe covers it well enough to distract from the whole mess. I'm so focused on my dress as I near my turn that it's not until I'm second in line that I notice Preston.

He's at the opposite end of the stage to me, his hands in his pockets and his navy suit obscured by his graduation robe while he leans back against the wall so casually that it's as if everyone else here is background noise. His green eyes are electric, his lips slightly curved as if taunting a smile, and his focus is so heavily on me that I'm suddenly certain he's been watching me this whole time.

As our eyes meet, I start laughing. My shoulders ease, my back relaxes, and the last thing I see as I step onto the stage is Preston's smile—teeth and all. Hell, he might be laughing too, and then suddenly everything seems so insignificant. My dress, the stage, my parents, my degree—the future. I'm still laughing as my name is called and I walk across the stage to take my diploma and shake the dean's hand, and I don't stop laughing until I'm at the other side. Even then, I'm wearing a smile so big that my jaw aches.

All at once, the advice Preston has parroted over the past however many months feels impossible to argue with. Just don't.

The rest of the graduation happens in a flash, the only break in routine being when Preston's cohort is called and he's on stage himself. His two complimentary tickets went to Anwen and Rhys, which saved me a lot of bother because if she wasn't here already for Preston, I secretly would've wanted to give my second to Anwen instead of Dad. Matty's here too, but is waiting outside under the questionable care of Aiden, particularly when you consider how well that went last time. Thankfully, Margot and Joe are also around.

What follows our graduation is what can be best described as theatre, despite physically leaving the theatre behind. Post-ceremony drinks are with Mum and Dad where, for Dad's sake and to the best of his knowledge, Preston and I are totally platonic friends. We're still working on breaking the totally non-platonic relationship news to him—or rather, I still am. Preston's assured me multiple times that he doesn't mind the potential consequence of being punched square in the face, but alas, I resist.

I don't need to be as guarded as I am about us. Dad no longer visibly hates Preston—hell, as we were standing around, he even chatted with him for maybe, like, a minute while I was distracted with some course friends—but it's something I need to figure out in my own time. Mum's as big of a star throughout our interaction as ever, and acts like this is totally normal and she knows no different.

We can relax a lot more when we head to dinner with Rhys and Anwen, who I dearly hope are way less subtle than Preston and I were with Dad because if we were anything like them, Dad doesn't have a doubt in hell that Preston and I are more than friends. Rhys and Anwen haven't so much as whispered a suggestion that there's anything romantic between them, but the way they look—no, gaze—at each other is so obvious that they might as well slap us in the face with a relationship revelation. They spend the majority of dinner acting like each other is the funniest person in the room, at least when they're not gushing over Preston and me as though we collectively cured cancer, and didn't simply graduate from university alongside thousands of other twenty-somethings across the country this summer.

At the end of the night, 'you owe me ten pounds,' is the first thing Preston says to me as we close our bedroom door.

I halt a few steps from the doorway as he wanders towards our bed while loosening his navy tie, but he doesn't catch my what the fuck are you talking about? expression because his back is to me. I quickly discover he doesn't need to see my expression because he can sense my perplexion from a mile off.

'Mum and Rhys,' he elaborates—a rare feat for him, so I consider it a win—as he turns to face me. 'You were convinced they'd tell us about them today, no?'

I scoff as I kick my black heels off my feet. 'Firstly, I do not owe you ten pounds. I bet that they were going to tell us at some point after we graduated generally, not the literal same day. Secondly, it was a joke bet. No actual money involved.'

A smirk fights its way onto Preston's face as he unfastens the top few buttons of his white shirt, and he's doing it on purpose—I'm so sure he's doing it on purpose. I've never so much as uttered the suggestion to him, but he without a doubt knows I have a soft spot for the formal-yet-slightly-undone look. When he proceeds to shrug off his blazer, then carefully roll up his shirt sleeves, it's no longer a suspicion; I'm certain he knows. It's hardly a far-fetched conclusion given the man inexplicably knows me better than I could ever dream of knowing myself.

Only now do I realise he's not answered me, just smirked while being offensively attractive. The realisation makes me stammer, my cheeks flushing, and the fact he still has this effect on me either makes me want to bash my head against a wall or consider starting a family with him. Maybe both.

'I don't owe you ten pounds!' I argue as if he did, in fact, say something.

He finally cracks, his smirk transforming into a smile—a proper happy smile—which he makes a poor attempt at hiding by glancing down at the laminate floor.

Then, because he's forever a shit, he lifts his head and returns his gaze to mine with a butter-couldn't-melt, 'okay.'

Naturally, my response is to make a beeline for him, and even more naturally, he sees it coming from a mile off. His fingers are wrapped around my wrists within seconds of me crashing his personal space, and it's less so playfighting and more so him having total control of my limbs as I squirm to free myself. I can't be trying that hard, mind you, given I'm giggling as if delirious as I give up on escaping and instead try to awkwardly shove him backwards onto the bed.

Preston's hardly putting up much resistance, and when he finally releases my wrists, he proceeds to lift me from the floor and flip me over his shoulder in one swift movement. I yelp, the blood rushing to my head as I pound my fists against his back.

'This isn't helping your case!' I yell, but the cackling sound I'm making kind of kills the delivery.

'You're considerably less threatening than you think,' is his reply as he walks me around the bed frame.

As swiftly as he lifted me over his shoulder, he lowers me to the bed with no chance of escape because as my back hits the mattress, he leans over with his hands either side of me. I'm still trying to act offended, or at least mildly frustrated, but I'm yet to stop laughing so I'm not sure I'm selling it.

'Don't be so heavy-handed,' I complain as if he didn't just lift and lower me with the delicacy of a feather.

'This bed has survived worse,' he murmurs like an afterthought, his lips brushing my neck.

I melt into the warmth of him, but manage a retort of, 'if you had it your way, we'd be sleeping on a mattress on the floor. I had to fight for this bedframe, goddamnit.'

His kisses have moved to my jaw, but I feel the smile on his mouth as he replies, 'touché, Euphemia.'

'Mia,' I correct him.

My name has barely left my lips when he lifts his head to look at me, and I'm not entirely sure who's soaking who in. His light hair has become increasingly disheveled as the day has progressed, and as my eyes follow the curves and patterns of his waves, I remind myself that I can touch it; that Preston won't mind—that it's a perfectly normal thing for me to do. I still forget, sometimes.

I lift my hand to run my fingers through it, then place my palm at the back of his head to inch him closer. Our kisses start off slow and delicate—careful, even—and as I sink into him, the anxiety I've been harbouring for months over what next? fades away.

I don't know what's to come after this, not for either of us. Preston's got multiple job offers across multiple—often conflicting—industries because he's nothing if not unforeseeable, and I'm still working on figuring out what to even apply for, but I'm okay with that. I'm suddenly sincerely, surprisingly okay with that. I haven't got a clue what's next, but whatever it is, I have faith in it. In me. In us. In the future.

We're still kissing, only we've become less cautious. His hand is cradling my jaw as I switch between unbuttoning his shirt and tugging it from where it's tucked into his trousers. I'm so caught up in it—in him—that I only remember the loosened tie still wrapped around his neck once all of the buttons are undone. He's laughing between kisses as I finally yank his tie loose, which makes the inevitably of my own laughter unavoidable.

'Smooth, Euphemia,' he teases.

'Mia!' I correct him. Again.

As if apologising, Preston's kisses become gentle once more, and I savour the moment to catch my breath as I swim in the familiar scent of his aftershave.

'Euphemia,' he whispers my name like a secret. 'I don't tell you enough, but it's a beautiful sound.' He places a kiss behind my ear, then again with a whisper, says, 'truly.'